WHAT THE LADY'S MAID KNEW

WHAT THE LADY'S MAID KNEW

The Riftmagic Saga Book 1

E.E. HOLMES

Lily Faire Publishing

Lily Faire Publishing
Townsend, MA

www.lilyfairepublishing.com
www.eeholmes.com

ISBN 978-1-7339352-5-8 (Print edition)
ISBN 978-1-7339352-4-1 (Digital edition)

Publisher's note: This is a work of fiction. Names, characters, places and incidents are either the product of the author's imagination or are used fictitiously.

Cover design by James T. Egan of Bookfly Design LLC
Author photography by Cydney Scott Photography

To Lily and Myles,

In your hearts, may you always know the worth of your own, irrepressible magic.

ALSO BY E.E. HOLMES

PROLOGUE

T HE BOY MOVED LIKE A SHADOW, a piece of the night broken off and slinking across the city. He melted seamlessly from one darkened corner to the next, untouched by the guttering orange light that danced in the glowing skulls of the streetlamps. It was not only his familiarity with the streets of London that allowed him to disappear so completely within its sooty labyrinth. He felt the tingling sensation within his body, the many points at which he could connect to the light and the darkness, twitching and coaxing them like cloaks on strings, drawing them closer, wrapping himself in them, or else casting them away. This was his gift. This, he knew, was why he was chosen.

It was a heretical thought. He thought it anyway, and grinned for good measure.

At the end of the cobbled road down which he now traveled, the fences of the Praeteritum rose up like so many arrows aimed at the sky. Every few minutes, the boy reached into his pocket and felt for the note, wrapping his fingers around it, running his thumb over its rough surface. He imagined it was a talisman meant to bring him luck. And luck he would need—that, if nothing else, was certain.

The shadows nestled in the threshold of the cobbler's shop welcomed him, embraced him, shielded him from view. Even a person looking into the doorway could stare directly at the place where he stood and still not see him there. He let out a long, slow breath. Now, he had to pick his moment.

The Praesidio, he knew from days and days of careful reconnaissance, patrolled the outer perimeter of the Praeteritum in pairs. Given the number of patrols and the frequency with which they

1

passed his chosen location, the boy would have less than five minutes to deliver his message, receive his reply, and vanish once again into the darkness. It was, at once, an eternity and a breathlessly brief window of time. And it would begin as soon as the next patrol passed his hiding place.

The shadow boy waited.

As he waited, the snow swirled around him. The first of the flakes had begun to fall as he'd set out, and he worried it perhaps might begin to stick, giving his presence away with footprints. Luckily, though, the cobbles were wet, and the snow was disappearing even as it fell. If the storm had begun but an hour sooner, he would have had to abandon the plan completely.

The sound of boots in lockstep stilled the boy's heart, and he sucked in a breath. The Praesidio approached. Moments later they appeared along the narrow walk that ran between the back of the cobbler's and the high iron fence that enclosed the Praeteritum, boots clomping, scarlet embroidered silver sashes laying across their chests, weapons gleaming in their gloved hands.

The boy, still not breathing, counted to fifty, slowly. By the time he had finished, his lungs were screaming for air and the sounds of the boots had faded to nothingness. He exhaled and peeled himself away from the darkness. There was no time to waste.

He approached the fence, squatting down in the deepest of the shadows he could find, tugging them in tightly around himself. Then, he reached into his pocket for the only other thing he carried: a round, smooth stone. Whispering a prayer to no one, he tossed the stone through the bars and listened to the clatter it made as it bounced on the cobbles. He held his breath and began to count again.

But before he had reached the number ten, he heard a shuffling of feet and a ragged drawing of breath. Five shadows lumbered toward him out of the darkness, one of them stooping to snatch the stone up off the ground. As they closed the distance to the fence, they were revealed to be men, all bedraggled and filthy. The boy fought back an urge to run. One man stepped closer than the others, who hung nervously back.

"I'm meant to deliver something to John Davies," the boy whispered breathlessly.

"You're looking at 'im, lad," answered the man who had approached the fence.

"I was told you would come alone," the boy replied, hesitating.

"And I was told the message would be coming in the hands of a trusted associate of the movement, not some cheeky little guttersnipe. Now hand it over," Davies replied, baring the remaining stumps of his teeth.

Shrugging, the boy retrieved the note from his pocket and handed it through the bars. Davies stood up and unfolded it hastily. The four other men hurried forward to read it over his shoulder. Almost at once, the angry muttering began.

"He's not coming."

"I knew it. I bloody well knew it. Didn't I tell you?"

"A coward, that's what he is, a blustering coward."

"How long are we to wait then, does he tell us that, at least?"

"No. Just that they aren't coming, and to be patient."

Davies raised his face and met the boy's eyes. His expression was full of something unsettling—something that made the boy's chest feel hollow at the sight of it. It would be many years before he came to understand that it had been despair.

"You're... you're meant to burn it, sir, when you've finished reading it," the boy whispered.

"Is that right?" Davies replied in a voice like a hiss.

"Y-yes, sir. And I'm to bring back your reply, if you've got one," the boy managed at last, prying the words free from the grip of the man's gaze.

Davies hobbled forward, crumpling the paper in his fist as he came. When he reached the fence again, he held up the wadded note and touched his finger to it. The paper began to smoke and within a few seconds, had been reduced to a pile of ash. "You want my reply, do you now? Well, here it is, and mind you deliver it in full: John Davies is done waiting. He's done wasting away in this hell pit, living on the dregs of broken promises. We'll take our chances without Eli Turner and his useless Resistance. You tell him that, from me."

The boy's eyes widened. If there was something he ought to have said to this man with the wild eyes burning out of his sunken face, he could not find the words. He swallowed and stepped back from the fence. "I'll... I'll tell 'im, sir."

John Davies turned his back on the boy and fell into huddled conference with the waiting men. The boy backed away from the fence, a strange lump in his throat. He felt something bearing down upon him, something vague and foreboding, and suddenly he could not take to his heels fast enough. He turned tail down the alleyway and fled, pulling the darkness with him as he went.

The boy had not yet reached the safety of his doorstep when the first shots echoed in the night, shattering the snow-muffled stillness.

(An excerpt from "The Book of the Rift": Chapter 1, The Reckoning, verses 1-7)

"…And thus it was that the world was so rife with sin and greed, so rotted from within, that the mighty Creator, in His wisdom, looked upon it in grievous distress, and did weep for the degradation of these, His greatest and most beloved works. But He loved them still, for all their wrongs and, in His infinite mercy, did not seek to vanquish His beloved creations, but to rout out instead the corruption and weakness that did infest them, and thereby purify His works and make them once again worthy of His power and His love. And thus, did He open the Rift and send forth the Bane, by which He could mark those among His people who, by their very nature, must fall to the perils of sin. These marked, known as the Riftborn, would be cursed, a curse that would forever tempt them to ill. But the Creator loved even these, the lowest of His people, and would not abandon them to fall to their curse, but gathered them within the arms of His embrace and declared unto them, "My children, enter thou into My service, and with thy bodies and thy spirits lift up My works in all things. If thou do this, thy curse shall vanish upon thy death, and thou shalt be welcomed into My arms, there to dwell for eternity. Go forth, and turn thy curse to blessed service in My Name."

And thus it was the Riftborn rejoiced in their lot, and took upon themselves their sacred burden: to serve, to toil, and to repent with gladness in their hearts, and the Creator's name upon their lips…"

ONE

"**W**HAT THE HELL COULD BE KEEPING THE BOY?"

It was well near dawn, and Colin had still not returned. Eli Turner paced the basement kitchen like a caged animal, watching the fire consume itself into a pile of glowing embers. Not one of the three men in the room moved to stoke it, allowing the cold to simply steal over them.

"It's possible he wasn't able to deliver the message," Zeke Doherty said, scratching nervously at his dark tangle of a beard. "Maybe the lad just couldn't get close enough."

"Then why wouldn't he just come right back here and tell us that?" Jasper Quinn growled. He had not moved from his post by the window, and stood squinting out into the darkness, arms crossed tensely over his chest. "We never should have sent him, Eli. I don't know how you talked us into it."

"I trust Colin," Eli snapped. "He's a good lad, and his Riftmagic means he's the only one who could have gotten near the fence without being seen."

"Might be ashamed o' himself, if he got spooked or couldn't make good on his promise," Zeke suggested. "Maybe he ran on home instead. He's jus' a kid, after all."

"Exactly," Jasper replied. "What kind of job was this for a child? We never should have sent him, damn it all."

"As I recall, you didn't take much persuading," Eli said through his clenched teeth. Over the last hour, everything about him had slowly become clenched, until it seemed that every muscle he had was coiled like a spring. He could feel the tension building unbearably, but he could do nothing to release it.

"That's right," Zeke added. "You didn't have any better ideas, and I certainly don't remember you jumping up and down all eager to take his place."

Jasper's hands balled themselves into fists. If the situation hadn't been so deadly serious, he might have gotten into a tussle with Zeke, thrown a few punches just to blow off some steam. Instead, he satisfied himself with tossing Zeke a vicious glare before returning to his vigil at the window.

"The point is, no one else's Riftmagic was better suited to the job," Eli went on, as much to himself as anyone else, talking only to relieve the silence that was pressing relentlessly down on them. "Any one of us would have been spotted in a trice, you know that. He's young, sure, but he's damn eager to prove himself, and he's tougher than he looks."

"Mighta been Davies what cocked it up," Zeke suggested darkly. "He always was a bit on the impulsive side. Rash, some might call him."

"It's no good casting blame on anyone until we know what's happened. Maybe there's nothing to worry about. Maybe Colin's just waiting it out until it's safe to return," Eli insisted stubbornly.

"Or maybe it's all gone to hell in a handbasket," Jasper muttered.

"Well, aren't you just a right ray of sunshine," Zeke cried out, throwing his hands up in exasperation. "Is he always like this? How do you put up with it?" he asked Eli.

Eli didn't answer. Yes, Jasper was always like this, spiraling into the darkest available void at the slightest setback, but it wouldn't do any of them any good to say so now. He put up with it because Jasper was his oldest friend. He was also loyal, and whatever his other faults, Jasper would step in front of a Praesidio soldier's weapon for him, that was one thing that Eli absolutely knew for certain.

"There's no use speculating. We won't know what happened until... until we know," Eli said. "We simply have to wait."

"Why not send someone out looking for the lad?" Zeke suggested. "I could take the long way 'round by the river, see if I can't..."

But Eli was already shaking his head. "It's no good, Zeke. We can't be out wandering the banks at this time of night. We can't afford to draw any suspicion onto any of us, not now. It's too risky, without knowing what's happened. We could be walking into a dangerous situation. We've got no choice but to—"

8

"Someone's coming!" Jasper hissed, pressing his face so close to the window that his breath fogged up the dingy panes of glass.

Zeke clapped his hands. "See, there? I told you Colin would—"

"It's not Colin. It's too tall to be Colin," Jasper snapped. "It's a man... I still can't..."

Eli and Zeke were on their feet now, ready to flee if the next pool of lamplight revealed a Praesidio uniform charging toward them.

"It's Fergus!" Jasper breathed, dashing from the window toward the door, hand outstretched to fling it wide.

"Hold it, lad," Zeke cautioned him. "We don't open that door without the signal, not to Fergus, not to anyone. He might be followed."

Jasper growled his frustration but pulled his hand away from the latch. They waited out the interminable next few seconds, listened to Fergus' frantic footsteps skid to a halt on the cobbles outside the door, and then...

Three sharp taps. A pause. Two taps. A second pause. Three more taps.

Jasper pulled the bolt from its catch and wrenched the door open. Fergus fell through it, stumbling in his haste to reach the safety of the kitchen. His breath was coming in great, shuddering gasps.

"Are you being pursued, Fergus? Have you been followed?" Zeke demanded, still tensed for flight.

But Fergus shook his head. "No. Not followed. Just ran here. Ran here as fast as my legs would carry me."

"Why? What's happened?" Jasper asked. "Is it Colin? Has he been caught?"

Fergus shook his head, but could not answer right away, as a deep rattling cough brought him nearly to his knees, and he collapsed into a chair at the battered wooden table.

Eli reached up and pulled at his hair, sure he would explode with the anxiety. Zeke, however, who had at least kept his wits about him, crossed the room and poured Fergus a glass of water from the chipped porcelain pitcher from beside the sink. He slid it across the table to Fergus, who snatched it up gratefully with a nod and began to gulp it down between rounds of coughing. At last, his breath came back to him, and he managed to choke out his message.

"Five Riftborn have been killed... attempted an escape... Praesidio caught them..."

Fergus might have been talking to an empty room, so silent and still had it fallen around him. It was as though the other three men had been turned momentarily to stone.

"Heard the shots... thought Colin might've... but he's alright... but the others..."

Jasper was the first to recover his voice. "They've shot them?"

Fergus shook his head. "Might've done... but they've dragged them to the public gallows. Hanged 'em all... already puttin' up the ladders to cut 'em down by the time I got there..."

Zeke's voice was barely more than a whisper. "Who was it, Fergus? Do you know who they..."

"It was Davies, Zeke. Davies and four accomplices."

For one long, silent moment, the name hung in the air among them, shivering. And then the pitcher on the table and the glass in Fergus' hand exploded. Zeke swore and fell backward into a cupboard, dislodging a shelf and sending potatoes rolling across the floor. Jasper flung himself to the ground, throwing his arms over his head to protect himself as the glass rained down upon him. Fergus, though, could do nothing but sputter, dripping wet, as the shock sent him into another violent coughing fit.

The shards of the glass and porcelain still lay glittering like a scattering of diamonds in the firelight. No one dared move. No one spoke. They simply sat, all of them stunned, in the aftermath of the news.

"The fool. The bloody stupid fool," Eli whispered into the glass-scattered silence. A kind of rushing sensation remained behind, coursing through his veins in the aftermath of his outburst. He could not remember the last time he had lost control of his Riftmagic like that. He was usually among the most careful and skillful of Catalysts.

Eli's voice broke the spell. Jasper and Zeke got slowly to their feet, and Fergus, still wiping water from his face, cleared his throat and stammered, "I- I'm s-sorry, Eli. I wouldn't have b-believed it if I hadn't seen it for myself. The Praesidio cut them down n-nearly as soon as they'd stopped wriggling, but it was him, I'd stake my life on it."

Eli collapsed into another chair at the table. "Why? Why couldn't they just have waited? Been patient just a little longer? I could have found a way... could have..."

"Men like John Davies are not known for their patience, Eli, you know that well enough," Jasper replied, his usually contentious voice subdued, so that he hardly sounded like himself. "Davies was a man of action. You can't ask a man like that to wait forever."

"I didn't ask him to wait forever!" Eli shouted, and the glass panels in the lamp began to rattle ominously. "He waited fifteen bloody years. Are you telling me he couldn't have waited another week? Just a bit longer, until we could be sure we had the right people in place to—"

"We put him off too many times," Jasper replied, shaking his head. "You can only tell a man 'just a bit longer' so many times before it starts to sound like the lie that it is."

"It wasn't a lie!"

"And it wasn't a guarantee either. He reached his limit, Eli, and that's an end to it."

Eli seemed to deflate. His face crumpled and dropped like a stone into his waiting hands. "Damn it all to hell."

"It's a blow," Zeke said with a grim nod of his dark, shaggy head. "It's a blow and it's no use pretending that it's not. We needed Davies. He was one of the only survivors of the Lamplighters Confederacy, and his Riftmagic was powerful, even under the influence of Riftmead."

"What are we to do?" Fergus asked.

"Without men like Davies, we've got to recruit now. Open rebellion won't be possible without the likes of him," Zeke said.

Jasper swore under his breath.

Eli sighed heavily and lifted his head to look at the others. "Zeke's right. Look, we all know you prefer open action, Jasper, but we can't afford to be fools, not now. We'll have to fall back on our other plans."

"Our other plans?!" Jasper snorted with disgust. "What other plans? Davies was the best chance we had!"

"I don't deny it, lad, but we can't dwell on what's done," Zeke replied soberly before turning to Eli. "What do you reckon, then, Eli? I know it's late, but we should get word to Sully, eh?"

"Yes, you're right, Zeke. I'd better be the one to go," Eli replied, rising from his chair.

"Yes, mustn't let anyone but Sully's little protégé break the news," Jasper muttered.

Eli and Jasper looked daggers at each other, but it was Jasper who dropped his gaze first. Eli clapped Fergus on the shoulder.

"Thank you for coming all this way to alert us," he said earnestly. "I know you risked much being out tonight. And I'm sorry about... well..." He gestured rather helplessly at the mess of sodden, broken glass.

"'S all right," Fergus replied stoutly. "I'll just be on my way then, if there's nothin' else you need from me?"

"No, Fergus, thank you. Send our regards to Madge, will you?" Eli replied.

"I always do. When do we meet, then?" Fergus asked.

Eli looked at Zeke, who shrugged. "Let me talk to Sully first. We'll send you word in the usual manner."

"Right, then. G'night, lads," Fergus said, getting to his feet. He shook hands all around, replaced his cap on his balding head, and slipped soundlessly out the door and back into the night.

"We'll have to lay low for a bit," Zeke said, his voice soft and serious. "Davies' escape will have the whole Praesidio on the alert. The Illustratum may even tighten restrictions. And as sure as I'm standing here, they'll try to keep Davies' name out of it. That'll have to be addressed. I'm not saying we give up, no, not at all. You'll never hear me say that, I give you my word. But we'll have to tread very carefully for a spell."

"You're right Zeke," Eli said, giving his friend a grim smile. "This changes everything. Davies wasn't our only hope, but he was our best one. We've got to start from scratch, but start we will." Eli moved toward the door and froze in his tracks, staring around him as though he had only just realized the extent of the damage he had caused. "Blast it all. Suppose I'd better clear all this up first then, eh?"

"Oh, just bugger off, will you? Sully will be waiting. I'll do it," Jasper muttered. He watched Eli's lithe form slip out the door before adding, "Someone's got to clean up your messes, it seems."

(An excerpt from the instructional text: "On the Identification and Categorization of the Riftborn," written by Elder Leander Potts, published 1802, commissioned by the Elder Council of the Illustratum)

"...The most important decision an Elder can make regarding the selection and training of servants from among the Riftborn is which type of Riftmagic is best suited to each role within the household. In this matter, though, guidance can be offered, and ought to be followed explicitly if a skilled and well-ordered household is to be maintained.

Though Riftmagic is specific to the individual who has been marked with it, there are general categories into which we can organize the various abilities that Riftmagic bestows upon those who must labor under its burden. By offering a post best suited to each established type of Riftmagic, we fulfill our Creator-given duty to provide a spiritual avenue of service for those who wish to stay the Path and overcome the constant and overwhelming temptation to use their Riftmagic for self-serving or sinful purposes.

Riftmagic can be generally organized into the following categories:

Manipulators: This is the most common type of Riftmagic, and it presents itself in perhaps the widest array of abilities. A Manipulator can, in one manner or another, move or manipulate things. This may manifest in an ability to shift large objects, for example, or else to mold or shape materials. A Manipulator will usually have an affinity for a certain kind of material upon which their Riftmagic is most effective; a Manipulator who works effectively with wood or stone is unlikely to work well with textiles. Manipulators are most often suited

13

to jobs that entail manual labor, such as masonry, ironworking, factory work, or other forms of goods production.

Catalysts: This type of Riftmagic can be among the most difficult to manage, and is considered a more volatile categorization than Manipulator. A Catalyst can affect energy rather than material, and hence can enact a reaction of some kind—the most common includes the ability to kindle fire, the ability to raise or lower temperature, and the ability to cause explosions. While this type of Riftmagic must be carefully monitored and heavily regulated, it can be exceedingly useful. Catalysts are suited to a great number of tasks dependent upon their particular abilities, including, just to name a few, military operations, blacksmithing, and cookery.

Temporals: A most peculiar type of Riftmagic, and one that has been studied extensively, though it remains mysterious. A Temporal can have small, concentrated effects on time itself; they might be able, for instance, to slow an object down as it falls, or else speed an object up. These effects are nearly always very small and temporary, but can be useful in the right type of service. Temporals can be found in many types of work, but are often to be found in household service as maids, chauffeurs, and other staff.

Influencers: By far the rarest and most dangerous of the Riftborn, Influencers are both coveted and heavily regulated. Once considered too dangerous for service, they have in recent years found their place in many prominent households as lady's maids, nursemaids, and governesses, as well as in hospitals as nurses and in stables working with horses and other livestock. Influencer abilities have been deemed useful in the role of maintaining decorum, subservience, and obedience in both women and children, and it is in this manner that a well-trained and well-regulated Influencer can most often be found in service to the Illustratum and, by extension, the Creator Himself.

In the chapters following this introduction, I shall further examine these categories in-depth, and offer guidance on the role the Elder must perforce play in the proper channeling of Riftborn abilities into service of the Illustratum..."

14

TWO

L ARKSPUR MANOR was one of those fortunate structures to
have lived many different lives in the time since it had first been
constructed. In its earliest days, it had served as an ancillary
royal residence, an outpost of courtly life, and the site of many regal
entertainments. When changing royal habits rendered it superfluous, it
had been given over to the church of the day, to be converted into a
nunnery, and where its halls had once been filled with gaiety and
excess, now they were heavy with reverence and reflection. Then the
ravages of wartime swept through, replacing prayer books and hymns
with hospital cots and the cries of the dying. When the last of the
soldiers had made their way home either to their families or to their
everlasting rewards, the place was converted into a prestigious private
school, and Larkspur Manor's imposing façade spent two decades
staring haughtily down at a generation of wealthy British gentlemen
navigating the rocky transition from boyhood to manhood. And then
at last, in the early days after the Awakening, the Illustratum rose to
power and the manor fell into their hands and was placed under the
stewardship of the Hallewell family. That was three generations ago,
and though Josiah Hallewell had never known a time that his family
had not occupied its hallowed halls, he still looked upon Larkspur
Manor with a distinct sense of pride and accomplishment. This place,
he told himself, was his just reward from the Creator, for all his good
works.

And as he rode up the long, gravel drive that afternoon, after a full
day of services and meetings, and as the front of the manor rose before
him, framed between two rows of ancient and stately plane trees, he
was filled once again with that sense of rightness, of satisfaction. The

very house itself seemed to reflect it—it sat on its grounds like a monarch on a throne, surveying the calm and quiet with a stately air.

As the carriage pulled to a stop, a footman hurried down the front steps to take Josiah's hat, coat, and carved ivory walking stick.

"Afternoon, sir," the young man mumbled, his eyes downcast, his tall and lanky frame bent nearly double in his attempt to show proper deference. Both his hands and his voice, Josiah noted, shook with nerves. Josiah frowned but said nothing, making a mental note instead to discuss the boy with Braxton when he had the chance.

Stepping into Larkspur Manor was, for Josiah, like stepping into a temple of sorts. He sometimes questioned whether there was a touch of blasphemy in this feeling, but always managed to dismiss this little nagging thought. After all, the house, and indeed all that was in it, had come his way as a result of his position in the Illustratum. If a hint of the divine breathed through the place, it was only right, surely. After all, wherever His servants lived in His name, wherever His will was being done, He was, by definition, present.

Within its hallowed halls, all was quiet, but for the echoing of Josiah's footsteps on the glistening floorboards. Somewhere above his head, he knew, his daughter flitted about her chambers, involved in whatever mysterious frivolity women occupied themselves with in private. And elsewhere in the house, insulated from the comings and goings of the Hallewell family, he trusted that preparations were well underway for the weekend's events, organized in the capable hands of Braxton and Mrs. Keats.

Josiah retired to his study and pulled the green velvet rope that hung beside his desk. Somewhere in the bowels of the house, a golden bell, hanging above a nameplate that read "Elder Hallewell's Study," began to tinkle expectantly.

Josiah let out a sigh and stretched his legs out before him toward the fire already crackling away cheerfully in the hearth. The day had been one in a string of trying days, and he was relieved to see the back of it. The challenges had begun even before the sun had risen, with the arrival of a messenger in the middle of the night.

The sound of the bell and the frantic knocking had woken half the household. His wife would be near hysterical with worry in her chambers if she heard the commotion, but that was Miss Spratt's concern—he would have enough to deal with that night, he realized, as he opened the letter to read it:

16

"Attempted escape at the Praeteritum. Five Riftborn apprehended and hanged upon the gallows. Your presence urgently requested at a convening of the Elder Council at once."

"Damn them," Josiah muttered. "Damn them all."

One bone-jostling carriage ride later, Josiah found the Elder Council chambers in a proper frenzy, with Elders arriving half-dressed and unshaven. Josiah spotted Francis Potter, the only other Elder to hold the rank of Counselor to the High Elder, and took his place beside him.

"Any rumblings as to what this might be about?" Josiah muttered by way of greeting.

"Hard to say. Morgan's not left his chambers, and the Moderator isn't here yet. The others are speculating about a high-security prisoner, but that's all it is at this point—speculation," Francis replied. He scratched at the white stubble on his chin and stifled a yawn.

"What about the valets? The secretary?" Josiah asked. Morgan's staff were notoriously persuadable when it came to providing hints to the other Elders, and were paid well for it.

Francis shook his head ruefully. "Haven't seen hide nor hair of them. Might be the lateness of the hour, but he may also have forbidden them to leave his chambers. I think we'll have to wait it out. Shouldn't be long now. Nearly all the senior members are here."

Francis was right. Within minutes, the door opened and the Moderator entered into the very top of the benches, where he carried out his role of maintaining order on the floor and facilitating the discourse among the Elders. The benches were still half empty and there was barely a quorum when the gavel came down and the High Elder proceeded into the room. A complete but grudging silence fell as he made his way to his seat at the top of the hall, and it was broken almost the moment he sat down.

"What's the meaning of this, then?" a deep voice boomed out before the meeting could properly begin. "Dragging us all from our beds because a few Riftborn scaled a fence?"

"Elder Garrison, take your seat. The matter is more serious than a scaled fence." The steely voice of the Moderator echoed down from his seat at the top of the benches, where he still fumbled to straighten his hastily donned wig and robe.

"But surely the Praesidio leadership can deal with something like this? I mean, they've already been hanged, haven't they? What trouble can they possibly cause now that can't wait at least until the damn sun comes up?" Elder Garrison shouted. His shirt was untucked and his stole hung haphazardly over one shoulder. There was a whiff of stale wine about him.

"I will have order on this floor! Order, man! I assure you, my brother, that if you cannot be bothered to carry out your sworn duty over a trifle like the lateness of the hour, the Illustratum is full of pious and devoted Dignus ready and willing to fill your seat," the Moderator barked.

Elder Garrison grumbled something incoherent about "didn't mean to imply," and "overreacting" before dropping heavily onto his bench.

The High Elder himself, John Morgan, cleared his throat and the chamber fell silent at once. All eyes turned to him, expectant.

"Brothers, we have before us tonight what may very well be a grave situation. A few short hours ago, five of the Riftborn incarcerated in the Praeteritum attempted an escape. They were apprehended by the Praesidio on patrol and subdued before being hanged at the gallows."

"Hanged with no audience? No Entreaty?" Elder Primrose asked in his cracked and reedy voice. "I assume there must have been extenuating circumstances to prompt such swift retribution?"

"Indeed," the High Elder replied. "The guards were met with violence. There were injuries. And... one of the men in question was John Davies."

A murmur ran through the benches. Josiah felt his fists close and then open at his sides. Davies was a name well known among both the Dignus and the Riftborn, a name always whispered, though whether with caution or with reverence depended upon the faith of he who uttered it.

"A man upon whom the mercy of the Illustratum was clearly wasted!" Elder Garrison spat. "He ought to have been hanged fifteen years ago, when he was first apprehended!"

"It was the will of this body that he be used as an example, to be broken and tamed and made to function within the system," Elder Potter replied. "Show him under the thumb of the Illustratum, and the will of other rebels would be broken. To have executed him would have been akin to martyring him. The damage would have been near impossible to contain."

18

"And the others? Who were the others that were hanged with him?" Elder Fields asked.

"Does it matter? His accomplices!" Elder Garrison snapped, his comment met with a smattering of applause.

"It will matter to the masses, when the names are printed upon the execution notices," Elder Fields pressed.

"Elder Garrison is right! What name will matter but Davies'?" Elder Smythe cried out, spit flying from his chapped lips. "It will echo through the Barrens, from White Chapel to Bethnal Green. We shall have unrest and discord among the Riftborn the likes of which we haven't seen since the early days after the Awakening."

"What were those officers thinking, hanging Davies in public? Bloody damned fools! They should be court marshaled!" Elder Perkins roared, swelling like a bullfrog. His words were met with much shouting and banging of fists by the other Elders. Josiah pressed his lips together, waiting for the bravado to pass—Perkins didn't know how to make a point at a reasonable volume, and many of the other Elders pounced on any opportunity to participate in an uproar. All bluster and no substance. Luckily, it was usually short-lived.

Moments later, the Moderator brought an end to the discord with the exuberant pounding of his gavel. "The Moderator reminds the Elders here gathered that the Praesidio has full authority to take punitive action as it sees fit when confronted with a threat. The actions of the guards in this matter have been reviewed by their Commander and the High Elder and have been judged appropriate. The matter under judgment here is not the actions of the guards, but how to handle the resulting circumstances. On that topic, we agree to hear discussion, so long as it remains civil and productive."

"Davies ought to have been hanged years ago. His continued presence in the Praeteritum has surely done nothing but spark resentment and breed discontent," Elder Garrison said in a voice which was, if not quiet, at least under control. "Good riddance, I say, and let us staunch the bleeding."

"Quite," Elder Smythe agreed. "We must issue a proclamation. Striking the proper tone will be essential. Get the word out before salacious versions of the truth spread like wildfire."

"And yet, we must also tread carefully not to make heroes of criminals," Elder Primrose cried out. "The wording, as you say, is the thing..."

Josiah rolled his eyes. Sometimes it was like attempting to govern with a room full of overly emotional children. He raised a hand almost lazily into the air and was acknowledged at once by the Moderator.

"What will matter most, I think, is the handling of how these events are disseminated among the masses. A standard proclamation of death will not be sufficient, regardless of how it is worded. We must consider a full range of responses, including possible retaliatory measures in the Barrens and the Praeteritum itself," he said.

The High Elder inclined his head in agreement. "Very astute, Elder Hallewell, thank you. This is why I have gathered you, my brothers. Certain measures must be taken. I welcome your suggestions. I call upon the Moderator to open the floor to discussion and to record the proposals."

There was a general flurry of activity as the Moderator went through his procedural rules, giving Josiah time to lean in toward Francis and murmur, "If they let Davies' name get out, they're fools, the lot of them."

"I quite agree," Francis replied. "Something needs to be done." He raised a hand politely in the air, waiting to be acknowledged by the Moderator, who quieted the benches and called upon him at once. "If I may begin with a question?"

"You may," the Moderator said, settling himself behind his gavel and papers.

"Who knows the identities of the men who were hanged?"

The Moderator frowned and turned to the High Elder, who replied, "It is hard to know. The guards, certainly. And there will, of course, be those within the confines of the Praeteritum. It will hardly be missed among the population there that Davies is gone, and the other men as well."

Elder Primrose creaked to his feet, pounding his walking stick upon the ground for emphasis. "Toward what purpose tends this line of questioning?"

"What was the manner of their escape?" Francis pressed on, ignoring Elder Primrose.

The Moderator frowned. "I'm afraid I don't..."

"Was it messy? Public? Did it draw a crowd or make a scene?" Francis clarified.

The High Elder turned to the Commander of the Praesidio, who stood nearby, guarding the door. The man stepped forward and cleared his throat. "There was gunfire when the guards first gave chase. That would have alerted the public that something was amiss."

"But it also would have sent them running for cover, surely?" Francis pressed. "People run from gunfire, not toward it."

"Indeed, sir," the Commander agreed with a sharp nod.

"And then?"

"Once they were subdued, the men were dragged directly to the gallows, sir."

"And did this not draw a crowd?"

The Commander considered. "A small crowd, yes, but not until after the men had already been hanged. It all happened..." the man gave a nervous glance at the High Elder before continuing, "... that is to say, it all happened very quickly..."

But Josiah saw his moment and took it; Francis' questions had set the stage perfectly. He stood up, gesturing his intention to speak. "Was Davies given the chance to make any sort of public declaration?"

The Commander shook his head. "No, sir. They bound and gagged him before they took him up the platform. The others as well. Davies, in fact, was barely conscious from the struggle."

"And their faces?"

"Covered, sir, as is traditional."

Josiah slapped his hand triumphantly down upon the ledge before him. "There, then. You understand what this means, gentlemen?"

The gentlemen, it seemed, did not. Josiah stepped to the middle of the floor and made quite a remarkable pronouncement.

"It means that John Davies is not dead."

Muttering rose up around him like a swarm of angry bees. Josiah weathered it calmly, catching Francis' eye, who gave a small but firm nod of approval.

"Explain yourself, please, Elder Hallewell," Elder Smythe demanded, clearly perturbed that he had not immediately divined Josiah's meaning. He was not alone. Many of the other Elders looked perplexed.

"I mean, we control the narrative," Josiah replied patiently. "John Davies is not dead. Whoever that man was, he was not John Davies. We publish a list of names in a public notice, and we put out our statement and our call for prayer and reflection and perhaps even penance for the names on the list. We never mention John Davies."

"You are suggesting we lie to the public?" Elder Primrose asked, his eyebrows disappearing into his flyaway nest of white hair.

Elder Carpenter snorted humorlessly. "We'll never get away with it," he insisted. "The Praeteritum will already be afire with the news. What's the point of telling a lie that the public already knows to be false?"

"The Praeteritum is hardly the public at large. If we can contain the news of Davies' death to that tiny corner of our territory, we should consider it a victory. Don't you see, my brothers? We must do what one does when a fire breaks out: we must contain the spread to minimize the damage," Josiah said calmly.

"But, how?" Elder Primrose asked. "How can we possibly manage to—"

"Enforce an edict. No travel in or out of the Praeteritum. No ministry there until further notice. No border visits or post."

"But we can't enforce such regulations permanently!" Elder Garrison pointed out.

"We do not need to enforce it permanently. Merely long enough for the worst of the scandal to blow over. A week or two, perhaps," Josiah said smoothly. "We've done so before, in times of illness or unrest."

"Very well. Let's say, for argument's sake, that we put in place such an edict. How do we justify it? What reason do we give?" Elder Carpenter asked. His voice was still harsh and yet his expression was intrigued.

Josiah turned and inclined his head toward the High Elder. "Perhaps we pray upon it. Consult with the Rift. See what guidance we can obtain on the matter. But I cannot think the Creator would begrudge us what means we find prudent to maintain His natural order and prevent an uprising."

"This is well reasoned, Elder Hallewell," the High Elder declared, nodding his head in agreement. "Let it be so. I shall consult with the Rift. In the meantime, let the barriers around the Praeteritum be reinforced, and all access points barred for the present. Commander, have your men enforce a curfew at once. All Riftborn within the Barrens will now be confined to their quarters until morning services, with no exceptions. Tell them the streets are not safe."

"Yes, your Eminence," the Commander replied, turning on his heel and exiting the chamber at a jog.

22

The High Elder rose, and all the men in the room rose with him, remaining respectfully on their feet while he swept toward the exit in his long robes. "Gentlemen, we shall take a brief recess while I Commune. Remain within the chamber, please. Moderator, please maintain order. And for Creator's sake, find someone to fetch us all a damn cup of tea! Josiah, Francis... a word?"

Josiah and Francis caught each other's eye and hastened up the benches to the back of the room, where the High Elder gestured them through the door behind his seat.

"You did well in there, the both of you," the High Elder declared when the heavy door had drifted shut behind them. "Our fellow brothers mean well, but I sometimes feel they lack the... ah... creative spirit necessary to govern effectively."

Both Josiah and Francis inclined their heads. "We are, as ever, only looking out for the welfare of the Illustratum and the furtherance of our noble work," Josiah replied smoothly.

"Indeed. Well, come along," the High Elder replied, shifting gears with something of a weary sigh. "There's something I need the two of you to see."

Francis and Josiah passed the obligatory silent question between themselves as they followed the High Elder down the hallway. Neither had the slightest idea what this was about, though their positions as the highest-ranking members of the Elder Council sometimes meant they were privy to information the rest of the Council did not immediately receive.

At the end of a long, wood-paneled hallway, a member of the Praesidio guard was standing at attention, evidently waiting for them. As they approached, the soldier clicked his heels sharply, gave a respectful bow, and turned to lead them through a door in the paneling and down a winding metal staircase, his boots echoing like cannon fire upon the stairs. At the base of the staircase, another door hidden within the paneling took them down another hallway, narrower and shabbier than the first, which seemed to go on for miles through the bowels of the Illustratum. Josiah lost all sense of direction as they twisted and turned. At last, the guard pushed open a door to their left and stepped aside for them to pass.

High Elder Morgan turned to face them in the doorway, blocking the room beyond from Josiah's view. "What I am about to show you, my brothers, must be kept entirely confidential, is that understood?"

"Perfectly, your Eminence," Josiah replied at once.

"Of course, sir," Francis added.

With one last look of patriarchal severity, the High Elder turned and entered the room, Josiah and Francis close on his heels. The space was small and dark, lit only by a couple of candles. In the far corner, what appeared to be a military cot had been set up, alongside a long, low table full of an apothecary's collection of glass bottles, vials, wads of cotton, bandaging, and metal instruments. A nurse in official Illustratum staff uniform was bent over the cot, tending to the occupant. Upon hearing the footsteps of the Elders, however, she scurried away into the corner like a frightened mouse. She kept her eyes cast downward, afraid, it seemed, even to look at them. A man was revealed lying upon the cot, heavily bandaged on both his arms and face. His breathing was quite labored, and he appeared to be unconscious.

"Who is that?" Josiah asked at last, when no one seemed inclined to speak or explain what was happening.

"This unfortunate fellow is Frederick Hewitt," the High Elder replied. "He is a member of the Praesidio guard. Promoted to Sergeant just last month, isn't that correct, Lieutenant?"

"Just so, sir," came a voice from the doorway—the soldier who had escorted them to the room, speaking for the first time.

"Sergeant Hewitt was part of the patrol earlier this evening that discovered and apprehended John Davies and his accomplices," the High Elder continued. "He is, as you can see, gravely injured."

Josiah stared at the aforementioned Hewitt, who seemed to be struggling mightily to take each ragged breath. "What's happened to him?" he finally managed to ask.

"That's just the question, brother," the High Elder said. Josiah knew him well enough to recognize the sharp edge in his voice for what it was: fear.

The High Elder stepped forward and reached down toward Hewitt. A sudden movement from the corner betrayed the nurse's impulse to stop him from disturbing her patient, an impulse she quickly and prudently suppressed. The High Elder did not seem to notice. He lifted the bandages away from Sergeant Hewitt's right arm. The skin there had been badly blistered and charred—the sinewy muscle was visible in places, the edges of the wounds angry and raw and reduced nearly to ash. Potter clamped a hand over his mouth as though he might be

24

sick. Josiah, however, in the grip of a kind of horrified fascination, bent closer to examine the injuries.

"Burned?"

"Yes," the High Elder replied.

"I don't understand. Did Davies and his accomplices carry torches? Were they armed? Improvised explosives, perhaps? The Commander never mentioned..." Josiah struggled to make sense of the human devastation before him.

"No, brother. It was Davies. His touch... just the touch of his hand."

Josiah felt as though the ground was shifting beneath his feet. He reached out and caught hold of the bedframe to steady himself. Only when he was quite sure that his voice would be steady and strong did he ask a question to which he already knew the answer. "His Riftmark. What is it?"

The reply came, as he knew it would. "Catalyst."

"But how?" Francis asked, fumbling to extract a handkerchief from his pocket with trembling fingers and pressing it to his clammy forehead.

"That is what we must determine, and with the utmost haste," the High Elder replied.

"It is not possible," Josiah whispered.

The High Elder's face was a mask in the wavering light of the gas lamps. "And yet, here we are."

§

A soft knocking upon the study door startled Josiah from the depths of his thoughts. He straightened up in his chair and cleared his throat.

"Come in."

Braxton entered the room, a gleaming silver tray balanced on his hand. He was a tall man, with broad shoulders, a proud bearing, and a full head of dark hair, now significantly greying at the temples. His voice, when he spoke, was always so measured and deliberate, as though he doled it out a teaspoonful at a time. "Good morning, sir."

"And to you, Braxton," Josiah replied. "You needn't have brought that yourself, surely."

"I was most distressed to see you out all night, sir, and wished to check upon you personally," Braxton said, setting down the tea tray. "I took the liberty of rearranging a few appointments and sending Jameson up to turn down your bed and lay out your night things, in case you were planning to retire for a few hours."

"Excellent, Braxton. I don't think I could suffer through a single decision about this blasted affair next month without a few hours of sleep under my belt. When do I need to rejoin civilization?"

"I was able to push everything back until after two o'clock, sir, without putting anything off until tomorrow."

"Very well. Thank you for the tea. I will head up to bed directly. Oh, Braxton," he added as Braxton handed him the delicate bone china cup and saucer.

"Yes, sir?"

"The new footman. What was his name, again?"

"You are referring to Bennett, sir?"

"That's the one. Tall fellow. Built rather like a hat stand."

"The very same, sir. What of him?"

"He still seems rather... nervous."

"Is that so, sir?"

"Yes," Josiah said, taking a sip of the tea and sighing with satisfaction. "Hands shaking so badly, I feared he might drop my hat right there in the drive. I wondered if you thought his temperament was quite suited to his post?"

Braxton's eyebrows rose in surprise. "Oh, I should think so, sir. He's very sharp. A quick learner. And he comes from highly respected service stock on both sides."

"And that's all well and good, Braxton, but breeding isn't everything. He's got to learn to pull himself together. Can you imagine a footman shaking and stammering his way through the arrivals at the Presentation next month? It will never do."

"Understood, sir. I shall see to Bennett personally. If he is not up to scratch by that time, he will not serve at the ball."

"Will you be able to manage without him? Won't that leave you short-handed?"

"Leave that to me, sir. I assure you, you needn't trouble yourself. We have capable staff enough to handle affairs, even if Bennett were to be relieved of his duties for the evening. That said, four weeks is plenty of time to cure him of whatever nerves are ailing him. Put it right out of your head, sir. I'll see to it personally."

Josiah smiled. "Thank you, Braxton. I know I can count on you."

"You can indeed, sir," Braxton replied with a deep bow. "Will there be anything else, sir? Something more substantial to eat, perhaps? I could have a tray sent up…"

"No, thank you very much, Braxton. I haven't got much of an appetite at the moment. You may leave me," Josiah replied, waving a hand to dismiss him.

Braxton bowed again and slipped soundlessly from the room. Josiah finished the tea and closed his eyes. He wanted to sleep. He knew he ought to. He just hoped the sight of Sergeant Hewitt's charred body wouldn't haunt him in his dreams.

(Excerpt from "The Riftborn Children's Primer," published 1804)

"One, Two, Three, Four,
Marked by the curse and barred the Door.
Five, Six, Seven, Eight,
Tempted to sin, to burn my fate,
Nine, Ten, Eleven, Twelve,
Help me, Creator, save myself!
Marked! Cursed! Burn! Fate!
Walk on the Path to reach the Gate!
Twelve, Eleven, Ten, Nine,
Salvation can as yet be mine.
Eight, seven, six, five,
Channel my curse to serve and strive,
Four, three, two, one,
Soul's great struggle, fought and won!"

THREE

EVERYTHING ABOUT THE GIRL was carefully arranged. Her gloved hands, arranged so that they rested one upon the other on the glossy countertop. Her golden hair, smoothed back and arranged into a neat bun at the nape of her slender neck. And the words upon the paper in her hand, arranged into a tidy little list from which she read to the shop girl in a careful, measured tone.

Measured. Yes, this was perhaps the best word to describe Eliza Braxton on this day, or indeed, most any day. Each word, each gesture, each decision, placed with delicacy on an internal scale, meticulously measured and deliberated upon before it was executed. It was this deliberation upon which Eliza prided herself. It was the reason the Hallewells so valued her contributions to the household.

As she waited for the shop girl to fetch an assortment of lace from which to choose, Eliza gazed around the shop with a contented sigh. She loved it when her duties brought her here. The place smelled of lavender and clean cotton and starch. The bolts of fabric hung upon the wall in a perfect gradation of rainbow colors, each flowing almost imperceptibly into the next. The wooden spools of ribbons were hung in neat and orderly rows. But for the shop girl's quiet voice and the occasional swishing and clicking of scissors, there was hardly a sound. It made for such a welcome change from the bustle and madness of life in the servants' quarters.

One of her father's habitual mutterings echoed in her head: "The mark of a well-run home is that the orderliness above belies the chaos beneath." Larkspur Manor was truly a reflection of this mantra, and Eliza was always grateful for the chance to slip away and catch her breath, though she would never admit that to her father, for whom running the manor house was both a calling and a point of pride.

"We've a lovely satin-edged lace, just come in," the girl at the counter said as she scuttled by with an armload of bolts. "Would you like me to fetch it down for you, miss, to get a peek? I think it will set off the new satin ballgown perfectly, but that's just me."

"Yes, I'll take a look, thank you," Eliza replied with a grateful smile. That was all she needed, for Miss Jessamine to hear that the latest in fine French lace had slipped past her unnoticed and onto the bodice of some other woman's frock. Eliza would never hear the end of it, especially if Sadie Carpenter got her hands on it.

"That Sadie must have a maid camped out night and day in front of every fine dressmaker in London, ready to pounce on the delivery crates before they even enter the doors," Miss Jessamine had pouted the last time Sadie Carpenter had floated into a gathering on a veritable cloud of imported French fabrics. Then she had turned to Eliza with a twinkle in her eye. "I don't suppose I could coax you into a night or two in front of Harrington's on Regent Street, could I, Eliza?"

Happily, upon this particular whim, Miss Jessamine had not insisted, and Eliza, with a gentle touch and a few choice words, soon had her feeling like the belle of the ball once again.

A touch, a few words. That was Eliza's gift, after all. Her blessing and her curse.

The shop girl, slightly out of breath, arrived back at the counter and deposited her armload of finery. "These are all the three-inch lace trims we have, miss, that've come into the shop since Miss Jessamine's last gown was completed. And this is the satin-edged I mentioned before, what just arrived." She slid the last bolt neatly toward Eliza so that she might examine it more closely.

With a practiced hesitation, Eliza waited to be sure that the young woman's hands were clear of the counter before she removed first one glove and then the other, laying them carefully to one side so that she could touch the delicate trimmings now spread out before her. As was customary, she made sure that the girl had a clear view of her Riftmark, so that there would be no confusion. The girl gave a nod of acknowledgment, and Eliza, noting it, began her inspection of the aforementioned satin-edged lace.

"You're right, it is lovely," Eliza replied, running her fingers along

32

the edge of the delicate needlework and then meeting the girl's eye with a wry smile. "The real question is, though, did it come in since Miss Carpenter's last gown was completed?"

The girl's face broke into a knowing grin. "Yes, miss. Just come in this morning. You're the first to see it, cross my heart!"

Eliza clapped her hands together delightedly. "Say no more, Lucy. Three yards of the satin-edged, and be sure to wrap it well. There's a drizzle on out there, and I've one stop yet to make. And if Miss Carpenter's maid comes calling, be sure she knows whose dress is already trimmed out with the stuff, will you?"

Lucy tipped a conspiratorial wink. "That I will, miss, you can be sure."

Eliza replaced her gloves and adjusted her cloak while Lucy busied herself measuring, cutting, and wrapping the wares in stiff brown paper before tying it securely with string. As Eliza watched, the subtle signs of Lucy's gift became apparent. The scissors slipped through the fabric just a little too easily. The edges seemed to seal themselves neatly, the strings tucking around each other smoothly. This girl was a Manipulator, and an elegant one at that: she could work at the bonds between things, pulling them together or apart as suited her. A useful gift, to be sure, when surrounded by so many delicate fabrics and trims. As though to silently confirm Eliza's conclusions, Lucy's sleeve slipped down toward her elbow, revealing the small, black tattoo—her Riftmark—upon her wrist: one small, complete circle linked with a second, slightly open circle.

"There you are," Lucy said at last, placing the four brown packages upon the countertop, along with the charges for Elder Hallewell. "And I do hope Miss Hallewell is satisfied with the details. The Misses Harrington will be out to Larkspur Manor promptly at nine o'clock tomorrow morning for her next fitting."

Eliza nestled the bill and the parcels carefully inside her shopping bag alongside a bottle of silver polish and a dozen new monogrammed handkerchiefs. Finally, with a wave to Lucy, she stepped out of the warm shop and into the damp embrace of a chilly, early March afternoon.

She knew she ought to be grateful that the rain had not yet turned back to snow, dirty grey piles of which were steaming and running in rivulets along the streets and sidewalks; but she was finding it hard to manage such a charitable thought as raindrops, propelled by a vicious wind, needled relentlessly at her face. She pulled the edges of her scarf up closer to her ears and walked faster.

Certain pockets of London could manage to be dreary on even the most delicious of warm summer days, and unfortunately, it was through one of these pockets which Eliza now had to trudge to meet the carriage that would return her to Larkspur Manor. She could have insisted that the carriage drop her at each door on her list and wait for her there, but that would have left Mrs. Keats on her feet too long. Though she had three able cook's apprentices beneath her now, Mrs. Keats always insisted on personally overseeing the choice of each and every cut of meat that presumed to enter her kitchen, and that meant, besides daily conferences with the gamekeepers and fishmongers, twice-weekly trips to the butcher, come hell or high water—or in this case, the remnants of a late winter storm. Eliza rounded the corner and sang under her breath to distract from the cold, picking her way carefully around the larger of the puddles. The song that came to her lips was a childhood rhyme, one she learned in children's services.

"One, two, three, four…

"Marked by the curse and barred the Door…"

A pair of grimy children darted out onto the sidewalk in front of her, clad in an assortment of too-large clothing and cast-off rags. One of them had no shoes to speak of, only a length of filthy fabric tied around his feet to keep them from the frozen cobbles. Eliza stopped, startled. It was unusual to see such shabbily dressed children in this part of the city—the poor masses of the Riftborn were typically contained to the Barrens. If a Praesidio guard or a constable saw them, they'd be packed off in a hurry.

"You two shouldn't be in this area," Eliza called, and the children stopped dead in their tracks. "The constables will have your hides if they see you here."

"The Barrens is in an uproar today, miss," the taller of them, a girl, replied in a mutter, wiping at her grimy face. "There was a spot of bother at the open market, fighting in the streets. Me mam told us to make ourselves scarce, so we did."

Eliza frowned. "An uproar? Fighting? What are you on about? Explain yourself and be quick about it."

"It's them hangings, miss. Everyone is real riled up about the hangings."

"Hangings?"

"It's all over them notices, miss. The notices what the Praesidio hung up all over the place," the girl said, frowning at Eliza as though she were mad. "Ain't you seen 'em, miss?"

"There aren't any such notices in this part of town, not so close to the Estates," Eliza replied sternly. "What did the notices say?"

"I don't know," the girl replied with a shrug. "I can't read, can I?"

Eliza pursed her lips at the girl's flippant tone, but said no more. It was clear she wouldn't get any more information out of her. She made to step around the children when the girl spoke again.

"Carry your parcels for you, miss?" she offered suddenly, shooting a darting glance from bloodshot eyes before dipping into a curtsy. The boy beside her, who could be no more than five or six and had said nothing at all during the exchange, coughed and dragged his sleeve across his face, staring blankly up at Eliza until the girl shot out a hand and yanked him down into an absurd bow.

"No, thank you very much," Eliza replied, knowing full well that if she handed her shopping over to these urchins, she'd likely never see it again. "But here's a venia for each of you. If things are as bad as you say in the Barrens, it might be best for you to keep your distance for a while. If you hurry, you can still reach the Illustratum before they close the gates for afternoon worship. Get yourselves a bite to eat now, off you trot."

The girl raised her eyes to Eliza again and seemed to assess her usefulness. The eyes were so shrewd, so expressive, that Eliza could practically read the child's thoughts in their depths. Was this, those eyes seemed to be asking, a woman from whom I could extract more than a measly venia or two? Might I be able to wring from her a bit more sympathy? If I grabbed those parcels and ran like the dickens, would she chase me? Eliza kept her expression blank, allowing the child to come to her conclusion. At last, nodding resignedly, the girl nudged her brother, and they each held out a gloved hand. Eliza dropped the coins onto their open palms and, with murmured thanks, the children splashed away. Eliza looked up at the clock dangling from the nearby jewelry shop. If they were quick about it, they might even manage to get a blessing before the Elders convened in the Sanctum.

Twice a day, in the morning and the afternoon, the Illustratum opened its doors to the city's poor. As many as could would cram themselves between the outer gates and the burnished golden doors before Big Ben struck the appointed hour, huddled together in a dirty jostling mass, waiting for the moment the Elders, shielded by the armed guards of the Praesidio, would venture forth onto the front steps to distribute bread and blessings. Eliza always smiled as she thought of the peculiar name of the bell that nestled high up in the highest clock tower of the Illustratum. When she was a child, passing through the tower's shadow with her father on the way to services, she had always imagined Big Ben not as a bell, but as a man—a jolly, round-bellied man in a golden waistcoat, consulting a pocket watch to confirm it was time to begin clanging away merrily with a great mallet to mark the hour for the city below. She wondered how the bell had acquired such a funny name, but had never dared to ask. In fact, the Illustratum itself, nestled along the Thames with its stunning array of turrets, towers, and gothic arches, had once had another name entirely. The palace of... West-something or other. Eliza couldn't remember. It didn't matter, really. That had been before the Rift. Before the Awakening.

What was the point, she asked herself, of dwelling on a world that was dead and buried long before she was born?

On her left, down the narrow alleyway between a cobbler's and a bakery, Eliza could see, from the corner of her eye, a short stretch of the high metal fence that separated the Praeteritum from the rest of the city. It was one of the only places where the boundary ran close to the Market District frequented by the Dignus. Eliza had heard Miss Jessamine complain about it on many occasions.

"Couldn't they just put up a wall?" she had asked her father once in rather a grumbling voice. "It's so terrible to look at. Surely there's no reason we must be subjected to it?"

But Josiah Hallewell had looked up from his newspaper and glared sharply down at his daughter over the top of his wire-rimmed spectacles until her cheeks began to redden like roses blooming and she dropped her eyes to the hands twisting in her lap. Only when she had assumed a posture of abject humiliation did he deign to reply.

"It is good for the Dignus to witness, with their own eyes, what becomes of those who do not stay the Path. It is vital, in fact. Only with a clear perception of the poorest and most sinful among us can we appreciate what has been bestowed upon us, both in blessings and in duty. We cannot lead those we do not understand."

And to drive the lesson home, Jessamine had been made to spend every day that week with her father on the steps of the Illustratum,

36

passing bread to grubby, snatching fingers, and holding ladlesful of blessed Riftmead to chapped and wrinkled lips. She did not dare mention the Praeteritum within her father's hearing again, though it did not stop her from grumbling about it to Eliza when they were out together.

Eliza said a little prayer under her breath for the poor souls on the other side of that fence and then quickened her pace. The Praeteritum was the place of childhood nightmares, the threat dangling over every Riftborn head, the ultimate punishment from which there could be no return. Even now, at eighteen years old, the thought of the place sent cold phantom fingers creeping up Eliza's spine and vague shadowy fears spinning in her head.

Eliza paused for a moment outside of the butchery to catch her breath and tuck a few rebellious strands of her blonde hair back into her cap before pushing open the door. A tinkling golden bell over the door announced her arrival.

At the counter, Mrs. Keats was deep in conversation with Madge MacCoul, the cook at Elmhurst Hall. Theirs was a friendship born out of necessity, commiseration, and a hearty mutual respect for one another's culinary talents. Mrs. Keats and Mrs. MacCoul ran two of the largest and busiest kitchens in the greater London area, as anyone who met them was immediately informed, and such responsibility was best borne when it could be shared.

"And then, if you please, he tries to sell me a brace of pheasants for more than twice what I paid for 'em only a week before," Mrs. Keats was blustering, her cheeks rosy with indignation. "And I says to 'im, I says, 'Samuel Keenside, what do you take me for?' And he looks at me, all innocent eyes and gaping mouth, and he says, 'Whatever do you mean, Lettie? I ain't tryin' to swindle you! It's the end of the season and pheasants are at a premium now.' And I replies, 'A premium, my foot! Unless them pheasants is stuffed with gold, you'd best be knocking that price right in half or I'll have none of your scrawny birds, and none of your mushrooms to boot!'"

Madge fairly hooted with laughter. "Bet he loved that."

"Oh, he huffed and puffed, to be sure, but he dropped that price right quick, I'm telling you," Mrs. Keats replied with a satisfied smile. "Imagine trying to pull something like that, and me with a dozen other hunters trying to get a foot in my door."

"Samuel Keenside is a ruddy poacher, and everyone knows it,"

Madge said, nodding sagely. "I've not reported him, mind, but someone will if he keeps carrying on like that. You'd think he'd keep his head down and his prices low, seeing as he hasn't got the proper licenses."

Eliza smothered a grin. There was about as much chance of those two turning in a poacher as there was of a Riftborn ascending to the rank of Elder: not a chance under the heavens, in other words. For all their bluster, they loved a good bargain almost as much as they liked serving that bargain stuffed and roasted on a silver platter, and no one could bargain like a poacher could. There was also the matter of sympathy, which both women had in spades. Times were hard, and honest work—or even less-than-honest work—was hard to come by. Lettie Keats and Madge MacCoul would sooner starve than see a family like the Keensides go hungry in winter.

Mrs. Keats paused in the throes of her story and caught sight of Eliza walking toward her. "Ah, there she is! And was it a battle to the death today over a scrap of lace?"

Eliza laughed. "No, thank goodness. The shops were very quiet this morning. I think perhaps the weather might have kept the hordes away."

"More likely it's the Praesidio that have kept the hordes away," Mrs. MacCoul replied under her breath. "Did you hear about that nasty business last night?"

"No!" Mrs. Keats replied, eyes widening.

The three women pulled together like a stitch, glancing around to make sure they were not being overheard.

"Has it something to do with the signs up all over the Barrens?" Eliza asked. "A child out in the street was just talking about it. She couldn't read, so she didn't know what they said, but she said the whole Barrens was in an uproar."

"It happened not three blocks from here," Mrs. MacCoul murmured. "A group of half a dozen men or so tried to scale the fence of the Praeteritum."

"Scale the fence?" Mrs. Keats whispered. "You mean they were trying to escape?"

"That's right."

"Creator save them, the bloody fools," Mrs. Keats muttered, shaking her head.

"Too late for that," Mrs. MacCoul said, her expression grim. "The

38

Praesidio on patrol caught them, of course. Dragged them through the streets and straight to the gallows, but they did not go quietly. Kicked up quite the ruckus, I've been told."

Eliza shook her head. "What would possess them to try something so foolish?"

"Desperation, no doubt," Mrs. MacCoul said. "I'm not sure but the mind can't think clearly when desperation sets in."

Eliza looked out the window and shuddered involuntarily. Over the chimney pots and rooftops, the great timbered structure of the gallows loomed like a nightmare shadow over the city. There were, thankfully, no figures dangling from it today, turning in the wind like grisly ornaments from branches. There had been days when she had looked up, heart in her throat, to witness such shapes, shells of humanity now empty. Sometimes the Praesidio left them as a lurid reminder of the consequences for breaking the Illustratum's sacred laws.

"...only hope the others have been properly chastened now," Mrs. MacCoul was saying as Eliza tore her eyes from the window and returned her attention to the conversation once again. "That kind of behavior can become contagious, like a bout of illness. One starts and before long the whole lot of them are restless and itching to cause trouble."

"Yes, well, they're predisposed to cause trouble, aren't they?" Mrs. Keats countered, drawing herself up with dignity. "Wouldn't be locked up in that place if they weren't."

All three women nodded in solemn agreement.

"To be honest, I'm surprised I even heard of it," Madge went on. "Wouldn't have done if I hadn't been concealed on the far side of a vegetable stand. Them Barrens lads hushed right up when they saw me, though. Suppose it was smart of them. Don't want to be reported, do they?"

There was an unspoken societal divide between the Riftborn in service to the Elders and the rest of the Riftborn masses. It was presumed that any Riftborn in daily service to the family of an Elder had attained their position through unswerving loyalty to the Illustratum and its teachings. Therefore, it stood to reason that any gossip or rumor that found its way to such a servant might then be passed along to the ears of the Elders themselves. In fact, if those children's parents knew that they'd been talking so freely with Eliza in the street without regard for her status, they'd likely punish them soundly.

"Your veal for you, Mrs. Keats, and the ducks dressed as well," came a hearty voice that made them all jump, as though they had forgotten they were in a shop at all. Mr. Hill, the butcher, dressed in a ghastly red-stained apron that left absolutely nothing to the imagination, plunked several brown paper-wrapped parcels upon the counter, his mustached face breaking into an amused smile as he looked from face to face, taking in their expressions. "My goodness, have we seen a ghost, then? Why the long faces?"

"Never you mind, Robert Hill," Mrs. Keats replied, as though the man were an impertinent child asking questions that ought not to be broached. "That'll do me for today, thank you."

"Always a pleasure," Mr. Hill replied, chuckling. "I'll see you Monday."

"That you will," Mrs. Keats said, almost wearily. She turned to Mrs. MacCoul. "You'll tell me if you want a hand for Friday night's do, won't you? The Hallewells will be out, of course, so I can easily spare you a girl or two. You just say the word, love."

"I'll not say no," Mrs. MacCoul replied. "Send them 'round about three, if you take the notion, and I'll put 'em to work and no mistake."

Eliza smothered a smile, knowing how Penny and Tess would kick up a fuss when they realized they'd just been robbed of a night off, casually lent to another kitchen like a cup of sugar to a neighbor. "We'd best be off, Mrs. Keats, it's near enough eleven."

Eliza said her goodbyes to Mrs. MacCoul and slipped back out into the rain, which had now turned to sleet. Martin, the coachman, was nowhere to be seen, and then Eliza remembered he had mentioned his own errand, picking up some chains and rope to repair another in the fleet of the Hallewell carriages. She sighed. She hoped he wouldn't take too long. Miss Jessamine would be up soon, and would expect Eliza there to dress her. Head bent, she hurried to the carriage, pulling the door open and stepping up inside. She was about to pull it shut behind her when a shout made her turn.

A young man was careening down the street, running at full tilt as though he were being chased, though there did not appear to be anyone following him that Eliza could see. He was tearing down the cobbles at such a pace that he could not stop in time to avoid an icy patch that sent him skidding right into the door of the carriage, nearly losing his grip on a pile of papers he had clutched to his chest. He caught hold of the door to right himself and, throwing a desperate look over his shoulder, flung himself inside the carriage, shutting the door behind him.

Eliza, finding herself suddenly trapped in the carriage with a strange man, opened her mouth to shout, "What in the world do you think you're—"

But the man, his eyes going wide with fear, threw himself forward onto her seat and clapped a hand over her mouth. "Shhhh!" he hissed.

Eliza could not at first summon the will to struggle, so shocked was she to find herself being restrained. Her heart was throwing itself against her ribcage as though it would leap from her chest as her fear paralyzed her. She stared at the young man, who, now that she was silent, was completely ignoring her and had turned his attention to the window of the carriage, peering out of it, waiting. His eyes were a startling emerald green color, set into a handsome, high-cheekboned face, pale under its smattering of freckles. She wondered if this would be the last face she would ever see, if this man was going to murder her right where she sat. A wild sob escaped her, and the man looked over at her as though surprised to still see her there.

"Are you mad? Be quiet!" he whispered, before turning back to the window again.

Eliza attempted to speak from behind his hand, but he shushed her again, more desperately this time, and then they both froze, staring right at each other, their faces barely an inch apart, as pounding footsteps and shouting sounded on the pavement outside the carriage. And in that moment, as they stared at each other, a strange thought flashed across Eliza's mind: I know him.

But before she could do more than register the thought, the man had thrown an arm across Eliza's chest and pinned her flat against the leather of the seat, at the same time drawing the little velvet curtain across the window, plunging them into semi-darkness. They both listened as the men—three of them, by Eliza's estimation—passed the carriage at a run, their cries echoing as they gave orders to each other.

"Take that alleyway!"

"On your left, that narrow lane, search it!"

"There were two of them, I saw a second!"

The men's voices and boots grew fainter as they split up and continued their pursuit, unaware that their apparent quarry was, at that moment, scaring a lady's maid out her wits. Eliza, meanwhile, was wondering if she ought to call out, to alert the men. Was she in danger? Was this man a criminal? Had she seen his image on a wanted poster: was that why he looked so familiar? How could she persuade him to let her go? In a flash of inspiration, she unclenched the hands now trembling in her lap and surreptitiously slid one hand out of its glove. She placed the hand on the man's elbow and summoned her Riftmagic.

In her fear, it surged as she had not intended, and the man turned to stare at her again. *Let go of me!* she screamed inside her head. *Let go of me right now!*

Miraculously, the man pulled both hands away from her as though she had burned him, and Eliza lost contact. He stared down at his own hands, and then at Eliza, his mouth falling open.

"How did you...?" But he had caught sight of her Riftmark and Eliza saw the light of understanding kindle in his eyes. "You're an Influencer! But how..."

He swallowed the question, his eyes moving instead to the badge upon her apron. "You... you work for the Hallewells."

The mention of her employer seemed to burn away the edges of Eliza's fear, and she raised her chin at this momentary reminder amidst the chaos of just who, exactly, she was. "Yes, I do," she said, almost defiantly.

The young man's expression twisted oddly. "Right in the belly of the beast. Creator help you," he muttered.

"What exactly is that supposed to mean?" Eliza snapped. The feeling was returning to her limbs, the numbness of shock ebbing away.

"What's your name?" the young man asked.

"Who are you to ask me such a question? What's *your* name, and how dare you lay a hand on me?" she snapped.

"Look, I'm sorry about that, I didn't mean to frighten you, but I couldn't let them..." but he seemed to be coming to his own senses, realizing where he was and, perhaps, whom he had just accosted. He looked wildly around the carriage, threw one glance out the window to be sure his pursuers were out of sight, and pushed the door open.

After wanting nothing more than for him to be gone, Eliza was suddenly furious that he was leaving. "Stop! Answer me! Who are you? Why were those men chasing you?"

The young man turned back to her and locked eyes once more. Something in them held her, tugged at her emotions in the strangest way. She realized she was afraid for him—afraid of what would happen to him when he left her sight. The realization left her breathless and confused, which was why, when he asked his next question, she answered it without thinking.

"Your name, please. I must know," he breathed.

"Eliza. Eliza Braxton."

The young man nodded. "Creator help you to see whom it is you serve, Eliza." He gave her one last, almost pitying look and took off, feet flying over the cobblestones. Then he darted down an alleyway and disappeared from view.

Free at last of his gaze, Eliza felt a return of her senses, twanging as sharply as the release of a hunter's bow. A strange surge of anger rose up inside her. Creator help her, indeed! She knew exactly whom she served! If anyone needed the Creator's help, it was a criminal who accosted young women and ran from the authorities! Meaning to shout the words after him, Eliza pushed herself up out of her seat and jumped down onto the cobbles. But her angry tirade died in her throat as she looked down at her feet and gave a cry of dismay. Her shopping bag had fallen to the ground in all the confusion and it now lay beside the wheel of the carriage in a puddle of slushy, muddy water.

"Blast it all!" she whispered to herself, bending down to retrieve it, terrified to see the state of the purchases within. A quick look through the bag was all it took to allow a sigh of relief to escape her lips; the lace, the handkerchiefs, and the rest of her purchases were still securely wrapped and unspoiled. As she made to sling the bag back over her shoulder, however, a flapping sound down near her feet caught her attention.

A piece of paper, splattered with mud, was caught beneath the heel of her boot. Instinctively, she bent to pick it up and smoothed it out so that the lettering upon it was clearly visible. It was one of the stack of papers her attacker had been carrying—he had dropped it in his haste to hide in the carriage, just as she had lost her bag. Taking the time to read it now, she realized it must be one of the notices that the ragged little girl had mentioned to her, the ones that were pasted up all over the Barrens. Eliza scanned the text and saw that it was more than merely an announcement of the executions Mrs. MacCoul had mentioned. It was also an official ordinance announcing a curfew within the Barrens, as well as a list of penances that the Illustratum was recommending to atone for the sins of their Riftborn brethren. Below all of this was the list of the men who had been hanged in the night. But as her eyes raked the text, something caught Eliza's attention: a scrap of paper had been pasted over the last name on the list, and upon it, in large red letters, so that it was sure to stand out to anyone who read it, was the name "JOHN DAVIES."

For the second time in a minute, Eliza was struck with a pang of recognition: was she supposed to know this name? Had she heard it before? But even as she pondered the question, two Praesidio guards came haring around the corner. Eliza barely had time to register their appearance before they were pointing at her and calling out, "You, there! Riftborn! What have you got there?"

At the same moment, Mrs. Keats emerged from the butcher shop, consulting her shopping list and muttering to herself. She looked up at the sound of the guards' voices, swelling like an angry bullfrog as they bore down on the carriage.

"What do you mean by shouting at her like that?" she bellowed.

Perhaps it was the shock of a Riftborn servant confronting them in such a manner but the soldiers, both of whom were very young, stopped in their tracks. They weren't deterred for more than a moment, though. The taller of the two stepped forward and snatched the paper from Eliza's grip, and grabbed her upper arm painfully tight.

"This paper! Where did you find it?"

Eliza pulled instinctively at the man's grip on her arm, the second such indelicacy in the last few minutes, but he did not relinquish her. "There was a young man... he dropped it."

The soldier narrowed his eyes at her. "A young man? Where did he go? What did he look like?"

What did he look like? Like a memory I can't place, or a dream half forgotten, Eliza thought. Out loud though, she stammered, "I... I hardly know. I wasn't looking properly. He was running down the street and... and collided with me." The lie slipped easily and readily from her lips, though she had not consciously decided to tell it. "I was knocked to the ground. He ran away after that, but not before he dropped this." She pointed at the paper in the soldier's hand.

He squinted at her, clearly unsure whether or not he ought to believe her. "How do I know you aren't one of his accomplices?"

Mrs. Keats stepped forward, puffing out her chest and pointing proudly at the badge of Larkspur Manor pinned to her jacket. "We are members of the Hallewell household staff. We were both inside the butchery here but a moment ago, on official household business. If you'd care to waste your time questioning the butcher, be my guest, but I think you'd be better served pursuing your suspect than questioning our loyalty to the house we serve."

It couldn't have been clearer that the soldier detested being spoken to in this manner, and he might have made a great deal of trouble for both women, but his partner, clearly anxious to continue the pursuit, nudged him in the shoulder.

Grudgingly, the first soldier turned back to Eliza. "You say he ran off? Which way did he go?"

This time she hesitated. She ought to tell them everything—the man was clearly a criminal, an upstart. No good could come from protecting a man like that. And then, those startlingly green eyes, that earnest face, flashed through her mind, and she found herself pointing in the complete opposite direction from the way the young man had fled.

"That way. He went that way, toward the river."

The first soldier released his grip on Eliza's arm, gave her a fleeting, malevolent look, then both men took off down the street in the direction Eliza had indicated.

The moment they disappeared, Mrs. Keats seemed to deflate. She turned to Eliza, her bravado wilting and her voice quivering. "Are you all right, Eliza, love?"

"I... I am, thank you," Eliza stammered. "You oughtn't to have spoken to them like that, Mrs. Keats. They might have arrested you!"

"Arrest me, indeed. For what? Telling the truth? I'd like to see them try," Mrs. Keats huffed, though still with less bluster than she'd shown to the guards. "What in the world were they harassing you for, anyway? What man were they talking about?"

Again, Eliza knew she ought to tell the truth about what had happened to her, and again, she could not bring herself to do so. "Just... just a man running down the street. He bumped into me."

"And the paper they grabbed from you? What was that all about?"

Eliza seized on the opportunity to tell the truth about something. "It was one of those notices I mentioned earlier, the one the Illustratum has posted all over the Barrens, in reference to the hangings last night."

45

Mrs. Keats rolled her eyes. "Well, what's so terrible about that? Unless the young man in question has been tearing them down?"

"I... no, I don't think so. I think he was... altering them," Eliza said.

"Altering them? How?"

"Well, one of the five names was obscured. Another name had been pasted over it."

"What was the name? Do you remember?" Mrs. Keats asked, fascinated in spite of herself.

"I'm not sure what the original name was—that was covered up. But the name that had been added over the first was 'John Davies'."

Eliza watched in shock as Mrs. Keats' face went from a rosy, flustered red to a pasty, bread-dough white in a matter of seconds.

"Creator protect us all," Mrs. Keats whispered.

"What is it, Mrs. Keats? Do you know John Davies?" Eliza asked eagerly.

Mrs. Keats bristled at once. "Know him? How dare you suggest such a thing!"

"I didn't mean to—"

"No faithful Riftborn in service would dare even utter his name," Mrs. Keats said, in a tone that left no doubt about just how faithful she considered herself to be.

"But why mustn't we utter his name? Who is he?" Eliza pressed eagerly.

"Never you mind. A good, respectable girl like you shouldn't let such a name pass your lips! Put it out of your head, Eliza. Keep your eyes on the Path as always," Mrs. Keats said severely.

Eliza knew better than to argue. She had known Lettie Keats all her life. The woman had bandaged her knees, wiped crumbs from her face, and even, on occasion, reminded her of her manners with a sharp tap of a wooden spoon on her backside. Once she put her foot down, there was no force Eliza knew of that would raise it again from the ground, and she was not fool enough to try.

"What's all the fuss over here?"

Martin had arrived at last, a clinking coil of chain and rope knotted over his shoulder and a bewildered expression on his face.

"Oh, never you mind, Martin. The moment has passed when you might have made yourself useful," Mrs. Keats snapped.

"But what did those Praesidio guards want?"

Mrs. Keats' eyes darted to Eliza before she set her face into an exasperated expression and said, "They wanted to know what great fool left a carriage parked here unattended for so long. Now, are you going to drive us back to the manor, or am I going to have to take the reins myself?"

Looking chastened, Martin grumbled to himself, tossing his rope and chain into the trunk on the back of the coach before hoisting himself up into the driver's box. Eliza stepped back so that Mrs. Keats could settle herself into the carriage first. Casting her eyes to the ground so that she could avoid soaking her boots in a puddle, Eliza noticed a scrap of paper half-hidden in the slush and, recognizing it, stooped swiftly to pick it up. She stared down at it curled between her numb fingertips: that name again, "John Davies." It must have come loose from the notice when the guard had grabbed it out of her hands.

If she'd had any sense at all, she would have flung the paper from her and let the winter morning have it, but she did not. For reasons she could not properly explain to herself, she slipped the name into the pocket of her skirt before ascending into the carriage and pulling the door closed behind her. Even as she settled herself against the seat, she felt as though the name was a weight dragging her down, a force of its own, and she was visited by a strange and unpleasant thought: that the choice to take the name with her, rather than casting it aside, had altered something. She shook the thought from the forefront of her mind, but she could not dislodge it completely.

The carriage rattled off at once in the direction of Larkspur Manor—the direction, in fact, that the young man had fled. Though she knew he must be long gone, Eliza could not help but press her face to the window as they clattered past the alleyway down which he had vanished. It was, predictably, deserted, and Eliza let out a breath she hadn't realized she'd been holding. She wondered if he'd gotten away, and found herself hoping, inexplicably, that he had.

As they rounded the corner of Regent Street, Eliza spotted the two children to whom she had given the venia. They were huddled in a doorway, and Eliza was gratified to see that they were gnawing on hunks of bread no doubt procured at the gates of the Illustratum. The sight of it restored, for a moment, a sense of rightness and order—this, at least, was how she knew the world was supposed to work.

Then, as though she had heard her name called, the little girl looked up and locked gazes with Eliza. Eliza, startled, smiled at the child, but felt the expression slip off her face. The girl's eyes, so bright and calculating when she had sized Eliza up upon the pavement, seemed dull and murky now, as though some light had been extinguished within them. Eliza felt the girl's eyes upon her all the way down the road, watching and yet not seeing at all, until the carriage turned the corner and the city swallowed the child whole.

FOUR

"**I**'M FAIRLY CONFIDENT that the last time I saw you, I told you we were going to have to tread carefully for the next few days," Zeke said, the words prying themselves free through his teeth.

Eli sighed. He had prepared himself for this confrontation, but it didn't lessen the sinking feeling in his gut as he looked into Zeke's stony face.

"All right, Zeke?"

"Don't you 'all right' me, you upstart lunatic. I expect this from Jasper, but not from you. Get your arse back here, now." Zeke threw down his rag and disappeared through the door behind the bar. Eli knew he had no choice but to follow him and face the verbal thrashing he had coming to him. Reluctantly, he hopped the bar and disappeared into the back room.

The Bell and Flagon was so small, dark, and unobtrusive, it might have sprung from between the other grimy buildings of the Barrens like a mushroom. No sign, emblazoned with the name of the place, hung outside the door to invite in the wayward traveler in need of a drink. No lights danced cheerily in the windows, and no barmaids laughed boisterously from the open doorway. In fact, if you hadn't spent all your life in the Barrens, gotten into a few fights, or nicked a few bits and bobs to survive, you'd likely never find the place even if someone had handed you a map. But if you'd scrounged yourself up from the gutters and managed to scrape a few spare venia together for a pint, The Bell and Flagon was the place into which you would most likely stumble. Zeke had been the barkeep since Eli was a child. He still remembered the first time he'd seen the place, in the dead of night, clinging to Sully's hand as they were ushered quietly through the door. He'd slept curled up on a pile of old sacking behind the bar while Zeke, Sully, and the others had met, scheming and planning by candlelight in the back room—the same back room in which Zeke now stood scowling at him, demanding answers.

"What in the devil did you mean by it?" Zeke asked, crossing his arms over his whiskey barrel of a chest, the damp rag with which he'd been wiping down glasses still hanging from his hand.

Eli closed the door carefully behind him before he answered. "They left his name off, Zeke."

"Of course they left his bloody name off!" Zeke replied, only just managing to keep his voice under control. "We talked it all through, didn't we? We agreed they were likely to try to bury the fact that Davies was among the dead. That's why we came up with the plan."

"The plan," Eli scoffed, snorting derisively. "Call that a plan, do you? A pack of women and children gossiping in the street?"

"You seemed all right with it when we all agreed to it."

"I changed my mind."

"You mean Jasper changed it for you. We had it covered, Eli. It was an organized system of passing information!" Zeke hissed.

"It was shite, Zeke, and you know it. How can you counter official state information by spreading a rumor?"

"Rumors can be powerful, especially when they're true," Zeke insisted.

"Yeah, well, direct contradiction is more powerful. Someone had to do something. Jasper's idea was a good one. He asked for my help and I gave it to him."

"So, you take your marching orders from Jasper now, is that it?" Zeke asked, and it was his turn to laugh. "Jasper, who can't open his mouth without losing his temper? Jasper, who wants to turn every trip to the market into a bloody revolution? Sully will be interested to know that."

"I know Jasper's... enthusiastic, but—"

"Enthusiastic? He's suicidal is what he is, and he's going to take you down with him if you're not careful, lad!" Zeke shouted. Both men stood staring at each other, trying to get their tempers under control before the patrons out in the bar realized something was wrong.

Eli felt his defiance faltering and fought to shore it up. "All right,

50

all right. It... wasn't the brightest thing I've ever done. But it wasn't the stupidest either. And it worked, didn't it?!"

"If by 'worked' you mean you avoided the hangman's noose, then yes, I guess it worked," Zeke grumbled.

"We got those notices changed. We got Davies' name on there where it ought to be. That's not nothing, Zeke," Eli countered, hating the sound of the plea in his voice.

"And how long did those notices last? An hour? Maybe two, before they tore them all down?" Zeke asked.

Eli swelled with indignation. "Two hours was long enough for hundreds of people to see Davies' name on an official Illustratum notice. And the ensuing searches and patrols by the Praesidio drew even more attention."

"People could have been hurt by those patrols. People could have been arrested," Zeke said.

"But they weren't!" Eli said, cringing at the defensiveness in his tone. He'd said as much himself to Jasper when Jasper had tried to talk him into helping to alter the notices, but Jasper, as he often did, managed to convince him he was being overly cautious. "And now the whole of Riftborn London knows that John Davies was killed. It was worth the risk, Zeke."

"The risk was your life, lad," Zeke said quietly.

"Well, I owed him that, didn't I?" Eli shouted. "For Creator's sake, it was my fault, Zeke. I was the one who called off the rescue. I was the one who decided it was too much of a risk. And because of that—because of me—Davies is dead."

"Oh, and the world revolves around you then, does it, lad?" Zeke asked. "Your actions alone trigger the way the wind blows?"

"That's not what I—"

"If it's not what you mean, then don't bloody well say it. A hell of a lot of people had a hand in shaping the events of the last two days. I don't give a rat's fart for most of them, and neither should you, but Davies... you deny Davies his agency when you talk like that. Davies wasn't a puppet, boy. He was a grown man and he made his choice. And he'd have made it with or without your help."

"We should have gone forward. We should have risked it," Eli muttered.

"Is that so? And what good would it have done, to have you strung up there, swinging in the wind beside Davies? No bloody good at all is the answer to that," Zeke spat. "The border couldn't be secured. We had good reason to doubt the information we'd been given, and the firing of that guard meant we had no ally. There wasn't a prayer of getting Davies out of that place alive, and you know it. We made the right decision. Davies made the wrong one. The Dignus has denied that man ownership of everything he's ever done. Let the man at least own his death. It's all he had left."

"What are we going to do without him, Zeke? We needed him," Eli asked, earnestly.

"We carry on, same as he would have done. Do you think Davies would have let the fall of one man determine the fate of all of them? I knew the Davies of old, boy. I was younger than you are now when he was at the helm of the Resistance. Look, lad, I know you younger lot are chomping at the bit, but you've got to use your heads. I'm an old bugger now, but I was young once—younger than you—when this fight began, and I couldn't wait to do my bit, to topple the Elders and burn the Praeteritum to ashes. But I've learned the hard way that there's no quick or easy way to win this. It's a slog, and you've got to make your peace with it if you want to keep your seat at the table. We can't afford rogue foolishness, not now."

Eli wanted to argue, but he knew Zeke was right. It was a bitter pill to swallow, but swallow it he did, along with a bit of his pride as he said, "I'm sorry, Zeke. It won't happen again, you have my word."

"I know it won't," Zeke said with a gruff smile. He slapped Eli on the back, making him stumble forward. "I know you've got sense, boy, you've just got to stick to it around the likes of Jasper. He's a headstrong fool and everyone knows it, but I can't convince Sully to chuck him out. Got a soft spot for him, and no mistake."

"I suppose I ought to go see Sully now then, eh? Get it over with?" Eli muttered, feeling like a naughty schoolboy.

"I would, lad. Face the music and move on. There's work to be done, after all," Zeke said solemnly. "And I'll bet every drop of whiskey behind this bar that Sully's already got another scheme cooked up to move us forward."

At this, Eli managed a grin. "I'd be a fool to take that bet."

"Too right you would. Now, come have a drink. I daresay you had a time of it today, even if it was your own damn fault."

Eli grinned. "Thanks, Zeke. Don't know how I'll face Sully without a pint or two."

Zeke shuddered. "I wouldn't be in your shoes for less than a bottle, lad."

52

**(Excerpt from "Duty and Service: A Lady's Maid Handbook"
By Ezekiel Stark, pub. 1867)**

"...It is a public misconception that a lady's maid's duties begin and end within the superficial realm of dressing, grooming, and proper organization of her mistress' private quarters. This is not to disparage the importance of such work, for it is a great service to assist the lady of the house in the onerous tasks of maintaining herself and her appearance. Wives and daughters of Elders are often called upon to be the public faces of the Church within our society, beacons of morality, cleanliness, and femininity, and they must appear as such at all times. This calls for great attention to detail in one's physical appearance, a duty that relies heavily on the talents of a skilled and meticulous lady's maid.

However, it is often the lady's maid who is confronted with the more mercurial whims of the female sex, and it is of this second, more private but no less important sphere which I now speak. In this more subtle of duties, the lady's maid must be as a port in a storm, a harbor into which the lady of the house can be safely moored until the tempest of the female temperament has blown itself out. It is in these ministrations that the lady's maid finds her true calling, for here can she do the most good in service to the Creator. In keeping her mistress firmly focused upon her duties and ready to serve both husband and faith, a lady's maid will discover her true value within a moral society.

And so, a lady's maid, if she is to fulfill her duties to glorify the Word, and to honor her commitment to walk the Path, must make it her most sacred of duties to serve as a constant reminder to her mistress of both her role and her responsibility, and ensure the adherence to both, all while keeping her influence in the matter nearly invisible.

In other words, a fine lady's maid is, perhaps, even more valuable to the master of the house than she is to the mistress..."

FIVE

J ESSAMINE HALLEWELL KNEW she ought to have been up hours ago, but she simply couldn't bring herself to do it. She lay in her bed, the hangings drawn, her breakfast tray cold and still untouched upon her bedside table.

She couldn't think what was wrong with her. She'd been looking forward to the ball at Larkspur Manor for months, but now that it loomed up before her, a solid reality rather than a lovely dream, a knot of fear had nestled deep in her belly, growing larger and larger every day until she could hardly breathe.

Jessamine had been to many a ball in the last few years, but this wasn't just another ball, and there was no point in pretending that it was. This was her Presentation ball, her first venture into society since celebrating her eighteenth birthday—her first ball as a woman. In a way, this ball was a presentation of sorts—a presentation of her to the world.

It was meant to be the true beginning of her life... so why did it feel like the end?

This thought inspired enough restlessness that it propelled her at last out of bed and across to her window. Eliza had mercifully left the hangings drawn, but Jessamine tugged them back now to gaze out over the grounds. It looked as though it might have snowed overnight, but a fine, misty drizzle had melted most of it away, and now only a few milky patches remained among the flowerbeds.

A Presentation was not merely a social event; it was the official coming out of a young lady into Post-Rift London society. And it marked, most significantly of all, a girl's suitability for marriage. Once she had been Presented, as the daughter of one of the most powerful Elders in the Illustratum, the fierce and frenzied competition for her hand among the young and eligible gentlemen of the Dignus would begin. This thought ought to have thrilled her; after all, what young lady would not wish to be the coveted prize among the most desirable bachelors in England? On the contrary, though: the thought filled Jessamine with the kind of dread that confined her to her bed until the morning had quite slipped away and left her blinking out into the noontime sun with a blank and desperate sort of despair.

"Miss Jessamine! Are you really only just now getting out of bed?"

Eliza had entered so surreptitiously that Jessamine had not even heard her. She turned to see the girl in the doorway, her hands on her hips and her face crumpled into a motherly scowl.

"I'm afraid so," Jessamine replied with a sigh. "You needn't scold me, Eliza. I promise you, I've been quite thorough in scolding myself."

"Begging your pardon, miss. I certainly didn't mean to sound as though I were scolding you. I just wondered whether you were feeling all right? It isn't like you to wile the day away in bed."

"No, I suppose it isn't," Jessamine said, stepping around the first question like a puddle. "I expected you to drag the covers off me ages ago—I suppose that's why I hadn't done it myself. Have you been out today?"

"Yes, miss," Eliza said. "I've only just gotten back. It's Thursday, remember?"

Jessamine whirled away from the window, her face lighting up. "The dressmakers! I'd forgotten all about it! And did you have luck? Oh, cheer me up and tell me you've found something simply breathtaking!"

Eliza smiled conspiratorially and pulled a small brown paper parcel from her apron pocket. "I'll let you be the judge of that, miss."

Jessamine let out a squeal of delight and hurried across the room to snatch the package from Eliza's hands. Then she sank to the floor in a twirl of white nightdress to tear open the paper. She gasped when she saw the contents.

"Oh, Eliza! It's just perfect! However did you find it?" she breathed, turning the lace over in her hands.

Eliza dropped to her knees beside Jessamine. "I'm friendly with the assistant at Harrington's Dressmakers. She tipped me off when the

56

new shipments of trims were coming in, and I made sure to be there when they opened the doors. It's just come from France. No one had seen it before she showed it to me."

Jessamine launched herself at Eliza, nearly knocking her flat with a fierce hug. "I just adore it! Sadie Carpenter will turn positively green with envy when she sees it!" Jessamine blanched and pulled out of the embrace. "You don't suppose there's any chance Harrington's would try to sell it to someone else, do you? There's still a month before the Presentation ball, after all."

Eliza shook her fair head, her expression utterly serene. "I have Lucy's word. No other lady's maid will dare to purchase it knowing it will already be trimming out the hostess' gown."

Jessamine's face fell. "The hostess. How tedious that sounds."

Eliza rose at once, pulling back the rest of the hangings and fetching Jessamine's dressing gown, a confection of blue silk embroidered with pink roses of which her father would have heartily disapproved had it come under his eye. "Tedious? I should think not, miss! A lavish ball with hundreds of guests, music, and dancing? What could be less tedious?"

"If all I had to do was laugh and dance the night away, Eliza, you would be entirely correct," Jessamine said, running her fingers over the embroidery, her happiness snuffed out as quickly as it had sparked. "But this won't be just any ball. This will be *my* ball, and I fear I won't be able to enjoy it."

"Whatever gives you that idea?" Eliza asked, now tutting over the cold breakfast tray. "I should think a ball would be that much more exciting, being given in your honor. Not that I would know about such things, of course," she added quickly.

"Oh, it's a lovely idea, I warrant you," Jessamine said. She rose from the floor and drifted over to her dressing table, sinking down into the seat. "I know I ought to want to be the center of attention at my own Presentation. After all, how many times have I watched other girls being Presented, and felt my heart ache for the same chance? How many of their gowns have I daydreamed myself into, how many of their suitors have I imagined whisking me away across the dance floor? But now that it's my turn, I must confess the dream is starting to feel like a nightmare."

"If it's not too bold to ask, miss, what part of it is troubling you?" Eliza asked. She had come up behind Jessamine now, gazing down at her mistress' distressed face in the mirror. "Is there something, in particular, that's worrying you? Something I can help with, perhaps?"

Jessamine's face flickered into a smile and then back into lines of misery. "I'm not quite sure, Eliza. I can't seem to pin down exactly what's bothering me."

"Well, I am confident that it couldn't possibly be your dress," Eliza said, reaching down and picking up Jessamine's silver-backed hairbrush. "It was a dream of a gown even before today's discovery of the lace trim, and with it, you'll be an absolute vision. The Misses Harrington have completely outdone themselves." She reached out and began to slowly and methodically run the brush through Jessamine's nest of dark curls.

"That's true enough," Jessamine said, closing her eyes and sighing. As Eliza's hands worked at her curls, a sense of calm and serenity began to steal through her, starting at the roots of her hair and spreading through her, a tiny trickle of tranquility.

"And certainly, you're no stranger to the spotlight, Miss Jessamine," Eliza went on, her voice a lullaby. "Why, in your duties as a Hallewell, you've always had all eyes upon you, and you have always handled it with poise and grace. Your reputation precedes you, miss, if you don't mind my saying so."

"Oh, I try, Eliza," Jessamine replied, her eyes still closed, breathing deeply. "Goodness knows I do try my best."

"And as for the Presentation... well, of course, I cannot speak from experience, miss, but it seems a simple enough ceremony, really. You don't need to give a speech or anything of that sort. Simply smile, and curtsy, and place your hand upon the Book of the Rift for your blessing by the High Elder. Certainly, nothing you can't handle."

"Oh, yes, I... I know all that. It isn't the ceremony I'm worried about, really. It's... it's more... I'm not really even sure..." She tried to snatch at the edges of her worries, to pull them into focus so that she could articulate them, but with each gentle stroke of the brush through her hair, they seemed to grow fainter—less substantial—until she could hardly recall them at all.

"And as for the suitors, well now, at the risk of sounding too bold, I think there's already a special young gentleman to whom you cannot fail to be the most glorious creature in the room," Eliza said.

Jessamine felt a smile spread slowly across her face. "Do you really think so?"

"Oh, indeed, miss. Master Teddy has set his cap for you, there's no question. And what a handsome and faithful young man he is. He's sure to follow in his father's footsteps as one of the most prestigious Elders in the Illustratum."

"He is handsome, isn't he?" Jessamine sighed, her voice taking on a dreamy quality. "And he's so kind... so gentle."

"That's right, miss," Eliza said encouragingly. "And he'll be waiting for you at that Presentation ball. If you feel yourself getting nervous, just think on him. Pretend he's the only one in the room."

Jessamine let out a girlish laugh. "Well, we both know that wouldn't be allowed."

Eliza permitted herself a small chuckle in return. "Begging your pardon, miss. That wasn't proper of me to say. But really, there's nothing to worry about, once you stop to think on it. You'll see. The Presentation ball is going to be wonderful—one of the best nights of your life, just as you've always dreamed it would be."

"You're right, Eliza," Jessamine sighed. "You're always right. I've worked myself up over nothing at all, as I often do. I can't even think of what I was anxious about. There's just so much pressure for everything to be perfect."

"'Perfection is not for such as we,' as my father likes to say. But you can be sure that everyone is working hard to bring it as close to perfection as the Creator will allow."

Jessamine's gaze clouded as Eliza's words finally struck at the root of her discontent. "But that's just it, Eliza. It can't be perfect, or even close to perfect, because I can't share any of it with my mother."

Eliza's face fell, and Jessamine almost felt guilty for speaking the thought aloud. After all, the girl had been working so hard to cheer her up, to calm her anxiety, and now it was clear all her efforts had been for naught. And she'd been so sure her gift was working. But here was something no amount of brushing and encouraging words and carefully applied Riftmagic could soothe away.

Her mother. Mrs. Hallewell. The mistress of the house, present but absent, at once a few flights of stairs and a world away, locked away not only in her own quarters but in the prison of her own grief.

Eliza did not reply for so long that Jessamine wondered if she ever would. But then her voice drifted down from above Jessamine's head, and the brush began its work through her curls again. "Your mother may not be well enough to... to participate the way you wish, miss, but..."

Jessamine let out a bitter laugh. "Participate? Eliza, she can't even acknowledge I'm alive! I'm not sure she even knows who I am anymore."

"Now, now, miss. A mother always knows her child in... in her heart, even if she can't express it."

Jessamine stared back into the mirror, and her eyes filled with tears. "There's only one child who lives in my mother's heart, Eliza. And when she lost him, that heart dried up in her chest. Perhaps if *I'd* been a boy as well, she could have found the strength to..."

"No more of this, miss!" Eliza replied, and Jessamine started at the sharpness in her voice. She looked up at Eliza's reflection and was startled to realize that her maid had the telltale glimmer of tears in her eyes. "We... we can't condemn what we cannot truly understand. Mothers aren't always there when we need them. We cannot let it define us."

Their eyes met and Jessamine understood that they were no longer only talking about her. Her heart sank. How could she have been so careless? How could she have forgotten?

"Oh, Eliza, forgive me. I... I wasn't thinking..."

"Nonsense, miss. There's no need to apologize. Now, let me tell you what I see when I look in that mirror." And she reached out and turned Jessamine's head so that she was facing her own reflection once more. "I see a young woman who knows her mind. I see a young woman who has prepared for this moment and is ready to meet it. I see a young woman who has every bit of self-assurance she needs, not only to get through that Presentation, but to enjoy every blessed minute of it. Now, if you can't see that girl yet, that's all right. But she's there, miss. I wouldn't lie to you, would I?"

Jessamine smiled, and was relieved to feel how easily the expression came to her face. "No, you certainly wouldn't."

"That's right." Eliza set the hairbrush down upon the table. "No more wallowing, miss. Ready to face the world at last?"

Jessamine examined her reflection. Her morning tangle of tousled black curls now lay in smooth, shining waves upon her shoulders, and her equally stubborn tangle of emotions, so dark and troubling a few moments before, had been tamed as well. Her own green eyes gazed back at her, clear and untroubled from the creamy porcelain planes of her face. Tentatively, she tried to smile again, this time at herself, and again, her lips complied.

"Yes. I believe I am. Or, to face my little corner of it, anyway. Thank you, Eliza."

"Not a word of it, miss," Eliza replied, laying down the brush and patting the tops of Jessamine's shoulders affectionately. "Now, let's get you dressed and then I'll see what we can persuade Mrs. Keats to surrender from the kitchen. We've got to keep you full up, or else the Misses Harrington will be forced to take in your gown again."

§

Eliza made quite sure the door was firmly closed between herself and Jessamine before she allowed the wave of light-headedness to sweep over her. The breakfast tray in danger of slipping to the floor, she tucked it in tightly against her waist with one hand and used the other to clutch at the doorknob in an effort to steady herself. It did not often take such an effort on her part to calm Miss Jessamine. Her mistress' concerns must have been overwhelming indeed. This, after all, was the heart of Eliza's duty to Miss Jessamine—the dressing and the grooming and the fetching of trays were as nothing compared to the use of her Riftmagic.

Eliza's earliest memory of her childhood involved using her Riftmagic, though it was unconsciously done at the time. She had been only three years old and walked into the servants' sleeping quarters at Larkspur Manor to find her mother sitting on the edge of a bed, sobbing desperately into her hands. The sight had struck her most terribly, for she had never seen her mother cry before, and it shook something at her core. Unable to bear the sight of her mother's tears, Eliza had climbed up onto the bed, grasped her mother's hand, and... it had simply happened. She summoned it from the depths of herself, a force over which she had not yet learned control. She felt it well up inside her, spilling from her fingertips, flowing into her mother like a river into the sea. Her only desire was to stop her mother's tears—to see the woman look down upon her and smile. The smile she craved lasted only a moment, to be replaced by shock and fear in a seamless progression.

There was another reason the memory remained burned in her

mind so vividly: it was one of the last times she ever saw her mother. She disappeared only a few days later, never to return.

This was how Eliza had learned that she was an Influencer. This was how she had discovered her soul-deep weakness, the innate and terrible curse with which she had been endowed from birth. With the mere touch of her hand and exertion of her will, she could influence the thoughts and feelings of others. Her particular kind of Riftmagic was the rarest, but also one of the most dangerous. It would be easy, her father had explained to his wide-eyed little girl, so very easy to use her Riftmagic selfishly, to work her own will, rather than the will of the Creator. If she succumbed to such weakness, her soul would be lost forever. Such terror he had struck into her little heart that day, but he had also fortified her with hope. All was not lost, he assured her. From then on, the sole focus of her young life had been to master her Riftmagic, to tame it, to utterly destroy any power it may hold to tempt her, and to channel it into the kind of devoted service that would be her one chance at salvation.

If she allowed herself to think about it for too long, she began to wonder if it had been the sudden appearance of her raw and untamed Riftmagic that had driven her mother away. Then she began to wonder where her mother might have gone, and what had happened to her there. Before she knew it, she had spiraled down into as deep and dark a place as she suspected could live inside her, and it was hard to climb back out. And so, she didn't allow herself to think about it at all, if she could help it. But when Jessamine got like this, it was hard not to tumble back in.

Two motherless girls. So similar in their struggle to understand, and yet, a whole wide world apart in every other way.

After a few deep breaths, Eliza felt steadier, and so she hurried down the hallway and through a concealed door in the paneling that led down into the servants' quarters.

The downstairs and the upstairs of any great house worked in exact opposition to each other. The calmer and quieter the floors above, the busier and more hectic the floors below, and with preparations in full swing for the Presentation ball, downstairs had rarely been so astir with activity. The kitchens were a madhouse—Eliza hardly dared even to peek her head in, and the whole of the staff knew not to bother Mrs. Keats with anything that wasn't the direst of emergencies unless they wanted their heads bitten clean off their necks. Every member of the kitchen staff was working madly—chopping, slicing, plucking, and kneading, while Mrs. Keats bustled between them, barking out orders in an increasingly frazzled voice. The Presentation might have been a month away, but every recipe had to be tested, timed, and coordinated before it could be approved for the final menu. Eliza waited patiently until Penny, one of the kitchen maids, passed the doorway. She caught the unsuspecting girl by the arm.

"What?! Oh! Eliza, you gave me a turn!" Penny's freckled face was smudged with flour and she was wiping her hands on her apron. Her eyes dropped to the tray in Eliza's hands and her face fell. "Don't tell me. She's gone and let it go cold and now you need another."

Eliza gave an apologetic smile. "I wouldn't ask, Penny, but she's in a right state today, worrying about her Presentation. Couldn't you do her up a quick tea and toast with that orange marmalade she likes? I'd be ever so grateful."

Penny rolled her eyes and blew a wisp of fair hair out of her face. "Worrying about her Presentation, indeed. And what's she got to do, I'd like to know? Just stand there smilin' while other people dress her, other people feed her, and other people swing her 'round a dance floor. Why, a girl could be Presented in her sleep! Meanwhile, I've been down here baking for a solid week and I'm not likely to sit down again for another four! I'd fancy a lie-in, let me tell you!"

"I know, and you're a marvel, Penny, truly you are," Eliza said soothingly. "But you know how she is. Please, she's got to eat something or she'll not be fit for company when the dressmakers come for her fitting this afternoon."

Penny grumbled and groaned, but she took the tray from Eliza's hands. Eliza gave her a grateful smile and backed carefully out before Penny could change her mind and thrust the tray back at her in a renewed tirade.

Eliza slipped down the hallway to the butler's office at the end of the hall. The door was slightly ajar, but she knocked all the same. Her father's deep voice answered, "Enter."

William Braxton smiled when he saw his daughter in the doorway, and beckoned her forward. His ledger lay open on the desk before him, and he set his pencil down upon it.

Eliza pushed the door wider but did not yet cross the threshold. "It's only me, Father."

"Nonsense. It's never 'only' you, Eliza," Braxton replied with a smile. "Do come in, there's no need to hover in the doorway like that."

Eliza stepped through the door and pulled it carefully shut behind her. "I'm sorry to disturb you. I just wanted to let you know that I'm back now, and Miss Jessamine's just told me she won't need me again until the dressmakers arrive this afternoon. I thought you might like to put me to work. How can I help?"

"Well, for mercy's sake, whatever you do, stay out of the kitchen," Braxton replied with a deep sigh. "Mrs. Keats is still waiting on a flour delivery, and there'll be no peace until it arrives."

Eliza suppressed a laugh. "Let's be honest, father. Is there ever peace in that kitchen?"

Braxton chuckled. "No, I suppose not. Even so, steer clear of that woman if you know what's good for you."

"I was with her all morning, you forget," Eliza said. "And a good thing, too, for it was a very strange morning to be in town."

Braxton frowned. "Strange? How so?"

"It was so quiet after... after what happened last night," Eliza began cautiously.

Braxton's face fell into an expression of deep disapproval. "Oh, yes. Elder Hallewell was out all night dealing with that. He was thoroughly out of sorts when he finally arrived home not long after dawn. I do hope he's getting some rest now."

"Did he... did he tell you much about it?" Eliza asked tentatively. It was like a carefully choreographed dance, trying to get information out of her father, a dance at which she often found herself to be completely wrong-footed. Still, it was worth a try.

"No, he did not," Braxton replied, with just a hint of a warning in his tone, but mild enough that Eliza could pretend not to notice it.

"The Market District was practically deserted. And everyone was talking about these... these notices that had gone up all over the Barrens."

"Everyone, indeed. Whoever would you be talking to who had knowledge of the Barrens? You know I don't approve of you mixing with that sort," Braxton scolded.

"I wasn't mixing, Father, I promise," Eliza said, though she flinched at the ugliness of the word. "I merely gave a venia each to a pair of beggar children."

64

"Beggar children? In the Market District? You had better have told them to clear off," Braxton said, wrinkling his nose.

"But that was the trouble, Father. They'd already been told to clear off—right out of the Barrens. Evidently, it was rather... unsettled there today, because of the hangings, and their mother said it wasn't safe," Eliza replied.

"It's a dangerous place at the best of times," Braxton said. "I don't even like you going there with your ministry group."

"I know, Father, you've told me many times," Eliza said, trying not to sound impatient, "but you know that Elder Hallewell says our presence there is important. We set a good example for the other Riftborn to aspire to."

"Just so," her father allowed grumpily.

"The thing is, Father, there were some notices that had gone up, and... and the Riftborn were talking about one of the men who they believe was hanged," Eliza plunged on before she could lose her nerve. "It seems there was... confusion as to whether he was one of the executed or not."

"Eliza for heaven's sake, whatever are you on about? What man?" her father asked impatiently.

"John Davies," Eliza announced, and held her breath.

The reaction was almost exactly the same as Mrs. Keats except, rather than going pale, her father's face was steadily reddening, as though he were being filled with boiling water. "Eliza!" he gasped. "I never want to hear that name escape your lips again!"

"But why? Who was he, Father? Why is it so terrible to speak of him?"

"That man flew in the face of everything we value and stand for. He's a traitor and a coward, and you will not sully your thoughts with his name anymore!"

"But—"

"Enough, Eliza!"

Eliza took an involuntary step back. It was the first time she could ever remember him shouting at her, and it took her breath away. Her father seemed to regret his loss of temper almost at once. He took several shaky breaths in an attempt to calm himself, and when he spoke again, it was in a voice of determined calm.

"You must trust me, child, that there are parts of Riftborn history that are best left buried. There have always been those who have chosen to reject the wisdom and mercy of the Creator, and they are best never spoken of again. We commit our lives and our Riftmagic to the Path, and we must remain focused and clear-eyed, or we will lose our way. Do you understand?"

"Yes, Father," Eliza whispered.

"I never want that name to cross your lips again. Is that clear?"

"Yes, Father."

"Good. Very good. You're a good girl, Eliza," her father said, attempting a smile and reaching out to pat her on the hand. "These are natural questions to ask, but you must content yourself with not knowing the answers."

Eliza nodded, trying to remember how to work the muscles of her face so that she could return the smile. She must have managed it, for her father's own smile broadened and relaxed, and he returned to his work.

"What's all this, then?" Eliza asked in a brave attempt to return to normality, stepping around the desk to peer down at the ledger.

"Expenses and supplies for the Presentation. Everything accounted for, right down to the last farthing," Braxton said with a sigh. "Or at least, it was, until I was sent a new list of requests from the kitchen staff and the coachmen." He tapped his hand on a stack of papers now piled beside the ledger.

"I'm sure you'll be glad when this is all over, but if anyone can manage it, I know you can," Eliza said, planting an encouraging kiss on her father's hair, which had just begun to thin on the crown of his head.

"I think we'll all be glad when it's over, Elder Hallewell included," Braxton admitted. "But he has certainly spared no expense and will not be outdone by any of the other Elders, that is to be sure. It will be the highlight of the social season. I don't envy the household staff of the next young lady to be Presented."

It was only because Eliza knew her father so well that she could detect the hint of pride in his voice. The truth was that the more elaborate and impressive the event grew to be, the more delighted her father was. Though he would receive none of the credit for it from the world of the Dignus, the Presentation would be as much Braxton's triumph as it was Elder Hallewell's, if it went off without a hitch. The service world had its own hierarchy, unacknowledged as it might be in upstairs society, and there was a great deal of healthy—and

66

sometimes unhealthy—competition between the staffs of the various Elder households. An Elder's family could see a boost in their own social standings when their staff was able to garner itself a reputation for competence. There was no position more envied and more admired in the Riftborn world than that of butler of an Elder estate, and by coordinating an event of this magnitude, Braxton was poised to perch atop the very pinnacle even of his fellows. The pressure, therefore, was immense, not that her father would ever betray for even a moment that he was affected by it. Eliza, now wracked with guilt for bringing up a subject that had so unsettled him, was anxious to assist him in any way she could.

"It's going to be a wonderful night, I have no doubt," Eliza said firmly. "If anyone can manage it all, you can. Now, what can I do? I've got a few hours before I've got to be back upstairs. Surely there's something I can help check off your list."

"I hadn't counted on your being available, Eliza. I was sure you'd be tied up with Miss Jessamine, what with one thing and another," her father said delicately, employing his favorite euphemism for the somewhat mysterious world of lady's maid's duties. "However, I shan't refuse your help, not when we're so snowed under. Perhaps you can see how Bridie and the others are getting along with the polishing of the silver, and speed things along if they've settled into gossiping like a brood of hens like they usually do," Braxton suggested in a weary sort of voice.

"Oh, don't you worry about Bridie. She can chatter and polish at the same time, never fear," Eliza said, squeezing her father's shoulder affectionately. "But I'll make sure they're coming along."

Down the hall in one of Larkspur Manor's many storage rooms, the audacious task of polishing the family silver was underway with, it was fair to say, a good deal of chin-wagging. Liesel Andrews, Bridie Sloane, and Millie Martin stood around an impossibly long table, polishing rags flying nearly as swiftly as the gossip through the air among them. Eliza rolled up her sleeves and took a place beside her best friend, Bridie, who graciously took a breath in the steady stream of her chattering to kiss Eliza on the cheek.

"Eliza! I didn't expect to see you until tonight! Grab yourself a rag, we're drowning in cutlery here, with no end in sight," Bridie insisted. She had the kind of voice that gushed up out of her, bubbling with emotion. Her eyes gleamed wickedly and she tossed her chestnut hair. "Honestly, is there a soul alive in England whom the Hallewells haven't invited to the ball?"

"They seem to have mislaid my invitation," Liesel Andrews said tartly, attacking the tines of a lobster fork with a vengeance. "But I'm sure it's on its way."

Millie's shrill piccolo trill of a laugh filled the room. "Oh, Liesel, stop it now. I can hardly polish for laughing!"

"I'm not sure where the joke came in, myself," Liesel said dryly, laying the lobster fork down and picking up a salad fork. "This tin's nearly empty. Slide that polish over here, would you, there's a good girl."

"So, what have I missed around the manor this morning, anything exciting?" Eliza asked.

"Oh, come off it, Eliza, and stop holding us in suspense!" Bridie hissed.

Eliza looked from one rapt face to another. All three women were staring intently at her, clearly waiting for her to speak. "I... what are you on about, Bridie?"

"Eliza, don't be mean!" Bridie cried resentfully. "You've got to tell us—Mrs. Keats wouldn't say a blessed word and told us off for vexing her, but I know you'll not be so cruel." Bridie dropped her voice to little more than a tremulous whisper. "Is it true, about the hangings in town last night?"

Eliza sighed. Of course, they wanted to know about such sordid affairs. One whiff of a scandal and the whole downstairs was abuzz like a hive of overexcited bees. "I would have thought, with all the preparations for the Presentation, that you'd have been too busy to hear about that."

"Well, of course we're busy, Eliza, but we're not deaf and dumb!" Bridie scoffed with a toss of her hair. Bridie could say more with a hair toss than most girls could say with a dictionary and a solid hour's time. "I wouldn't have heard about it at all, if it weren't for the fact that I used the last of the coal in my scuttle and had to go to the cellars to refill it, and wouldn't you know, there were James Whippet and that new footman, what's his name?"

"Peter Bennett," Millie supplied, checking her reflection in the back of a soup spoon.

"That's the one. Well, Peter and James were out by the cellar doors, having a cigarette, you know, and I overheard them speaking of it. Of course, when they saw me coming, they hushed right up, and when I asked them what they were talking about, they fell to flattering me instead." She rolled her eyes. "As though I'd give the time of day to a pair of overgrown schoolboys like those two. Barely out of knickers, the pair of them. Anyway, I couldn't get another sensible word out of them. But surely you must know, Eliza, all the shops must have been brimming with talk of it!"

Eliza bit her lip. The subject had already gotten her into so much trouble. She decided to say as little as possible. "Well, yes, I did hear something about it, but not much, mind you," she added quickly, for all three women had leaned in eagerly. "It was Mrs. MacCoul who mentioned it."

Liesel nodded sagely. "No one's got their ear closer to the ground than Madge MacCoul. It's a miracle the woman can walk upright. What did she say?"

Eliza shrugged. "Not much. Just that several men had attempted to escape the Praeteritum and had been caught and hanged."

Bridie's face fell. "That's all? Did she even tell you their names?"

Eliza shook her head and feigned disinterest. "I'm afraid not. And anyway, I'm not sure what difference that should make to me. If they were in the Praeteritum, they were criminals, so it's not as though I should know them."

"It's just..." Bridie shrugged, her expression falling. "Peter and James were discussing it so eagerly. I thought it might be... be more than just a common hanging of a few thieves. It was as though I'd interrupted them in something real secret-like. They clammed right up when I tried to get them to give me the details. Peter's face went all red, and James Whippet wouldn't even look at me in the eye."

"I should think not. Imagine being caught like two old spinsters trading gossip. I'd be embarrassed myself. I daresay the menfolk around here are as foolish as the womenfolk," Liesel countered. "I'm not sure I've ever heard two words of sense spoken together out of the likes of James Whippet—or any of the Whippets, come to that. I've known two of his brothers and they've both been prattling fools. And Peter Bennett's not been here a fortnight. He'd do well to hold his tongue and fix his mind on his work if he means to stay on in this household."

Eliza nodded approvingly, relieved that Liesel had put an end to the topic. Of all the maid staff in Larkspur Manor, only Liesel had been with the family since before Master Josiah had become the head of the household. She owed her longevity not only to the quality of her work, but also, as she was wont to say, "knowing when to keep my eyes open and my mouth well and truly shut." There was little Liesel didn't know about the goings-on in Larkspur Manor, sure enough, but there was even less that you could drag out of her.

Bridie's countenance was slipping by the second. "So, that's it then? You haven't heard anything else, Eliza?"

Eliza hesitated a moment. She normally told Bridie everything, but for once in her life, she had an experience she wanted to keep entirely to herself, though she could not give herself a satisfactory explanation as to why that was. All she knew was that she couldn't bring herself to tell Bridie about the young man who had leapt into the carriage—at least, not in front of the others, and not until she had taken a moment on her own to sit and reflect on what she was only now beginning to understand was a traumatizing experience. Resolved, she shook her head.

"When it comes right down to it, it doesn't sound like the kind of thing we should bandy about for gossip, now does it?" Liesel concluded. "A bit of prayer for the families bearing their disgrace might be more fitting."

Bridie mumbled something that sounded like... "Just wanted to know..." and returned to her polishing with a meek and humbled expression. Liesel had that effect on Bridie. Bridie had come to the Manor from a workhouse, hardly an auspicious beginning, but Liesel—who had been trusted with selecting a new maid to work beneath her—had seen promise in Bridie and taken her under her wing. It was not quite as maternal a gesture as it sounded. She scolded Bridie incessantly and was never what one would call affectionate, but she also taught her and guided her and shielded her from the common pitfalls that led a maid to be dismissed. She drilled her in her duties until she was as competent as it was possible for her to be, and she defended her so thoroughly that no one dare say a bad word about her in Leisel's company.

"Do you suppose the staff will be invited up to see the Presentation?" Millie asked, with the bright air of someone eager to change the subject. "Because my sister, Ellie, is a scullery maid at Elmhurst Hall, and she still talks about how the whole of the downstairs staff was invited to stand along the back of the hall when Elder Potter's eldest daughter was Presented."

"I haven't heard anything about it," Liesel said at once.

"Nor have I," Eliza said, "and I'm sure my Father would have told me if he'd heard of any such plans."

"Ellie said it was ever so grand—like watching a garden come to life. So many brightly colored dresses, all whirling around. And the music... she still dreams about it, sometimes." Millie's eyes glazed over dreamily.

"Well, I, for one, will be staying downstairs where I belong," Liesel replied curtly. "We've no business being upstairs while the Dignus are gathering."

"But if we'd been invited, you'd have to come," Bridie said, beginning to perk up again. "You wouldn't dare refuse Elder Hallewell if he asked us to attend."

"No, I daresay I wouldn't," Liesel said with a grudging shrug of her shoulders. "But it doesn't seem right to me, mixing like that. We've got our sphere and they've got theirs. I don't know that it would give me any pleasure to watch such goings-on."

"Well, it would certainly give me pleasure," Bridie sighed, taking hold of her apron and holding it out like the skirt of a ballgown as she spun around the room. "It must be such a sight to see!"

"Ellie went on and on about it," Millie agreed. "Oh, I'd love to have a story to match hers."

"What do you think, Eliza? Can you imagine yourself in a ballgown like Miss Jessamine's?" Bridie asked eagerly.

Eliza smiled and shrugged vaguely but did not answer. Of course, she'd imagined herself in every one of Miss Jessamine's vast collection of gowns, especially in her earliest days as a lady's maid, when she'd found herself handling such finery for the first time. She'd run her fingers over the lush silks and satins as she'd hung them up and imagined how they would feel against her skin. She'd polished and arranged every piece of jewelry, mended every flower crown, and pressed every lace-edged handkerchief, and though she'd imagined doing so many times, she'd never once tried a single one of them on herself. The thought of it filled her with an overwhelming fear, like crossing a boundary from which there could be no return. She couldn't help but think that Miss Jessamine would know instantly what she had done, as though the very contact with Eliza's Riftborn skin would alter the garments in some tangible way.

Eliza stayed and helped with the polishing for another two hours, and thankfully, the conversation never returned to the unrest in London—it seemed Liesel had shamed the others out of daring to bring up the subject again. When she was at last able to excuse herself, it was with an air of extreme relief; Eliza enjoyed the women's company, but all the while she was working with them, she felt as though there were an ember slowly burning a hole in her apron pocket.

Alone in her room, with the door safely locked behind her, Eliza carefully extracted the scrap of paper that had been pasted over the Illustratum notice. Staring down at the name written upon it, a name that was meant to strike fear and shame into her very core, all she could feel was... curiosity. Why would no one tell her who this man was? What had he done? And why should this very knowledge have some sort of negative impact on her? Was she so weak, so faithless, that the mere mention of a criminal was sufficient to knock her from the Path on which she had trod faithfully all her life? Indignation rose inside her, transforming the letters from a simple identity to something like a challenge. She knew she ought to throw the paper into the grate—to burn it to ashes before someone discovered it. But she did not do it. Instead, she folded the paper up as small as she could, tucked it inside a handkerchief, and placed it carefully in the drawer of her bedside table.

And as she did so, she thought of the young man who had leapt into the carriage, the one who felt it so important that the world see this name, that he risked serious trouble—maybe even death—at the hands of the authorities. Eliza didn't know for sure what would happen to a man who tampered with official Illustratum communications, but she was willing to bet that he was risking his life. Who was he? And why, in the face of his own rather desperate situation, did he seem to pity her? His words echoed in her head, haunting her like a persistent specter: "Creator help you to see whom it is you serve."

"Creator help me, indeed. Creator help *you*, whoever you are, before you find yourself swinging from the same noose as the man whose name I've just buried in my drawer," she whispered to herself.

But even as she crossed the room a few minutes later, a fresh apron tied around her middle, preparing to return to Miss Jessamine's room for her fitting, she fancied she could feel the name of John Davies and all its unanswered questions, like a sentient thing, its eyes following her until she closed the door.

**(Letter from the Private Archive of Dr. Josiah Fenwick,
Physician, Westminster Hospital, 19 February, 1798)**

Dr. Alexander Monro
Royal Infirmary of Edinburgh
Edinburgh, Scotland

Dear Sir,

*It is with grave concern that I write you of a most peculiar
condition that has cast its shadow over the city of London, the likes of
which neither myself nor my colleagues have seen before, and which
is of such a disturbing nature that we cannot begin to conceive of the
cause.*

*A child was brought to us in the early spring who had, according
to the girl's distraught parents, developed most abnormal abilities. It
must be admitted, as I listened to their story, that I gave it very little
credence at first. They were uneducated, dragged up from the very
gutters of the city and, bless them, very superstitious. It was a marvel
they even thought to bring the child to us, given that they surely had
no money with which to pay for medical services. They were insistent,
however, that we keep the child under observation, and her peculiarity
would become abundantly clear. It was my colleague, Dr. Martin, a
man whose heart has always been far too soft when faced with the
dregs of our society, who relented and agreed to keep the child in
hospital for the night.*

*I have enclosed a copy of our detailed notes from that night
for your inspection, but what we witnessed was indeed remarkable.*

75

The child could, when worked into an emotional state, physically manipulate inanimate objects without touching them. As we watched in astonishment, she made first a lamp, then a book, then a chair fly across the room at us as she shouted and cried to be allowed to return home. We were forced to vacate the room to avoid grievous injury at her hands, and the staff only just managed to sedate the child.

No amount of testing or examination can find a root cause of this phenomenon, and now I am told that there are rumors of others...

SIX

E LI STARED UP at the imposing façade of the brownstone, gnawing at a fingernail. He felt like a naughty schoolboy, anticipating a sound whipping at the hands of a stern schoolmaster. Sully was far from a schoolmaster, and there would certainly be no whipping involved, and yet Eli could barely drag his feet across the road to face what he knew would be a devil of a verbal thrashing.

The neighborhood itself was known simply as the Commons, and it was as far from the Barrens as a Riftborn could possibly get without crossing into Dignus territory. The streets were well-lit and no vagrants crowded the doorways or built fires in the rubbish bins on the corners. Carriages trundled freely through, with no fear of thieves or orphans hopping onto the running boards. Respectable businessmen and merchants whose storefronts lined the Market District made their comfortable homes here. There was nothing ostentatious about the Commons—it was simply clean and well-kept, which for a Riftborn in post-Rift London, was about as close to paradise as one could dream. It was a status so difficult to attain that many of the houses were vacant, which was a bloody good thing, or it would have been a damn sight harder to run an illegal literature trade and a safe house of the Resistance from Sully's basement. A person would have to be mad to operate such an enterprise in such a respectable area, particularly in light of the fact that many of the Riftborn who lived there worked directly with the Illustratum.

But that was Sully, Eli thought. Mad as a hatter. Always had been.

On a typical day, Eli might have used the front steps, but today he decided he was in enough trouble to warrant a trip around the side to the kitchen door. He slipped through the narrow alleyway between Sully's house and the brownstone next door, descended the steps to the sunken kitchen door, and knocked.

Louise's ruddy face appeared in the little leaded glass pane in the door so fast, she might have been lying in wait beneath it. She squinted at Eli for several seconds, as though she hadn't seen him every day since the time he was four, and then wiped her hands on her apron, pulled the latch on the door, and stood back to allow him entry.

"Louise," Eli said, flashing his best smile and doffing his cap. "And how are you this fine day?"

"Don't see what's so fine about it," Louise replied, returning to the counter, where she was plucking a chicken with unnecessary vigor.

"Well, I get to see you, don't I? That's fine enough for me," Eli said, nudging the woman with his elbow.

"Oh, save that charm for someone it works on," Louise scoffed, but a smile tugged at the corners of her lips just the same. She pointed a feathery finger at the pantry door. "There's scones just come out the oven there, but I've not finished the clotted cream yet, so there's none to be had and you'll just have to make do."

"You're a treasure, Louise," Eli said, grinning and pocketing two scones for himself. "I'll be more than glad to make do."

"Go on, get that gigglemug out of here. I've got enough work to be getting along with without your interference," Louise said, as Eli knew she would, having ushered him out of her kitchen in such a manner since he was in short-pants. He turned to go.

"Oh, and Eli?"

He turned back, half a scone crammed in his mouth.

"Sully's in a right state. Watch that tongue of yours."

Eli grimaced. If the uproar had reached Louise all the way down in the kitchen, things must be worse than he feared.

He trudged up the stairs to Sully's office, the scone feeling as though it were turning to sawdust the longer he chewed it. He swallowed it with some difficulty as he found himself standing outside the door, palms sweating. Screwing up all his courage, he made a fist and knocked upon the door.

"Enter at your own peril," came the familiar voice.

Eli turned the knob and pushed the door open to find Sully standing behind the large mahogany desk, arms crossed, face a storm cloud.

"Well," she said. "You've got a hell of a nerve coming back here. Give me one good reason why I shouldn't boot your ungrateful arse from the ranks of the Resistance right this blessed moment."

Lila Sullivan was a tall, angular woman of forty-five with a mane of unruly chestnut hair, a high cheek-boned face, and a penchant for eschewing corsets and skirts for suspenders and trousers. She was also in possession of a pair of steely blue-grey eyes that could burn a hole through whomever found himself unfortunate enough to be fixed with her glare. At this moment, the unfortunate party was Eli, and he felt every degree of the heat as he stared down the lioness in her den, who also happened to be the woman who raised him.

"Well, it would be a shame to throw me out before I at least had the chance to apologize," Eli replied.

"Oh, is that so? And what good will an apology do me if you're swinging from a hangman's noose?" Sully demanded, red spots appearing on her cheeks where, in happier times, dimples made their impressions.

"I didn't get caught, Sully. Neither of us got caught."

"And you think that's because you're both clever? Or skillful? Or whatever nonsense boys fill their heads with when they don't want to admit they've done nothing more than stumble cock first into a scrap of dumb luck?"

Eli stiffened at this. "I'm not a boy anymore."

"When you act like a boy, I'll bloody well call you one!" Sully shouted. "How dare you ignore the will of the group, Eli? We agreed to use other channels to get the word out about Davies, to ignore the notices. But, no, that wasn't good enough for you, was it? You needed your own plan—"

"It wasn't my plan, it was Jasper's plan!" Eli cried, stung.

"And where is he? Slunk into some whorehouse to wait out my wrath, no doubt, not that he can afford to engage any company for himself," Sully snapped with a harsh laugh. "And I expect he knew you'd come back here with your tail between your legs. He's more than happy to let you bear the brunt of my temper while he hides like a coward."

"Are you going to let me apologize or not?" Eli asked.

Sully crossed her arms over her chest, her expression stony. "Go on, then. I like watching a good exercise in futility as much as the next person."

Eli took a deep breath. "I'm sorry, Sully. I know it was stupid and reckless, and all the other things you said. And I wouldn't blame you if you wanted to throw me right out of the Resistance. I never should have listened to Jasper. He's always had too much of an influence on me, as you know, and I've yet to outgrow it, so I guess calling me a 'boy' isn't off the mark after all."

Sully was still glaring at him, but Eli noted with a scrap of relief that something in her posture had softened. "Every time I had to whip you as a child, it was a result of that boy's mischief."

Eli allowed himself a small shrug. "What can I say? He's always been hard to resist."

Sully pointed a finger at him. "Well, you'll resist him next time or you'll be out on your backside. And Jasper had better find a new place to hang his hat for a while unless he wants to feel the back side of my hand."

Eli knew this was an empty threat. Sully had thrown Jasper out a dozen times since the age of twelve, and yet he still called the place home. It seemed Eli wasn't the only one easily influenced as far as Jasper was concerned.

"As if I didn't have enough to worry about without the two of you running around like a pair of miscreants without any sense. There's a holdup in my shipments from France, and I've lost a translator to influenza. There's been a crackdown in the Barrens since this Davies business, and it's hard to move people in and out. I'm not sure when I'll be able to secure another location for the Riftborn we've already promised to take." She slammed a hand on the desk, sank into her chair, and closed the text she had been examining when he walked in. "I suppose you heard about Nigel Barrows?"

Eli frowned. "The fellow from the smithy? What about him?"

"Dead. Broke curfew and got into it with a Praesidio guard when they tried to arrest him."

"Bloody hell," Eli whispered. "I don't believe it. I knew he was a fool, but..."

"Oh, you don't have to take my word for it. Take a stroll into the Market District and see for yourself. He's still up there, waving in the breeze," Sully replied with a bitter laugh. "I suppose they want to leave him as a warning to the rest of us to follow the rules." She looked him square in the eye. "That could have been you, Eli. It could be any of us if we don't stick together and follow the plans."

"I know," Eli said solemnly. "Zeke already dressed me down, good and proper. I won't let you down again, Sully, you have my word."

"You start keeping your promises to me, Eli, or that word won't be worth the breath it takes you to utter it, you hear me?"

"Yes, ma'am."

Sully held his gaze a moment longer, then pressed her lips together and nodded once, firmly. It was a nod that Eli knew well, and the sight of it released a knot of tension in his gut. Things between them might be tense for a while, but he was forgiven.

"I didn't just come here to apologize," Eli said, hoping to redeem himself slightly. "There's something I need to tell you—something I discovered that might just make up for all the worry I caused you."

"Is that so?" Sully replied, her voice full of sarcasm. "Go on, then. Dazzle me."

"There's an Influencer working for the Hallewells," Eli said.

Sully raised one, decidedly unimpressed eyebrow. "And why wouldn't there be? Hallewell is second only to Morgan in the chain of command. And anyway, our records have indicated such."

"No, Sully, you don't understand. They've got a real, powerful Influencer, like nothing I've ever felt before," Eli said.

Sully narrowed her eyes. "Explain. Now."

"Well, when I was altering the notices, I... sort of ran into a servant from Larkspur Manor," Eli began hesitantly.

"And by 'ran into' you mean...?"

"I... all right, I was running from the Praesidio and leapt into her carriage," Eli blurted out.

Sully stood up, her face flushing with anger, and opened her mouth, no doubt to castigate him again, but Eli cut her off.

"I know, I know! We've already established I'm a fool, all right? I concede the point. I had to cover her mouth to keep her quiet, and—"

"You didn't run into a servant from Larkspur Manor, you accosted her!" Sully shouted. "She could have had you arrested on the spot!"

"She didn't need to! She placed her hand on mine and before I knew what had happened, I was on the opposite side of the carriage," Eli said.

Sully froze. "What do you—"

"I mean she compelled me across the carriage! I certainly had no conscious intention of letting go of her, but suddenly I had done it."

81

Sully's face had become rather flushed. "But a servant of the Hallewells—she'd be at services every Sunday without fail. She is absolutely under the influence of Riftmead."

"Yes, ma'am. No doubt about it," Eli said with a nod.

"So then how could she possibly—"

"I don't know, Sully, but that's what happened, sure as I'm standing here."

Sully stared at Eli in silence for so long that he wondered if she were having some kind of fit. Then she launched back into action with such suddenness that he jumped in alarm. She began pacing back and forth behind her desk, her arms tightly crossed over her chest, her fingers drumming on her upper arms, like they always did when she was scheming.

"This servant—who was she? What was her position? Did you find out anything about her at all?" The questions came out so rapid-fire that Eli flinched.

"She... I'm not exactly sure what she does, but if she was out in the carriage on her own, she'd have to be pretty high up. A lady's maid, I'd say, based on her uniform," Eli replied.

"Yes, that makes sense. How old was she, would you say?" Sully countered.

Eli shrugged. "Quite young. Just a girl, really. Seventeen? Maybe eighteen? She told me her name."

Sully stopped pacing, her face tense. "And? What is it?"

"Eliza Braxton."

Eli watched in alarm as Sully's face drained of color, going from an almost feverish pink to grey in a matter of seconds. "Sully, are you—"

But Sully had already recovered herself. "That will be William Braxton's daughter, I'll bet my life on it. He's the butler there, has been for more than thirty years now." She sighed. "It would be madness, I've got to say, trying to bring a child of William Braxton into our ranks. He's as indoctrinated as some of the Elders, from what I've heard, and I don't doubt any daughter of his would be cut from the same cloth."

Eli felt his excitement starting to ebb. "But isn't she exactly what we need?"

"Oh, that she is," Sully said. "We've been trying to get a spy into Larkspur Manor for years. The stable boy, Whippet, is sympathetic, but he's not what I'd call reliable, and what the hell use is he to us out in the stables mucking out stalls? We need someone on the inside—someone with real access."

"Yes! That's exactly what I'm saying. And anyway, an animal Influencer isn't going to be much good to us anyway, is he? But someone who has daily direct contact with Hallewell family members? Just imagine what we could do with that!"

"And that's exactly what we'll have to do, Eli. Imagine it," Sully said, shaking her head. "Trying to turn a Braxton is too risky."

"But, Sully—"

Sully's eyes flashed. "So help me, Eli, if you question me again today, I might just change my mind and kick you out after all. I thank you for telling me this—I think you're right, it's information we should have, even if it isn't information we can act on right now. But you've given it to me, and now I want you to put it out of your head, all right?"

Eli could think of a dozen things he would rather say, but what came out of his mouth was, "Okay, Sully. Whatever you say."

Sully stared at him for a long time before she finally nodded that she accepted his words. "Now that you've gotten this utter foolishness with Jasper out of your system, I want you to focus on our next plan, for which a stable boy's level of access will be more than sufficient. Have you met this second servant, the one he's enlisted to help him?"

"Not yet."

"Name's Bennett. He was at the last meeting, the one you missed, and he's green, Eli. Looked about ready to vomit just hearing about our plans. I won't lie to you, I don't feel good about it. They're going to need a lot of guidance. Can I count on you to oversee them?"

"Of course, Sully."

"Good. We'll be finalizing the details tomorrow night. Eleven-thirty at The Bell and Flagon. Maybe someone can drag Jasper out of whatever filthy hole he's crawled into and bring him along. This next plan's a bit more his style, although I'm sure he'll be bitterly disappointed he doesn't get to light the match himself."

She settled a pair of gold-rimmed spectacles on the end of her nose and settled back down to her document, which in Sully-speak was the same as a proper dismissal, and Eli took it as such. He backed out of the room, eased the door shut behind him, and retreated to his bedroom, which was located on the third floor of the house, up in the eaves.

Once in the privacy and quiet of his room, Eli removed his shoes, flopped onto his bed, and heaved a sigh. On one hand, he was glad he'd managed to retain Sully's trust—the woman was the closest thing to a mother he could remember, and what she lacked in maternal warmth, she made up for in loyalty and grit. He would be lost without her to turn to, and that was a bone-deep truth he could not deny. On the other hand, he was tired of being treated like a kid, even if his behavior did, on occasion, warrant such treatment. Sure, his stunt with Jasper had been both ill-conceived and recklessly carried out, but it had also worked. Eli reflected on the way his heart had soared, to see the way the Illustratum's official lies had been plastered over with the truth, and he knew he was far from the only one. The Barrens was positively writhing with the news of Davies, and each subsequent action by the Illustratum to try to bury the truth had only served to increase the buzz. The execution of Jasper's plan had left much to be desired—namely, it had involved a bit too much running for his life for Eli's taste—but the concept had been a good one.

No, Eli decided. He could not regret his part in it.

And then there was the question of the lady's maid, for she *was* a question—a gaping, gnawing unknown, plaguing his thoughts. The strength of the magic that had surged through Eli at her behest still seemed to tingle in his veins. He looked down at his own hands, remembering the way his head and body had been filled with the instant and overwhelming desire to release her, how he had done so without the slightest reservation, how he had come to his senses moments later, completely unable to account for his actions. This girl—Eliza Braxton—was a phenomenon of Riftmagic to be able to affect him so, even under the influence of regular dosing with Riftmead. Hell, it would have been remarkable even if Riftmead had never passed her lips. It was raw power, pure and simple, and the thought of harnessing it for the good of the Resistance was intoxicating.

Eli thought about what Sully had said, about how it would be mad to try to recruit a Braxton. He thought back to his conversation with the girl; could she really be so impossible to turn? She had been proud, certainly, like every manor servant he had ever interacted with. But once she'd freed herself from him, she hadn't screamed. She hadn't shouted for help at the top of her lungs or caused a scene. She owed him nothing at all, and yet, she gave him her name when he asked for it, though he had given her no such courtesy—he could not have done, as he was running from the Praesidio at the time.

And yet, as he remembered the moment they had spent staring into each other's eyes, he felt he could have told her his name, told her exactly what he'd been doing to the notices, and he would still have been safe. Somehow—and he didn't dare say it out loud, for fear of sounding like a bloody fool—but somehow, he knew that she wouldn't have turned him in. For that moment inside the carriage, he had been safe.

The instant the thought materialized in his head, Eli snorted at himself. Making decisions based on feelings rather than facts was exactly how people like Nigel Barrows ended up swinging from a noose. And whatever dreams of glory Eli might have had as a part of the Resistance, they all ended with himself still very much alive. No, he could not fling himself on the mercies of a manor girl, no matter what he may or may not have imagined in the depths of her eyes.

But, he promised himself, as he rolled over to go to sleep, he was not going to give up on her, either.

**(Prayer of the Riftborn:
A call and answer, to be repeated after the High Elder)**

"We know we are unworthy and unclean.
We accept our weakness, we acknowledge our sin.
And though we cursed be, there is yet hope
For life eternal, for a soul unsullied and free.
And as this blessed Riftmead passes our lips,
We take the Creator's promise within us,
We let it fill us up, we nourish ourselves with it,
And renew our commitment to the Path.
We reject the temptation of our Riftmagic
And we pledge it to service. In the Creator's name, we drink."

SEVEN

"**E**LIZA? ARE YOU EVEN LISTENING TO ME?"

Eliza surfaced from her thoughts like a sleeper from a dream. "I'm sorry, miss, my head was quite in another place. What was it you said?"

Jessamine's face broke into what was unmistakably a pout. "I said, do you think I was right to ask for the additional tuck at the bodice?"

"The... I'm sorry?"

"The extra tuck! My goodness Eliza, my dress! What else in the world would I be talking about?"

Of course. The fitting. The Presentation gown. With what felt like a gargantuan effort, Eliza tore her mind from her own reality and fixed it firmly on Jessamine's, in which nothing could be of more vital importance than the placement of a scrap of fabric.

"Oh yes, miss. I think the extra tuck at the bodice was an excellent choice. It suits your figure perfectly, and sets off the rosette at the hip," Eliza answered, dragging the details from the back of her mind and trying to smile.

"I agree," Jessamine replied, and she sounded mollified. "I shan't be out-tucked by the likes of Sadie Carpenter, I can tell you. Why did I ever tell you..."

And off she launched into another tirade about the many sartorial escapades of Miss Carpenter, leaving Eliza free to nod along and sink once again into her own thoughts.

Getting back into the carriage had brought all kinds of feelings flooding to the surface, so much so that Eliza was desperately trying to find nooks and crannies within herself where she could stuff them all away. Sitting upon the leather seat, she was revisited by the feeling of a hand covering her mouth, and a pair of green eyes wordlessly begging for her silence. Her mind lingered on the young man's features, wondering if he had gotten away, or if even now he occupied a cell in the Praeteritum or, even worse, a noose upon the gallows. This last possibility left her cold and jittery with fear which, she reasoned with herself, was ludicrous because she didn't know the man from any other stranger on the street.

And yet... and yet she had told him her name. Why had she done that?

Eliza scolded herself for brooding and pushed the feelings away again. She was on duty, with her mistress, and as such it was incumbent upon her to be attentive and engaged. She forced her full concentration back onto Miss Jessamine, who was now expounding broadly on Sadie Carpenter's social transgressions.

"...don't know how I'll stand her company this evening. She's sure to be insufferable, what with my Presentation just around the corner. I wish I could beg off and skip the whole affair."

"I know you do, Miss Jessamine, and I can't say I blame you one bit. But it is a charity gathering, after all, and your absence would be remarked upon. We mustn't give Miss Carpenter another reason to wag her tongue. You walk in there with your head held high and keep your mind on your good works. Think of all the Riftborn families who will be properly fed and warmed by your handiwork. Keep your thoughts there, and Miss Carpenter's words can't touch you."

Jessamine sighed. "You're right, Eliza. Of course, you're right." She narrowed her eyes. "Sometimes I wonder if it's really you under that cap, or if my father hasn't stolen your uniform to lecture me in disguise."

Eliza dropped her eyes. "Begging your pardon, miss. I had no intention of lecturing you."

Jessamine laughed and reached out to squeeze Eliza's hand. "Oh, dear Eliza, I'm only teasing you! Of course you aren't lecturing me. You are simply offering your sound advice as usual. It's a compliment, really, even if I didn't manage to make it sound like one. Tell me, do you always find it easy being so naturally good?"

Eliza felt her face reddening. "I'm... I'm not so naturally good, miss. I am not Dignus. I must work hard to stay the Path upon which your feet have been placed by virtue of your birth."

Jessamine laughed again. "And yet you always seem to be the

one reminding me not to lose my way. Oh, don't be cross, Eliza, I'm sorry. I've embarrassed you. I didn't mean to, truly." She drew her face into an exaggerated pout. "Tell me you forgive me, or I'll wallow in boundless misery forever."

Eliza smirked in spite of herself. "There's nothing to forgive, miss."

Jessamine feigned a dramatic swoon, throwing herself across Eliza's lap and pressing the back of her hand to her forehead. "Say it, Eliza! I feel the boundless misery about to swallow me whole!"

Eliza's smile broke open and she laughed aloud. The sound of it made Jessamine look up and grin. "All right, all right. I forgive you, miss. I should never recover from the guilt if you were swallowed whole."

Jessamine sat up again, patting at her hair and winking genially. "There. That's better. You see? I am instantly recovered. That's the power of forgiveness, I suppose."

The two young women continued to laugh as the carriage rolled and bumped along toward the Illustratum. It was Sunday, and time for services. The hordes of Riftborn who gathered at the gates before every service had already been blessed and fed and forced back to the other side of the bars, where they remained, pressed in on each other, jostling and craning their necks for a glimpse of the great ladies and noble gentlemen of the Dignus who attended the Sunday noon service. It was customary for the families of the Elders to attend, clad in their absolute finest.

"It is aspirational," Elder Hallewell had explained to his daughter. "When they see you, a physical manifestation of the blessings of good works and faithful living, it inspires them to stay the Path."

"I daresay it inspires them to never don a bloody corset as long as they live and breathe," a younger Jessamine had muttered in reply, much too quietly for her father to hear her at his far end of the table, and took her frustration out on her poached egg instead, smushing it mercilessly with her spoon until she had properly vented her feelings.

Now several years later, it was without complaint but with a sense of detached resignation that she allowed herself to be dressed and primped and decked out every week to sit in a stiflingly hot and crowded pew for hours at a time, merely so that a crowd of strangers could goggle at her for a handful of seconds as she descended from the carriage and climbed the front steps into the church.

As for Eliza, that handful of seconds each week were perhaps the proudest of her life as she accompanied her mistress through the massive doors and into the central lobby. The opulence never failed to stun her into a reverent silence so profound that she dared hardly breathe for fear of disturbing the very motes that hung, consecrated, in the air. She allowed herself a few moments of raising her eyes to the vaulted ceilings, the gothic arched windows, glistening like jewels set with stained glass, the magnificent golden chandeliers, and niche upon niche full of statues looking down on her like the eyes of Heaven itself, before dropping her gaze again respectfully in the presence of wonders that did not truly belong to her — or indeed, to any Riftborn.

Only Riftborn in the highest standing with the church were allowed to enter the hallowed halls of the Illustratum for services — the others were forced to congregate in the courtyard and at the gates to hear the Book of the Rift. Her father had always taught her not to take her presence within those walls for granted, and she tried to send up a prayer of gratitude every time she followed Miss Jessamine down the hallway and into the Sacrarium proper.

At the doorway, the two women parted company, Jessamine for the family pew at the very front of the room, and Eliza for the servants' benches against the back wall. There were no parting words or nods of goodbye — they were within the inner sanctum now. Only the Words of the Creator were to be spoken here, and only when prompted. Eliza walked along the row, her head bent, eyes upon the pairs of shoes of the other lady's maids as she passed, counting them until she reached the place, seven pairs of glossy black buckled shoes along, that was hers. She took her seat, clasped her hands in her lap, and waited. When she lifted her face, she knew who she would see: Peppa Milton, lady's maid to Rebecca Potter, on her right; Mary Carter, lady's maid to Katherine Primrose on her left. In the row before her, the valets, butlers, and other male servants of the various houses, including the back of her own father's head just in front of her. And behind her, if she turned, she would see Mrs. Keats, Bridie, and the other women in service to the Elder households. All was silent, every head bent in prayer, waiting for the Elders to process in and the service to begin.

Eliza loved the pomp and pageantry of the service. She felt her heart soar as the familiar music began, echoing grandly through the chamber, played upon a pair of trumpets she had never seen, for their players were masked high up in the corners of the balconies above her head. As a child, she imagined that music emanated not from something so commonplace as instruments played by human lips, but rather that the melodies lived within the very walls and stones of the sacred space in which she sat, drawn forth into the air around her by the power of the faith in the room. She could half-believe such fancies even now as she allowed the music to sweep her away, grateful for the opportunity to stop thinking, stop wondering, stop worrying. Here, everything was as it should be—everything was predictable, down to the word. There were no surprises, no decisions to make. This was a place of answers, of rules, of simple truths that she could follow. Even marked—cursed—as she was, salvation could be found here.

Some tiny part of herself broke away from the reality of crowded benches and squeaking shoes and stifling heat and soared upward, like a sparrow on a current of wind, and she joined in song as the congregation rose to their feet out of respect for the Elders now filing in from the doors on either side of the front of the room. They walked, heads bent, to their seats facing the rest of the assembly, twelve on either side of the great golden altaria behind which the High Elder himself would momentarily appear.

A fanfare announced his arrival, and a door behind the altaria opened. Two young boys acting as attendants processed out, holding red flags with the crest of the Illustratum upon it, and behind their flutterings, the High Elder appeared. The music swelled, and every Riftborn member of the congregation sank, as one, to their knees, prostrating themselves before the man who could convene directly with the Creator, to receive his definitive word, by means of the Rift. The Dignus, on the other hand, stayed standing.

The opening chants began, and Eliza fell into the familiar patterns as easily as sinking into water. The Dignus all lifted their prayer books before them; the servants were not allowed their own prayer books—were not, indeed, even permitted to touch them, but like Eliza, they had all learned the chants and prayers by heart now, and could recite along when invited to. She listened to the Welcome of the Faithful, the Call to Commune, the Cries of Mercy, and the Prayers of the Path. She felt her knees beginning to protest against the stone of the floor, but she did not care.

The moment arrived for the Prayer for the Riftborn, and the servants, as one, lifted their arms into the air, reaching up above them

93

as though to receive the words that filled the air around them. This was the moment that reminded them who they were, what their duty was, what would await them should they fail. Many in the seats around her succumbed to tears during this moment in the service; Eliza was used to the words of this prayer punctuated by much sniffling and even the occasional quiet moan. But it never moved her to tears, not once in all the years she had heard it. Rather, it seemed to turn her insides to iron—she felt not sorrow, but resolve, steely and unyielding, filling her from toes to fingertips.

She would not fail, she told herself. She would stay the Path.

The High Elder's attendants now walked up the aisles, each carrying a large golden goblet brimming with Riftmead. They passed by the rows where the Dignus were sitting but did not stop. It was not until they reached the benches in the very back where the servants remained kneeling that they turned and offered the cups.

"And as this blessed Riftmead passes our lips,
We take the Creator's promise within us,
We let it fill us up, we nourish ourselves with it,
And renew our commitment to the Path.
We reject the temptation of our Riftmagic
And we pledge it to service. In the Creator's name, we drink."

The words were repeated, over and over again, as the goblets were passed down the rows of Riftborn servants, and each of them drank deeply. An almost fearful anticipation built in Eliza's heart as the cup drew nearer to her, although what ephemeral thing she feared, she could not grasp.

"In the Creator's name, we drink," she whispered, and raised the goblet to her lips, drinking deeply, before passing it along to Mary Carter, who received it with a rapt and tearful expression upon her face.

At once, a feeling of deep, abiding calm came over Eliza. Her entire body was flooded with a knowledge and a certainty that was almost weakness. Her head spun. Her hands shook. Her legs trembled beneath her, and she struggled to remain on her knees. Her thoughts felt as though they were expanding endlessly within the confines of her skull. The space within her had become at once vastly, staggeringly expansive, and she was an infinitesimal speck in a universe she could have balanced upon the head of a pin. And, for a brief but glorious moment, she felt completely severed from her

Riftmagic, that constant reminder of her weakness and shame. It floated away from her, into that infinite space, and she felt free.

Free.

So lost was she in this moment that she didn't notice at first that some kind of disturbance was going on. The chanting cut out suddenly as shouts and banging reached the ears of the congregation, but many, like Eliza, were slow to realize that something was amiss. It wasn't until four guards stationed up front near the Elders jogged up the aisles and exited through the back doors of the Sacrarium and into the central lobby, from which the sounds were emanating, that everyone finally came to their senses. At the same moment, two more guards escorted the High Elder swiftly through the door behind the altaria, slamming it shut behind him. Like everyone around her, Eliza turned in confusion to the back doors of the Sacrarium, through which the sounds were penetrating from the room beyond.

The echoing cavern of the central lobby made it nearly impossible to make out what was being said — all that Eliza could distinguish was a great deal of shouting and scuffling and banging. And then a voice rose over the tumult, shouting for all it was worth, and Eliza's heart seemed to freeze in her chest as she comprehended the words:

"Davies is dead!" it cried out.

Bang. Bang. Bang.

Screams erupted around the Sacrarium. Many people ducked down into their pews. Several of the Elders fled for the doors through which they had entered. Half a dozen more Praesidio guards charged up the aisle toward the back doors.

"Silence! Everyone stay where you are!"

The voice that echoed through the hall was so commanding, so full of authority, that everyone did exactly as it said. The room transformed into a still life — and Eliza didn't need to turn her head toward the altaria to know who it was that had spoken.

Elder Hallewell stood framed by the hulking golden structure of the altaria, his face blazing with controlled fury.

"Do not panic. Remain in your seats. You are in the house of your Creator and you are safe. Guards, secure those doors."

The Praesidio soldiers, who had frozen like everyone else, resumed their jog up the aisle and began to unwind chains that were hidden in a niche beside the doors that Eliza had never noticed before.

But before they could properly fasten the chains, a voice from the lobby rang out.

"All is well! Stand down!"

The guards paused in what they were doing and turned back to Elder Hallewell for direction. He nodded, and they dropped the chains at once, opened the door, and slipped through it, closing it behind them. A breathless moment later, both doors were pulled open and the guards returned to their regular positions, where they stood at attention, faces impassive, as though nothing had happened.

Clearing his throat, Elder Hallewell began again the Prayer for the Riftborn in a deep, resounding voice, nodding significantly at the attendants, who resumed the passing of the goblets. All around her, people seemed startled at the sudden continuation of the service, and it took several minutes for the buzz of conversation to die away and the chant to fill the Sacrarium. Heads kept craning toward the back doors, and the spell of the service was broken.

Eliza did not notice when the High Elder, accompanied by his bodyguards, slipped discreetly back into the Sacrarium, barely noted when his voice joined the next prayer. In fact, the rest of the Illustratum's noon services could have been conducted in French, and Eliza wouldn't have noticed the difference. Her pulse was still racing, and her palms were sweating. What had happened in the lobby? Who had caused the disturbance? And those bangs—they had certainly sounded like gunshots, but then again, sounds were magnified and distorted in such a large space—surely the service would not have simply continued if someone had been shot just on the other side of the door?

It was only when she noticed that the Book of the Rift had been laid upon the altaria that Eliza forced her whirling thoughts back to the service itself. The High Elder was reading from some kind of proclamation.

"... for crimes both violent and heretical. Let it be so recorded on this day that the following Riftborn are stricken from the Book of the Rift, and their souls Cast Out forever from the kingdom of our Creator. So must it be, according to His word and His will, which we, His humble servants, carry out in our devotion to Him."

Elder Potter stepped forward, carrying five sheets of parchment upon which the names of the criminals were recorded. At the same time, Elder Carpenter approached carrying a candle, its flame dancing in the air. The two attendants brought forth a golden bowl, so large and heavy that they were clearly straining under the weight of it as they lifted it and placed it carefully onto the altaria. Once the bowl was in place, Elder Carpenter tipped the candle forward, allowing the flame to vanish from sight for a moment, and then, with a great whooshing sound, the contents of the bowl ignited. Flames leapt from it, casting a winking golden light. Then Elder Carpenter handed each paper, one by one, to the High Elder, who read the name upon it and then dropped it into the bowl, from which curls of black smoke announced the utter destruction of both paper and soul.

"William Tucker."

"Lawrence Taylor."

"Frederick Kingsley."

"Liam Guiffery."

Eliza held her breath as the final paper was lifted above the bowl, as the High Elder opened his mouth. Was it possible...

"Thomas Woodwright."

A tiny, muffled cry sounded behind her, and Eliza turned to see Mrs. Keats, her hand over her mouth, tears in her bright blue eyes. Their eyes met, and Eliza's silent question passed between them, but Mrs. Keats merely shook her head, dragged her hand across her face to mop up the tears, and composed herself, raising her eyes to the altaria once more. Eliza turned to face the front as well, recognizing defeat when she saw it.

A prolonged silence always followed the Casting Out—it was meant to be a moment to reflect on one's own commitment to the Path. But there was something in the silence now that had never been there before—the weight of unasked questions and unsaid things. Its gravity came, today, not from certainty, but from uncertainty. As Eliza realized this, her blood ran cold.

Her head was still spinning when the service ended. She missed the dismissal entirely, and it took a tug on the sleeve from Peppa and a whispered, "Get a move on or our mistresses will have left without us!" to pull Eliza back into reality. She shuffled along the row with the rest of the servants, hardly seeing where she was going, and only when Mary Carter nudged her hard in the back did she manage to step out into the aisle at the right moment to follow Miss Jessamine like a shadow.

The central lobby, usually quite deserted after services, was full of

Praesidio soldiers stationed in rows around the room, all staunchly at attention. They were the only sign that some disruption had occurred during the services. Eliza might have made it through the lobby, might have looked up at the chandeliers and the statues and the great arching glory and snatched just a scrap of comfort from it—all might have been well—were it not for the blood.

It was not much—if she had not glanced down at just the right moment, had the nearest guard not shifted his foot at just the same time, she might never have seen it at all. But there it was, a smear of scarlet blood upon the marble floor, just beyond the line of blank-faced soldiers.

Eliza felt the bile rise in her throat, and she fought to swallow it back, to keep her face calm and reverent and docile—all the hallmarks of a good and faithful lady's maid. Whether she succeeded she would never know—moments later she had followed Miss Jessamine through the front doors and into the dull and misty London afternoon, where a light rain was spitting down upon the steps, masking what may have been tears upon her face.

"What in the world was that all about?" Jessamine gasped the moment the door to the carriage had been shut behind them.

It took several attempts for Eliza to reply. "I... I simply don't know, miss. It was all very strange."

"Strange? It was terrifying! And those were gunshots, I'm sure they were! What possible circumstances could have led to shooting in the Illustratum?"

"I... I can't say," Eliza barely managed to mumble. And then, remembering her duty, she hastened to add, "Whatever it was, we can be... be confident it was dealt with swiftly and decisively, miss. I'm sure there's nothing else at all to worry about."

"You may be sure, Eliza, but I am certainly not," Jessamine replied indignantly. "And you can also be sure that I have every intention of asking my father about it on the ride home."

Eliza would normally have advised against the questioning of Elder Hallewell on such a topic, but she was too desperate for answers to say a word. Elder Hallewell typically joined his daughter for the ride back to Larkspur Manor on Sundays. It was his custom to discuss with her the readings from the Book of the Rift, and the contents of the sermon—to test her, in a sense, on the material that had been presented to her, and to expound upon his own thoughts and interpretations, thereby instilling them in his only child. Jessamine had learned over time that her role in these conversations was simply to nod along, and then to parrot back what her father wanted to hear. But judging from the high color in Miss Jessamine's cheeks and the fire in her eyes, Eliza could predict that her mistress would submit to no such passive acceptance of her father's words today.

But the confrontation did not come — at least, not at that moment. When the door to the carriage opened again, it was not Elder Hallewell who stood there, but his aide and secretary, Brother Goodwin.

"Miss Jessamine," Brother Goodwin huffed as he mopped his round, shining face with a handkerchief. "Your father sends his deepest apologies that he will not be accompanying you back to Larkspur Manor. His presence has been requested at a meeting of the Council, and he cannot be missed."

"When can I expect him home?" Jessamine asked, her face falling.

"That I cannot say with any authority, miss," Brother Goodwin replied with an unpleasant simper. "He is one of the High Elder's nearest advisors, after all."

"And what is it, precisely, he needs to advise the High Elder about?" Jessamine demanded. "What happened during the service?"

Brother Goodwin's rosy face flushed, if possible, even ruddier. "Nothing at all that need concern you, miss, I assure you."

"But I *am* concerned," Jessamine replied. "I am deeply concerned, and I am not interested in being told not to bother my pretty little head about it! I want to know what happened!"

"I... I'm not at liberty to..." Brother Goodwin was looking downright terrified now, the sweat beading upon his brow faster than he could wipe it away. "It was nothing, miss. A mere trifle, handled at once by our excellent Praesidio guards."

"It certainly didn't sound like a trifle," Jessamine replied, pouncing on the man's words like an alley cat upon a mouse. "Those were gunshots, I'm sure they were! Gunshots, within the hallowed halls of the Illustratum! Now, why were they shooting?"

"I... I really don't... there were no... I'm terribly sorry, miss. Your father will speak to you when he arrives home, I am sure. Drive on!" Brother Goodwin pushed the door shut in Jessamine's face and rapped smartly upon the side of the carriage, signaling for Martin to depart.

"Blast him!" Jessamine cursed, kicking the door panel with the pointed toe of her boot and slumping back against the seat as the carriage began its bumpy progress back home. "I've never liked him, not from the first moment I met him. A smarmy little snake, and that's the truth. How dare he not answer my questions!"

Eliza simply nodded sympathetically, but she knew how he dared. Brother Goodwin had Elder Hallewell to answer to, and it was more than his job was worth to say anything to Jessamine he hadn't been expressly commanded to convey to her.

"If Father's been called into session, he'll be hours," Jessamine went on, still grumbling. "I probably won't see him at all before I have to leave for the charity circle this evening." She slapped her hand impatiently against the seat. "I'll just have to find out what I can from the other girls tonight. Surely one of them will be able to wheedle the truth out of her father, or at the very least overhear something."

Eliza pressed her lips together, making a vague sound of agreement that she hoped would suffice for a reply, and turned her gaze out of the window. First, the young man in the street had risked his life to alter official Illustratum notices with this man Davies' name, and now it seemed another person had given theirs to make sure that Davies' name was heard by those who were witnessing the Castings Out. It could, she realized with a pang of horror, even have been the same young man. The thought made her blood run cold and her palms sweat, though she couldn't have explained why, even to herself. But the fact remained, there were people desperate for Davies' name not to be forgotten or buried. Why would people die for such a thing? What was so important, so special about this name and this man?

There was another thing to consider, a thought that made Eliza's heart feel like a stone lodged in her chest. Could it be... was it possible... that the Illustratum was concealing this man's death for some reason? Might it be true that the name on the notices and—more disturbingly—the last name to be Cast Out in services today—was not in fact the fifth man to be hanged? What could justify a falsehood about the identity of a man executed by the Praesidio?

For there must be a reason, and a very good one at that, Eliza told herself firmly. If the Illustratum had chosen to keep John Davies' name from the people, clearly they had just cause. What could be more just, more unassailable than the actions of the Elder Council, who took their direction from the Creator Himself? These... these upstarts, whoever they might be, were flying in the face of the Creator's will!

100

Eliza felt her resolve stiffen, her surety return. She would forget this man Davies and those seeking to reveal his name. Whoever they were, they were nothing to her. Nothing at all...

The words shriveled in her heart, though, as the carriage rounded the corner and the gallows came into view over the tops of the buildings. A single body, face obscured, swung lightly in the breeze from a noose.

(Letter from James Whippet to Eli)

E—

Please don't abandon the plan. I promise you, you've put your trust in the right person. Peter will come around. He's sympathetic to the cause and I'd trust him with my life, but he gets cold feet when he thinks about the possibility of being caught. I keep telling him that if we plan properly, we won't get caught, but he can't help worrying just the same. I'm going to bring him to The Bell and Flagon with me Friday night so he can talk to you properly. I think he'll feel more reassured if he hears the plan straight from you.

His biggest fear is that someone will get hurt. I explained to him that isn't the intention—we only mean to get their attention, to scare them a bit, so that they know we mean business. He agrees we cannot let them bury Davies' death, but as I said, he's a bit of a nervous lad, and he's going to need some encouragement because Jasper was right, I can't do it alone, and we can't afford to raise suspicions by bringing any more outsiders onto the grounds on such an important night. All eyes will be on Larkspur Manor, and that's both a blessing and a curse for our purposes.

Until Friday then,
James Whippet

EIGHT

"IT'S NOT WORKING. Despite our best efforts, the name of Davies resurfaces again and again."

Francis and Josiah stood upon the balcony ignoring the light mist now settling upon them, their cigars sending plumes of smoke into the purpling sky over their heads. It was the first break they'd had during the long and contentious session.

"If these are our best efforts, we might as well paint Davies' name on the side of the Illustratum itself and let it shine out over the Thames for all to see," Josiah muttered, disgusted.

Francis grunted and nodded, puffing vigorously on his cigar. "A bunch of blasted washerwomen gossiping over their tubs would be making more progress, that's for damn sure and certain."

"I can't say a word but I'm shouted down," Josiah said. "Carpenter is waiting to pounce before I draw breath."

"Yes, well, that's Carpenter, isn't it?" Francis scoffed. "You should have seen his face when you called the service to order today."

"Someone had to take charge, Francis."

"I agree, but Carpenter never will, as long as that someone is you," Francis replied. "He's never forgiven you for being appointed councilor, and he's not the only one."

Josiah snorted, but Francis pushed on.

"I'm not telling you anything you don't already know, Josiah. If there's anything you want said, you'd best let me say it. Carpenter won't allow you any more victories today."

"It wasn't a victory, it was a necessity!" Josiah cried, pounding his hand on the railing. "For pity's sake, what's happened to Morgan?

Time was we could count on him to take the reins in any situation, and now he flees when he should fight."

Francis shrugged. "He's getting old, Josiah."

"So are we all. Bloody hell, I've never felt so old," Josiah said, running his hand through his hair. His head was beginning to ache.

"Yes, but he's showing it," Francis said. "Haven't you noticed? His hands have started shaking."

Josiah didn't reply. Yes, he'd noticed. He'd have been a fool if he hadn't.

"The fact is, the balance of power among us is shifting," Francis said. "And you'll have to be prepared for a landslide of unpleasantness heading your way if it looks at all like it's tipping in your direction. Steel yourself, Josiah. It's coming."

Josiah shook his head. "We're years away from that yet."

"Perhaps," Francis conceded, with a puff on his cigar. "Perhaps not."

Josiah looked Francis in the face. "Are you always this calm? It's infuriating."

Francis laughed, a jovial boom that echoed out over the grounds and frightened a pair of pigeons into flight from a nearby ledge. "Just wait until my Teddy and your Jessamine are married. I'll be infuriating you every week at Sunday dinner."

§

Beyond the walls of the Illustratum, across the bridge, and down the winding, narrowing roads of the Barrens, Eli thrust his hands into his pockets, partly to warm them against the persistent chill and partly to hide the fact that he kept tensing his knuckles. He stood across from Lavender's place, convincing himself that he wanted to go in.

It wasn't that Lavender's didn't have its allurements—to suggest so would do a great disservice to the proprietress of that notoriously welcoming establishment. In fact, even as he stood there, indecisive, two girls lingered in the doorway, batting their eyelashes and enticing him to join them. The problem wasn't going in; it was getting out and, preferably, getting out with Jasper. He smothered a grin. Only Jasper could get neck-deep in trouble and neck-deep in beautiful women at the same time. Although, there was an argument to be made that that was simply two kinds of trouble.

106

One of the girls peeled herself off of the door frame to greet him as he approached. "Well, well, well, here he comes, the heart-breaker. What's kept you away, Eli?" she said with an exaggerated pout. Mariah was barely older than twenty, a curvy blonde slip of a thing with curls piled high on the top of her head and breasts in a permanent state of near escape from her too-tight corset. She held out a hand as though she were royalty and Eli, smiling indulgently, bowed low to plant a kiss upon it. She giggled, bringing the hand up to her brightly rouged cheek.

"You're looking as lovely as ever, Mariah," Eli said.

"You're welcome to keep right on lookin', love," she replied. "And there's more to see, if the price is right. Fancy a drink?"

"Actually, I fancy a word with my wayward brother. Is he here?" Eli replied. Through the doorway he could see the brothel was crowded tonight.

"Hmmm... your brother... your brother..." Mariah tapped her chin in mock thoughtfulness and turned over her shoulder to the other girl in the doorway, who was trying to entice passersby with shouted invitations. "Did I even know you had a brother? Peg, you remember Eli's brother?"

Peg caught on at once. "Doesn't ring a bell," she answered, shaking her head regretfully, but smirking all the same.

"I could just go in and look for him, you know," Eli pointed out.

"Yes, but the view is much nicer out here, don't you think?" Mariah said, striking a demure pose. "Besides, who knows where he's run off to and with who. It could take you half the night."

Eli rolled his eyes and dug into his pocket, extracting two venia. He tossed one to each girl, and watched them disappear handily into two ample bosoms.

"Oh, now that I think on it, I do remember your brother," Mariah said, her eyes going wide and innocent. "Enjoying Paulina's company when last I saw him, isn't that right, Peg?"

"Sloshed he was," Peg agreed. "But you'd have to be to enjoy a scag like Paulina, wouldn't you?"

The girls laughed boisterously, and Eli, seeing his chance, slipped between the two of them into the tavern-like room beyond. Mariah's hand shot out and caught his wrist, pulling him toward her.

"I'd be willing to earn whatever you've got left in those pockets, Eli Turner," she whispered into his ear.

"A tempting offer I'll be sure to keep in mind," Eli replied, gently prying himself free from her grasping fingers and escaping inside.

All around the room, girls in garish gowns sat on laps, carried trays, and poured drinks, floating around like so many brightly colored feathers, flitting here and there, laughing loudly. Hardly any of the customers were from the Barrens, that much was clear—it would take a bloke from the Barrens half his life to save up enough money to take a turn with one of Lavender's girls, if he ever managed it at all. The men who occupied the seats and bid on the girls were all from the Market District, business owners and merchants, men who had slunk like thieves guiltily down the pavement to reach the place but soon drowned their consciences with a surfeit of booze and feminine wiles.

Eli scanned the room for Jasper, but didn't see him anywhere. He wasn't fool enough to attempt a search of the rooms upstairs; there was no faster way to get yourself thrown out of Madam Lavender's than by entering rooms you hadn't expressly paid to enter. Instead, Eli dodged an attractive yet aggressive looking redhead and made his way to the back office, knocking sharply and waiting for a reply.

"Who is it?"

"Eli Turner."

"About time. Come in and be quick about it."

Eli pushed the door open just enough to slip through it, and closed it carefully behind him. Madam Lavender was revealed to be lounging on a settee, a monocle jammed into one eye as she sipped on a tiny glass of wine clutched in one hand and perused a stack of papers held in the other. She was a decidedly large and curvy woman, once considered a great beauty, but age, hard-living, and hard-drinking had long since claimed her looks. Her silk dress, embroidered with seed pearls and fine lace, strained at its seams to rein her in—an apt metaphor for her personality, which expanded to fill any room that dared try to contain her.

"You're late," she boomed, still not looking up from her reading.

"I'm sorry?"

"I said, you're late," Madam Lavender replied, draining the last dregs of wine from her glass and setting it down with a clink of annoyance on the table beside her. "Your brother's been eating and drinking me out of house and home for two days, and he ran out of money not long after he arrived. How long am I expected to keep him on as a charity case before I'm forced to put him in a dress and sit him on some laps?"

Eli snorted. "If I'd known you were planning to dress him up, I would have waited another day or two."

Madam Lavender did not return his smile, but shifted her bulk up from her lounging position and allowed the monocle to fall from her eye and onto the silken folds of her dress, where it swung amidst the lace on a fine golden chain. "If he were anyone but Sully's boy, I'd have him arrested for non-payment."

Eli sobered his expression. "I realize that. I'm sorry. I'll drag him out of here with me tonight, and Sully will make sure you're compensated."

Madam Lavender nodded once curtly, then rose to pour herself another glass of wine. Eli knew better than to expect to be offered one. "Sully and I have much in common," she said with a sigh as she lifted her crystal decanter and pulled the stopper from it. "Both women in a man's world, both trying to run a business, to survive, to walk that very fine line between prosperity and the noose." She rummaged in a tin of chocolates and popped one into her mouth, chewing slowly, savoring it. "She has done me a great service, and I do not regret it, but I have a business to run."

"Of course," Eli conceded. He knew the service of which Madam Lavender spoke. Many years ago, her husband had been convicted of a crime and sent to the Praeteritum to serve his sentence. Sully had helped orchestrate his escape, along with several other prisoners, and hidden them in her safe house until she could help them arrange passage to France. He died shortly thereafter, before Lavender could join him, but she had never forgotten what Sully had done for him. Since then, with the establishment of her brothel, she had become a valuable resource to the Resistance, especially when it came to information; nothing happened in the Barrens that Madam Lavender did not know about.

"There was another reason I wanted to see you," Eli said, "but I'd rather you didn't mention it to Sully."

Madam Lavender raised an eyebrow. "Is that so? If you're looking for company here, I don't think Sully will mind. She's not a fool; she knows what young men are."

"No, it's not that," Eli said, shaking his head. "Meaning no disrespect to your girls, of course," he added quickly.

"Well, what is it, then?"

"I need information."

Madam Lavender gave a harsh laugh that dissolved into a hacking cough. "You sound like a constable."

Eli smiled. "Does that mean I get to be on your payroll?"

Madam Lavender continued to cough and laugh. "Constables on my payroll keep me in business and my girls out of trouble. When have you ever been so useful?"

Eli ignored the question. "Do you ever have contact with any of the servants from Larkspur Manor?"

The question caught Madam Lavender off-guard. She paused, looking intrigued. "Not as such, no. Hallewell runs a tight ship. I've never had any of his men in here, as far as I know, though they are paid well enough to afford the occasional fling."

"And the girls?"

Madam Lavender cackled again. "Can you see one of those uptight little prudes coming within a hundred meters of this place? Their bleeding bonnets would catch fire."

"What about elsewhere in the Barrens? Have you ever seen them within the district limits? Are they even allowed to come here?" Eli tried to keep the plea out of his voice.

Madam Lavender thought for a moment or two, then nodded. "As a matter of fact, yes. Some of the maids come into the Barrens on Tuesday mornings to deliver food baskets to some of the families in the tenements. It's usually the lady's maids, but Larkspur Manor only has one lady's maid now, so she'll have someone else with her—a kitchen maid or scullery maid, perhaps."

"Tuesdays, you say? What time?" Eli asked, perking up.

"How the devil am I supposed to know?" Madam Lavender snapped, devouring another chocolate. "Am I a ruddy timekeeper? Early. Well before morning blessings."

Eli held up his hands as though in surrender. "And they come on their own? No Dignus with them?"

Madam Lavender snorted. "What Dignus would be caught dead in the Barrens? Yes, they come alone, but their carriages are always nearby, within a block or two, and the drivers with them. They gather on the High Street, make their deliveries, and go. I've seen 'em as close to here as Barrow Street. A right little pack of nuns they are, all bent heads and smug condescension. I'm not really sure what else I can tell you."

"That's enough, thank you," Eli said. "That might just be enough."

"Say, what are you getting yourself into here?" Madam Lavender asked suddenly, her eyes narrowing shrewdly. "Not about to make a fool of yourself with a manor girl, are you? Nothing but trouble tends that way, and you damn well know it."

Eli shook his head. "Of course not. I have no intention of making a fool of myself with anyone."

Madam Lavender gave a dry cackle. "No one intentionally makes a fool of themselves, lad, but fools they become all the same. What are you caught up in? Does this have anything to do with your brother?"

"No," Eli insisted. "As for Jasper, that was foolish, but that's over with. I'm not taking his advice anymore, you've got my word."

"The word of a man. Be still my bleedin' heart," Madam Lavender snorted. "Well, just remember, Turner, like you said, I've got eyes all over these streets. If you're fixing to get tangled up in some nonsense with a manor girl and I get wind of it, I'll go right to Sully, you can count on it."

Eli nodded. "Fair enough. I'm only looking for information right now, Lavender. I'll take it to Sully myself if it turns out to be anything worthwhile."

Madam Lavender surveyed him suspiciously through her monocle for a long moment, then gave a sharp nod. "I'll say this for you, you've got more sense than your brother. Now, off with you. Get him out of here before I have him thrown out."

"Yes, ma'am," Eli said, standing up and doffing his cap. He reached hesitantly toward his pocket. "Is there anything I can..."

Madam Lavender waved him off. "Buy a few of the girls a round. It's an ugly crowd out there tonight. They'll need all the courage they can find at the bottom of a pint or two."

Eli gave a bow and backed out of the room. Once he had eased the door shut, he slunk back down the hallway and out to the bar. The room wasn't quite as crowded as when he'd entered—apparently, some customers had already made their way upstairs. He approached the bar, slapped a few coins down on it, and leaned across to the bartender.

"Buy a drink for whoever's going to have a rough night of it," he said under his breath.

The barkeep looked up from his bottles, scanned the room quickly, then gave a grim nod. Eli knew he didn't have to say more.

A familiar musical peal of laughter rang brightly from the far end of the room. Eli turned to see Jasper stumbling down the stairs in the wake of a disgruntled-looking redhead.

"Paulina, come now, I'm good for every farthing, cross my heart," Jasper pled, clinging precariously to the railing as he struggled to put one foot in front of the other.

"Sod off, Jasper," Paulina grumbled, arriving at the bar just as the barkeep put four pints on the counter. Eli handed one to her, along with a handful of coins. Paulina looked up, suspicious.

"With my apologies, on behalf of my brother, whose desires are deeper than his pockets," Eli said. "And if he owes you any more, let Madam Lavender know and the account will be settled in full."

Paulina's face broke into a smile, and she lifted the drink to her lips, draining half of it before setting it down again. She gave Eli an appraising look. "Sure I can't tempt you to stay? You look like the kind of man who might just turn my night around."

Eli grinned and cocked his head over toward Jasper, now teetering at the bottom of the stairs. "Another night, Paulina. I've got to get him out of here before he makes an even bigger prat of himself than he already has."

Paulina nodded, downed the rest of her drink, and turned to face the room, plastering on a winning smile that did not quite reach her eyes. She flounced off toward the door and was in another man's lap before Eli had picked Jasper up off the floor.

"Hands off me, you varlet, you rogue!" Jasper hollered, before collapsing into Eli's arms in a fit of laughter. He blinked up at him. "Doth mine eyes deceive me, or are you considerably less attractive than the last person who had her arms wrapped around me?"

Eli chuckled and then gasped as the hot stench of whisky wafted over him from Jasper's breath. "Are you suggesting you can actually see?"

Jasper crawled up his arm to whisper into his ear. "Truth be told, I'm seeing several of you at the moment, and any one of them might or might not be a member of the fairer sex."

"Come on. Let's get you home while you can still get your legs under you," Eli grunted, slinging Jasper's arm over his shoulders. He was actually relieved to find Jasper so intoxicated on this particular

112

occasion. Sober Jasper was stubborn and combative. Drunk Jasper was silly and sad and reflective, even if he couldn't remember the more profound of his reflections when he woke up. Even if Eli had to carry him all the way back to Sully's, it would be easier than fighting with him about it.

"Shouldn't I sober up first?" Jasper said in a whisper that wasn't a whisper at all.

"That's the problem, mate," Eli replied. "If you stay here, you'll never sober up, and then Lavender will have you carried out and carted off to the lock-up."

"Lavender would never do that," Jasper scoffed. "She loves me."

"I hate to be the one to tell you this, but you're growing less lovable by the moment," Eli grunted as he staggered toward the door. Jasper didn't put up a fight, for which he was grateful.

"She's going to chuck me out," Jasper said gloomily, once they had made their way outside.

Eli didn't have to ask whom Jasper meant. "She might, if you make a stubborn fool of yourself," he allowed. "But if you stand there and take your tongue lashing like a man, I think you'll come out of it all right. She didn't chuck me out."

"It wasn't your idea. Besides, you're her favorite," Jasper mumbled.

Eli rolled his eyes. "Oh come off it, Jasper. Sully doesn't have favorites."

"Spoken like a true favorite child," Jasper slurred.

"Imagine having the nerve to call anyone else a child when you're in this state," Eli muttered. Jasper, still mumbling, didn't seem to hear him.

They stumbled on through the streets weaving this way and that every time Jasper's balance failed. Before long, Eli was aching and wishing he could just hail a carriage to take them the rest of the way. But they were still too deep into the Barrens—no self-respecting cabbie would dare venture into this neighborhood at this time of night. They would have to walk to the edge of the Market District at least.

"I wasn't wrong, you know," Jasper said suddenly, as though he were continuing a conversation aloud that he'd been having in his head.

"About what?" Eli asked with a sigh.

"About the notices. It worked," Jasper whispered.

"Is that right?" Eli asked.

Jasper nodded, and his face broke into a smug smile. "I heard people talking about it in the brothel and around the Barrens during the day. They whisper, but they're talking. They're not letting the Illustratum bury Davies' death."

"Keep your voice down, Jasper," Eli said. "It's suicide to talk too loudly about Davies with all the extra patrols around."

"But that's just it," Jasper said. "The Riftborn don't care. Not anymore. There's rumblings of discontent and demands for answers. For once they aren't satisfied with the Illustratum's explanation of things. And we did that. We did it." He looked at Eli, a bit blearily perhaps, but with pride. Eli couldn't help it. He returned the smile for a moment, before it slipped off his face again.

"Sully's afraid. Afraid we're going to lose control," Eli said. "She doesn't think we have enough infrastructure in place, enough of a plan for the Riftborn populace to rebel. We can't organize or control it if it gets out of hand too soon. That's why she wanted to control the news of Davies' death."

Jasper gave a scoffing laugh. "Sully's problem is she thinks a revolution is something you can control. She thinks you can lay it out, chapter by chapter, word by word, like one of her bloody books."

"And you'd prefer mass chaos, would you?" Eli asked sharply.

"I'd prefer action," Jasper replied, and his voice suddenly sounded steadier than it had since Eli had found him. "So much waiting and planning, and for what? If there's never any risk, there's never any reward, never any progress."

"Risks should be calculated," Eli said, even as he felt the truth of Jasper's words twist in his gut.

Jasper swiped his hand, the simple motion making him stumble and nearly fall. "What's happened to you? I can't even talk to you anymore. It's like talking to Sully in trousers."

"Bold words from a man who looks like he's about to piss his at any moment," Eli retorted, stung.

Jasper looked stunned into silence for a moment, then suddenly threw back his shaggy golden head and burst out laughing, the raucous sound of it echoing through the quiet street, startling a scrawny cat out of a nearby alley. Eli felt the corners of his mouth turn up, but he smothered his own laughter.

"There's the edge of the Barrens up ahead. Keep your feet under you a bit longer and maybe we can hail a ride back," Eli said.

Jasper wasn't listening. He'd begun singing a song, still laughing to himself. Eli continued to half-drag him toward the better-lit street ahead, his brain buzzing. Jasper was an idiot on occasion, but every once in a while, he made a hell of a lot of sense. It was in these moments that Eli found himself wrapped up in whatever recklessness Jasper had up his sleeve, but he did not always regret it. Some of the best and most exciting times of his short life had been because he'd said yes to Jasper even as his common sense was telling him no. He wondered if it was Jasper's influence that had him seeking information on the Hallewell's lady's maid in the first place. Sully had told him to let it go, but somehow he couldn't. It bothered him that he couldn't put into words exactly what he thought he would accomplish by finding the girl, but the idea would not let go of him.

He looked down at Jasper, still singing his slurred and plaintive song, and sighed. It was going to be a long night, and he had to be up early tomorrow to find another spot of trouble to get into. At least he had a hunch Jasper would be too hungover to want to accompany him.

And as though to confirm that hunch, Jasper looked up at Eli, grinned lazily, then dropped to his knees and vomited in the gutter.

NINE

T HE DOOR TO THE CARRIAGE STOOD OPEN, and the
footman stood by expectantly, but Jessamine still had not
moved to alight. To an outside observer, she might have
appeared to have lost the ability for forward ambulatory motion, but
in reality, she had merely lost the will.

She sighed. An evening spent in the company of her friends. Oh,
how she dreaded it.

It hadn't always been this way. Once upon a simpler time,
Jessamine had spent many a gay and giggling hour sporting with the
other little girls whom she had called her friends. They had woven
daisy chains and crowned each other queen of the castle. They had
whispered secrets and traded sweets. They had been dear to each
other, and promised always to remain so. She wished she could
remember the moment when it had all changed, but then, it hadn't
been a single moment at all, had it?

Over time, secrets had become weapons, and compliments had
become barbed. Conversations had developed so many layers that it
was nearly impossible to know what one was really talking about.
Invitations were extended or denied with all the deliberate tactical
strategy as the moves in a game of chess. And while it could
sometimes be intriguing, or tantalizing, mostly it was just exhausting,
and Jessamine was in no mood to navigate those waters tonight.
Kitty Price was really the only one she thought she could call a
true friend anymore, and Kitty would likely have to stay home, as
she had lately suffered from a cold, and her mother was notoriously
overprotective. Without Kitty's friendly face, Jessamine felt that she

was being thrown to the wolves—a pack of smiling, nodding, lace-clad wolves.

Her father had not come home, as she had predicted. She had taken her tea and eaten her dinner in solitude. Not one of the staff would dare to offer comment on the afternoon's events beyond, "I cannot say, miss," or "That's surely a question for Elder Hallewell, miss." This, she felt sure, would put her at a distinct disadvantage this evening, for she was certain that the only topic of discussion would be the events that had transpired at the noon services, at which all of the charity circle members were in attendance. She would, of course, be glad at last to have her questions answered, but she despised being the one with questions rather than answers. Not every Elder ran as tight a ship as her own father did, and Jessamine was sure that several of the other girls would have been able to wheedle information out of servants and family members—information they would horde jealously and dangle temptingly over the heads of the others before they would disperse it with a nauseating magnanimity. Perhaps it was because Jessamine had done so herself when she knew something the others didn't, that she so loathed being the one fishing for scraps of information this time around.

"Well," she told herself, "I can't very well sit out here all night, so into the fray it is. Besides, if I don't go in, the night's only compensation will be lost entirely."

Tonight's charity circle was being hosted at Elmhurst Hall, the seat of power for the Potter family. Rebecca Potter, who would act as hostess for the evening, was two years younger than Jessamine, and the silliest nit ever to be strapped into a corset. She had a laugh like a mad hyena and looked desperately to the older girls for approval, which they were forced to give, seeing as her father was so powerfully placed. But Jessamine would tolerate hours of Rebecca's tiresome company (and would, no doubt) for just a passing glimpse of Rebecca's older brother, Teddy. A kind word from him, a short exchange, even a nod in passing was enough to make her heart soar. And she knew, though she dared not say it out loud, that Teddy would not miss the opportunity if it were within his power to see her.

Bolstered by this knowledge, Jessamine stepped down from the carriage and strode across the gravel to the open front door, where the servants stood at attention to receive her. With barely a word spoken, her wrap was taken, her umbrella hung, her basket whisked away, and

118

her person escorted with military precision to the sitting room off the library where the ladies lay in wait for her, coiled like silk-clad snakes, ready to strike. She heaved a sigh, composed her face, and nodded her readiness to be announced.

"Miss Jessamine Hallewell of Larkspur Manor."

"Jessamine!"

At least a dozen voices rose in a chorus of enthusiastic greeting. Jessamine's face lit up with the most practiced and diplomatic of smiles as she sailed across the room, the picture of delighted anticipation.

"Ladies! A pleasure to see you all tonight. The Creator bless our hands and our work," she said, to which a chorus of murmurs had no choice but to vociferously agree.

Kitty Price smiled broadly—a genuine smile—and patted the seat beside her. "I've saved you a seat, Jessamine," she said, with a shadow of a wink.

Jessamine nodded gratefully and took a seat beside Kitty at the long table that had been set up in the center of the room. The girls all sat around it, each with a task set up before her. In front of Jessamine's seat were the blessing cards, a dip pen and inkwell, and a stack of labels.

"I've assigned you the signing of the blessing cards and the labels for the preserves, Jessamine, as you've such an elegant hand," Rebecca Potter said nervously, gesturing to the materials. "The others agreed it was just the right task for you."

"There's nothing I'd like better," Jessamine replied, transforming Rebecca's anxious expression into a beaming smile. "Mrs. Keats truly outdid herself this week. Orange marmalade and strawberry preserves. I've brought enough for two for each basket." The servant who had taken the basket from her was now arranging the jars along the end of the table.

"Splendid!" Rebecca said. "And just in time for the Feast of the Chosen."

"Honestly, Jessamine, how does dear Mrs. Keats find the time?" Katherine Primrose chimed in. "What with all the preparations for your Presentation, does the poor woman ever sleep?"

Jessamine kept her smile firmly in place. "She is a marvel, to be sure. And of course, our entire kitchen staff is such a blessing to her.

Father's taken on three extra kitchen maids for the month to ensure the workload is properly managed."

Katherine simpered. There were a few exclamations, but no retorts. Jessamine smiled and turned to Kitty. "Kitty, I'm so pleased to see you. I was sure your mother would keep you home another week at least."

"She nearly did," Kitty said, rolling her wide blue eyes. "I was perfectly well enough to come last week, but you know my mother—she's beside herself with worry at the merest sniffle. However, Father insisted I was well enough to come to services this afternoon, and once I was seen at services, it was easy to convince her I ought to come tonight."

"Easy to convince her? I should think not," Jessamine laughed. She knew Mrs. Shaw to be as immovable a woman as she had ever met. "However did you manage it?"

Kitty grinned slyly. "I simply lamented the fact that the rest of the girls would surely gossip that I was shirking my responsibilities to the circle, and lo and behold, she had my basket packed in a trice."

Rebecca looked scandalized. "We would never do such a thing!"

Sadie Carpenter snorted and tossed her glossy auburn curls. "Wouldn't we?"

Kitty shrugged. "It doesn't matter whether you would or not, for my purposes," she said. "All that matters is that my mother believed it, and here I am, back in society again at last."

Bette Smythe frowned severely, which was entirely predictable as Bette Smythe did everything severely. "We don't want a reputation for gossip when the purpose of our group is fully in service of the Creator and His good works." She stood up from the table to fetch more loaves of bread to wrap.

"For heaven's sake, don't get your corset in a knot, Bette. Our reputation's in no more danger of being tarnished than you are of being courted," Sadie muttered, so quietly that Bette wouldn't hear. She was rewarded for her wit with a chorus of tittering laughs from the rest of the circle.

Jessamine laughed as well, though she felt rather guilty about it. Bette was seven years older than her, with not a suitor in sight. Her father was an Elder, it was true, but he was quite an old man, with a cantankerous nature. He had squandered away most of the family's money with poor management, and had long since lost his opportunity to move up in the hierarchy of the Elders in any meaningful way. Poor Bette would have needed an abundance of physical and social charms to elevate her into a marriage with another Elder family, but sadly she had been blessed with very little of either—awkwardly tall, beak-nosed, and homely, with a nasal voice and no gift for conversation or humor. Bette was widely acknowledged by this time to be a spinster, though her father doggedly continued to trot her out at every social event in the vain hope that someone would take her off his hands. She might have made a fair marriage to a well-to-do Dignus without Illustratum status, but her father was far too stubborn to entertain proposals from such social climbers. And so here poor Bette Smythe was, surrounded by younger and younger women, watching them get married off one by one as she remained behind, sermonizing and tutting over the contents of charity baskets.

"Don't be unkind, now, Sadie," Adelaide Shaw scolded, though she was stifling a laugh like the rest of them. "We mustn't make her feel badly."

"Hark who's talking," Sadie retorted. "You wave that ring right under her nose every time you hand her something. Honestly, Adelaide, who returns a pair of scissors like this?" And Sadie scooped up a pair of scissors, making an exaggerated show of waving her hand around back and forth and wiggling her fingers before setting the scissors down again. More titters of laughter.

Adelaide blushed prettily, fingering the ruby glittering on her slender finger. "Don't be ridiculous, Sadie. I'm doing no such thing."

"That's right, Adelaide, you ignore her," Kitty replied, patting Adelaide on the arm and grinning wickedly. "Sadie's the one who can't stop staring at it. I must say, Sadie, you can carry almost any color off beautifully with your complexion, but green is a dreadful look for you."

It was Sadie's turn to blush now. Kitty smiled wickedly and added. "Ah, there we are. Red's a much more flattering hue."

Adelaide and Sadie had made no secret of the fact that they'd both set their sights on Will Garrison, Elder Garrison's oldest son. The competition between them had been fierce down to the very day he had proposed to Adelaide, and the two had only just begun speaking to each other again. Personally, Jessamine hadn't seen what all the fuss had been about. Will Garrison was handsome, she supposed, but his manner was stodgy and he had the kind of voice that could put a roomful of listeners into a sound sleep within moments. He would be, without question, the dullest husband Jessamine could imagine. It was almost a shame, really, that Sadie hadn't managed to get her claws into him first—as far as Jessamine was concerned, Sadie deserved to be bored to death. But of course, when it came right down to it, the girls' rivalry mattered little. Marriages were decided by men behind closed doors, not by girls dazzling on dance floors.

Bette returned to the table, leaving the girls no choice but to pivot the conversation away from matrimony for the moment.

"How are we to get the baskets into the Barrens this week? Has anyone heard?" Adelaide asked, returning to her stitching of the sachets.

"Whatever do you mean?" Kitty asked. "Our lady's maids will deliver them, the same as always."

"I'm not so sure about that," Rebecca said, shaking her head. "The last I heard, there was still a strict curfew in place, and people weren't being let in."

"Surely they'll make an exception for charitable works?" Jessamine asked, eyebrows raised. "The need in the Barrens won't have lessened simply because of a hanging."

"Yes, but Father told me they fear unrest in the streets. It mightn't be safe to deliver baskets in such conditions," Katherine added in a whisper.

The entire table of young women tensed at these words. They had come at last to the topic they'd all been eager to discuss since they'd arrived.

"What I can't understand," Rebecca said, "is why this hanging should cause any greater of a fuss than any other hanging. After all, the Praesidio hang criminals all the time."

"If anything, the Riftborn should be eager to show their restraint and faithfulness at a time like this," Bette sniffed. "This is a moment to set themselves apart from the riffraff, not join them."

"I heard," Sadie began, and every girl leaned in eagerly, "that these criminals were no ordinary thieves or vagrants, but rebels of some sort."

Adelaide looked affronted. "Rebels? You mean blasphemers!"

Sadie shrugged. "If you prefer. They questioned the Illustratum's authority, and that's why they were hanged. In fact, it might have been

122

one of their accomplices who got through the front doors and caused the disturbance today at services."

Jessamine pretended not to look aghast at this extraordinary pronouncement, but could not be sure she had managed it. Several of the other girls' mouths had simply fallen open, and Rebecca had dropped her spool of ribbon, which rolled away across the table unnoticed.

"How do you know that?" Rebecca breathed, awed. Clearly, her father had told her nothing of the day's events, just like Jessamine's.

Sadie preened. "I overheard my brothers discussing it. Charles and Leander never bother to keep their voices down when I'm around. I suppose they must think me deaf or perhaps they just assume I've no interest in such things."

"This isn't a proper subject for discourse," Bette announced, her nose in the air.

"And why not?" Sadie countered. "We were all there. We have every right to discuss events at which we were present!"

"My mother said that whoever made the disturbance today won't even have made it out of the Illustratum alive," Kitty whispered. "Do you think that's true?"

"Of course, it's true!" Adelaide hissed. "Didn't you hear the gunshots?"

For a moment, the shots seemed to echo in all of their memories, and a collective shudder ran through the assembled party.

"I was ever so scared," Katherine admitted after the silence had stretched on.

"So was I," Jessamine admitted, patting Katherine on the hand. "But we had nothing to fear. The Elders had everything well in hand."

"Your father certainly seemed comfortable taking charge, Jessamine," Sadie replied, with more than a touch of coolness.

Jessamine lifted her chin. "Yes, I daresay he did."

"There might be some who would say it wasn't his place to do so," Sadie went on, her voice casual, but with a malicious gleam in her eye.

"I beg your pardon?" Jessamine replied, feeling anger rise in her chest.

"I certainly don't presume to be one of them," Sadie insisted, widening her eyes innocently. "I, for one, thought he handled the situation admirably. But after all, there were nearly fifty Elders there…"

"Many of whom were fleeing for the doors," Jessamine snapped. "My father is one of the advisors to the High Elder, and as such—"

"But so is Rebecca's father," Sadie pointed out. "I wonder if he felt your father's taking of the reins was entirely appropriate."

Rebecca's eyes went wide as she looked back and forth between Jessamine and Sadie, clearly horrified that she had somehow wound up in the middle of the discussion. "I... I'm sure he wouldn't... that is to say... I can't imagine..."

"Someone had to step up to ensure the safety of the congregation. My father did so. I'm quite sure that if anyone took issue with his actions, including Elder Potter, they would address my father directly, not send snide insinuations on the lips of their daughters," Jessamine cut in over Rebecca's babbling. "I can't imagine your father would have much to say about my father's handling of service today, Sadie. After all, it would have been hard to hear much from wherever he was cowering out in the hallway after he fled at the first sound of disruption."

Sadie looked as though she had been slapped in the face, which was gratifying, as that was exactly what Jessamine would have liked to do to her. She stood up, swelling with indignation. "How dare you—"

"Oh, I know exactly how I dare," Jessamine said, and though her voice remained utterly calm, she rose to her feet, and her green eyes flashed. "I am a Hallewell first and foremost, and I do not forget what is owed to that name and that legacy. Let me disabuse you of the notion that I will sit by and smile and tie ribbons while you make snide insinuations against my father's character. Whether they are your insinuations or your father's, I don't know or care, but I will say this: only a coward would send his opinions through the idly gossiping tongue of a girl rather than voice them himself. Now, unless one of you intends to show up on our doorstep tomorrow so that you can share your concerns with my father directly, I suggest you sit right back down in that chair, close your mouth, and keep your mind on your work where it might actually do some good. If your intention was merely to wound me with your words, I assure you, you have failed utterly, a sensation with which I can only assume you are intimately acquainted."

Sadie's chest heaved as she struggled to bring forth a stinging reply. Jessamine held her gaze steadily, waiting. Finally, with no more answer than a flare of her nostrils, Sadie sank slowly back into her seat, picked up a square of fabric with shaking hands, and resumed her wrapping of the produce bundles.

"Rebecca, excuse me, please. I need a moment to gather myself," Jessamine said, holding her hands tightly together to stop them from shaking as she stepped away from the table.

"Of... of course," Rebecca said, sounding flustered.

"Would you like me to come with you?" Kitty asked, throwing a malevolent look at Sadie and half-rising from her seat.

"No, please," Jessamine said. "I just need some air. I'll be right back." And holding herself with as much dignity as she could manage, she strode from the room, out into the entrance hall, and onto the balcony overlooking the gardens.

In the stillness of the cool night air, Jessamine placed her hands upon the stone ledge and took several slow, deep breaths. She could feel the beginnings of tears threatening to spill out, and she would not give Sadie Carpenter the satisfaction of seeing her return to the charity circle swollen-eyed and red-cheeked.

Jessamine hated confrontation, especially when it devolved into a messy public spectacle, but there were affronts that could not be borne, and this one upon her father's reputation had certainly been one of them. As much as she had insisted the opposite, Sadie's words had worried her—had her father committed some kind of infraction? Would he be met with censure for stepping up so bravely and taking command of the service when it seemed destined to devolve into chaos? Surely not—and yet, Jessamine knew there was much to the hierarchy of the Illustratum that she did not understand and was not allowed to ask about. She knew her father could handle himself; she only hoped he wasn't going to be made an object of ridicule for what he had done.

"Well, well, what light through yonder window breaks? It is the east, and Jessamine is the sun!" came a voice from the darkness below.

Jessamine leapt back from the railing and gave a small shriek of surprise, which she quickly stifled with her hand before returning to the balcony's edge and peering over it. She gasped.

"Teddy? Is that you down there?"

"Of course it is! How many gentlemen do you have spouting verse at you from a darkened garden?"

Jessamine laughed. "Well, none, until this very moment."

"What a shame," Teddy replied, stepping forward so that he was illuminated by the light shining down from the window. "Not that I want the competition, you understand, but beauty such as yours should be inspiring volumes of the stuff."

Jessamine smiled down at the good-natured face. Teddy Potter was tall and dark-haired, with an easy smile and warm brown eyes. He had all of his father's humor and none of his bluster. A thrill ran through her. She ought not to be speaking to him alone—propriety would not allow it. And yet, he was down below and she was up on the balcony—it wasn't as though they were in close proximity to each other. She decided to risk prolonging the conversation. "I've never read any poetry."

"Nor have I, much. Well, there isn't much of it to be had, is there? If it weren't for my father's involvement with the historical archive, I might not have read any at all. But that bit was quite famous once, so I understand."

"Who wrote it?"

Teddy thought for a moment. "Do you know, I simply can't remember the fellow's name. No one of any consequence, I suppose."

"Well, having now experienced poetry, I must admit, I quite liked it. In fact, I look forward to my next poem, which I demand you compose yourself. When shall I expect it?" she asked.

"At such time as I discover a heretofore untapped talent for writing. Until then, I'll have to steal them, I'm afraid," Teddy replied with a shrug and a grin.

"Mr. Potter, I am afraid I cannot associate myself with a thief," Jessamine said, leaning onto her elbows so that she could get a better look at him all the same.

"Then I shall reform at once," Teddy replied, saluting. He leaned forward, a slight frown on his face. "What's this, now? You haven't been crying, I hope?"

Blast it all, Jessamine thought. Aloud though, she laughed lightly. "Of course not. My eyes simply sparkle. Ask any poet you meet."

"Who's upset you? Do I need to challenge someone to a duel in the name of your honor?" Teddy asked.

Jessamine laughed again, genuinely this time. "No, indeed. Sadie Carpenter is a deadly shot, I hear."

"Ah," Teddy said, nodding his understanding. "Feminine warfare, is it? I'm afraid I'm out of my depth there, Miss Hallewell."

126

"Never fear," Jessamine smiled. "I am more than capable of defending myself on that particular battlefield, if on no other."

Teddy laughed. "Of that, I have no doubt. Miss Carpenter is likely shivering in her crinolines. Are you nearly done with the charity circle?"

"I fear we've only just started, really. The list of families to serve seems to get longer every week. Is that why you're hiding in the garden?"

Teddy held up both hands. "Guilty. I didn't want to disturb. Father's still at the Illustratum, and I've no one to lecture me. I'm desolate."

Jessamine raised her eyebrows. "Your father still hasn't returned?"

"No sign of him yet," Teddy said.

"That means my father is likely still out as well," Jessamine said.

Teddy took a step forward. "I've worried you. I'm sorry, that wasn't my intention."

"No, not at all," Jessamine said quickly. "I'm not worried. I just... wish I knew a bit more about what happened at the service today, and I'm not likely to find out if Father's going to be out all night. Unless," her face lit up, "unless you can tell me anything about it."

Teddy looked discomfited. "It's not my place, Jessamine. Besides, why would you want to worry yourself with such matters?"

Jessamine felt her smile fade. "I don't want to worry myself, I just want to know what's—"

"You young ladies have so many other things to occupy your minds with—the charity circle, your Presentation coming up..."

"My mind has room for many things, I assure you, Mr. Potter..."

"Then let them be pleasant things. Chaos in the Barrens and Riftborn run amok are hardly the kind of—"

"Chaos? What kind of chaos?" Jessamine asked.

"No, I will not be responsible for ruining what might otherwise be a lovely evening," Teddy said, holding up a hand.

"Spoken like someone who's never had to endure a charity circle before," Jessamine replied, trying to keep the coolness out of her voice. It seemed not even Teddy would answer her questions. Would everyone insist on treating her like a child?

"Let me rescue you, then," Teddy insisted. "What do you say to a moonlit stroll with me?"

Jessamine's heart fluttered in spite of her annoyance. "A scandalous suggestion, Mr. Potter."

"Oh, come now, not on a night like tonight," Teddy said innocently. "Just look at that moon. Why it's as bright as day out here in the garden."

Jessamine looked up. The great swollen curve of the full moon was indeed doing its best to imitate her daytime counterpart. The moonlight had leeched the color from the flowers and the grass, giving the garden the appearance of a fresh sketch to which the artist had not yet applied his palette.

"I ought to go in," Jessamine said with a sigh, pulling her eyes from the moon. "Kitty will come looking for me, and I'll never hear the end of it if she finds I've been out here conversing with you without so much as a chaperone."

Teddy put his hand over his heart and staggered backward, as though Jessamine had shot him. "I suppose I shall have to nurse my devastation until we next meet. Until your Presentation, then, Miss Hallewell. I hope I may safely lay claim to your first and last dance."

Jessamine smiled, dropping her eyes coquettishly. "They are yours to claim, Mr. Potter, as you very well know."

Teddy gave a sweeping bow, and Jessamine returned a low curtsy before slipping back through the doors. She closed them carefully behind her and turned, bumping right into Kitty.

"Goodness Kitty, you startled me!" Jessamine gasped.

"There you are! I was starting to wonder if you'd simply gone home!" Kitty said with a pout. "Please, Jessamine, do come back. I can't stand another minute of them without you. I have half a mind to fake a coughing fit and claim that my mother was right after all and my cold has come back."

"There's no need to reward your mother's overbearing nature so," Jessamine laughed, patting Kitty on the hand and taking her arm. "I'll come back to the circle with you. We mustn't give Sadie the satisfaction of thinking she's run me off."

And arm in arm, they returned to the smiling, simpering fray.

TEN

T HE BODY SWUNG LIGHTLY IN THE BREEZE, with a
gentleness that seemed to mock its very presence upon the
scaffold. A burlap sack had been pulled down over the head,
obscuring the face. Eliza stepped slowly across the creaking wooden
planks, unable to tear her eyes from that sack, both wanting and not
wanting desperately to know who was hidden beneath it. She was so
intent on discerning the features that she nearly lost her footing at the
edge of the open trap door. Her arms windmilled for a moment and
she stifled a scream, but managed to keep her balance.

As her own muffled shriek echoed in her ears, she could have
sworn she heard a second voice, no more than a breath of a whisper,
say her name.

"Eliza. Eliza Braxton."

She froze. Could it have been just the creaking of the rope she
had heard? She stared at the body still swaying before her. The noose
around his neck, the stiffness and stillness of his limbs, left her in no
doubt that he was dead. And yet...

She reached out a trembling hand, grasped the burlap sack, and
pulled.

Those green eyes. That chiseled face. She knew him.

Even as she recognized the boy from the carriage his whole head
turned to look at her, and a whisper escaped his blue lips.

"Eliza Braxton."

Eliza woke with such a start that she had to catch herself before
she toppled over the edge of the bed. Bridie cried out beside her and
sat up, staring around wildly into the darkness.

"Eliza! Are you all right? What's happened?"

Eliza worked to get her breath under control—it was coming in great, heaving gasps, as though she had just surfaced from the water. "I... I'm sorry, Bridie. I... it was... just a nightmare..."

Bridie pressed her hand to heart. "Creator above, Eliza, you gave me a turn. I thought we were about to be murdered in our beds. That must have been quite the nightmare."

"It was... I... I'm all right now," Eliza said, trying to play off her terror with a shaky laugh.

"You still look very pale, Eliza," Bridie said, looking at her with some concern. "Do you want to tell me what it was about?"

Eliza tried to shrug casually. "I can hardly remember anymore. You know how dreams just slip right out of your head like that when you wake up."

The lie seemed to convince Bridie, and she lay back down and rolled onto her side, her mumbling soon subsiding into quiet, even breathing. Eliza slumped back against her pillow, afraid to close her eyes again, lest the image of the young man's face retain its terrible imprint on the insides of her eyelids.

A strange tension had filled Larkspur Manor over the last two days, that heaviness that comes when a subject cannot be discussed openly, and so it just looms over everyone like a summer rain cloud. Eliza did not dare ask her father or anyone else about the disruption that had taken place at the services. Even Bridie, who had never before managed to hold her tongue on any topic, had not dared to speculate about it. The only person in the house who did seem to want to discuss it was Miss Jessamine, who was firing questions at anyone who stood still long enough in her presence. She had mused about it to Eliza several times, when Eliza attended her in the morning and evening.

"I just can't understand why my father won't explain it to me. What can be so terrible about me knowing the truth about what happened? How can the truth be bad? Isn't that what we're supposed to be seeking?" Jessamine had sighed as Eliza brushed her hair before bed.

Eliza had simply nodded, but inside, her heart felt ready to burst. With a start, she realized it was the first time in her entire life that she understood exactly what her mistress was feeling. There had always been a kind of wall—and understandably so—between Eliza and Jessamine. Eliza was Riftborn, Jessamine was Dignus. Eliza was a servant, Jessamine was a mistress. What common ground, really, could these two young women have, despite their age and sex? And at this precise moment, that common ground was a much wider expanse than ever it had been. They were both daughters whose fathers refused to answer their questions. They were both young women whose gender precluded them from certain knowledge and privilege. They were both being shut out of understanding the very same events. Never had Eliza felt that she and Jessamine occupied the same space until now as they stood on the outside looking in at the troubling situation encroaching upon their lives and routine.

The following morning, Eliza rose early and entered the kitchen as she always did on Tuesday morning, prepared to make her weekly trip to deliver baskets for needy families in the Barrens. As it was Bridie's job to start all the fires in the house, she was already up, dressed, and well along in her work by the time Eliza got up, but Eliza knew that Bridie would meet her at the carriage when she had finished so they could ride in together. She and Bridie took the drive into the city every week, often meeting up with maids from other households who had been charged with delivering their mistresses' baskets. Just as the Elders' daughters were obliged to serve the Illustratum by creating the baskets, their maids were required to engage in their own form of service by venturing into corners of the city in which their mistresses would never be permitted to set foot and see that the baskets reached their recipients. Bridie detested the task, apart from the opportunity to trade gossip with the other maids. Bridie never specified just what about it bothered her so, though Eliza suspected that the knowledge of how close Bridie herself had been to being a creature of the Barrens made the experience a somewhat uncomfortable one. But as for Eliza, she always arrived back at Larkspur Manor afterward with a feeling of contentment that she had done her duty and that many a family would eat better that night because of her efforts.

Eliza looked around the kitchen, but found no baskets waiting for her on the tabletop, as she expected. It was very odd, indeed—she knew that Miss Jessamine had gone to her charity circle two nights ago to put them together, as Eliza had had to stay up late waiting for her to arrive home. Puzzled, she grabbed Penny, who was passing with a fresh loaf of bread still steaming from the oven.

"Penny, do you know what's become of the charity baskets?"

Penny looked at the table in mild surprise and then looked up at Eliza, shrugging. "I'm afraid I don't. I'd have thought they'd be right there as usual. You'd best ask Mrs. Keats." And she bustled off again, humming quietly.

Eliza groaned inwardly. Bothering Mrs. Keats in the midst of Presentation preparations was a risky proposition, but she could hardly deliver charity baskets in the Barrens this morning if the baskets were nowhere to be found. It seemed more prudent to have a look around for the baskets herself, rather than risk incurring Mrs. Keats' wrath. A cursory search of the dry goods pantry revealed the baskets tucked onto a lower shelf, covered with cheesecloth. Breathing a sigh of relief, Eliza gathered up the baskets, sliding three into the crook of each arm, and slipped out of the kitchen and up the back passage to the waiting carriage.

The morning was brisk, but not as chilly as recent days, and Eliza took a deep breath as she loaded the baskets into the trunk strapped to the back of the carriage. She fancied she could feel something of spring in the air, and the thought that they would soon be out from under winter's damp, grey thumb cheered her slightly. Eliza stepped up into the carriage and pulled the door shut behind her before she saw Bridie was already in the carriage waiting for her.

"Bridie! You've finished early! I thought I'd have to wait at least a few more minutes for you to—"

Eliza started, staring into the face beneath the white cap. It wasn't Bridie at all: it was Jessamine. She was dressed in a maid's uniform, her face hidden and her magnificent dark hair tucked up under a lacy white cap identical to the one that Eliza wore upon her own head. She sat with her shoulders hunched and a deferential tilt to her chin, rendering her almost unrecognizable. It was only when she raised her face to look into Eliza's eyes that Eliza realized with whom she was sharing a carriage.

"Miss Jessamine! What are you—"

"Shhhh!" Jessamine hissed. "Hold your tongue, Eliza, or you'll get me caught. Is that what you want?"

Eliza thought it might be exactly what she wanted, but she held her tongue just the same. The carriage jerked to a start, rattling its way out of the drive, and under cover of the noise, Eliza ventured another attempt at her question, this time in a whisper.

"Miss Jessamine, what are you doing here? And why are you wearing that uniform?"

Jessamine gave something of a sheepish grin, which Eliza was much too anxious and bewildered to return. "Well, I would have thought that was obvious. I would have been caught and sent right back into the house if I'd been wearing my own clothes."

"But where's Bridie?" Eliza asked, looking around the carriage in a bewildered sort of way, as though expecting Bridie to materialize from the leather seats.

"I caught her this morning while she was stoking the fire in my rooms. I demanded that she allow me to take her place, and swore her to secrecy. I also compensated her, just to ensure she wouldn't get cold feet. We swapped clothing; at this very moment, she is wearing my nightgown and pretending to be asleep in my bed."

Eliza threw a hand up over her mouth in horror. "Oh, but if she were to be caught!"

"But who would catch her? You are always the first person into my chambers in the morning. No one else would dare enter, not even my father, before I was properly dressed. As long as you don't give us away, no one will ever know."

Eliza's brain conjured a brief vision of Bridie luxuriating in Jessamine's four-poster bed, having a lie-in for perhaps the first time in her life, before panic wiped it blank again. "But miss... I still don't understand what you're doing here," she pressed.

"I want to come with you."

"With me?"

"Into the Barrens."

Eliza's heart, already galloping, seemed to stop. "Miss, you mustn't! You aren't allowed! None of the daughters of the Dignus are allowed to—"

"Eliza, for heaven's sake, I know the rules, so there's no point in spouting them at me. I am fully aware that I'm not allowed to go, hence my elaborate disguise and plan."

Jessamine's eyes were filled with a wildly excited light, and it was all Eliza could do not to reach right across the carriage and shake her. She suppressed the urge, however, and tried another tack.

"Miss, you've never shown even the slightest interest in going into the Barrens before. On the contrary, you've never even liked passing too close to the borders. What would possess you, all of a sudden, to need to visit the place?"

Jessamine bit her lip. "It started with the disturbance at the services on Sunday. No one will tell me anything—not the slightest detail. I don't understand why it's being kept from me. First my father, then the servants, and even Teddy refused to say a word."

"I'm sure they're only trying to... to protect you, miss," Eliza replied, trying to sound reasonable.

"But I don't want to be protected. What kind of protection is ignorance?" Jessamine snapped. "I am not a child, Eliza, and I am perfectly capable of understanding complex issues."

Eliza tried to retort but could not. Had she not had the very same argument with her own father? With Mrs. Keats? Even as she hesitated to reconcile her lecture with this fact, Jessamine went on.

"One of the girls at the charity circle let slip that there might be some... unrest in the Barrens. She thought perhaps you and the other maids mightn't be allowed to go deliver the baskets this week."

"I... I hadn't heard anything like that," Eliza said slowly, now wondering if that was why the baskets had been tucked away in the first place. "But if that's the case, that's all the more reason for you to stay home, miss. It mightn't be safe there."

"But you're going!"

"It mightn't be safe there for *you*," Eliza clarified.

Jessamine stiffened. "I can handle myself as well as you can, Eliza. I'm not completely helpless. And I suspect what you mean is that it isn't safe for anyone who looks like a Dignus. Well, I'm not dressed as a Dignus. I'm dressed as a Riftborn servant, so unless you have plans to give me away—"

"Of course I haven't!" Eliza gasped, hurt.

"Well, then, what's the problem? I won't say a word. I'll just follow along with you. I'll do whatever you want me to do." Jessamine folded her hands in her lap as a sign of compliance, and composed her face into a docile expression.

"I want you to go home, miss!" Eliza cried.

"All right, anything but that," Jessamine corrected herself.

"But miss, if someone should recognize you..."

"But why should they? No one in the Barrens has ever come within a hundred yards of me, with the exception of the week I spent handing out blessings at the Illustratum with father, and that was ages ago. No one will recognize me dressed like this. Please, Eliza, I just want to understand what's going on."

Eliza bit her lip. She hated to admit that Jessamine was in any small way right about her desire to go into the Barrens, but the truth was that it might be the only place where she could find answers to the questions raging in her own breast. People spoke freely in the Barrens. They did not adhere to the same strict social restrictions as the Riftborn who worked in service. And though they often tread warily when Eliza and other servants were present, Eliza always came away with a very different perspective than she garnered from her life downstairs at Larkspur Manor. How could she blame Miss Jessamine for having the same questions and longing for the same answers?

"Couldn't you just let me go, miss, with the promise that I'll share whatever I find out with you upon my return?" Eliza asked in a last, desperate bid to end this madness.

Jessamine crossed her arms. "No, Eliza. I've made up my mind. I'm coming. You know you are very dear to me, but your first instinct will always be to protect me and I'm done being protected."

"Please, Miss Jessamine. Please think of how much trouble we'll both be in if we're caught," Eliza practically whimpered.

"I have thought about it," Jessamine shot back at once. "And let's be very clear; you will be in no trouble at all. I am perfectly prepared to say that you tried to dissuade me by every possible means, but that I forced you to bring me along. I shall take full responsibility for this outing if we are caught, but I honestly don't see why we should be. I'm not going to announce my presence in the Barrens, Eliza. I want to be an observer—that's all. We shall deliver the baskets, observe and listen, and return home. Father will be at the Illustratum all day, and you're the only person who might have seen me in the intervening time. No one will have any reason to suspect I've done anything but keep to my bed for the morning. As long as we stick together, everything will be fine."

Eliza looked into Jessamine's earnest, pleading eyes and felt her resistance crumble. Perhaps she was right... perhaps they could both find the answers they sought and return home without anyone being any the wiser.

Or perhaps this would all end in disaster. But she supposed it was a risk she was going to take.

"Very well, miss," Eliza replied at last, her tone sharper than she had ever dared use with her mistress before, though Jessamine did not seem affronted in the least. Eliza realized she had a chance to set some rules and she leapt upon it. "If I am forced to acknowledge you at all, I am going to introduce you as..." she plucked a name from the air, as common a name as she could think of, "…Agatha Hix, a new kitchen maid in our household. Everyone knows Mrs. Keats has taken on extra help in preparation for the Presentation, so it shouldn't be difficult to convince someone that you are among them. You are to say as little as possible, and keep your face obscured as much as you can. Pull that bonnet down, and keep your gaze lowered—that will help. And for the love of the Creator, keep your hands hidden when you can. No one will believe you're in service with hands as lovely and smooth as that, and anyway, you haven't got a Riftmark."

Jessamine looked down at her hands, clearly having never considered such a thing before. Then she looked at Eliza's hands and pointed. "What about your gloves? Can I wear them?"

Eliza pulled her hands to her chest instinctively. "No, miss. As an Influencer, I'm required to keep my hands covered, as my Riftmagic is one of touch. It would be unpardonable for an Influencer such as myself to go out among people without gloves."

Jessamine cocked her head to one side, curiously. "But you hardly ever wear gloves when you're with me," she pointed out.

"Yes, but I use my gift in service to you, miss," Eliza explained patiently.

"I'm surprised you didn't use it just now, to try to talk me out of this," Jessamine said with a smirk.

"So am I," Eliza muttered.

"Well, what am I to do about my hands, then?" Jessamine pressed.

"Perhaps… perhaps just keep your hands in your pockets as much as you can?" Eliza suggested. "And tug your sleeves down as low as you can, to cover your wrists."

Jessamine nodded and then quickly stuffed both hands into her apron pockets. "Like this? All right, I can certainly do that. What else?"

"I realize there are things you want to know, but please, don't ask any questions. We can't be drawing attention to ourselves like that. And if anyone hears you speak, you'll be discovered at once."

"But why—"

"You haven't had much opportunity to converse with kitchen maids," Eliza said with a grim smile. "Trust me, miss, your poise and polish have no place in a manor house kitchen."

Jessamine gave a laugh. "Fair enough. All right, I shall be Agatha Hix, she of the pocketed hands and closed lips. Anything else?"

136

"If we see too much of this... this unrest you spoke of... if it seems at all unsafe, we will turn right around and head home, even if it means not a single basket gets delivered or a single question gets answered," Eliza said, and there was a steely resolve in her voice that wiped all humor from Jessamine's face.

"But don't you think—"

"I will not be moved on this point, miss," Eliza said. "I am already agreeing to this excursion against my better judgment. I will turn around right now and reveal the entire plan if you will not agree to this condition."

Jessamine hesitated a moment, and then nodded, solemnly. "Very well, Eliza, if you insist."

"I do," Eliza replied, her cheeks flushing as she realized she was giving orders to a Dignus, and her mistress at that. However, she forced herself not to drop her gaze.

Jessamine grinned and settled back against the seat, looking quite pleased with herself. "I'm rather excited, you know."

Eliza grimaced. "I'm pleased one of us is."

Eliza kept waiting for something to happen that would force them to turn around, for the carriage to be stopped, for a Praesidio guard to step out of nowhere into the street and halt them, demanding Jessamine show herself. She was almost hoping for it, hoping she wouldn't have to be responsible for her mistress within the borders of the Barrens. But no such barrier presented itself; the carriage bumped along unimpeded as the intrepid rays of morning sunlight crept through the narrow gaps and alleys of the city, lighting it up a single windowpane and roof tile at a time. But soon they would be in a part of the city that no amount of sunshine could brighten.

The further they drove, the more the city seemed to undergo a transformation, as though it were aging and withering before their eyes. The Dignus sector melted into the hustle and bustle of the Market District and then, as though the bridge over the Thames were a kind of gateway into a new world, the city shifted again, transformed by the barriers of water and status and magic into an almost unrecognizable place.

The Barrens loomed up before them, a den of squalor and poverty sprawling over the East side of post-Rift London. The cobbles gave way to muddy ruts and wheel-wrecking ditches. Eliza felt the carriage slow as Martin began the arduous task of making sure his rig was not destroyed by the poor conditions of the roads. Soon, he would have to give up altogether, pulling over in front of some sordid pub or another, leaving Eliza and—on this mad occasion, Jessamine—to traverse the last few blocks into the tenements on foot.

Doors hung open, where doors were to be found, revealing squalid conditions within—fires stoked in filthy grates, with children huddled around them, meager meals being scrounged up and distributed from last night's scraps. What might easily have been mistaken for bundles of rags were revealed to be vagrants curled up to sleep on thresholds. On one side of the carriage, a harried-looking woman was emptying a stinking chamber pot into the gutter while a red-faced baby screamed on her hip. A few doors down, a man wove drunkenly along the pavement, shouting incoherently at no one in particular. In a Dignus neighborhood, he would have drawn every eye, a novelty and a nuisance, but here in the Barrens, he was summarily ignored, a fixture of the morning routine.

Upon the corners, small transactions took place—the selling and bartering of meager goods for services or what little grubby coinage could be scrounged up. An elderly, toothless woman sang a tuneless song meant to draw customers to her wares—a tray of tarnished spoons, half-spent spools of thread, some scraps of ribbon, and half a dozen shriveled potatoes. Jessamine pulled back from the window, her face an awed mixture of fascination and revulsion.

As the carriage trundled through the road, eyes met it with trepidation. A few of the shadier characters melted into the shadows as it approached, and did not resurface. Some children stared until their mothers cuffed them on the ears or shooed them into the buildings. Those who remained dipped into awkward bows or inclined their grubby heads as a sign of deference, faces unsmiling, even hostile.

"They… they don't look very happy to see us," Jessamine said, her voice awash in confusion. "Don't they know why you're here?"

Eliza didn't answer; she was too busy taking in the unfamiliar current of tension in the air. No one ever cheered at their approach, it was true—the distribution of charity was usually a fairly quiet event. The families for whom the week's baskets were meant were always glad for them and expressed their gratitude, but even so, there was no fanfare. But today there was something amiss. People seemed to be fleeing the presence of the carriage, and there was much more pointing and staring than Eliza had ever encountered before. She felt the creeping fingers of nervous energy stealing their way up her spine.

Before she could process the change in atmosphere, the carriage bumped to a halt and Martin called out, "This is as far as she can go today!" Eliza peered around; they had stopped just a block away from where the rest of the maids sometimes convened before splitting up to distribute their baskets, but the street was so much more crowded than she had ever seen it before; then she remembered the curfew that had been imposed, and wondered if this might account for more early risers?

The door beside her swung open, startling her, and she found herself facing Martin, whose face was quite tense. He looked Eliza in the eye as he took her hand and said, in a low voice, "Best be quick about it today, I think, miss."

Eliza nodded once, decisively, and allowed him to help her down out of the carriage. She held her breath as Martin reached for Jessamine's hand, too, but Jessamine did just as she had promised: she kept her head down and her eyes on the ground, saying nothing. When Martin turned to take his place back on the driver's seat, Eliza was quite sure from his distracted expression that he had noticed nothing amiss with the second of his passengers.

"Here, take these," Eliza said quietly, passing half of the baskets to Jessamine.

"What? Oh, yes. Yes, of course," Jessamine stammered, holding quite still as Eliza slid the baskets onto her forearms.

"Remember what I said. Eyes down, not a word, if you can help it," Eliza reminded her in a whisper. She waited for Jessamine's nod of assent before turning and setting off down the road.

Eliza kept her chin up and her eyes on the path in front of her. She was a servant of the Hallewell home. She had the official crest upon her uniform. She had no reason to fear any trouble from anyone in the Barrens. She repeated these statements over and over again to herself, even as she felt glares upon her. Eliza always felt out of place in the Barrens—after all, her life was in the hallowed halls of Larkspur Manor, not the filthy slums of this most dejected of Riftborn districts. But she had always felt as though the people of the Barrens regarded her as a novelty at best, a weird aberration at worst. But now, she could not shake the notion that there was something more—something darker—than idle curiosity in the stares that met her.

They approached the corner of the High Street and Commercial Road, a fairly busy impasse where a number of vendors usually gathered, selling off what remained of their unsold Market District wares. This was where the maids usually met up, trading nuggets of gossip with each other before setting off to make their deliveries, moving in a group, like a little flock of black and white birds, clucking and pecking together. But her momentary relief at not seeing them gathered there added another log to the fire of anxiety now crackling away in the pit of her stomach. Where was everyone? Surely she hadn't missed them. They always waited for each other.

Eliza turned back to look at Jessamine and forced her face into a smile. "We're in luck. We don't have to pass you off as anyone."

Jessamine did not return the smile. "Why aren't the other maids here?"

Eliza shrugged. "Maybe you were right—maybe we weren't supposed to come into the Barrens today. We'll just be quick about our deliveries and head home. Keep your head down. Try not to make eye contact with anyone."

This seemed a tall order for Jessamine, who was staring all around her with her mouth hanging open, as though the Barrens and the people residing in it were from a different planet altogether, rather than a different district of the very same city in which she had grown up. Eliza tugged lightly on her sleeve, and Jessamine started. One look at Eliza's expression and she realized she was drawing attention to herself. She nodded penitently and dropped her gaze, which was lucky because she barely managed to sidestep a steaming pile of horse manure.

"Stay right on my heels," Eliza murmured, before turning around and marching back in the direction of the carriage. Before they reached it, however, she turned right up Middlesex Street. A knot of small children glared at her for interrupting their play and scattered. Then she turned right onto Wentworth Street, where the first of their deliveries was located. A tiny face loomed in the grimy ground floor window of the house on the corner, vanishing as they appeared in the lane and then reappearing in the doorway, belonging to a small boy of perhaps six or seven years old, though he was so scrawny and underfed that he looked younger.

"Mum, they have come, they have, I told you it was our turn!" he screeched over his shoulder before turning his eyes back on the girls and their baskets with a greedy expression. He dared not approach them, but lingered on the very edge of the wooden threshold, hands twisting the frayed edge of the ragged smock he wore.

"Billy, I told you—oh!" A woman came tearing into the doorway, a dripping rag in her hand, reaching with the other as though to yank the boy back into the house, but then she caught sight of Eliza and Jessamine. Her face went blank, then wary. "Begging your pardon, misses. We hadn't thought to see you today."

"Good morning, Mrs. Barry. I hope we're not intruding," Eliza said, trying to smile, but finding it hard to shake the way the woman looked at her, as though she were holding something other than a basket of rations—perhaps even something dangerous.

"No, of course not. Not... not at all, miss," the woman said hastily, dropping the rag into her pocket and wiping her hands on the apron.

"Is there jam this week?" Billy piped up, licking his lips and craning his neck to get a better look at the baskets.

Eliza gave him a mock-serious look. "Jam? Hmmm... no, I don't think so. No one around here likes jam, do they?"

The boy's face lit up. "Yes, they do so, miss! I like it! I like it more 'n anything!" Billy cried, now positively writhing with excitement.

Eliza laughed. "Well, then, I guess it's a good thing we've made extra jam this week!"

Billy let out a whoop of glee, for which his mother immediately scolded him. She did not laugh, as she might normally have done, and seemed to cast a suspicious eye at the offering before pressing her lips into the semblance of a smile and reaching out for the basket. Eliza stepped forward and handed it to her.

"What flavor?" Billy hissed at her as the basket changed hands.

"Strawberry preserves and orange marmalade," Eliza whispered back, winking.

The boy grinned and disappeared behind his mother's skirt. Mrs. Barry shifted the basket onto her hip, the forced smile still on her face. "Well, I thank you both for your kindness, and for coming all this way on... on a day like today." She threw a tense glance down the road. "I'll not keep you. I'm sure you're very busy."

Eliza felt the smile threatening to slip from her face, but she managed to keep it in place. "Yes, thank you. We have got more deliveries to get on with. Creator keep you, Mrs. Barry, and all your family."

Mrs. Barry gave a shadow of a curtsy and vanished into her house, closing the door with a snap.

"Well!" Jessamine huffed, trotting up alongside Eliza as she started for the next address they had to visit. "That woman wasn't very friendly at all! She acted like we might be trying to poison her!"

"Don't be silly, Miss Jessamine. She was very grateful. I'm sure she just has her hands full, what with all the children," Eliza said, trying to sound unconcerned when inside she was rather flustered. Mrs. Barry was usually a boisterous woman. She'd been known to talk to Eliza and Bridie for so long that they had to make their excuses and run to catch up with the other girls. Today, though, she clearly couldn't wait to be rid of them. Something was indeed amiss.

The next two deliveries took them up Bell Lane to Butler Street, where they were met with similar wariness. Twice they caught sight of Praesidio patrols passing up or down a neighboring street. At the third door, though they could clearly hear voices from inside, no one answered Eliza's persistent knocks. Hesitant though she was to simply leave the basket on the doorstep—from which it would almost surely be stolen—the dark narrowness of the street and the crooked leaning of the sagging old buildings made her feel claustrophobic. She set the basket against the door, called out, "Your basket is here, Mrs. Hewitt! Creator keep you!" and set off again, making her way as quickly as she dared to Goulston Street.

"Eliza," Jessamine panted from a few steps behind her. "Can't you... slow down, please? These shoes aren't mine, it's hard to—"

"Of course, miss," Eliza said, coming to a stop so abruptly that Jessamine bumped into her from behind. "I'm so sorry, miss. Are you all right?"

"Perfectly well," Jessamine replied, straightening her cap and making sure it was still pulled safely down to obscure her face. "Please do go on, just... a little slower, if you would be so kind."

They set off again, heading for the house on the far lefthand corner of the street. It was darker here, more cramped than some of the other roads, and the buildings seemed to be struggling to hold each other up. The walls were nearly black with chimney soot. A lanky man lolled about in the doorway of the house as they approached it. Eliza pulled back, wondering if they mightn't just skip it—she had encountered Mr. Green before, and he was an unpleasant man on the best of days.

Today he had another man with him, shorter and squatter, with a newsboy cap perched precariously on his enormous bald head.

"Ah, here they come—the shame patrol," Mr. Green slurred, eliciting a hoarse laugh from his companion. Eliza noticed for the first time the bottle in Mr. Green's hand. She felt Jessamine shrink back behind her as she took another step forward.

"Good morning, Mr. Green," Eliza said, as pleasantly as she could. "I've brought your family's basket. Where would you like me to leave it?"

"You got anything worth my time in there," Mr. Green asked, narrowing his eyes at her, "or will it be a load of frilly nonsense like usual?"

Jessamine stiffened, but Eliza pressed on. "I believe it is quite the same as usual sir, but I do hope you'll find use for it."

"I'll tell you what I could find use for... a bit more of this right here," he replied, tipping his bottle upside down and pulling a grotesquely sad face, like an actor in a pantomime. "I don't suppose you've stashed some Riftmead in there, have you now?"

Eliza shook her head, blushing. "Of course not, sir. We're not allowed to—"

"Then I've got no use for it," he shouted. "What do I want with a prayer card and a jar of jam, eh? Will it get me a decent payin' job? Will it get me out of this Creator-forsaken wasteland of a tenement district? What good is that to me?"

"No good at all," the other man chimed in, wheezing with laughter again.

Indignant, half-formed thoughts raced through Eliza's mind, a hundred lessons drilled into her from infancy, about the importance of prayer, of the Creator rewarding the faithful, but she could not think how to express them to these drunken, belligerent men. Instead, she drew herself up and said, as smoothly as she could. "Nevertheless, I'll leave it here for you, sir. Perhaps one of your children might—"

"I said be gone with it!" Mr. Green suddenly shouted. "You must have an iron nerve, comin' into the Barrens today."

Eliza turned to go, but Jessamine had given a small gasp and clutched tightly at Eliza's sleeve. She didn't need to speak for Eliza to understand her meaning: this man was talking about the very unrest Jessamine had been so keen to understand. Eliza gritted her teeth, forcing a smile.

143

"Not at all, Mr. Green, sir," she said. "Merely my own conviction that the baskets make their way to the people who need them, nothing more than that." And she set the basket down on the ground.

"You don't belong here, you understand me? You may have a Riftmark on your wrist, child, but the similarity ends there. You eat at a Dignus table. You sleep under a Dignus roof. And you have the nerve to think you can set foot here and look down on us all. You're a traitor, that's what you are!"

Eliza's mouth was opening and closing like a fish as she fought to muster a reply. It was true that she'd never thought of herself belonging in the Barrens—but a traitor? What was the man talking about? How had she ever possibly betrayed other Riftborn? Hadn't she always done all she could to help them?

Mr. Green's raised voice had brought several of his ten children to the windows. A moment later, his wife appeared in the doorway behind him, looking flustered and red-cheeked, her frizzy hair escaping from her bun.

"Alfie? What's all this, then? Let the poor girls be," Mrs. Green hissed.

"Poor girls, my arse!" Mr. Green barked. "Sweeping through here like they belong, lording it over everyone, looking at me like I'm some bloody cockroach beneath their shoes." He pointed a shaking finger at Jessamine, who, in her shock at being addressed in such a hostile manner, had quite forgotten to keep her eyes down and was staring in open-mouthed horror at Mr. Green.

"He don't mean that. Never you mind him, he's on the drink, he is," Mrs. Green said, trying to muster a smile for the girls and shoving past her husband, hand extended for the basket.

"Don't you dare, Bessie! Don't you bring that poison into my house!" Mr. Green roared, lunging forward to snatch the basket, but tripping and sprawling into the dirt instead.

"Poison, indeed. I wouldn't have need of any of it if you'd spend your bloody wages on food for your children instead of gambling it away at the pubs," Mrs. Green screeched back. "You rant and rave that we're at the mercy of the Dignus, but who's the one stumbling home half-pissed with empty pockets? You ain't takin' this food out of my babies' mouths, not today, I don't care where it came from."

Mr. Green roared but could not seem to get himself up, and so his

144

wife swept back into the house, where her pack of children descended upon her before she could even shut the door.

Eliza backed away a few steps, but Mr. Green called out. "We know. They tried to hide it from us, but we all know. We know what they did to Davies. We know they covered it up."

"Hold your tongue, Alfie, there's a lad," the other man hissed, the grin wiped clean from his face as he glanced nervously at Eliza and Jessamine. "The patrols are out today."

"To who?" Jessamine asked, the question bursting from her lips before Eliza could stop her.

By now there were heads poking out of nearly every doorway in the crowded road, mouths agape at the scene unfolding on their doorstep. Eliza tried to tug Jessamine along, but she had rooted herself to the spot.

"Who, she asks. Who, as though he didn't matter, as though she ain't even one of us," Mr. Green scoffed, spitting on the ground in disgust. "No, of course they wouldn't want you knowing about that, would they? Wouldn't want any dangerous ideas in those pretty little heads. Of course they don't want you to know about the man who nearly saved us all."

It was Eliza who froze now. "What do you mean, saved us all? Saved us from what?"

But Mr. Green ignored her question with a snort of disgust. "You tell your fancy masters when you crawl back to serve them. You tell them that us what lives in the Barrens, we ain't fooled. We know what they did to Davies, and we won't be lied to anymore." And with a grunt, he hurled his bottle at the wall over his companion's head, causing the man to duck and curse as it exploded into shards.

The sound shocked Eliza back into action. She shoved Jessamine hard in the small of her back. "Miss, we have to go. Now."

"But what does he think they—" Jessamine began, but she caught Eliza's eye and something in the wildness of Eliza's expression finally shook her from her singular focus. She darted a look around the road—among the dozens of faces now staring at them, there was more than one hostile expression. She stumbled forward, allowing Eliza to pull her along, Mr. Green still shouting incoherently after them.

They half-ran the rest of the road but found they had taken it in the wrong direction in their haste—they were on Wentworth Street again—the High Street had been in the other direction. Swearing under her breath, Eliza pulled Jessamine to the right—they would go around the block and reach the High Street that way—it would take longer, but they could avoid Mr. Green and those of his neighbors who looked quite ready to join in the shouting.

Wentworth Street took them back past the Barry house. Eliza glanced at the window automatically, expecting to see little Billy there, perhaps with a jam-stained face. Instead, she saw shuttered windows and the basket she'd left with them sitting untouched on the doorstep. Her heart, already pounding, seemed to speed up. She broke into a run and reached the corner of Commercial Street with her breath searing in her lungs.

"Eliza, listen! There's something wrong," Jessamine gasped, grasping Eliza's sleeve and pulling her to a stop.

"What, what is it?" Eliza cried. "We need to keep moving!"

"Just listen!"

Eliza stared at Jessamine's wide, terrified eyes and suddenly she heard it too. There was shouting and loud bangs and screams echoing faintly up from the High Street—the direction they needed to go to return to the carriage.

"What is it? What's happened?" Jessamine squeaked.

"I don't know. Stay with me. We've got to get closer."

"Closer?! But—"

Eliza glared at her. "How else are we supposed to get back to the carriage? Martin is waiting for us there!"

Jessamine gave a faint whimper but nodded and the two girls started off again toward the High Street at a much more cautious pace. A few people ran past them in the opposite direction. They jumped as a bang echoed close by them, but it was only the shopkeeper of a grungy little pawnshop, slamming his shutters closed.

"Get yourselves inside, if you know what's good for you," he barked at them, before disappearing behind the faded green shutters.

The commotion grew louder as they approached the cross street. They could see people running, and there was smoke in the air. As they watched, a barrel rolled across the road. They saw men in red uniforms flash past—the Praesidio, already in the fray. They cut over to the right, pressing themselves against the buildings for more cover. It was clear, by the time they reached the corner, that a full-scale riot had broken out where the market carts had been gathered. One makeshift stand was ablaze—several men were running around it,

146

trying to smother it out with burlap sacks while others ran toward them with buckets of water. Two of the large wagons had been pushed together, and men and women were gathered behind them, hurling produce and tools and bottles, anything they could find, and shouting abuse at the Praesidio guards who were dodging around, firing their weapons and fighting with other Riftborn who were running for cover. Even as they watched, spellbound, five more guards burst onto the road from an alleyway, their faces fierce and set.

"What do we do, Eliza?"

Eliza tore her gaze from the chaos to find Jessamine looking imploringly at her. Her face was flushed with the effort of running, and her cap was askew.

"I... I don't know. I have to think..." But she couldn't think. She could barely breathe. They had to get out of here. They had to get back to the carriage. She took a deep breath and closed her eyes, blocking out the worst of the distraction.

"We have to turn right up there to get back to where Martin's parked the carriage," Eliza said. *If the carriage is still there, if Martin hasn't fled*, she thought desperately, though she did not say it out loud. She swallowed back her fear and continued, "Don't run out into the street. Stay as close to the buildings as possible. Tuck yourself in doorways as we go. When we've got a clear path to the carriage, we'll run on my say-so, and we won't stop, won't turn around, until we reach it, all right?"

Eliza watched as Jessamine's saucer-round eyes blinked once, twice, three times before she finally nodded her understanding. Eliza reached down and grabbed Jessamine's hand, clinging on like a mother to her child. Perhaps it was simply the adrenaline of the moment, but she could have sworn she felt just a shadow of her Riftmagic passing through the fabric, willing her mistress to remain calm, to stick to the plan, for she thought she saw a fraction of the sheer animal panic fade from Jessamine's eyes. Squeezing her hand, she took a deep breath and crept around the corner.

The scale of the madness was even more alarming once they entered into the High Street and could see the extent of it. It stretched for several blocks, Riftborn and Praesidio, locked in skirmishes everywhere they looked. The Praesidio were ruthlessly taking down one dissident after another, and the ground was littered with barely stirring bodies and smoking piles of debris. Eliza and Jessamine edged as quickly as they dared along the walls as the madness unfolded around them. The smoke was thick in the air, forcing Eliza to pull her apron up over her nose and mouth. She abandoned the rest of the baskets still dangling on her arm, simply dropping them in the street, and Jessamine, noticing what she was doing, did the same.

Someone threw a brick, and it shattered a pane of glass not five feet from where they stood. Eliza dropped to her knees, shielding her face, but Jessamine lost her head completely. She let out a terrified scream and broke into a run, taking off in the direction of the carriage.

"Miss Jessamine, no! Wait for me!" Eliza shrieked. She stumbled awkwardly to her feet, tripping on the hem of her dress, and took off after her mistress, heart in her throat. If anything happened to her...

As she passed the mouth of a dingy alleyway a shout over her left shoulder caused her to turn around. A cart was hurtling toward her, completely out of control, barrels rolling off its back end and bouncing away across the cobbles. She froze on the spot, unable to force a connection between her muscles and her brain to get out of the way, and anyway, there was nowhere to go. She threw up her arms and closed her eyes, bracing for impact.

ELEVEN

E LI COULD FEEL THE TENSION IN THE AIR almost from the moment he crossed the border from the Market District. The streets were crawling with Praesidio patrols—it was as though the Barrens had suddenly become an extension of the Praeteritum, and the citizens scraping a living within its borders were nothing more than prisoners.

He squirmed uncomfortably and lowered his hat a bit over his eyes. He knew his own actions had been partially responsible for the uptick in security—if he and Jasper hadn't doctored those notices—

"You there!" A sharp voice rang out and Eli's head shot up.

A Praesidio guard was marching toward him, stony-faced. Eli kept his face smooth and his feet planted while fighting a primal urge to run.

"Yes, officer?" he asked, eyebrows raised in what he hoped read as mild surprise.

"Your papers. Let's have them," the guard barked.

"Certainly. Here you are," Eli reached carefully into his pocket, slowly pulling out the small leather-bound booklet in which he kept his identification papers. He opened it up and handed it to the guard who snatched them and examined them closely.

"It says here you live in the Commons."

"Yes, that's right," Eli confirmed.

"What are you doing over here then, so early in the morning?"

Eli bit back the retort he longed to throw at the guard, who looked barely old enough to grow whiskers. "I'm meeting a friend on a matter of business."

The guard snorted. "Business? In the Barrens? If I were you, I'd find me some better friends, Riftborn." He handed Eli back his papers and Eli pocketed them.

"Am I free to go?" Eli asked politely.

He could tell the guard longed to return a different answer than the one that escaped through his gritted teeth. "Conduct your business swiftly and be on your way. There's trouble brewing in these streets today, and you would be smart to steer clear of it."

"I am grateful for the warning," Eli replied, tipping his cap. "I assure you, officer, I shall make all haste."

The guard narrowed his eyes at Eli, clearly detecting the note of derision in Eli's tone, but there was nothing he could do about it. He threw Eli one last, disdainful look and marched off in the direction of the High Street.

Eli watched him go and then took off down the road toward The Bell and Flagon, avoiding the groups of people that were gathered around, muttering and glaring at the patrols. He knew he ought to head over to the High Street as well, knew that was where Madam Lavender said the manor servants would be congregating to deliver their baskets, but he needed to talk to Zeke first.

Zeke answered the pounding on his door with a roar of impatience, blinking blearily into the early morning light.

"What the devil—Eli? That you?"

"Yes," Eli replied. "Let me in, I need a word."

He pushed through the door and Zeke stepped back to let him through, scratching at his face and yawning.

"It's early for a social call, lad. You know the hours I keep."

"This isn't a social call. Have you seen the patrols out this morning?"

Zeke snorted. "I ain't seen a blessed thing but the insides of my own eyelids, lad. What are you on about?"

"The patrols," Eli said, a bit impatiently. "There are dozens of them, swarming the streets. They must be expecting trouble today."

"Aye, there was talk of that last night. The pub was full of it. So they've made good, have they?"

"Yes. It looks like the Praeteritum out there."

"Blimey," Zeke muttered, rubbing at his beard and blinking the sleep out of his eyes. "But what are you bothering me for? I've got two eyes, lad, I can see patrols well enough. There's no need to—"

"Isn't Seamus supposed to make a delivery today?" Eli interrupted.

Zeke frowned. "That's Tuesday, that is."

"Zeke, it *is* Tuesday. That's what I'm telling you. You've got to get word to Seamus to hold off on delivery until tomorrow at least. They checked my papers just for walking down the street."

Zeke swore under his breath. Seamus Taylor and his crew of bootleggers had been making weekly deliveries of black-market whiskey and ale to The Bell and Flagon for years, ever since they'd discovered the Illustratum was linked to the local supply chains. Zeke would rather have closed his pub and starved than knowingly serve his own clientele Riftmead-laced booze.

"Right, I'm on it," Zeke said, slapping his cheeks several times to wake himself up. "Thanks, lad." Then he blinked and narrowed his eyes at Eli as though he'd only just seen him. "Is that the only reason you're here so early?"

Eli smiled grimly, his excuse ready. "Jasper stumbled home last night—or I should say, I dragged him stumbling home. I didn't want to stick around for when Sully finds him—I expect we'll be able to hear that explosion from here, don't you think?"

Zeke let out a low whistle. "From here to kingdom come. Well, get off the street at least. Getting caught up in a scuffle here will only give Sully one more thing to shout about. You can stay here, if you like, but..."

Eli shook his head. "No, you take care of matters with Seamus. I'll make myself scarce."

"Be careful, lad."

"And you."

Eli stepped back out into the damp morning, relieved he had, at least, managed to help Zeke avoid a messy situation. The Illustratum had their hands in everything to do with distribution, importing, and exporting goods, from books and liquor to textiles and foods. Not only did they tightly regulate what was allowed in and out of the country, but they had inserted themselves into the production chains of nearly everything made within the borders, so that a man could hardly exchange a coin for a good without the Elders having profited from it at some stage. Sully had made it her life's work to uncover all the places in which the Illustratum were secretly pulling the strings, even as they touted England as a shining example of free enterprise. The average Riftborn on the street had not a clue how the Illustratum's long and dirty fingers had touched every tiny aspect of their lives. Eli watched them as he passed, drinking from flasks, trading meager scraps of goods, scolding their children, and scrubbing fruitlessly at decades of grime that would never wash clean, each of them harboring a gift they could never realize because they had been taught to fear and suppress it. He kicked a rock, watching it skitter along the gutter.

Eli turned off Brushfield Street and started walking south, which would take him out of Spitalfields and into the area that locals still called White Chapel. He hadn't quite worked out what he would say to Eliza Braxton even if he managed to find her. He wasn't even sure he would speak to her. Maybe he'd just observe her routine, track her route, see if there was any chance of getting her on her own. Even as he thought it, he knew he sounded like some sort of predator stalking his prey, and he knew he would have to tread carefully. If she caught on that he was following her, she'd get spooked, and then he might never have the chance to speak to her at all. For all he knew, she thought of him as a dangerous and subversive criminal already.

Two small children ran past him back toward Spitalfields, their faces white and stricken. A minute or so later, a harassed-looking woman followed, her arms loaded with parcels.

"What's going on?" Eli called out to her.

"Some bloody fools have gotten into it with the patrols," the woman huffed, barely looking at him. "Steer clear of the High Street."

Eli picked up his pace, jogging now. As he drew closer, more Riftborn hurried past him, some wheeling carts, others carrying shopping. Some even seemed to be nursing injuries—a young man was swearing and holding a bloodied and torn piece of sacking to a gash on his forearm. A burly, bearded man carried a second, unconscious man over his shoulder. "Bloody murdering cowards!" he roared as he staggered past.

Eli took the last block of Commercial Street at a run, the sounds of the conflict growing louder and louder with each step. By the time he reached the High Street and was met with the full sight of the chaos, his heart was nearly in his throat.

Had the lady's maids convened here as usual? Was Eliza caught up in this madness?

Keeping his back pressed to the wall of the building on the corner, he scanned the High Street for some sign of her, but the smoke made it hard to make out much more than the vague shapes of bodies, tussling, fleeing, and falling. Gunshots rang out through the madness, but how the guards could see where they were firing, Eli couldn't imagine. He spotted the source of the smoke at once—a group of makeshift booths were ablaze nearby. Coughing, he covered his face and took off down the cobbles, his eyes burning, searching for a sign of a manor uniform, a white-capped head.

A man stumbled into him, his fists swinging wildly. Eli ducked the blows and drove his shoulder forward, plowing past the man and sending him tumbling to the ground. He jumped over the shattered remains of a barrel, slipping in the puddle of whatever was leaking out of it, but managing to remain on his feet. Ahead, he heard the high-pitched scream of a young woman and he ran blindly toward it.

A clattering sound on his left made him stop and stare around. A cart was careening out of control—barreling across the road. He swung his head right and spotted her: a slender girl in a starched manor uniform, blonde hair blowing around her face, standing frozen with terror as the cart bore down upon her.

With speed born of sheer animal fear, Eli shot forward, reaching for the girl. He caught hold of her just as the cart drew level and, wrapping both arms around her shoulders, threw himself sideways, lifting her off her feet and sending both of them tumbling into the mouth of the alleyway just beyond. He heard the crash of the cart as it smashed into the wall, felt the debris sailing over their heads. He looked down at the girl, now pinned beneath him. Her eyes were closed but she was stirring feebly. As he stared down at her, her enormous grey eyes fluttered open, and he watched recognition spark in their depths.

§

Eliza was still breathless from the shock and pain of the fall into the alleyway as she opened her eyes. A face swam into view above her, a face twisted with fear and concern.

A face she knew.

"It's you! I thought you were—" Eliza abruptly bit off the end of the thought.

"You thought I was what?" the young man asked, his eyes searching.

Eliza bit her lip. She'd been about to say, "I thought you were dead," but of course, she had no real, tangible reason to admit such a thing. That had been a nightmare, nothing but an invention of her exhausted and overwrought brain. To admit otherwise was to admit that she'd been thinking about him, and that felt too personal an admission to make to a stranger who was still practically lying on top of her. He was staring down at her as though he was afraid she'd been knocked senseless by the fall to the ground. She propped herself up onto her elbows and he immediately pulled back from her.

"I thought you were done forcing yourself upon me and scaring me out of my wits," Eliza replied at last, and she was pleased to hear that her voice sounded quite steady. She made to stand up, but something else large went whizzing by and smashed against a nearby wall. She flopped back to the ground once more, throwing her hands over her head.

The young man's face broke into a grin, and he actually laughed with relief. "That's a funny way to say thank you for saving my life."

Eliza ground her teeth together, biting back a retort. "Do I at least get to know who I'm thanking?"

He hesitated for a moment and then seemed to come to some sort of decision. "Eli. Eli Turner," he said.

"Thank you, Mr. Turner."

"I prefer Eli."

Someone in the High Street let out a piercing scream and some sense of reality came back to Eliza. "I… I have to find Miss… the… the other maid who was with me. Did you see her? Did you see which way she went?"

Eli frowned. "I'm afraid not. I was too distracted by the runaway cart that seemed hell-bent on killing you. I must say, Miss Braxton, we do seem to meet in the most exciting of circumstances."

But Eliza hadn't listened beyond the first three words. Miss Jessamine knew they were headed for the carriage. Perhaps she had been lucky enough to reach it? Eliza clambered to her feet, turned on her heel, and bolted back toward the High Street, but Eli caught her.

"Are you mad? You can't go back out there!" he cried. As though to underscore his point, another bottle smashed in the mouth of the alleyway. They both covered their faces as the pieces flew through the air.

Eliza pulled against his grip. "I must. Please, I must find her."

154

"I understand you're worried, but I can't let you go back out there!"

"Let me? *Let me?* You don't have any power over what I can and cannot do!"

Eli crossed his arms, looking stubborn. "Arguably, I just saved your life. I've got a vested interest in it now. You owe me a favor."

"A favor? Is that so? It just so happens, Mr. Turner, that I may very well have saved *your* life the very first time we met," Eliza shot back. "I could have told those guards exactly where you disappeared to, but I didn't. I sent them in the opposite direction. So, by my calculations, we are square."

Eli blinked. "You lied to the Praesidio guards? For me?"

Eliza felt her face flush. "Yes."

"Why?" Eli asked, blankly.

Eliza hesitated. It was a question she'd asked herself a hundred times since that day, and she still couldn't come up with a satisfactory answer. "I... I don't know, but I'm starting to regret it."

"I'm fairly certain you could just take off that glove and force me to let you go," Eli said, all trace of humor gone.

Eliza looked down at her hand and felt shame, fear, and confusion curdling into a lump in her throat, making it difficult to speak. "I... let my fear cloud my judgment. I don't want to do that ever again. That's not what my Riftmagic is for," she replied, in barely more than a whisper.

Eli stared at her for another moment, then craned his neck to look past her into the road. "This is only getting worse. We'll need to find another way back to your carriage."

"But what's happening? Why are they fighting?" Eliza asked, throwing her hands up in the air.

"People are angry. Things... things have happened recently that have people on edge, and the Praesidio stir up that anger just by their very presence."

Eliza felt her heart speed up. "Are you talking about John Davies?"

Eli's eyes went wide. "What do you know about John Davies?"

"I... hardly anything, really. But you dropped one of your... one of the notices with his name pasted on it that day. And then at the services on Sunday, there was a disturbance. I... I thought I heard the intruder shout his name."

"I've no doubt you did," Eli said quietly.

Eliza tried to stop it, but the question she'd been longing to ask burst from her lips. "Who was John Davies?"

Eli pulled her back further into the alleyway. "We've got to get out of here. Where's your carriage waiting?"

"But aren't you going to answer my —"

"We'll walk and talk," Eli said curtly. "Now where is it?"

Eliza was so relieved that she didn't even take offense to his tone. "Further down the High Street, across from Duke Street."

Eli nodded, brows drawn together. "Okay, good. I think I can get us there without getting near the High Street. Keep close to me and keep an eye out for your friend."

Eliza nodded her agreement, her heart giving a great thump of fear as she was reminded once again of Jessamine. She followed Eli up the alley and between a stinking tenement building and a rotting wooden fence. The gap was narrow, and they had to turn sideways to manage it. Her boots sunk into the mucky ground, and she had to tug them out again with each step.

"John Davies is dead," Eli said, his voice barely more than a whisper so that Eliza had no choice but to stay very close to him. "He was one of the five men the Illustratum hanged after the break out from the Praeteritum last week."

Eliza shook her head. "That can't be right."

"That's exactly what the Illustratum would like you to believe," Eli said.

It was a bold thing to say and Eliza gasped. "You mean to say you believe they lied about it?"

"I know they lied about it," Eli said calmly. He was now shoving against a loose plank in the fence, trying to force his way through it.

"How could you possibly know such a thing?" she asked.

"Because I knew Davies. And because a friend of mine saw it happen," Eli said. He managed to slip through the gap and held the board back for Eliza so that she could follow him.

"Perhaps your friend was mistaken, have you ever considered that?" Eliza asked. "It's much more likely that one man made a mistake than that the entire Elder Council of the Illustratum is lying."

Eli's face twitched — almost as though he were trying not to smile. Eliza stiffened — was he laughing at her?

"He was not mistaken," Eli said, with such finality that Eliza gave up with a roll of her eyes and moved on to her next question.

"But on Sunday the Illustratum performed a Casting Out with another man's name. How could they do that? And who was that other man?"

"All good questions the Illustratum should answer for," Eli said, his teeth gritted. They were in a squalid courtyard. Several tenement houses backed up to the same, grassless square of mud. It was littered with trash and strung across with clotheslines hung with clothes that, though dripping wet, could not have been called clean by any stretch of the imagination. Eli cut across, waving off a woman who shouted at them from an open doorway.

"The Illustratum answers directly to the Creator!" Eliza hissed indignantly.

Eli turned to look her in the face. "The Illustratum ought to answer to the people they rule," he said.

It was such an extraordinary pronouncement, such an absurdity, that Eliza could only blink stupidly at him, her mind groping for a response that would not come. Eli raised an eyebrow at her and then turned away again, continuing to cut a path across the court. Eliza had to run to keep up with his stride.

"How did you know John Davies?" was her next whispered question. Several other people had poked their heads out of windows to stare at them as they cut through the yard. A child paused his amusement of drawing shapes in the mud with a stick to stare open-mouthed at them.

"I can't answer that," Eli said.

"You can't, or you won't?"

"Both."

Eliza sniffed. "Well then, who was he? Why would the Illustratum even bother to cover up his death?"

Eli paused, his face tense. "John Davies was a hero."

"A hero?" Eliza scoffed, earning such a sharp look from Eli that she took a step back from him. "What was he doing locked up in the Praeteritum if he was a hero?"

"There are plenty of heroes in there," Eli replied.

"They're criminals," Eliza said, surprised by the vitriol in her tone.

"Just because someone commits a crime doesn't make them a bad person. Sometimes the right thing to do isn't the legal thing to do. A law isn't right just because it's the law."

Again, Eliza could not muster a response at first. Every sentence out of Eli's mouth felt like a swing with a hammer at the very foundations she was built on.

"Well, what heroic crime did John Davies commit?" Eliza asked. "Go on. Astonish me."

Eli stopped cold and turned around. "He saved my life."

Eliza felt the breath go still in her lungs. "He..."

"Saved my life, yes. And not just mine. Many others as well."

"Oh," Eliza said lamely. "That's... how did he save your life?"

Again, Eli paused, as though he were making a decision. Then he turned and started walking again, leading Eliza between two houses and back out into a wider road. He turned left. "Have you ever heard of the Lamplighters Confederacy?"

"The... the what?"

"The Lamplighters Confederacy," Eli repeated, more slowly.

"I... no," Eliza said, frustrated to have to return the answer.

"Of course you haven't. Barely anyone has. And that's the way the Illustratum wants it. Every word ever written about it has been confiscated—I imagine some of them might even be residing in the very house you live in. They would tell you everything you could ever want to know about John Davies, and the crimes that made him a hero."

"But why don't you just tell me what—"

"Eliza!"

The shrill voice echoed in the distance and Eliza looked up to see the carriage stopped in the road up ahead. She gave a cry of relief to see Jessamine leaning out of the window, waving frantically to her.

"There you are, then," Eli said, with a sigh of relief. "Go on, before the fight breaks out of the square."

"But..." Eliza turned to him, unsure what to say. She still had so many questions she wanted to ask him, so many things left unsaid and unexplained. "You're not going back there, are you?"

"Me? No. I know a fools' fight when I see one. I'm staying clear," Eli said.

"Eliza, what are you waiting for?!" Jessamine shouted, her voice full of tears.

"Get a move on, girl, we can't stay here!" Martin shouted from

158

the driver's seat, his face white and tense with fear. The horse gave an anxious snort and shook its head, pawing at the ground.

Eliza turned back to Eli. "I have to go. I... thank you again. For saving my life."

Eli touched his cap. "It was my pleasure. I'm sure we'll see each other again, Miss Braxton. I'll just look for another life-threatening situation and there you'll be, no doubt."

Eliza managed a small, embarrassed smile and then turned, running as fast as her legs would carry her until she reached the carriage. Jessamine flung the door open for her and she clambered hastily inside. The door had barely latched when Martin gave a sharp "Git-up there!" and the carriage took off. Eliza chanced half a glance out of the window to see that Eli was still standing there, hands in his pockets, looking after her, but a moment later Jessamine pounced upon her, pulling her into such a violent hug that Eliza cried out in shock.

"Eliza, I'm sorry! I'm so sorry! I panicked. I didn't think at all, I just ran. I was so scared, I thought you must be... I thought..." she was sobbing into Eliza's shoulder.

Eliza ripped off her gloves and began stroking Jessamine's hair, her entire body flooded with relief that she was all right, that she had made it to the carriage. She focused her energy on Jessamine, on coaxing her to take deeper breaths, to calm her storm of crying.

"There, there, Miss Jessamine," Eliza intoned. "It wasn't your fault. Anyone would have panicked. I'm just so relieved you got to the carriage. Are you hurt at all?"

"N-no," Jessamine managed to reply through the tears. "Are... are you?"

"Fit as a fiddle," Eliza said soothingly. "Not a scratch on me, cross my heart."

"Oh, I'm so glad. I'm so glad." Her sobs were quieting under the influence of Eliza's Riftmagic. "And you're wrong. This was my fault. All my fault. We never should have come today."

Eliza shushed her mistress and continued the stroking of her hair, though she did not disagree with her. They'd had no business being in the Barrens today, that much was now abundantly clear. The sounds of the confrontation in the High Street could be heard even as they drove away. People were scurrying from house to house around them, huddling together and whispering, looking panic-stricken.

"Who was that man?" Jessamine asked, lifting her tear-stained face from Eliza's shoulder at last.

Eliza's heart skipped a beat. "What man?"

"The man you were talking to when we found you," Jessamine said, frowning.

"Oh, I don't know. I've never seen him before. But he pulled me out of the way of a runaway cart in the High Street and was trying to help me get back to the carriage," Eliza replied.

Jessamine gasped. "Oh! He... he saved your life!"

Eliza shrugged. "Yes, I suppose he may have done."

"Your very own guardian angel, Eliza!" Jessamine said in an awed voice. "Didn't he even tell you his name?"

Eliza shook her head. "No. There was no time for pleasantries. We were too busy trying to get out of there."

The cart bumped to a sudden halt. Eliza looked out the window and saw that they had reached the outer limits of the Barrens. The buildings on either side were better kept, the people milling about were cleaner, more presentable. She wondered for a moment why they had stopped when Martin appeared suddenly in the window, his face livid. He pulled the door open and stuck his head inside, speaking in a lowered but very angry voice.

"I don't suppose anyone is going to explain to me what's going on here?"

Eliza opened her mouth, but Jessamine, having regained her composure, spoke up at once. "It was all my doing, Martin. Eliza is not to be blamed, she was only following my orders. I forced her to bring me along. And you certainly can't be faulted, you didn't know it was me in the carriage. I was disguised, after all."

Martin tried to sound respectful, but he was so exasperated. "But... but why in the world would you want to come here, miss? Even on a normal day, it's just not safe."

Jessamine lifted her chin. "My business in the Barrens today is of a private nature and is none of your concern," she said in a tone that brought her father to mind. Martin was instantly chastened.

"I meant no disrespect, miss. But what's happened today could get me sacked, so I'm trying to understand what—"

"No one is going to be sacked," Jessamine said firmly. "We will return to Larkspur Manor at the usual time, or close enough. Eliza will take me in through the servants' entrance. We shall tell Bridie

160

everything, and she will say she was the one in the carriage with Eliza today. There is no one to refute it—no one recognized me, dressed like this."

"And what if someone asks us about the disturbance today? What will we say?" Martin asked.

"You shall simply say that you heard it, but luckily you were several streets away at the time. You came to fetch us and we left at once," Jessamine responded calmly. "If you pretend you saw nothing, no one will press you for details."

Jessamine looked at Eliza, eyebrows raised, clearly seeking her approval of the plan. "If we can get into the house without anyone seeing Miss Jessamine, I think it just might work."

"And if it doesn't work?" Martin asked.

"Then the responsibility for the entire incident lies at my feet. I'll be the only one to blame," Jessamine replied, echoing what she had said to Eliza when they'd first gotten into the carriage that morning. Eliza looked at Martin, whose face was full of the same doubts that she had—there was no way, if anyone discovered what had happened, that she and Martin would escape without consequences. It was only Jessamine's naïvety that allowed her to believe such a thing. Servants knew better—if there was blame to be had, it would certainly be laid at their feet.

What could Martin say, though? The damage had been done—they just had to hope they could get back to Larkspur Manor without being discovered and forget the whole thing. He tipped his cap to Jessamine and said, "Very well, miss. I'll keep it under my hat, as you request. I'll not say a word to anyone."

"Thank you, Martin. Thank you very much for your discretion," Jessamine said with a smile. "And I... I'm very sorry to have put you in this position. Both of you." She turned to look at Eliza as well. "I assure you, it will not happen again."

Martin inclined his head in acknowledgment, looking frankly stunned that a member of the Hallewell family was apologizing to him. Then he pushed the door shut, climbed back up onto the driver's seat, and resumed the drive back to Larkspur Manor.

TWELVE

E LIZA WOULD NOT HAVE THOUGHT she could be as
anxious again as she had been running through the High Street,
but her nerves were on fire as the carriage pulled up at the
manor. Jessamine had her cap tugged down low over her face, and
Martin pulled up as close as he could manage to one of the back
kitchen entrances of the house. They peered through the glass, making
sure the hallway was clear of servants, but no one was about. They
slipped through the door, up the back servants' staircase, and along
the third-floor corridor without seeing a single soul. They took the last
few steps at a run, flung Jessamine's door open, and practically fell
through it, closing it behind them.

Bridie leapt up out of Jessamine's bed, looking terrified.

"Saints alive! You startled me!" she cried, before blushing
crimson from neck to crown. "I mean, begging your pardon, miss."

But Jessamine waved the apology off and the girls got
immediately to work. They got Bridie and Jessamine into their
appropriate clothing and then they sat Bridie down on the settee and
told her every detail she needed to know about their adventure into the
Barrens. Bridie listened to all of it with wide eyes, her hand pressed
over her mouth to stem the flow of exclamations she was surely dying
to make. When at last they had finished, she lowered her hand and
shook her head slowly.

"I can't believe, after three years of delivering charity baskets
in the Barrens, I missed the one day that something interesting
happened," she said in an awed whisper.

Jessamine laughed, but Eliza rolled her eyes. "Interesting isn't exactly the word I'd have settled on. You should be thankful you were safe here in Miss Jessamine's bed. I certainly wish I'd been."

Bridie grinned shyly. "It is the most comfortable bed I've ever lain in, miss. I felt like I was floatin' on a cloud. I don't know how you convince yourself ever to get out of it, miss."

Jessamine was still laughing. "I confess it is often a struggle. It's Eliza's unfortunate task on many a morning to drag me from its depths."

"Bridie, we've got to get downstairs. Someone is bound to be looking for us soon," Eliza said, standing up and checking her reflection in the mirror. She still looked pale, but her dress was, miraculously, fairly clean, and her hair was tucked neatly back up under her cap again. Her boots were a mess, but her skirts hid the worst of it, and she could clean them properly once she got back to her room. "Miss Jessamine, I'll have your tray sent up. I imagine you'd like to rest a spell, though?"

"Yes, thank you, Eliza. I'll ring when I'm ready for it," Jessamine replied.

And just like that, normalcy was restored. Everyone slipped back into their roles. Eliza and Bridie curtsied and left the room.

"Do you think you've got the story straight, Bridie?" Eliza whispered as they made their way back downstairs.

"Yes, yes, but I want to know more about the young man who saved you!"

Eliza stared incredulously at Bridie, whose face was aglow with the possibility of a romantic tale of adventure and chivalry. She had to remind herself that Bridie hadn't been present for all the terrifying events of the morning before she answered.

"There's nothing to tell. I don't know who he was. It was kind of him to pull me out of the way of the wagon, but that's all there is to it."

Bridie's face fell. "Didn't he even tell you his name?"

"No," Eliza lied.

"Oh," Bridie said, frowning a bit. Then she sighed again. "A nameless rescuer. That might be even more romantic!"

"I promise you, romance was the last thing on either of our minds, Bridie," Eliza replied through slightly clenched teeth. Now was not the time for girlish fantasies. They had to be alert, ready to stick to their story, ready for—

164

"Eliza! Bridie! There you are, thank goodness!" Mrs. Keats was standing in the entryway to the kitchen, her face red and blotchy, her eyes bloodshot as a wave of fresh tears spilled down her cheeks.

"Mrs. Keats!" Eliza gasped. "What in the world—"

But Mrs. Keats was already barreling toward them, reaching for them, crushing both of them to her bosom as she shrieked. "I thought for sure the two of you were dead in a gutter somewhere! What were you thinking, going into the Barrens today?! Didn't you know—I couldn't believe it... when I saw the baskets were gone, I nearly lost my head!"

"We didn't know, Mrs. Keats," Eliza said, glad, at least, that this part of the story was true. "No one told us we weren't to deliver the baskets today."

"I was meant to tell you!" Mrs. Keats replied, exasperated. "I thought you'd come to me for the baskets when they weren't out, and then I could explain!"

"I considered it, but I thought perhaps you were too busy with the Presentation preparations to lay them out as usual, so I found them myself," Eliza explained. "I'm terribly sorry, Mrs. Keats, I thought I was helping you out."

"Well, all I can say is, thank the Creator you're both all right. Your Father's been beside himself all morning. He was getting ready to send another carriage after you! You can't imagine the state he's gotten himself—"

"Eliza!"

Eliza jumped and turned to find her father now bearing down on her, his face a storm cloud.

"Father!"

"What can you mean by it? What would possibly possess you to enter the Barrens today?" he shouted.

Eliza flinched. He sounded angry, but he always did when he was afraid, and his eyes, now glaring down at her, were bright with fear.

"Forgive me, Father, but we didn't know! I took the baskets before Mrs. Keats had a chance to explain," Eliza replied.

"She came and went before I could tell her, Mr. Braxton," Mrs. Keats chimed in, hanging her head.

Her father seemed ready to turn on Mrs. Keats, so Eliza pounced before he had the chance. "It wasn't her fault. It wasn't anyone's fault. It was a... a simple miscommunication!"

"A miscommunication that could have gotten you killed!" Braxton shouted. He ran his fingers through his meticulously slicked back hair, rumpling it so that he looked quite unlike himself. "Didn't you have sense enough to stay away? Surely you must have realized—"

"How?" Eliza interrupted, feeling her own anger rise now. "How would I have realized the state of the Barrens today? No one bothers to tell me anything! I have a hundred unanswered questions about the goings-on of the past week, but no one seems to think me worthy of the answers! If you want me to make informed decisions, inform me!"

Eliza couldn't remember the last time she'd raised her voice to her father, and it seemed he couldn't either, for he was looking at her as though he'd never seen her before. "Eliza, take care of the way you speak to me," he warned.

"I have said nothing disrespectful," Eliza insisted, crossing her arms over her chest and standing her ground. "But I am being blamed for being ignorant of something no one would tell me, and that's not fair."

Braxton's mouth opened and closed several times, searching for a counterargument, and then, quite suddenly, he seemed to deflate. "No. No, that's not fair. I was just... very worried. Are you hurt?"

"No, I assure you, we are quite unscathed. The disturbance took place several streets away from where we were. We only ever heard it, didn't we, Bridie?"

"That's right, sir," Bridie said stoutly. "We... we knew something wasn't right, though, so we returned to the carriage."

Braxton sighed. "Well, thank the Creator for that. And there will be no more trips into the Barrens—or even into the Market District for that matter—until I tell you otherwise, all right?"

"Certainly, Father. I promise you, I had no desire or intention to disobey you," Eliza said, perhaps more meekly than she might normally have done, in an effort to dampen the effects of her outspokenness a few moments before.

Braxton's face seemed to soften. When he spoke, his words came haltingly. "I know you have questions. But you must remember our place—our position. It requires of us that we set a certain example, you see—that we model faith. It requires that we do not allow ourselves to be caught up in the histrionics of those who have strayed from the Path. It can be such a temptation to be swept up in such things—but we must be stronger than that. We must turn away. If we

166

stay the Path and serve, we will always walk in righteousness, do you understand me?"

All three women nodded, but even as Eliza's head bobbed up and down, a nagging thought crept into her head: what good was faith if it demanded you be blind to what was around you? Shouldn't faith withstand the storm around it? Was it even faith at all, if it crumbled so easily at the very first test?

She wondered if her doubts were showing on her face, for suddenly her father was staring down at her, his face a strange and unreadable mixture of emotions. "Sometimes when I look at you—speak to you—I feel like I'm face to face with your mother all over again," he murmured.

Where her heart had been abuzz with questions only a moment before, it now felt hollow. She thought she felt Mrs. Keats stiffen beside her. Her father never mentioned her mother—never. She was one of those distractions he had spoken of—the thing at which they never looked back, never dwelled upon—and she had never felt so present to Eliza as she did in this brief and oddly charged moment.

Before she could muster a reply, her father shook his head and frowned, as though displeased with himself, and turned to march down the hallway, disappearing into his office and shutting the door quietly behind him. Eliza stood staring at the closed door until Mrs. Keats squeezed her hand.

"How about a spot of breakfast, love? You must be exhausted after all that excitement." Her voice was much gentler than usual.

"I... yes, but first I need to see to Miss Jessamine's tray," Eliza said, trying to regain a hold on herself.

"I'll see to it, don't you worry. She hasn't even rung yet—having a lovely, long lie-in, I suppose. Go and have a bite to eat, the pair of you. We haven't cleared the staff table yet."

§

Eliza felt like she was perpetually holding her breath for the next few days, waiting for the inevitable moment when someone would discover the truth of their ill-conceived adventure in the Barrens. But the hours and days passed, and no one questioned them. She snuck out to the garages every morning to check in with Martin, but he had nothing to report. Her father spoke with him when they first

167

returned. Martin had assured him that they had been removed from the danger, and that he had taken them home the moment they realized a disturbance was taking place. He hadn't heard a whisper about it from anyone since, and was quite ready to forget the whole thing had ever happened.

"If we were to be caught, Eliza, I reckon it would have happened right off," Martin said, scratching his chin. "Once a story's stuck, it ain't likely to come unstuck. It's getting it to stick in the first place that's the trick."

Eliza tried to adopt this attitude and put the events behind her, but it was hard to do. In the first place, Jessamine insisted on continuously discussing it when they were alone together. No matter how hard Eliza tried to refocus her on other things—her Presentation, her social obligations, Teddy's latest letter—all her mistress wanted to do was rehash the details of the morning in the Barrens.

"I've never heard anyone speak about the Illustratum that way!" Jessamine said, with an equal measure of awe and indignation. "What in the world could they be thinking, accusing my father and the other Elders of lying? Lying! As if my father were capable of such deception and in the name of the Creator, no less! It's unfathomable!"

"Indeed, miss," Eliza agreed, because she could hear the same niggling doubts in Jessamine's tone that were swirling around in her own mind, and she knew it was her duty to soothe them into submission, not encourage them. With every huffy exclamation, Jessamine was silently begging Eliza to reconfirm the foundational beliefs she'd always held, the fundamental truths of her world. And Eliza did so, because not to do it would be to shatter her own tenuous hold on those same beliefs.

Because as much as she longed to put the events in the Barrens far behind her, Eliza could not stop thinking about Eli Turner and his words to her. Again, a brief and frightening chance encounter with the man had turned her universe upside down. And this time, instead of leaving her with nothing but questions, he had left her with the tantalizing possibility of answers within the very walls she now occupied.

The Lamplighters Confederacy.

She turned the words over and over in her mind. What did it mean? She was positive she had never heard them before, and yet she had a nagging feeling that she ought to understand them. Eli had said there were probably books about it right there in Larkspur Manor. Eliza found herself scanning the shelves in the library and the sitting rooms every time she entered one, hoping the words would jump out at her from one of the gold-gilded spines. Then she would reprimand herself. In the first place, if the books had been confiscated and hidden from the public, they wouldn't be sitting out on the shelves where anyone who entered the home could see them. And even if she did happen to stumble across such a book in plain sight, she would never dare to take it from the shelves without permission, much less read it. It was madness—more than her life was worth to do such a thing. And yet, she could not stop herself, every time she passed a book anywhere in the upstairs rooms, from stealing a glimpse at the title.

Ironically, if ever there had been a time she would be less likely to be caught with such a book in her hands, it was the present one. The staff had had barely a glimpse of Elder Hallewell in the days since the uproar at the Sunday service. Braxton gathered the servants together below stairs to inform them all that the master was under extraordinary pressure at the moment and was under no circumstances to be disturbed, even on the rare occasion he graced the halls of his own home. Her father did not discuss the source of this extraordinary pressure, but Eliza was quite sure she had seen it firsthand. The Riftborn were restless, and the Elders would surely not allow it to continue.

§

Josiah sat in the chair closest to the fire in the High Elder's chambers, trying to rub some feeling back into his numb hands. The cavernous Elder Council chamber had long since lost all warmth from the day, but proceedings had carried on much longer, and by the time Josiah had been summoned here, he was damn near frozen right down to his toes inside his boots.

It had been relentless for days, with no sign of letting up. It had not been this way in more than fifteen years, not since the days before Davies had first been caught and imprisoned. He had hardly seen the light of day outside the Illustratum, much less his own house, in three days; which was surely a blessing, as the Presentation was a mere two weeks away, and he could not stand to feign interest in things like canapés and lace trimming and flower arrangements when the ground was falling away beneath him.

Beneath all of them.

Despite the Elders' best efforts—or perhaps, it seemed, because of them—the city was beginning to roil with unrest. Every day there were new reports of violence or confrontation in the Barrens. The population had not been this unsettled in years, and the usual measures were failing to quell them. Josiah was under extreme pressure to alleviate the situation, for it had been his suggestion in the first place to cover up Davies' death, and Elder Carpenter and some of his more severe critics were wasting no opportunity to lay the blame at his feet. The bloody fools. As though it wouldn't have been unfathomably worse to shout Davies' death from the rooftops.

Josiah rubbed at his temples. He could feel a headache coming on and knew there would be nothing he could do to abate it. The Elders had adjourned in a state of shouting and disarray. When they came back together in half an hour's time, there would be more of the same. Half of them were petulant children who only wished to hear the sound of their own voices echoing off the walls as tangible evidence of their own importance—it mattered little whether the words they spoke made a modicum of sense, as long as they were louder than the words being spoken by the man sitting beside them. How much worse would things have to become before they finally woke up and realized the work wasn't going to do itself?

The door behind the desk opened and the High Elder shuffled in. If Josiah felt exhausted, it was nothing to how John Morgan looked as he sank down into his chair and removed his ceremonial cap. Josiah made to stand, but Morgan waved him off impatiently, and Josiah, taking his cue for informality, sat down again.

"Am I simply growing impatient in my old age, or are things downstairs as hopelessly bungled as I think they are?" Morgan asked in a weary voice.

"I would not blame you for impatience at this stage, Your Grace. And yes, it's a bloody disaster down there," Josiah admitted with a sigh.

"I thought so. I knew you would be honest with me," Morgan said.

"I strive always to be so."

"Yes, I know you do. And so shall I be, and brief too, for we haven't much time before we have to return to the fray," Morgan said.

Josiah sat up a little straighter, eager to show his readiness.

"I am worried about my son, Josiah."

Josiah struggled to keep his face free of the surprise he felt. Whatever topics he had expected of the conversation, a heart-to-heart about offspring had not been among them.

"I have done my best to guide him, but I feel that Reginald has not found his footing in the assembly. He does not show the initiative to move up the ranks, does not strive to distinguish himself as I had hoped he would. He is not his brother, and I do not believe he ever will be."

Josiah nodded sympathetically, but silently professed the High Elder's words to be a gross understatement of the situation. Peter Morgan had been a paragon of faith and duty. He had followed in his father's footsteps, shooting up through the lower ranks of the assembly with a series of eloquent speeches and well-executed legislative efforts. He had been the clear successor to his father's legacy, until tuberculosis claimed him in the prime of his career. Elder Morgan had never fully recovered from the devastation of the loss, now five years past. With an older brother to shoulder the burdens and responsibilities of the family name, Reginald Morgan had been somewhat neglected, and as a result, had grown into a notorious cad, regularly missing the assembly meetings and squandering his time, talents, and fortune in gambling halls and dens of iniquity. His father had wasted incalculable resources in his efforts to reform his son, but it had all proven too little, too late. None of this, however, could Josiah bring himself to say out loud.

"I do not deny the boy is struggling, but it is a heavy mantle he has been handed. Give him time, Your Grace, and I'm sure he will—"

"I am running out of time, Josiah," Morgan interrupted.

"Oh, I don't know about that. He is young yet."

"No, you misunderstand me. Reginald may reform yet, but it will not be under my guidance."

Josiah frowned. "I'm afraid I don't follow."

"I'm dying, Josiah."

The words fell like stones between them. Josiah stared into Morgan's face, the shock reverberating around inside him. Morgan simply stared steadily back, and Josiah grappled around for a response.

"What do you mean, Your Grace?"

171

Morgan slammed his hand onto the desk impatiently, making Josiah jump. "What could I mean? Do you not comprehend the words? I am dying, I tell you."

"You are ill?"

"Yes. Gravely."

Josiah continued to stare at Morgan, who had been looking thinner and paler of late, but not in a manner to cause alarm. Josiah assumed that he, like the rest of them, was feeling the strain of their current struggles with the populace.

"I... am terribly sorry to... you have no idea how it grieves me to hear this, Your Grace," Josiah finally stammered. "And there is nothing to be done?"

"My doctors tell me no. It is only a matter of time."

"How much time?"

"Months. Maybe less. A tumor."

Josiah ran a hand over his face and through his hair, trying to pull himself together, to absorb the news. This would be a devastating blow to the Illustratum, to lose the High Elder in the midst of such disarray.

"Who knows?" Josiah asked, his voice barely more than a whisper.

"No one outside of this room, apart from my doctors. And I intend to keep it that way, at least for the present. But the reason I've told you this, Josiah, has nothing to do with me, and everything to do with Reginald."

"What about Reginald?"

"He is going to need guidance, Josiah. He is going to need a firm hand to continue steering him along the Path. I need you to be that hand."

Josiah blinked, struggling to find the right reply. "You know I would do anything to help you, Your Grace; but respectfully, sir, why would Reginald ever listen to me? I hold no sway over him whatsoever."

"You would if you were his father-in-law," Morgan replied.

"His... I don't..."

"Reginald has nothing to bind him to his responsibilities right now — it is high time he settled down, and marriage to the right woman might make all the difference in helping him to find his way. I know you have made other arrangements. I know that your daughter is all

172

but promised to the Potter boy, and it is not my wish to create bad blood between you and Francis. But an alliance between our families could solve everything."

Josiah's mouth opened and closed several times before he could respond. "Your Grace, I am incredibly humbled by your faith in me and your desire to join our families, but my daughter's Presentation a mere fortnight away. How can I—"

Morgan raised a hand to silence Josiah. "I know all of that. I know that you cannot make this decision lightly. And I do not intend to do this solely out of your sense of duty to me. I know you, Josiah. I know what you seek, and I can help to put it within your grasp."

"Your Grace?" Could Morgan possibly mean what Josiah thought he meant?

"I must make arrangements for my successor to the role of High Elder. By putting forth a name and casting my vote before my death, I all but assure the installation of my hand-chosen candidate. If we can come to this agreement, Josiah, I intend to name you."

There in his chair, staring at the man who held his future in his hands, Josiah saw the deepest ambitions of his heart laid bare before him, naked and exposed to the harsh light of day, and yet more tangible than he had ever allowed them to be before.

All he had to do was reach out and grab them.

"You are the right man for the job, Josiah. Your devotion to the Council has been unflinching. You are not afraid to take bold action to preserve our rule. You will not stand by and let all we have built crumble."

Josiah's head spun. How many times had he looked at his own reflection in the mirror and whispered those very words to himself? How ardently had be wished to be granted the chance to prove them true?

"I do not mean for you to make such a consequential decision right now, Josiah," Morgan said, mistaking Josiah's shock for indecision. "There is much to be considered, and you must weigh all of it carefully. And I can promise you that I will speak with Francis myself. He will not be forgotten in all of this, and I shall ensure that the sacrifice on his part is well rewarded, you have my word. But as you yourself have pointed out, time is of the essence. Will you promise to think it over?"

"I... I shall, Your Grace, with all due expedience and gravity."

"Good man. I shall summon you again in twenty-four hours' time, and we can discuss it then."

"Very good, Your Grace."

"Excellent." Morgan stood up from his chair and smiled. "Now pour us a brandy, would you? If there's one thing a dying man deserves, it's a drink whenever he damn well pleases."

(Letter from Eli to James Whippet)

James—

The last of the supplies we were waiting for came in last night with Zeke's barrels of ale. No run-ins with patrol, no problems at the border. I've arranged for them to be delivered to you with the grain on Friday morning—that way, you only have to conceal them for a day, and there's less opportunity for them to be discovered. If you need anything else, send word with Colin. He'll know where to reach me.

As we discussed, time the signal for maximum impact—that means waiting until all the guests have entered the ballroom. It will be tempting to set things off earlier, but be patient. Make sure to give yourself as much deniability as possible—it will be tempting to conceal yourself in the aftermath, but avoid that impulse. Everyone will be running to see what has happened, and you must attempt to give the same impression. Ask questions. Join the discussions. Volunteer to assist the guards and other servants who will be enlisted to help. Make yourself visible, for your absence would be far more suspicious and might therefore be remarked upon.

We're counting on you, James. Creator be with you.

—E

THIRTEEN

T HE SUN WAS SETTING OVER THE GARDENS of Larkspur
Manor, admiring one last glimpse of its fiery reflection in the
mirrored surface of the lake before dipping behind the trees, just
as the first of the carriages began to arrive. The manor house was
aglow from every window, winking golden eyes down at the guests,
welcoming them with promises of untold delights.

Every Riftborn servant was impeccably dressed, starched, and
ironed. Not a curl nor a thread dared to be out of place. To look at them
now, attending to their duties with placid and competent expressions,
one would never know the frantic and sleepless lengths they all had
gone through to ensure that the home and everything in it met an
impeccable standard of grace, cleanliness, and quality. The tables
were laid for a sumptuous banquet, each and every newly-polished
utensil set out with measured precision around the Hallewells' finest
gold-rimmed china and cut-crystal goblets. White and ivory blossoms
spilled artfully from arrangements on every surface, and the light
dazzled off the magnificent chandeliers, scattering tiny rainbows
across the ceiling, echoing the stars winking to life in the darkening
sky outside. Music wafted through the house like a sweet perfume,
mingling with the delectable smells that escaped from the kitchens
below each time a door was opened. Flutes of champagne floated
from room to room atop gleaming silver trays carried deftly by white-
gloved servers. Larkspur Manor was nothing short of a beautiful
dream.

Jessamine stood before her mirror, gazing blankly at her own
resplendent reflection, but seeing nothing. Eliza stood just behind her,
adjusting the last of the frills and tying the last of the silk ribbons.

177

"There now, miss. Aren't you just a vision to behold?" she said with a satisfied sigh.

Jessamine was indeed a vision. Her gown swept out around her in a splendor of pale lavender. Every bow, every lace tuck, every fabric rosette was perfectly placed. Her dark hair was piled on her head in a glossy arrangement of curls, into which Eliza had artfully tucked an array of flowers and sparkling pearl combs. An amethyst, surrounded by a halo of diamonds, nestled in the hollow of her throat, suspended there by a triple string of glossy white pearls. Even the nervous flush in her cheeks only served to enhance her loveliness.

"Thank you, Eliza," Jessamine whispered, turning first this way and then that before her reflection, staring at it as though it were a stranger that stood before her. "I hardly know what to say. It's all just... just perfect."

Eliza beamed. It had been no simple feat, and secretly she had been just as nervous as Jessamine when they'd begun the lengthy process of getting ready. For hours she had bathed, perfumed, brushed, pinned, tucked, laced, powdered, and flattered, until the vision stood at last completed before her, all the while probing the emotional energy that pervaded the room, bestowing compliments and reassurances at just the right moments, so that Miss Jessamine's vague worries would not resurface to mar the anticipation of the night's events.

"Oh, I know I mustn't be seen at the window, but I simply must know—have the carriages begun to arrive yet? Oh, won't you peek through the drapes for me, Eliza?" Jessamine fluttered.

Eliza raised an eyebrow. "Do you think a single member of the Dignus would dream of refusing the invitation?"

"Please, Eliza. Please, I haven't had a glimpse downstairs all day. I simply can't stand it a moment longer!"

Eliza smiled indulgently and crossed to the window, where she parted the curtains just enough to glimpse the drive four stories below. "A whole line of carriages, miss, and more coming down the road even now. The ballroom will be full up with guests in no time at all."

Jessamine pressed her fingers to her mouth to suppress a girlish squeal and executed a twirl on the spot. "I can't believe it's finally here! I feel as though my feet are hardly touching the ground." The dazzling smile slipped from her face, replaced by a look of wistful sadness. "I wish my mother could see me in this dress."

Eliza's smile almost faltered as well, but she managed to keep it in place. "You look so much like her, Miss Jessamine, in her portraits. She would be very proud to see you looking so lovely for your Presentation."

Jessamine turned on the spot and looked at Eliza very seriously indeed. "Yes, Eliza. I do think she would be proud. That's why I want you to take me to see her. Right now."

Eliza's tenuous hold on her smile broke. "Miss Jessamine, you know I can't do that."

"Of course you can!" Jessamine said eagerly, rushing forward and snatching up Eliza's hand in her own white-gloved one.

"Miss, there isn't time! The guests have already begun to arrive, as I've just told you, and—"

"And I won't be needed for an hour yet!" Jessamine replied, pointing to the clock. "You know very well that I'm not allowed downstairs until I'm announced, and that won't be until eight o'clock!"

"Miss, please don't ask me," Eliza pleaded. "You know your father has forbidden anyone to disturb her, especially on a night like tonight, with every important Dignus in the country right downstairs!"

"Eliza, please! I'll never ask you for anything else again as long as I live!"

Eliza raised a skeptical eyebrow and Jessamine laughed.

"Okay, you're right, that's a foolish promise if ever I made one. I'll probably ask you for ten more things before I even make it down the stairs. But you said it yourself—I've been waiting my whole life for this night. All I want is for my mother to have one tiny glimpse of me in my Presentation dress, Eliza. I'm sure she would want to see me, don't you? Don't you think it will cheer her heart?"

"That's just the problem, Miss Jessamine. We don't know what it will do. Your mother's state is... well, unpredictable. She becomes upset at the slightest provocation. Mrs. Spratt works very hard to keep her calm, and if we just barge in there now unannounced..."

"I have no intention of barging in anywhere, Eliza," Jessamine replied, sounding stung. "I just can't imagine that my mother would want to miss her only chance to see me on the day of my Presentation. I know it's out of the question for her to come down for the ceremony, but surely a little turn about her room in my dress could do no harm."

Eliza bit her lip. The truth was that it could do harm—a great deal

179

more harm than Jessamine could ever know. She opened her mouth to say so when Jessamine spoke again.

"Eliza, please. It isn't just of Mother I'm thinking, although I do think it terribly mean to leave her out completely. You said it yourself a few weeks ago: a mother always knows her child in her heart. I want to see my mother. I need to see her on today of all days. It's important to me. Please."

"You've been planning to ask me this all day, haven't you?" Eliza asked, and if she had been any less careful, an accusatory note surely would have crept into her voice.

Jessamine flushed. "Not exactly. But I think it's at the heart of what's been bothering me for weeks now. She's missed everything, Eliza—every important milestone of my life from the time I was three years old. I don't want her to miss this one, too. Don't make me face this night without her. Please."

Eliza looked into Jessamine's lovely, earnest face and felt her resistance crumble. She never had been able to refuse her mistress, even in such a foolish endeavor as this was certain to be. Muttering a silent prayer to the Creator under her breath, she nodded once and turned for the door. "We can only stay a moment, Miss Jessamine. And you must keep very calm and quiet."

Jessamine nodded solemnly. "Yes, of course."

"And if Mrs. Spratt says your mother is already in a state, if she asks us to leave, you must accept it," Eliza went on, refusing to budge from the door until the rules had been established.

"I promise, Eliza. I don't want to upset her," Jessamine replied. With her face so solemn and her hands clasped before her, she looked like a china doll come to life.

"Very well. Let's go, then, before I come to my senses." Eliza groaned and gently eased the door open.

Eliza knew they were unlikely to run into anyone, since the entirety of the staff was assigned to duties relating to the celebration happening several floors below, but that did not stop her nerves from jangling as she glanced up and down the hallway, which was as deserted as she could have dared to hope. Closing the door behind them, Eliza led the way down the corridor toward the back staircase. She did not dare use the main staircase, for fear of being seen.

They slipped quietly past the main sleeping quarters because Lillian Hallewell did not sleep in any of the main sleeping quarters.

The grand bedroom, sitting room, and dressing room that had once been hers on the third floor had long been empty, dusty, and locked away from prying eyes. Jessamine had once ventured to ask her father if she might not occupy the space, and was met with such a storm of rage that she never dared to mention it again.

The rooms in which Lillian Hallewell now dwelt had, for many years now, been tucked away in the most secluded corner of the top floor of the estate, far removed from the daily lives of the rest of the inhabitants of the house. Her presence within the walls of Larkspur Manor was akin to that of a ghost—more rumor than substance, and always spoken of in hushed and somber tones. Even among the guests now circulating below, there was an occasional whisper of curiosity. Was it possible that she might emerge from seclusion? Might they glimpse—if only for a moment—the mysterious mistress of Larkspur Manor?

If only they had known the truth of her condition, they would not have bothered to engage in such foolish speculation. Lillian Hallewell would not attend the Presentation. Lillian Hallewell had not left her remote hideaway in the furthest reaches of the house in more than fifteen years, having retreated so very far into her own mind that no one could reach her.

Eliza had only one memory of Lillian Hallewell before she became something of a wraith in the rafters of her own house, a memory that felt half a dream. A dazzling smile on a porcelain face, beneath a frilly white parasol, reaching out a slender white-gloved hand to offer a sweet scone to a shy child.

"It will be our little secret, Eliza. Now run along and play, darling," she had said, with an indulgent smile upon her glorious face. And Eliza had run along, her treat clutched delightedly in her tiny hands.

In the years since, Eliza had only had a few glimpses of the woman who had once won her childish heart with a sweet. On occasion, when the kitchen staff had been overwhelmed, she had been asked to carry a tray up for Mrs. Hallewell or else for her caretaker, Mrs. Spratt. Each time, as Mrs. Spratt carefully opened the door to receive the tray, Eliza had a momentary view of a figure in a white nightdress, thin shoulders hunched, greying hair streaming down her back, huddled in a chair by a small, round window. On the rare occasion when her duties took her around to the back gardens, Eliza would chance a glance up toward the eaves of the house and find the little window there, partially obscured by creeping green fingers of ivy. Sometimes she would fancy that she could see the shadowy outline of a face looking down, and a shiver would run like a mouse up her spine.

The circumstances which had rendered Mrs. Hallewell little more than a rumor to the outside world were well-known, and yet Elder Hallewell had forbidden its mention, and therefore only the most intrepid of servants or foolish of guests would ever dare speak the name of William Elias Hallewell. Even Jessamine had not allowed her brother's name to pass her lips in more than fifteen years.

Eliza remembered the eldest Hallewell child the same way she remembered a dream—a vague impression, blurred around the edges, unsure whether the details were real or imagined. Only a year older than both Jessamine and Eliza, he had been, according to whispered account, the pride and joy of both Elder Hallewell and his wife. But then, one morning, the family awoke to the nursemaid's screaming from the nursery and discovered that William had disappeared from his bed in the night. He might have vanished into thin air but for the fact that the window in the far corner of the nursery had been left open. It had been concluded that the boy had been abducted.

A great search commenced, but no trace of the boy could be found. The Illustratum ordered sweeping raids of the Barrens and the Praeteritum district to no avail. Curfews were imposed and arrests were made, but all of their efforts came to nothing. William Hallewell was never found. It was one of the enduring mysteries of the city of Post-Rift London, and a darkness in the heart of Larkspur Manor. Despite being only three years old, Eliza remembered it all well, tangled up as it was in her mother's own disappearance; for Emmeline Braxton had run off only a week before, leaving a note that she had fallen in love, renounced her faith, and fled the country.

Now, as they traversed the last corridor that would lead them to Mrs. Hallewell's chambers, that shiver Eliza always felt when she thought of the mistress of the house returned, raising goosebumps upon her arms even as she tried to suppress it. The carpet muffled their footsteps, but still they tiptoed, their breathing coming faster now that they were so near to her quarters. As they turned the last corner and the door came into sight, Jessamine froze.

Eliza turned to look at her, taking in the sudden papery paleness

182

of her cheeks and the way her pupils had dilated to swallow the deep brown of her eyes.

"Miss Jessamine? Are you quite well, miss?"

"I... I am, thank you, Eliza," Jessamine replied, though she looked anything but.

"We don't have to go, you know," Eliza said softly.

Jessamine closed her eyes, took a deep breath, and blew it out again. Then she lifted her chin defiantly and declared, "I want to see my mother. Kindly knock on the door."

Eliza did as she was bade, knocking softly and waiting, hardly daring to breathe, for Mrs. Spratt to open it. Mrs. Spratt did so in short order, peering through a crack just wide enough to reveal her look of shock at seeing who stood waiting on the threshold.

Eleanor Spratt was the kind of woman whose every care hung upon her outward appearance like clothes upon a line. She had been handsome once, tall and chestnut-haired, with bright eyes and a warm smile. If Eliza strained her memory, she could remember Mrs. Spratt this way, back when she had served as Mrs. Hallewell's lady's maid rather than her caretaker. Now that hair had dulled to a steely grey, just as the gleam had dulled from her eyes. Her once easy smile had sunk into a thin, grim line, and her shoulders had rounded into a defeated-looking hunch. Everything about Mrs. Spratt was faded now, like a flower that had been pressed mercilessly between the pages of a book.

"Eliza, what are—Miss Jessamine! Miss, whatever are you—" the woman began in a cracked voice, but Jessamine cut her off.

"I've come to see my mother, Mrs. Spratt. Will you kindly permit me entry?"

Mrs. Spratt hesitated. She glanced at Eliza, who gave a helpless shrug, a gesture that any servant would surely understand—that she had had no choice in the matter but to indulge the whim of her mistress.

"Miss Jessamine, I know that we sometimes make exceptions to allow you to visit—for Christmas and the like, and I know today must be... must be a special sort of day for you, but your mother is already agitated. It's as though she senses that something unusual is happening in the house—all the noise from outside, I expect, and the staff flying all about the house readying things. I don't know but that the sight of you might... might upset her further," Mrs. Spratt replied.

"I don't know why it would," Jessamine said with something of a pout. "I should think she'd be happy to see me looking so well."

"Of course she would, miss, if she were... that is... if she were able to..." Mrs. Spratt struggled to find a term delicate enough to use with Jessamine, but in her surprise seemed unable to conjure it.

"And if she does get a little... well, worked up, surely you can calm her down. That is your job, after all," Jessamine said, her impatience creeping into her tone now, turning it cool. She looked pointedly at Mrs. Spratt's wrist, where her Riftmark was clearly visible: a tiny black hooked shape, like a wave, just like Eliza's.

Mrs. Spratt blushed. It was not common for Riftmagic to even be acknowledged among the Dignus, let alone referenced so directly. Tugging ashamedly at her sleeve to hide the mark, she addressed her shoes when next she spoke. "I certainly always endeavor to do my duty to the best of my ability, miss, in service to the family."

"Of course you do," said Jessamine smoothly. "Now, open the door, if you please. I haven't much time before I'll be summoned downstairs to the Presentation."

Looking for all the world like she was doing it against her better judgment, Mrs. Spratt opened the door and stepped back to allow Jessamine to pass. The room beyond was dim and quiet, lit only by the fire in the fireplace and a single lamp set upon a bedside table. Mrs. Spratt's embroidery lay half-finished upon her chair, and the remains of a solitary dinner sat on the small tea table beside it.

In a rocking chair by the tiny, ivy-covered window sat Lillian Hallewell, gazing out over the grounds. At first glance, she did not appear agitated, as Mrs. Spratt had claimed. But Eliza had a great deal of experience in recognizing the outward signs of the inward plight, and within a moment or two, she had noted with concern the way that Mrs. Hallewell's hands twisted together in her lap, how the knuckles were white with tension, how her knees beneath the skirt of her nightdress were locked tightly together. Her face might have been impassive, but the rest of her body told an entirely different story.

Jessamine, possessing none of the same skills, recognized none of the silent warnings as she slowly crossed the room, patting at her hair and smoothing her gown nervously. She cleared her throat and said in a quiet, gentle voice, "Hello, Mother."

If Lillian Hallewell had heard her, she did not let on. She

continued to stare out the window, eyes fixed intently on the gathering darkness.

"It's me, Mother. It's Jessamine," Jessamine continued. "It's the evening of my Presentation tonight."

The thin white hands clenched and unclenched. Eliza felt Mrs. Spratt tense beside her, but neither woman made a move to stop Jessamine.

"I... know you would be down there with me if you could," Jessamine went on in a doggedly determined impression of cheerfulness that nearly broke Eliza's heart. "But since that's not possible, I wanted to be sure that you had a chance to see me in my dress."

Mrs. Hallewell's gaze did not waver. As the silence lengthened, Jessamine's determined smile began to slip. She tried again.

"It took them ages to get the fit right," she went on, as though she and her mother conversed about such trivial matters as dress fittings all the time. "I wasn't sure about the trim they chose at first, but Eliza found a new lace edging that's finished it off just right, don't you think?"

She twirled slowly on the spot, but it made no difference. Her mother's gaze would not be drawn from the window.

It was all too sad. Eliza was not sure she could bear to watch another moment of it. She made to step forward, but Mrs. Spratt touched her arm gently, and she stayed where she was.

Jessamine finished her twirl and came to a stop. A spasm of something desperate momentarily twisted her features before she composed them yet again. "I'm not sure it's as lovely as your Presentation dress. I've looked at it so many times, in your portrait above the drawing-room fireplace. I chose the same color, though. I thought it suited you so beautifully that it might suit me, too. What do you think?"

Eliza's eyes blurred with tears, but she quickly batted them away, knowing she needed to keep her wits about her, and her view of the encounter unclouded and clear. There was no room for error, not tonight.

"Oh, can't you look at me? Just this once, Mother? I need you today," Jessamine whispered. There was a long, dreadfully silent pause and then, without warning, Jessamine flung herself onto her knees before her mother's chair, grasped the woman's face between her hands, and forced their eyes to meet.

"Look at me! I'm still here!" the girl shrieked.

Mrs. Spratt cried out and lunged toward them, but it was Eliza who stopped her this time. Arms about each other, frozen with shock, they watched as Lillian Hallewell's eyes stared into her daughter's, as a dim light of recognition kindled within them, as her mouth opened as though to speak...

"They're coming for him," she whispered in a hoarse croak of a voice long disused.

Jessamine's face twisted in confusion. "What?"

"They're coming. You must protect him, Lillian. You must hide him."

"I'm... I'm not Lillian. I'm Jessamine. Don't... don't you know me?" Jessamine cried out.

"Protect him! They're coming! They'll take him from you, don't you see?" Lillian's voice was rising now in a hysterical shriek. Her hands shot up out of her lap, gripping Jessamine's arms with surprising strength.

"Ouch! Mother, you're hurting me! Mother, let go!" Jessamine cried out.

"Protect him! Protect him, Lillian!" Mrs. Hallewell screamed, tears springing into her wild eyes.

"Mother, let go!" Jessamine cried again, but Eliza and Mrs. Spratt had already descended upon them, Eliza prising Mrs. Hallewell's fingers gently away while Mrs. Spratt pulled Jessamine's hands away from her mother's face, and cradling the sallow cheeks in her own hands, beginning a soft, steady stream of calming words and soothing platitudes under her breath.

Eliza tugged the now sobbing Jessamine away from the chair, hoisting her to her feet and taking her by the elbows, leading her across to the other side of the room so that Mrs. Spratt could work.

From a chest beside the bed, Mrs. Spratt hastily pulled out what appeared at first to be a bundle of fabric or blankets, but which Eliza soon recognized, with a realization that felt like a punch to her midriff, was an old and battered baby doll wrapped in a bunting. She thrust the doll against Mrs. Hallewell's chest and wrapped the woman's flailing arms around it, pinning it against her. She then began, in a voice of unearthly calm, completely at odds with their physical struggle, to sing a gentle lullaby.

Entranced, Eliza and Jessamine watched as Mrs. Spratt used both her skill and her Riftmagic to coax Mrs. Hallewell down from the heights of her hysteria, stroking her hair and her face as a mother might her child's, moving Mrs. Hallewell's arms back and forth in a rocking motion, encouraging her to focus on the bundle in her arms. In the throes of her work, Mrs. Spratt came to life, her cheeks flushed, her eyes aglow, her voice vibrant and powerful. She became—strangely beautiful. Eliza found herself unable to look away, breathless with wonder.

Slowly, painfully, Mrs. Hallewell's breathing slowed, her sobs quieted, and her body sank into a languid posture. Her cracked voice began to echo snatches of the lullaby between sobs, until finally, she settled into a quiet repetition of the tune, rocking her chair slowly, still cradling the baby doll in her arms. When Mrs. Spratt had finally satisfied herself that her charge was calm once more, she stepped away, her hands shaking, her breath coming in gasps as though she had just run a great distance. She staggered back to her chair and collapsed upon it, all color and glow fading from her features as though someone had blown out a candle.

"Go," Mrs. Spratt gasped. "Please, Miss Jessamine. You must go, now."

Jessamine gave a dry sob but did not argue. She was shaking from head to foot, and a bruised rose blossom, crushed and browning, was dangling from her hair. Eliza guided her toward the door. She knew she ought to be using her own Riftmagic to likewise calm and soothe her mistress, as Mrs. Spratt had done, but she was so distressed by what had just occurred that she found herself quite unable to focus her mind. It was all she could manage to guide a distraught Jessamine back to her chambers.

Thankfully, they met no one on their way, and once the door was safely closed behind them, Eliza felt the cold, iron grasp of fear release her lungs at last. Jessamine sat upon the stool at her dressing table, staring blankly at her own reflection in the glass. Having recovered herself, Eliza joined her there and began at once to repair the damage done to Jessamine's formerly flawless curls. As she worked, she summoned her Riftmagic, so that her hands could restore much more than the outward show of what had just occurred. By the time every curl had been smoothed and pinned back into place, and the battered roses replaced with fresh ones, Jessamine had regained her composure, and it was with a solemn, almost detached voice that she broke the silence at last.

"You were right, Eliza. I ought to have listened to you. We shouldn't have gone."

Eliza had no desire to scold, not now. "It was only natural, miss, that you would want to see your mother on a day such as this. You mustn't be too hard on yourself."

"Don't excuse me now, Eliza. I don't deserve it. I ought to have known better. I *did* know better. I simply pretended not to. I suppose I convinced myself that today would be different, that she would somehow know that, deep down. But it was a child's foolish dream, and nothing more."

"I don't think it was foolish, miss," Eliza replied, and she meant it. She and Jessamine had grown up together, after all, on opposite sides of the cultural divide, perhaps, but sharing the experience of the motherless daughter. Sensing that Jessamine's energy had at last calmed, Eliza stepped back to ensure that every hair and thread was back in place. Jessamine rose from her chair and did the same, examining herself once again in her mirror. Seeing her standing there again, Eliza was visited by the strange sensation that the past hour had been a dream, that it had never happened at all, and that Jessamine was looking into the mirror at her Presentation gown for the first time—a sensation that was quickly shattered as Jessamine opened her mouth to speak.

"She thought I was her, didn't she? My mother. She thought she was looking at herself."

It took several moments for Eliza to try to find the right words to reply. At last, she stammered, "I... I think so, miss. You do look so very much like her, it would be an easy mistake to make, in... in her condition."

"It is as I always feared. I don't exist anymore, not to her. I'm just a reflection. Her sorrow over William has swallowed me whole," Jessamine replied.

Eliza fought back a sudden desire to cry. There was no sadness in Jessamine's voice as she uttered the words. It was simply a statement of fact, and all the more terrible for its baldness.

"It seems a selfish thing to abandon one child simply because you've lost another," Jessamine said, her voice flat.

Eliza looked up, unable to conceal her shock, nor to stop herself from crying out, "Miss Jessamine, that's not fair!"

Jessamine returned Eliza's gaze frankly. "I know it's not. It's a terrible thing to think. I thought perhaps if I said it out loud, I would hear how truly awful a thing it is, and exorcise it from myself. But, there. I've done it, and the shame still hasn't burned it out of my heart. It's still there, rotting away. What do you say to that?"

Eliza hesitated. She thought of her own mother. Of the ache and anger and confusion she felt every time she stared into the hollow, empty place in her life where her mother ought to be. Of the many tears she had shed into her pillow, tears that were not composed entirely of sorrow, but also of darker, more bitter things she dared not name.

"It's not my place to say anything," she replied at last.

Jessamine sighed as though she were disappointed and turned back to her reflection. "Yes, I thought you might say that."

A sharp rap upon the door made them both jump, and Jessamine took a deep breath. From somewhere inside her—Eliza could hardly imagine the depths of such a place—Jessamine mustered up the glowing smile that the assembled crowd below would expect to see upon her face when she descended the staircase on her father's arm. She arranged it carefully on her face, clasped her hands, and turned toward the door.

"Please come in," she called in a clear, untroubled voice.

The door opened and Elder Hallewell stood framed in the dazzling light from the hallway. Even with his face in darkened silhouette, it was clear that the sight before him—that of his only daughter bedecked like royalty—was an arresting one. His face struggled for a moment, perhaps to overcome the uncanny resemblance to his wife, and then fell into its usual lines of composure. Eliza watched the brief moment of vulnerability with a sense of shame, as though she were eavesdropping.

"Jessamine, my dear, you look lovely," Elder Hallewell declared. "It is time for your Presentation." He offered his arm formally.

"Thank you, Father. Yes, I'm ready," Jessamine replied. She nodded once in Eliza's direction, a silent acknowledgment of what had transpired between them; and then, taking her father's proffered arm,

189

sailed from the room, her proud bearing betraying not a hint of the fact that she carried with her the unspeakable weight of the ghost who haunted the eaves.

FOURTEEN

A S HE GLANCED at the silent and slender figure sweeping along beside him, Josiah was met with a strange sensation — a sensation that passed so quickly he barely had a chance to recognize it — that his own daughter had, in the time since he had last seen her, become a stranger to him. He brushed the thought away like an irksome fly. It was surely the gravity of the moment — and the symbolic shift into adulthood that it represented — that made him feel this way. After all, it was only a matter of time before she would not belong to him anymore, but to another man. The thought did not sadden him exactly — this was the way of the world, after all — but it did leave him with just a touch of something like regret. The house would be terribly empty without her.

He wondered at the very serious look upon her face — Jessamine was hardly a solemn girl. Indeed, he spent entirely too much of their time together reprimanding her for the kind of giggling foolishness to which girls of her age were often prone. He decided it must be nerves that had her looking uncharacteristically grim, and then, because he realized it was perhaps his duty to address it, cleared his throat.

"No need to be nervous, my dear. This is a happy occasion, after all."

Jessamine turned to her father and rewarded him with a small smile for his efforts. "Thank you, Father. I am not nervous anymore."

He experienced a moment of madness as he looked into her face, an irrational impulse to tell her what was coming after the Presentation itself had been completed. He knew she had certain expectations — and after all, who could blame the child, as he had been encouraging those expectations for years now, sure the whole thing had been settled to

191

everyone's satisfaction and to his daughter's greatest advantage. But such arrangements were not set in stone—circumstances changed, and he would be a fool not to reach for the stars on her behalf when they came suddenly within reach, even if she had set her heart on the moon.

She would understand, he told himself. She was a good girl, a faithful girl. She knew where her duty lay. With these words, he put the last nagging remnants of guilt to rest. This was no moment for weakness or sentimentality. This was a moment for commitment, and he would honor it as such.

Together they descended toward the second floor and waited upon the landing. A herald from the Illustratum stood there, waiting to announce them to the crowd below, as well as a valet, ready to give the signal to the string quartet playing below. Both men looked expectantly at Josiah, who straightened his Elder vestments and glanced at Jessamine.

"Ready?"

"Yes, Father."

Josiah inclined his head to the valet, who waved his arm over the side of the banister. Seamlessly, the lilt of the waltz being played below became a regal march—the official processional of the Illustratum Elders. At the familiar sound, ceremony took over, and Josiah found that his feet began their descent of the stairs without his conscious thought.

The Presentation had begun.

§

Jessamine heard the music transform on the air, and for a moment she was sure she would not be able to move. She was sure the stairs would fall away, sure she would just tumble and tumble into nothingness. But then the thought that had taken root in her head as she left her mother's room grew louder, more insistent.

She did not exist in this house. To her father, she was a child to be reprimanded. To her mother, she was nothing at all. Once she was Presented, she was her own woman. She could leave this place. Teddy would come and carry her away from the emptiness and the loneliness.

But it could not happen if she didn't swallow her fear and walk down this staircase.

Josiah and Jessamine descended toward a sea of upturned faces, all murmuring and gasping at the sight of the young woman bedecked in her Presentation gown. For Jessamine, the sound was as welcome as the first breath of air after submersion in water—it filled her with life. It wasn't vanity—it was duty, she reminded herself. It was incumbent upon the daughter of an Elder to make the most faithful and advantageous match possible, and a young woman's care for her appearance was a part of that, regardless of how shallow that might seem. "To care for oneself is to show that one is grateful for all the Creator's blessings," her governess had drilled into her as she combed the knots mercilessly from a young Jessamine's hair. Jessamine had heeded her words, and so she allowed herself the thrill of satisfaction that ran through her as she saw the faces below light up, all except for one that glowered. Sadie Carpenter's pout of disappointment made Jessamine's heart flutter with an unabashed glee that probably had little to do with duty.

The music continued as Jessamine and her father rounded the final sweeping curve of the staircase and came to a stop upon the landing facing the grand entrance hall. Waiting there for them was none other than the High Elder himself and his attendants, ready to conduct the rite of Presentation. The candlelight gleamed off the golden threads woven through his vestments, and the jeweled medallion in the three-peaked cap he wore. A silence fell over the assembled crowd as he raised his hands.

"Creator bless you, my child," the High Elder said, his voice rising clear and resonant over the cavernous hall. He held out a hand and Jessamine, sinking gracefully to her knees, bent forward to kiss the sparkling emerald in his ring.

"Thank you, High Elder," she murmured, and bowed her head, waiting, her heart thundering against her corset.

"The Creator has Called the women of the Dignus to serve Him, to spread His word, to obey His Call, and to bring forth His servants in abundance, so that His works can continue to shape the world He willed into being," the familiar ceremony began. Jessamine knew the words by heart. "And so, the time must come in every girl's life, that she leave the service of her father and enter the world as she is Called to do, to be Presented to the Dignus among whom she will fulfill the next chapter of her service along the Path set out for her. Elder Hallewell, do you Present your daughter freely to walk along this Path?"

"I do, your Grace," Josiah replied solemnly, head bowed.

"And do you, Jessamine Rose Hallewell, commit yourself fully to this service, to fulfill your duty, to submit to your Calling as the Creator has intended?" the High Elder went on.

A cold stab of fear pierced Jessamine's heart, but she found her voice nonetheless, and she was pleased to hear it did not tremble as she replied, "I do, your Grace."

The High Elder turned and beckoned forward his stewards, one of whom carried the Book of the Rift, and the second, an inkwell and peacock feather quill. The two stewards stood before her, staring fixedly over her head, as the High Elder opened the book to the page whereon Jessamine was to sign her pledge. He murmured a prayer over the Book, and then pulled the quill from the inkwell and held it out for her.

As a younger girl, watching older girls sign the Book at their own Presentations, a wicked thought had sometimes flashed through Jessamine's mind. What would happen, she would ask herself, with a delicious shiver of dread, if the girl had refused? What if she had tossed the quill aside and—sacrilege of sacrileges—knocked the Book to the ground? The thought visited her again in this moment, as the quill hovered over the page, and she imagined, for the briefest of instants, the quill cast aside, the Book flying through the air, the gasps, the cries...

And then she placed the quill tip to the paper and signed.

FIFTEEN

A T THE SOUND OF THE APPLAUSE BELOW, Eliza felt the
breath escape her in a long sigh of relief, and she wondered
how long she'd been holding it. She couldn't see what was
happening—it would have been unthinkable to be caught peeking over
the railings—but she could hear the words of the ceremony echoing
into the upper reaches of the house, and so she stood in the hallway,
her back pressed to the wall, listening with all her might and trying to
visualize the scene below. She could not help but feel a sense of pride,
to know that she had played a part, however small, in the success of
the night. The nerve-wracking part was over, she knew. The rest of the
night would be a brightly colored dream of dancing and drinking and
eating and laughter.

And a dream it would have to remain, for she was not meant to
be a part of it. She would have to satisfy herself with the whispered
stories from the serving staff and the glimpses of the gaiety and
glamour from the windows. Even now, Bridie and the other maids
would be gathered around the scrubbed wooden table in the servants'
dining quarters, eagerly awaiting her return so that they could wring
details from Eliza like water from a sponge. She sighed.

There were several concealed staircases in Larkspur Manor, which
allowed the servants to traverse the house like mice within the walls.
Eliza descended one such staircase now, knowing it would be
unseemly to be spotted on the main floor by any of the guests. This
particular staircase led to a back storage room and then a door took her
outside, where she could follow a path along the back of the house and
access the downstairs through a kitchen door concealed from the main
gardens by the garages. She hurried along it now, her breath billowing

out behind her like steam from a locomotive. The grass was crisp with frost, and the stars were brilliant in the still deepening darkness. She turned the corner and walked right into Peter Bennett.

"Peter! For goodness sake, you startled me!" Eliza cried, stumbling back from him and catching herself against the side of the house. "What in the world are you doing back here?"

"I... that is... I'm on a break," Peter stammered. His face was pale and sweaty, and he had loosened his bowtie. His jacket lay upon a barrel behind him.

"A break? Surely not! The dinner ought to be starting at any moment!" Eliza said, frowning. "Are... are you ill?"

Peter made a strange sound, somewhere between a laugh and a whimper. "Aye, there certainly seems to be something wrong with me."

Eliza stepped forward and peered into Peter's face. "You look dreadful, Peter. Do you want me to fetch someone? If you're not well, you shouldn't be—"

"No!" Peter cried, dragging the back of his hand across his face and shaking his head as though to clear it. "No, please, Eliza. Don't fetch anyone. I... I don't want anyone to see me like this."

Eliza placed a sympathetic hand on Peter's forearm and gave it a little squeeze. "I understand, Peter. It can be very intimidating, working directly with an Elder family, especially one as powerful as the Hallewells. I still get anxious sometimes, especially around Elder Hallewell. And on a night like this, with even the High Elder in the house—it's enough to make anyone anxious. Why even my father is on edge, and we all know nothing rattles him."

Peter tried to smile, but the expression wouldn't quite take. His face fell back into lines of misery.

"Is there anything I can do to help?" Eliza asked. "Would you like a cup of tea or..."

"No. No, there's nothing," Peter said softly. "I've... I've got a job to do and I've got to do it, that's all."

"Exactly! That's the spirit!" Eliza said with an encouraging smile. "Stiff upper lip, and all that, right?"

Peter let out a laugh that bordered on hysterical. "Yeah. Something like that."

Eliza peered closer at him. "Are you sure it's just nerves? You can tell me. I won't say anything to the others."

Peter looked her in the eye and opened his mouth. For a moment, it seemed as though he was going to tell her something. She watched as the words bubbled up, right to the verge of speech. But whatever he had planned to say, she wouldn't find out. Peter closed his mouth, swallowed it back, and, with seemingly great difficulty, shook his head.

"No. No, it's nothing, Eliza. I just... just need a moment."

Eliza gave him a last, encouraging squeeze on the arm and decided it was best to leave him. Her father had once told her that a man could suffer many things, but the loss of his pride was not to be borne. He was clearly already ashamed of himself—no need to rub it in, especially tonight, when he would need every ounce of confidence he could muster. She wondered if she ought to inform her father of Peter's whereabouts, in case he was looking for him, but thought better of it. Peter deserved a moment to pull himself together, and she wouldn't be the one to deny him that. Besides, there were footmen enough if her father needed one, and every one of them had more experience than Peter.

She took the long way around the kitchen, knowing better than to interrupt the workings of that inner sanctum tonight. She retreated instead to the dining hall, where, just as she suspected, the maids were gathered to hear of the splendor above. Eliza allowed their giddy excitement to wash over her as she indulged their wishes, sparing no detail about Jessamine's appearance, and the music, and the glamour of the crowd. She allowed herself to be congratulated for her role in it all. She didn't even bother to scold Bridie when she began to giggle.

"And the next time I see that Mary Whitson in the street, I'm just going to wave my hand at her like I'm a duchess riding by in a carriage. Ooh, she was insufferable for weeks after Miss Carpenter's Presentation. Imagine a scrawny little scullery drudge like her, putting on airs," Bridie declared, much to the delight of the other girls, who could claim no more right to airs than the aforementioned Miss Whitson, but laughed and preened all the same.

"Of course the next big event will be the engagement, won't it?" Bridie said when the last of the laughter had died down. "I wonder when that will be?"

"One thing at a time, Bridie, love," Liesel sighed, slipping her boot from her stockinged foot and massaging the sole. "The longest week of work of our lives is barely over, and here you are, already signing

197

us up for another one! I'd be perfectly content for ten years to pass before we have to throw another gala like this!"

"I do wish we could see them dance together, she and Mr. Potter," Bridie said, her gaze going all misty, as she swayed in her seat to a waltz she had playing in her head. "What a lovely pair they make. I don't suppose there's any chance that we still might be invited up to watch?"

Eliza shook her head. "Father would have told us, to ensure we were ready and waiting. No, I'm afraid we'll just have to imagine it, Bridie, like the rest of the night."

§

The ballroom was a whirlwind. Jessamine felt as though she were being spun around the room on a kind of carousel—faces flashed past her, hands reached out to grasp hers, heads bobbed up and down in front of her in a parade of bows and curtsies. Voices blared around her in a discordant symphony of congratulations and compliments. She soaked in as much of it as she could, tried to memorize as many details as possible, so that she could look back on it all the next day and revel in it. The champagne made her feel heady, like she was floating, and as she floated she kept looking for Teddy Potter. Where could he have got to, she kept asking herself. Why hadn't he fought his way through the crowd yet, to flash that brilliant smile at her and claim every dance on her card?

She had nearly given up on him when at last she spotted him standing by the fireplace, a glass in his hand, engaged in conversation with his father. Emboldened by her social triumph—and, if truth be told, by the champagne—Jessamine steered her Father in the direction of where they stood.

"Why, Mr. Potter, wherever have you been hiding yourself?" Jessamine teased, flashing a luminous smile.

Teddy returned her smile, but it was… off. It did not quite reach his eyes. "Miss Hallewell, my apologies. Your throngs of admirers presented such an obstacle that I dared not fight the crowd. But please, let me offer you my deepest congratulations on your Presentation."

He bowed, but did not reach for her hand, did not bestow a kiss upon it, as she might have hoped.

"Indeed, Miss Hallewell, a splendid occasion. You have never

198

looked lovelier, my dear," Elder Potter added sweeping into his own very low bow.

Jessamine curtsied in kind, and raised her eyes again to find that Teddy was staring fixedly down into his own glass again. She couldn't understand it. Why wasn't he looking at her? For heaven's sake, didn't he realize she didn't care if a single other person in this room looked at her except for him?

"A triumph of a night, Josiah," Elder Potter was saying now, turning his attention to her father. "Quite the turnout, too. I daresay the biggest event of the year."

"Now, now, the year is young. We're very pleased to have so many of the Dignus leadership here, honoring us with their presence, and celebrating with us," Josiah replied diplomatically. "And of course, it's an honor to have the High Elder here to perform the Presentation. We are much blessed."

He turned to Jessamine who nodded and smiled automatically, pretending that she was listening to her father's idle prattle rather than paying attention to Teddy and how he was still determinedly not meeting her eye, the way his fist was clenching and unclenching at his side.

"Well, I certainly hope you enjoy your night, Jessamine," Elder Potter continued genially. "I'm sure your dance card is very full already."

"Not *very* full," Jessamine replied, with an attempt at a coy smile. She lifted her wrist from which the card dangled and patted unnecessarily at a curl which was still perfectly in place. There were only two dances that truly mattered at a Presentation: the first and the last. No man in the room had dared claim either dance for himself, though many of the others were now spoken for. It was widely, if quietly, known that the Potters and the Hallewells had an arrangement, and that it was only a matter of time before the engagement between Jessamine and Teddy would be formally announced; and therefore those two dances belonged, by default, to Teddy.

And yet he still stood there, silent. Jessamine knew it wasn't her place to ask or invite him to take the dances—it was his place to claim them. So why wasn't he? She tried another, indirect route.

"And I'm sure Mr. Potter will be quite busy himself. We all know he is one of the most accomplished dancers in the city," Jessamine said, offering up another winning smile.

199

Teddy glanced up at her with a nod of acknowledgment at the compliment. "High praise, indeed, Miss Jessamine. I do not deserve it, I promise you."

"I should say he doesn't!" laughed a loud voice. Jessamine whirled on the spot to see Reginald Morgan cutting across the dance floor toward her, his father at his side. Tall and angular, with thick dark hair, a square jaw, and startlingly blue eyes, Reginald Morgan struck an elegant figure, and many a pair of female eyes furtively followed his progress across the ballroom. Jessamine knew he was handsome and well-connected and, by all objective standards, what she and her friends would call "a catch." But she had also heard the rumors of his many vices– the gambling, the women, the drinking. There was also the matter of his eyes which, though they were a dazzling blue, revealed no warmth in their depths. No kindness.

Reginald came to a stop beside her and swept into a low bow. She curtsied as courtesy dictated, and when she lifted her face again to look at him, found herself staring right into those icy blue eyes. She felt her smile falter.

"You are looking ravishing tonight, Miss Hallewell," Reginald said, extending a hand, which Jessamine had no choice but to take. He bent again to bestow a kiss upon her white glove.

Jessamine felt rather than saw Teddy tense beside her. Even Elder Potter, known for his jovial nature, had a rather strained expression on his face now.

"Reginald! High Elder! What a night, eh?" he boomed a little too loudly.

"Indeed, it is," High Elder Morgan concurred.

"A success in every respect," Reginald declared, with a respectful bow to Elder Hallewell. "That is, except for one."

Jessamine raised an eyebrow. "Is that so, Mr. Morgan? And if I may ask, in what respect do you find the evening has not met with your expectations?"

Reginald's smile broadened, reached into his pocket and extracted a pen. "It is a shortcoming of my own making, Miss Hallewell, and easily remedied. I have not yet claimed your first and last waltz."

Jessamine gasped. She could not help it. "I… I beg your pardon?" she stammered, stalling for time.

"Your first and last dance. I've come to claim them, as I see they are still blank on your card," Reginald repeated, his smile widening.

200

Jessamine could not think what to say, what to do. "I... I am not sure that they are unclaimed, Mr. Morgan. Mr. Potter and I were just in the midst of discussing my dance card, and..." She turned and threw a desperate look at Teddy. She wanted to scream at him. Why wouldn't he speak up? Why wasn't he fighting for her? Why wouldn't he even look at her?

"Oh, I'm sure Mr. Potter doesn't mind, do you Teddy, old boy?" Reginald said with a cold laugh, slapping Teddy on the back as though they were the best of chums.

Teddy's face might have been made of stone as he replied through gritted teeth. "Not at all, Reginald. The dances are yours."

"Teddy!" Jessamine gasped, but her father lay a warning hand upon her arm and she pressed her lips together.

"Now, Jessamine, let's not have a scene," he murmured in her ear before addressing the group at large. "I think the young men know their own minds."

Jessamine's eyes were swimming with tears. She could not help it—they would not be repressed. Desperately, she looked first at Teddy, who was still determinedly avoiding her gaze, and then at Elder Potter, who was bouncing awkwardly on the balls of his feet and pretending to survey the room, and lastly, at her father, whose expression was so calm, so unreadable that he might have been sleepwalking through the breaking of his own daughter's heart. It was only when her eyes fell again on Reginald that her silent plea was met with any reply—one of unmistakable amusement.

"Miss Jessamine, I can hardly be expected to sign the card if you keep it hidden away in your skirts like that."

Blushing with a combination of anger and humiliation, Jessamine lifted her arm so that the card hung within Reginald's reach, and then stood by helplessly, fighting back tears, as he signed his name twice upon it.

"Why the long face, Teddy?" Reginald asked as he placed the pen in his pocket. "After all, I see there are still a number of other dances free. I'm sure Miss Hallewell will be only too happy to take a turn with you as well. Mustn't keep her all to myself, after all. It wouldn't be sporting."

Teddy raised his head and stared right at Reginald. The rage in his eyes was so intense that Jessamine took a step back, sure the men would come to blows. But the moment passed, the fire quelled, and

Teddy, still looking at Reginald, said in a tense and strained voice, "Might I be so bold as to claim a quadrille, Miss Hallewell?"

Jessamine nodded wordlessly, and held out her card yet again, watching as Teddy signed his own name, an emptiness settling over her. Every man standing around her at this moment—this moment that ought to have been hers—Elder Potter, High Elder Morgan, Teddy, Reginald, even her own father—had understood what was to happen. Only she had stood there, ignorant to the fact that some transaction had taken place, and that the life she thought she was stepping into had been negotiated away right out from under her feet.

"Excellent, glad to see it all settled," High Elder Morgan said, a look of smug satisfaction on his face. "Come along, Reg. We still have some important people to greet, as does Miss Hallewell. We shan't keep you."

"Thank you, High Elder," Elder Hallewell replied, inclining his head and returning the smile.

"I'll see you on the dance floor, Miss Jessamine," Reginald murmured, taking her hand once again and planting another kiss on it.

Jessamine did not reply. She couldn't see. She couldn't think. Her eyes were brimming with tears and her brain was filled with a blank sort of humming that echoed in her ears and made it impossible to think. She felt a tug on her arm—her father was pulling her away, making their excuses, shepherding her along to greet some more guests. The manner in which she was allowing herself to be pulled along caught his attention. He looked her in the face for the first time since approaching Teddy.

"Jessamine, pull yourself together," he murmured, a snap in his quiet voice.

"What does this mean, Father?" Jessamine asked, finding her voice at last.

"What does what mean?" he asked, though he did not quite meet her eye.

"Reginald Morgan. I thought that Teddy Potter... that Teddy and I... that we..." but the rest of the sentence was swallowed by a sob that bubbled up out of her mouth before she could stop it. She clamped a hand over it to stifle it, sure that if she let one escape, she would be completely unable to control the others and she would fall entirely to pieces.

"This is neither the time nor the place for a scene," her father hissed.

Which is precisely why you chose it, Jessamine thought bitterly to herself, though she didn't dare to say the words out loud.

Her father went on, tightening his grip on her arm, "You have a part to play tonight and you must play it, or you will disgrace the entire family. Is that what you want?"

Jessamine felt his fingers digging into her arm, saw the anger twisting his features, and knew she could only give one answer.

"No, Father. I have no wish to disgrace you," she whispered.

"Very well, then," Elder Hallewell replied, looking mollified, and then reaching into his breast pocket for a handkerchief. "Now, wipe your eyes. Gently and discreetly, please, so you do not redden them. There, now let me look at you. Yes, that's passable. We are going to greet Elder Primrose and his family. Smile, for Creator's sake, Jessamine."

With an enormous effort, she forced her face into a smile once more, and her father led her away across the ballroom, his hand raised in greeting.

And she followed. Because that was all that was permitted of her.

SIXTEEN

THE REPORTS FROM THE SERVING STAFF trickled down to the servants quartered anxiously below. The flower arrangements were universally admired. The wine choices were discussed at great length among the Elders and found to be most satisfactory. Compliment after compliment about the food were delivered glowingly to Mrs. Keats, who took great care not to look too pleased with herself, as the night was not yet over and there were still many dishes to be brought up, although she did allow herself one giddy smile and several pats on the back when it was reported that the High Elder had complimented her roast lamb as "the most tender and flavorful he had ever had the pleasure to taste."

Eliza barely caught a glimpse of her father, as his place was upstairs overseeing the carefully orchestrated dance of servants' duties, but the one time he appeared on the stairs with a special wine request from the High Elder, she managed to give him a fleeting smile, which he returned despite his haste, and she knew from that brief interaction that all was proceeding to his satisfaction. It was not until the meal had ended and Mrs. Keats had allowed herself a few moments to put her feet up with a small glass of sherry that Eliza was suddenly summoned.

"Eliza!" Michael Stone, one of the valets, appeared upon the stairs, his face red and strained.

"Michael? What is it? Is everything all right?" Eliza asked, jumping up at once and throwing a panicked look at the clock, even though she knew it would be several hours before she ought to be in Miss Jessamine's room.

"You're wanted upstairs, Eliza."

"Whatever do you mean? Upstairs where?"

"In the master's study off the library," Michael replied. He was panting as though he'd taken the stairs at a run. "You're to take the South staircase and enter through the hall, so no one will see you."

"But why—"

"I don't know, do I?" Michael cut her off, exasperated. "Elder Hallewell requested you come at once, he didn't tell me why!"

Heart racing, wondering what on earth this could mean, Eliza dashed past Michael and up the stairs, smoothing her hair and making sure that her white cap was still pinned on straight.

The staircase split off at the first landing, and Eliza was able to skirt the festivities through a narrow servants' hallway full of linen cupboards and cleaning supplies. She counted the doors carefully as she ran, arriving at last, breathless, in front of the twelfth one, which she knew opened up onto Elder Hallewell's study. She pressed her palm against it, took a few steadying breaths, composed her features, and knocked softly.

"Eliza?" Elder Hallewell's voice was sharp.

"Yes, sir."

"Enter."

Eliza pushed the door open and froze on the threshold. Elder Hallewell was standing over the settee, struggling, along with her own father, to calm Jessamine, who was crying hysterically and begging to be allowed to go to her room. A candlestick lay broken upon the marble hearth, and broken glass glittered in shards on the floor near the door.

"I—you sent for me, sir?" Eliza managed to stammer.

"Yes, Eliza, please, we require your gifts. Miss Jessamine is not well, and she needs your help," Elder Hallewell said, his voice flustered. Even as he spoke, Jessamine managed to get a hold of a small crystal ashtray from the table beside the settee and flung it, with a hysterical wail, into the fire, where it smashed.

Eliza couldn't move for shock. "I... I don't underst—"

"Eliza, now! Please!" her father shouted. The desperation in his voice catapulted Eliza into action. She dashed forward, dodging several pillows that had been cast to the ground, and climbed under the wrestling arms to sit beside Jessamine on the settee, peeling off her gloves as she did so.

"Eliza!" Jessamine cried. "You've got to help me! It's Teddy! They've taken him from me, Eliza!"

"Sssssh, it's alright, Miss Jessamine," Eliza replied in a voice of determined calm. "You must calm yourself, miss, I can't understand you. Take a deep breath, now, and tell your Eliza what's wrong."

She reached forward to place her hands on Jessamine's arms, but Jessamine slapped them away. "No! No, you mustn't! Don't touch me! I don't want to calm down, I tell you!"

Eliza pulled her hands back as though burned. Never, in all the time she had worked for the Hallewells, had Jessamine not welcomed her ministrations. She didn't know what to do. She balled her hands into fists and turned to her father, asking wordlessly for help.

"What are you waiting for!" Elder Hallewell cried. "Subdue her!"

"I..." Eliza hesitated again. "I... can't..."

"Eliza! You mustn't!" Jessamine sobbed. "Please! Don't you understand? Teddy and I were meant for each other! We had an agreement, and they've broken it, don't you see? They've bargained my life away to the highest bidder..."

"Jessamine, that's enough!" Elder Hallewell hissed, but Jessamine would not be silenced.

"They knew! Everyone knew that Teddy and I... that we love each other..." Jessamine sobbed. "And now he won't even look at me..."

"It is not his place to look at you!" Elder Hallewell replied, struggling to keep his voice down. "I am your father and the arrangement of your marriage falls to me. It is my decision to whom I betroth my daughter. Enough with this histrionic foolishness! I will not have it! I will not have it, I tell you! Eliza, calm her! Now, I command it!"

Eliza couldn't move. The devastation in Jessamine's eyes had captured her, and she could not look away from it.

"Eliza, I can't... not Reginald Morgan... not a man I despise... I can't!"

"Eliza!" her father's voice cut in now, sharp with something other than the effort of restraining Jessamine — was it fear? The sound of it frightened Eliza so much that she whirled around to look at her father. "You must calm her! Please, the Presentation, the Elders, they're all here!"

"But..." Eliza could hardly string her emotions into words. She didn't want to calm Jessamine. She wanted to embrace her... to cry with her... to mourn with her the loss of the life she was so sure had been waiting for her. She wanted—and this scared her—to shout at their fathers to leave Jessamine be... to let her grieve and rage and storm as she had every right to do.

"Subdue her! Now! The Illustratum demands it!" Elder Hallewell shouted. Flecks of saliva had gathered at the corners of his mouth. His face was flushed. He looked quite mad.

Terror and duty overwhelmed her. Eliza turned to Jessamine, who was still sobbing, still fighting, and whispered, "I'm so sorry, miss. I have no choice."

Jessamine flailed and fought, but there was nothing she could do—the men had her held down so tightly. Summoning her Riftmagic, Eliza reached out and placed her bare hands on Jessamine's shoulders.

"It's all right, miss. Everything is going to be all right. Just calm yourself, now. Calm yourself," Eliza intoned, though her own voice broke with emotion she could not contain. Jessamine continued to moan and sob and plead.

"Why isn't it working?" Elder Hallewell gasped, still struggling to keep his daughter on the settee.

"I've never seen her like this before, sir," Eliza replied. "I've never had to... this isn't what I..."

"Well, try harder, damn you!" Elder Hallewell cried.

Eliza shuddered at his harsh words, and redoubled her efforts. She reached down, deeper into herself than she had ever allowed herself before, and felt her Riftmagic intensify in her palms, in her fingertips. She focused her intention, and it became a command rather than a suggestion. She felt the moment that it shifted, felt the magic twist in upon itself as it fought the control she tried to give it. Her heart began to race, her pulse to pound in her ears, but still, she did not let go.

Slowly, the panic and pain faded from Jessamine's eyes. It terrified Eliza to watch it—like watching the life snuffed from a dying person. Jessamine stopped struggling, her body went limp, and then she sagged back upon the settee. Her sobs and tears slowly ebbed away, like the ragged traces of a storm blown out to sea.

"There now," Eliza was saying over and over again, full of revulsion for the words. "That's it, miss. Just calm yourself. Stop crying now. It'll be all right, you'll see."

At last, Elder Hallewell and Braxton were able to step away from the settee. Elder Hallewell staggered back to the fireplace, where he stood for a moment, breathing hard, and then crossed to a nearby table, where he poured himself a large brandy and knocked it back in one. Braxton immediately set about tidying his rumpled appearance, as though the worst thing that could come out of the scene was that someone might see him with a thread out of place. He brushed off his jacket, straightened his bowtie, and smoothed his slicked hair back into place. He then wrestled his expression back into one of untroubled competence.

The adrenaline of the moment draining from her, Eliza felt weak and feverish. Her vision was hazy, her teeth chattered, and her hands, as she pulled them away from Jessamine's arms, were shaking like mad. She folded them in her lap to hide the trembling, and dropped her eyes to them, unable to face for another second the awful vacant look in Jessamine's face.

"I underestimated her attachment to the Potter boy, I confess it," Elder Hallewell muttered, and it was unclear whether he was speaking to himself or to Braxton. "But I never imagined she was capable of behaving in such a manner on tonight of all nights."

You ought to have known. The thought slipped through to her consciousness before Eliza could stop it. She very nearly spoke it aloud.

Braxton, who could not hear his daughter's thoughts, cleared his throat. "Sir, the time. The dancing is scheduled to begin at any moment. Already the servers are clearing the plates and moving guests along back to the ballroom. Do you want me to delay things, sir?"

"No!" Elder Hallewell cried, then closed his eyes and pinched the bridge of his nose, exhaling slowly. "No," he repeated, more calmly this time. "I do not want to draw any attention at all to the fact that something is amiss. She must finish the night as planned."

Eliza looked up, horrified. "You want her to go dance? Now?"

Elder Hallewell's face darkened dangerously. "Yes, now. Do you suppose all those Dignus waiting out there will simply go home and come back tomorrow night so she can try again? The Presentation must continue as planned. Too much is riding on this night. We cannot fail."

Eliza pressed her lips together, fighting against a rising tide of anger that was swelling inside her. Wasn't it bad enough, what Jessamine had had to endure already, discovering her father had promised her to a man she did not love? Must she also perform like a rosy-cheeked marionette the rest of the night, her father pulling the strings? She stared into Elder Hallewell's face and realized that yes, she must.

Hating herself, fighting back a violent urge to vomit, Eliza turned back to Jessamine and took her mistress' hands in her own. She summoned her Riftmagic again, but found it still so close to the surface that it began flowing between them at once.

"Miss Jessamine, it's time to go dance now. It's time to enjoy the rest of your Presentation ball."

Jessamine stared at Eliza as though she were trying to communicate with her in a foreign language. "Enjoy... the ball?" she asked, her brows knotted together in concentration.

"Yes," Eliza said, encouragingly. "Yes. You must go dance, now. The music is about to start. Everyone is waiting for you."

Jessamine shook her head sadly and pouted like a child. "No. I don't want to."

"But you must," Eliza went on, her Riftmagic surging, making her head spin. "You must smile and laugh and dance until the last song has been played. That's what everyone expects of you, remember? And isn't that what you want, miss? To enjoy your Presentation? You've waited so long for this night."

A slight smile crept into the corners of Jessamine's mouth. "Yes. I have waited. For so long."

"Don't let anything else worry you tonight, miss," Eliza went on. "All those worries? They'll keep until tomorrow, but your Presentation will not wait. Go on, miss. You earned this night. Go on and enjoy yourself."

The smile broadened, but it still did not quite reach Jessamine's eyes, which still had a clouded and empty quality to them, but Elder Hallewell did not seem to notice. He sighed with relief as his daughter rose from the settee and allowed Eliza, who was still trembling from head to foot, to smooth her dress and re-pin her errant curls, all the while whispering platitudes and soothing words under her breath that only Jessamine could hear. By the time Eliza had finished, her mistress stood tall and picture-perfect once more, her smile still dazedly in place.

"Are you ready for your first dance, Jessamine?" Elder Hallewell asked tentatively.

"Yes, of course, Father," Jessamine replied, in an even voice.

210

"Please forgive me. I am determined to enjoy the evening and do my duty, just as you wish."

"Very good," Elder Hallewell replied, acknowledging Eliza with a curt nod before offering his daughter his arm, which Jessamine took. Together they strolled out of the room and into the library beyond. Braxton hurried along behind them, sliding the doors shut so that he and Eliza were left alone in the study. The only sign of the chaos that had erupted there were the remnants of the ornaments Jessamine had thrown, twinkling benignly in the firelight.

Braxton looked at his daughter. His face was ashen, his expression one of bewilderment.

"Father..." Eliza began, her voice and eyes filling with tears, but before she could say another word, a wave of darkness rolled over her and closed above her head.

She had fainted dead away.

SEVENTEEN

S OMEONE WAS PATTING A COOL, damp cloth on Eliza's forehead. Her eyes felt like heavy stones in their sockets. She tried to open them, but the lids felt as though they glued themselves shut. She moaned.

"There, there, love. Just rest," said a familiar voice. It was Bridie.

Eliza peeled her eyes open. She was lying on the sofa in the study. The fire in the hearth had been stoked and was now crackling and popping merrily. Someone had propped a cushion under her head and removed her boots.

"I shouldn't be here," Eliza said thickly. Her tongue felt too big for her mouth and her throat was dry. "The Presentation... someone might walk in."

"Just calm yourself, Eliza," Bridie replied, her voice taking on the same kind of soothing tone that Eliza herself always employed with Jessamine. "No one's going to come in. The doors are locked from the inside, and there's a valet posted directly outside."

"Please, Bridie, it's not proper. Take me downstairs, I beg you."

"I can't," Bridie said, more bluntly now, and sounding much more like herself. "Elder Hallewell has instructed that you stay close at hand, just in case Miss Jessamine needs you again." Bridie's eyes widened. "What in the world happened to you, Eliza? No one would say a word about how you wound up in this state, not even your father."

"Of course not," Eliza replied, trying and failing to sit up. Bridie pushed her unceremoniously back onto her pillow. "My father is that last person who would want any rumors circulating that something had been amiss at the Presentation, and there's no better way to spread a rumor than starting it among the staff."

Bridie looked completely unabashed at this remark. In fact, she nodded in agreement. "Well, Creator knows that's true enough. But come now, Eliza, you'll not keep me in the dark, will you? What's happened?"

"I am going to tell you Bridie, but only because the reason for it will be common knowledge very soon. Everyone in that ballroom will most likely already know by now. It will be all over the society pages by morning, and news vendors will be shouting it from every filthy street corner."

"What, Eliza? What is it?" Bridie asked, her voice barely more than a breathless whisper.

"Elder Hallewell has made some sort of arrangement. Jessamine is out there even now, dancing her first and last dances of the night not with Teddy Potter, but with Reginald Morgan."

Bridie threw a hand up over her mouth. "Eliza, you don't mean it!"

"I do," Eliza replied, but even nodding her head made the room spin, so she concentrated on keeping perfectly still until her bearings returned. "Miss Jessamine had no idea. She went into hysterics, as you can imagine, although I think she had the sense to wait until she and her father were in private. He couldn't calm her and sent for me to help."

"Eliza, that's... that's terrible!" Bridie declared, dropping her hand, her shock replaced by an expression of indignation. "Why, all of London knows that Miss Jessamine and Master Teddy have been in love with each other since they were children! Their marriage has been a foregone conclusion for years! What on earth happened?"

"I don't know," Eliza said. "But I... I was made to calm her down so that she could perform as required for the rest of the night."

Bridie sighed sadly and wrung out the cloth she'd been using to mop Eliza's brow. "Well, you've always been a great help to her, Eliza. I'm sure she was grateful for—"

"No, Bridie, that's just the trouble. She wasn't grateful at all. She... she begged me not to use my gift," Eliza whispered.

Bridie frowned. "What do you mean?"

"I've... I've always prided myself on my ability to help her, Bridie. I was so pleased to know the way she relied on me. But tonight... tonight was different. She begged me not to use my gift. She didn't want to be out there, to be dancing and smiling and putting on a show when her heart was broken into a thousand pieces. But he made me, Bridie. He commanded me, in the name of the Illustratum, to... to *subdue* her. And I... I did it. I forced her to calm down, to follow instructions, to obey..."

Eliza's voice caught on a sob and her eyes filled with tears. She tried to brush them away, but the blasted things just kept right on coming, welling up and spilling over down her cheeks.

Bridie looked quite alarmed to see her crying like this, and no wonder; Eliza couldn't remember the last time she'd allowed someone to see her cry—Bridie was usually the one in hysterics over one thing or another. Bridie tossed her rag into the bowl of water and threw her arms around Eliza, who lost all control, sobbing into her friend's shoulder with a ferocity that frightened them both.

"It's... it's okay, Eliza," Bridie murmured into her hair. "You were only doing as you were told. You had no choice."

"Didn't I?" Eliza asked between sobs. "I'm not so sure about that."

"But what else could you have done?" Bridie asked, taking Eliza by the shoulders and looking into her face.

Eliza gave a half-hearted shrug. "Refused?"

Bridie's eyes widened. "Refuse a direct order from an Elder of the Illustratum? Are you out of your head? Of course you couldn't refuse!"

A sound escaped Eliza, a slightly hysterical thing, somewhere between a laugh and a groan. "Couldn't I?"

"Eliza, I can't believe I'm the one telling you this, but be sensible!" Bridie said, giving Eliza a little shake by the shoulders. "The Illustratum's word is law. Refusing an Elder's command would be akin to refusing the Creator Himself! You've known that better than I have since your father dandled you on his knee. We serve the Dignus. Our Riftmagic is at their disposal. It's the only way to save ourselves!"

"But, Bridie, that's just it. Using my Riftmagic that way... it felt *wrong*. I've never compelled her to do anything before. I've only ever been there to soothe and guide her, to help her stay the Path, not... not to control her!"

"But it... it comes down to the same thing, doesn't it?" Bridie asked, patting Eliza's hand. "You're an Influencer. You've always

Influenced her in the direction of good, to follow along with her father's will. Each time you convince her to go to services, or to attend to her charitable duties. Why, I even remember it was you who first convinced her to accept the Potters' invitation to a boating weekend all those years ago. She wasn't sure about Master Teddy in those days, and you persuaded her to say yes."

Indignation flared in Eliza's breast. "But that's different. They fell in love with each other!"

Bridie shrugged. "But they might not have done. And if they hadn't, I expect you'd have kept persuading her to accept his invitations anyway, because that's what Elder Hallewell wanted, at the time."

Eliza longed to say she would have done no such thing, but she couldn't, because it wasn't true.

Bridie mistook her silence for agreement and gave her a smile. "You see? You mustn't beat yourself up, Eliza. It wasn't so terrible, what you had to do tonight. It was only a bit more... powerful than what you've always done, but it all comes to the same thing."

Eliza stared at her friend in horror. Bridie was right. Of course, she was right. How had Eliza never seen it before? All this time, she'd been sapping Jessamine of her own free will. Her revulsion at the realization rose up inside her making her instantly, violently ill. She sprang up from the settee, knocking both Bridie and her bowl of water to the floor in her haste, dashed across the room, and vomited into the ashbin.

"Eliza! Oh dear, you're still not well! Perhaps I ought to get you to bed. Millie or I could undress Miss Jessamine, or perhaps Mrs. Spratt could be spared while you—"

"No!" Eliza gasped, dragging a shaking hand across her mouth, feeling a bead of cold sweat trickle down her cheek. "Don't bother Mrs. Spratt, that's the last thing we need." She hadn't told anyone downstairs about the visit to Mrs. Hallewell's room and she didn't intend to. "I'll... I'll be all right now. I just... I've never pushed my Riftmagic so far before. I just need some water and a little time to rest, that's all."

"You really don't look well, Eliza."

"Stop fussing, Bridie. I can't leave. If Elder Hallewell summons me, I have to—"

Eliza's voice trailed away as she realized exactly where she was.

216

In the chaos of Miss Jessamine's hysteria, she had not been able to properly appreciate the fact that she was now sitting in a room she had walked by many times, but never before entered in her life: Elder Hallewell's study.

Later, she would try to understand exactly what possessed her in that moment. She would try to dissect the exact combination of feelings that led to the madness that followed that simple realization. All she could remember was the aching horror at what she had been forced to do to Miss Jessamine and Eli Turner's words ringing in her ears:

Creator help you to see whom it is you serve.

Eliza was suddenly on her feet, though she did not remember standing up. Before she could question herself, she was halfway across the room, standing in front of Elder Hallewell's bookcase. She began to run her fingers along the spines of the volumes there, pulling out the ones that had no visible titles and riffling through them.

"Eliza? What are you doing?" Bridie asked, her voice uncertain, even frightened.

"I... there's something I need to find."

"In the master's study?" Bridie asked, her voice rising now.

"Yes," Eliza said tersely, without further explanation. If it was anywhere in this house, of course it was here, it *had* to be here.

She continued along the book shelves but though they were crammed with volume after volume, none of them seemed to be the book Eliza was looking for. She stumbled away from the shelves and stared wildly around the room. Her eyes fell upon the desk in the corner and a madness came over her. She descended upon it and started pulling open drawers.

Bridie leapt up from the settee where she had been sitting, and hurried across the room, wringing her hands together. "Eliza, what's gotten into you? You mustn't touch the master's private things! Why, no one, not even your father, is permitted to—"

"I don't care. I don't care, Bridie. I need to find it."

Eliza pulled open the last of the drawers, revealing a narrow compartment in the left-hand corner of the desk. She found three books piled there, beneath a collection of papers and a letter opener. The first was revealed, after a cursory search, to be some kind of financial log. The second was a lengthy work entitled "On the Identification and Categorization of the Riftborn." And there, on the

217

very bottom of the pile, a slender volume with no title at all. Eliza pulled it out, flipped it open, and scanned the first page.

"An Historical Account of the Downfall of the Lamplighters Confederacy."

Eliza stared down at the words, reading them several times before they finally penetrated her shock. Eli had been right. Somehow, he had known. Bridie was still hissing admonishments at her, tugging on her sleeve, begging her to return the book to its rightful place, but Eliza waved her away.

Finally. *Finally,* she would understand the heart of what had turned her world upside down.

Fueled by her horror at what her Riftmagic had just been used for, all sense of caution and propriety burned away, she hastily turned the page, determined to know everything.

She had not yet read a word when an ear-splitting explosion rent the air.

Boom.

EIGHTEEN

E VERYTHING WAS A DREAM—a dream from which Jessamine could not wake. Her feet moved forward—she tried to remember why. She felt dazed.

Oh, yes. That's right. The ball. It was time for the dancing.

She smiled at that thought. She did so love to dance. She heard applause around the room and the smile grew. What a lovely night.

She turned to see her father leading her across the dance floor. Was she to dance with him? Oh, that was nice. Her father never danced, not anymore. Jessamine smiled at him, and he smiled back. He was holding her arm rather tightly, she realized. How odd. Did he think she was going to fall? Of course she wouldn't fall. She was as light as air at a waltz. Everyone said so.

But then another man stood before them, and Jessamine's father released her arm and backed away with a bow. Jessamine looked up. He was tall—taller than she expected.

What had she expected? Or rather, whom? Her smile slipped just a bit as she tried to remember, but then the music began and that man took her hand, and she began to twirl around the room and she forgot to wonder, forgot to worry, forgot all about the feeling that there was something dark and terrible in the periphery of her vision, a something she would not allow herself to look at or the dream would end.

And she didn't want the dream to end, she thought, as she spun around the room. It was too pleasant.

Remember how much you love dancing? she reminded herself in a voice that was not quite her own.

After a minute or two, other couples joined in the waltz. The music swelled, and the room became a carousel of whirling gowns, of pink

219

satins and plum velvets and blue silks. Jessamine's smile grew. It was easier to ignore the dark thing in the corner now. It would not ruin her night, whatever it was. She sighed contentedly.

The dances bled into each other, partner to partner, song to song. Jessamine floated through them all without a care in the world until...

A man stood before her, bowing as he took the lead in the next dance...

A quadrille, Jessamine noted. What fun.

But the man did not smile at her. His face would not stay a pleasant blur. She tried to keep smiling, to keep forgetting, to keep spinning, but his face was like a storm cloud, blotting out the sunshine of her dream.

What did he mean by it? Jessamine wondered. *Doesn't he know how fond I am of dancing? Doesn't he realize this is my night?*

The man was speaking. She vaguely noticed his mouth was moving, that his words were now mingling with the music. She felt... irritated. Why was he ruining things? Didn't he realize she just wanted to dance... just dance and forget... forget...

Forget what?

No, no, don't ask yourself that, she told herself in that voice, the one that did not seem to belong to her. *If you ask yourself that, the dream will vanish, pop like a bubble.*

But the man kept talking... and his voice... she knew his voice. A few of his words permeated her haze.

"...must forgive me... had no choice... the High Elder commanded... won't you speak to me..."

Jessamine frowned. This wasn't fair. He was ruining everything. Teddy was ruining everything.

Teddy.

And suddenly she knew with whom she was dancing. And she knew why his face, which she could now see, looked so stricken. And she knew what that terrible dark thing was on the periphery of her vision...

She stopped dancing. She stared at him, seeing the hurt in his eyes, the anger, the frustration... and the love.

"Jessamine?"

She opened her mouth to speak to him.

"Teddy, I..."

Boom.

The explosion rattled the chandeliers and the panes of glass in the south-facing windows, through which a blinding flare of orange light could be seen. The guests screamed and shouted, threw themselves to the floor, and ran for the far side of the ballroom. Teddy pulled her to the ground, shielding her with his body.

"What the devil was that?" he gasped.

But now the guests were running toward the windows, pointing and shouting. The women were gasping and crying. Jessamine watched as her father and the other Elders began trying to push the crowd back, shouting at the servants to go out at once, to secure the grounds.

"Jessamine, don't!" Teddy cried out, attempting to hold her back as she rose to her feet, but she shook him off and ran for the windows. Not caring whom she jostled, she elbowed her way to the front of the gasping, pointing crowd, until her bodice was pressed right up against the glass. The sight below left her unable to draw breath.

§

Eliza and Bridie both screamed. The book tumbled from Eliza's hands and fell, open, onto the carpet. Down the hall, the sounds of more screaming and shouting echoed down from the ballroom.

"What in the world was that?" Bridie gasped.

"I don't know! It came from outside!" Eliza replied, struggling shakily to her feet. The two girls dashed for the windows, wrenching the heavy brocade curtains aside and staring out into the grounds.

One of the garages, the one closest to the manor house, was ablaze. Great, orange tongues of flame were leaping from the roof and out of the windows, which had been blown out by whatever explosion had just taken place. But Eliza's eye was drawn not to the fire, which ought to have drawn every eye for miles around, but to the words, splashed across the garage wall in garish, dripping red paint.

"LONG LIVE JOHN DAVIES."

Bridie gasped as her eyes fell upon these same words, her hands clamped up over her mouth in horror.

"Eliza! What does it mean?"

"I... I don't know," Eliza said. Her heart was pounding. This was the name that had caused the Barrens to erupt into violence. The name on the lips of the ragged street urchins in the Market District. The name her father had grown so angry to hear when she'd asked him about it. The last words uttered by a dissident who was then shot dead by guards in the lobby of the Illustratum. The name, according to Eli Turner, of a hero. And now here it was, glinting in the light of the flames on the wall below them, as though it were screaming at every living soul within the walls of Larkspur Manor.

But whatever the mystery surrounding the name, whatever she still had left to discover about it, one thing remained clear, illuminated fully by the fire's glow: she was witnessing an act of Riftborn resistance. And she was about to commit another.

She did not know how much time she would have—perhaps only seconds. She flew back across the room and snatched the fallen book up from the floor. She pushed shut the drawer in which she had discovered it, making sure everything else within it was carefully replaced. Then she ran back to the window, where Bridie was still staring, spellbound, out at the raging fire.

"Bridie, I need your help. Quickly," Eliza hissed at her, tugging on her sleeve and forcing her to look around.

"Huh?" Bridie turned blank and bewildered eyes on her, the orange light of the inferno reflected in them as she struggled to focus.

"Take this book downstairs with you right now and hide it in our room," Eliza said, thrusting the book into Bridie's hands.

Bridie looked down at the book as though she had never seen such an object before. "I... what?"

"Take it down with you. Now, before someone comes in here! Put it under the mattress!"

Understanding flickered in Bridie's eyes, and they widened in alarm. "Eliza, you can't be serious! This belongs to Elder Hallewell! Have you gone mad? Put it back, before he realizes it's missing!"

"I haven't gone mad—or perhaps I have, I don't know anymore," Eliza murmured, shaking her head. "But I'm not stealing it, and I *will* return it, Bridie, I promise you, and very soon. But I'm going to be summoned to Miss Jessamine at any moment, so I need your help. Please. I've never asked you for a favor in my life, Bridie, but I'm asking you now. If our friendship means anything to you, you will put that book in your pocket and take it down to our room for me. Please."

Bridie was still shaking her head, but she slipped the book into her pocket with a resigned expression. "What's happened to you, Eliza Braxton? I feel as though I hardly know you anymore."

"Well, you're in good company then, for I hardly know myself," Eliza replied with a slightly hysterical laugh. "Now, go, please!"

Bridie gave Eliza one last, searching look, and scurried away across the room, disappearing through the opposite door.

§

Jessamine had no clear memory of how she got back to her room. The ball ended in chaos. Someone had pulled her away from the windows—her father, perhaps? She couldn't be sure. She heard words like, "protect her!" and "get her away from the windows! They might be armed!" She had been handed off, it felt, to servant after servant, until at last she felt Eliza's familiar hand in her own, recognized the surroundings of her bedroom, and seemed to come to her senses.

"Miss Jessamine, are you all right, miss? Can I get anything for you? A cup of tea? A glass of water?"

Eliza was speaking to her. Jessamine focused on her anxious face and felt the dregs of her haziness leave her. A cold lump of dread settled in the pit of her stomach.

"No, I... could you just help me get undressed?"

"Of course, miss."

Jessamine sat in stunned silence as Eliza worked expertly, getting her out of her gown and corset and undergarments, and into the nightdress laid out in waiting for her on the bed. Then Eliza guided her over to the vanity table, sat her down, and began to take down her hair. All the while, Jessamine said nothing, as wave after wave of horror washed over her. Not until the last of the pins and combs and blossoms had been removed from her hair and her curls had been brushed into long, silky waves, did she finally speak.

"What was that all about, Eliza?"

"I'm sure I don't know, miss," came Eliza's predictably safe reply.

"Why would anyone want to ruin my Presentation? And our garage—it's destroyed! Who would do such a thing, and why?"

There was just a breath of a hesitation before Eliza spoke, but Jessamine didn't miss it. "I... I really don't know, miss. It was a terrible thing to happen, to be sure."

"It's getting worse, isn't it?" Jessamine asked.

Eliza frowned. "What's getting worse?"

"The anger and violence we saw in the streets, that day in the Barrens. They can't contain it anymore. It's spilling out everywhere."

"Yes, miss. I reckon that's so."

"But how can anyone believe that doing something like this—destroying someone's property, I mean—how can they believe that will do any good?" Jessamine sounded truly bewildered. "Ruining my Presentation won't help their cause, whatever that might be."

"I... I don't know, miss," Eliza hedged, stalling for time.

Jessamine turned to look at her. "But you're Riftborn," she said, almost imploringly. "Surely you must understand something of their point of view?"

Eliza stiffened.

Jessamine felt a flush creep into her cheeks. "I didn't mean to imply you... you have any knowledge of criminals, Eliza. I just meant... oh, I don't know what I meant."

Eliza was quiet for so long that Jessamine thought she must be too upset with her to speak. But then she answered, and her voice had no trace of anger at all. On the contrary, it was very gentle. "Sometimes... sometimes I don't think people feel as though they are being seen or... or heard. And when they feel that way for too long, when talking and then shouting are no longer enough... well... they find other ways to be heard."

"Oh." Jessamine sat, absorbing this answer. "Well," she finally said with a detached sigh, "I suppose we heard them tonight."

"Yes, miss, I suppose we did. All of the Elder Council did. I expect that's why they chose tonight—all of the most important people they wanted to reach were all gathered in one place."

Jessamine rose from her seat, walked over to the window, and peered out onto the grounds below. "The guests have nearly all gone, but it looks like a good number of the Praesidio have turned up. What's happening down there now, do you suppose?" she murmured.

"I'm sure I don't know, miss," Eliza said, her eyes on the many hair accessories she was now organizing into little porcelain boxes and filing away into the vanity drawers, "but I expect they'll have extinguished the remains of the fire and will be searching the grounds for whoever did it."

"I suppose I ought to be sad about my Presentation ending the way it has," Jessamine said softly, watching the many figures milling around on the grass, the glint of the soldiers' uniforms in the darkness, "but I can't manage it, somehow. I suppose that makes me selfish, or something akin to it. Do you know what I kept thinking, even as I watched that garage go up in smoke?"

"No, miss," Eliza whispered.

"All I could think was that I was so glad that the last thing all those people would see tonight wouldn't be me dancing with Reginald Morgan."

There was a strange, muffled sound behind her that caught Jessamine's attention. Had it been a sniffle?

"Eliza, are you crying?" Jessamine asked, shocked out of her confession. She crossed back from the window and returned to the vanity, where Eliza was still needlessly tidying trinkets.

"Nonsense, miss," Eliza said, and there was a definite tearful sound to her voice now. "I'm just fine, don't you worry your head about me. You've got more than enough worry to be getting along with."

"Eliza," Jessamine shot out a hand and caught Eliza's sleeve, causing the latter to jump back with a start and look up. Her eyes were indeed full of tears.

"Eliza, please, won't you tell me what's—"

"Oh, miss, please forgive me!" Eliza said, and she fell suddenly to her knees and clutched at the skirt of Jessamine's nightdress. Jessamine stared down at her, utterly at a loss.

"Eliza, I don't understand. Forgive you for what?"

"For... for doing as your father bid me. For using my Riftmagic to calm you so that you would proceed with the Presentation ball. I'm... I'm just sick over it, miss."

Jessamine cocked her head to one side. "Why, Eliza, that... that wasn't your fault. You were only doing as my father bid you. You mustn't feel badly for..."

"But I shouldn't have!" Eliza cried rashly. "I shouldn't have done it. You're my mistress, and you asked me... you begged me not to! I shouldn't blame you if you never wanted to see my face again."

Jessamine slid down to the floor so that she could fold Eliza into her arms. She felt the young woman stiffen, sure she was shocked at the familiarity, then felt her relax and slump against her shoulder and throw her own arms around her.

"Please, Eliza. I'm not angry with you. I promise I'm not,"

Jessamine cooed over the sounds of Eliza's continued sobs of apology. "You've always been such a good friend to me."

"Have I?" Eliza sniffed. "I'm suddenly not so certain."

"Of course you have," Jessamine said, in an almost scolding tone. "You've only ever done your job, and done it well."

Eliza's voice was tiny as it mumbled, "But what is my job, really? I'm not sure I know anymore."

"Why, it's to take care of me," Jessamine said with a small smile. "And to help me stay the Path, of course."

"But you… you and Master Teddy…"

"That's all Father's doing, not yours. I don't blame you, Eliza, not one bit."

"But I'm scared, Miss Jessamine," Eliza whispered.

"Scared? Of what?" Jessamine asked.

Eliza lifted her head from Jessamine's shoulder and then looked at her squarely in the face. "I'm afraid of what they'll command me to make you do next, miss."

The two girls stared at each other, and a fleeting moment of understanding passed between them, a glimpse into a future over which neither of them had any control. And in this moment, they were closer than they had ever been to realizing how very the same they were, in a world that told them they were irreconcilably different and, indeed, derived its very power from reinforcing that difference.

It was the closest they had ever yet come to being the friends that they might always have been.

NINETEEN

ELIZA SAW THAT JESSAMINE was safely tucked into bed with the draperies drawn before she made her way back downstairs. She was half-desperate to get down to the tiny bedroom she shared with Bridie, to shut the door and pull that book out from under the mattress and finally find some answers to her questions between its pages.

So much had happened to shake her to her very core in such a short period of time that she found herself looking around in bewilderment, wondering if she weren't dreaming—if the walls surrounding her and the floors beneath her feet weren't just an illusion, a dreamscape that would melt away the moment she tested their solidity.

Morbidly curious as to what was happening downstairs, Eliza did not slip down one of the back staircases as she might usually have done, but ventured instead down the main staircase where, only hours earlier, Jessamine had descended in such splendor for her Presentation ceremony. It felt like a lifetime had passed between that moment and now, as Eliza turned the last corner and gazed out over the main entry hall. There were no women left that she could see—presumably, they had all been sent home in their carriages while the Elders sorted out what had happened. The High Elder himself was also nowhere to be seen, though Eliza supposed this was to be expected as well. If there were dangerous rebels about, the rest of the Illustratum would make it a priority to protect the most senior of their number. After all, if these rebels were capable of setting fires and explosions, what else might they be capable of?

She recognized the other Elders still present by the red sashes they wore over their formal attire. Each of them wore, too, a very serious expression. She caught sight of Elder Hallewell straight away; he was conversing in hushed tones with one of the Praesidio Commanders. Eliza got the sudden feeling that she shouldn't be there, and paused on the steps, trying to decide if she should turn around and take the back staircase after all, when Elder Hallewell looked up and caught sight of her.

"Eliza! Come here at once, please," Elder Hallewell called.

Every eye in the entry hall turned to stare at her as she nodded obediently and descended the rest of the staircase, her face scarlet with mortification. She kept her eyes so downcast that she could only be sure that she'd reached Elder Hallewell when she saw his glossy black shoes before her. She dipped into a curtsy and mumbled, "Yes, Elder Hallewell."

Elder Hallewell leaned in, dropping his voice and excluding the Praesidio Commander from the conversation. "How is Jessamine faring?"

"As well as can be expected, sir," Eliza replied, trying to conquer the tremble in her voice. "I got her settled into bed, and I'm just going to ask the kitchen staff to send up a strong cup of tea for her. I expect she'll be asleep soon."

"Excellent. Excellent," Elder Hallewell replied, sounding relieved. "I was afraid she might give you trouble."

"No, sir," Eliza assured him, dipping a second curtsy and turning toward the hallway that led down to the kitchens.

Without warning, Elder Hallewell reached out and grabbed Eliza by the wrist. She was so startled she thought she would scream, but sheer shock kept the sound lodged in her throat. In all the years she had lived in that house, in all the years she had worked for the family, Elder Hallewell had never once touched her. The man seemed not to notice her terror as he held her wrist with one hand and, with the other, pushed the sleeve of her dress back just slightly, so that her Riftmark was visible. He ran a thumb over it and cocked his head to one side quizzically. Did he expect to feel something of the magic through the mark itself? Or was he wondering, perhaps, what it would be like to feel its Influence? At last, after a long moment during which Eliza could not draw breath, he raised his eyes to Eliza's face and gave her an appraising look that made her skin crawl. "Quite a remarkable Riftmagic you possess. You did well tonight. You served your Elders and your Creator well. It is clear that you are a valuable asset to our household. You have our gratitude, Eliza. And I shall be sure to express these sentiments to your father, as well."

At any other time before this night, those words would have sent a thrill of joy through Eliza, a pride that would have filled up all the empty places inside her. Now she was left only with a dreadful hollow ache and an urge to get as far from the gaze of those cold, dark eyes as she possibly could.

She could not vocalize any of this, of course, and so she simply nodded, forced her face into a demure smile, and curtseyed again. To her intense relief, he let go of her and she was able to slip away down the stairs.

§

Josiah watched the lady's maid scurry away, her face flushed. The poor thing could barely look him in the eye—a common reaction, he had found, among the Riftborn. He was, after all, a very important man in the realm of the Illustratum. Still, he stared after her for a long time after she disappeared. When he had asked the girl to compel Jessamine's cooperation, he had not expected the result to be so very... effective. He shuddered to think how the girl's Riftmagic might manifest itself were she not regularly dosed with Riftmead.

He had perhaps been foolish to spring the match on his daughter in such a public way. He could see that now, but at the time, he could see no way around it. If he had not done so, he wondered if he would have been able to get her down the stairs and through the Presentation ceremony to begin with. Jessamine was—and always had been—a force to be reckoned with.

He had always been too indulgent with her, he knew it. It was a weakness he could not help—she looked so damned much like her mother, after all, and had lived nearly all her life without her. If he had been less strict than he ought—if he had spoiled her a bit or given her her way too often, was he really to blame? If he was, he thought ruefully, he was certainly reaping his reward now that their future demanded her unswerving obedience. It was possible the lady's maid had saved them all. She was undoubtedly an invaluable card to have in his hand, and he would not hesitate to play her again.

"Sir? May we continue?" The voice of the Commander broke into his thoughts, and Josiah started. He turned back to the man and nodded his head.

"Of course. Forgive me, it has been a long night."

"No need to apologize, sir. We're nearly done. I just need a list of your servants."

Josiah blinked. "My servants? Whatever for?"

The Commander frowned. "All Riftborn on the premises must be questioned, sir. It's standard protocol."

Josiah shook his head. "You... you think one of *my* servants may have done this?"

"We're certainly not prepared to rule out the possibility, sir," the Commander replied. "Unless, of course, you have some kind of objection to..." His voice trailed away uncertainly as he studied Josiah's face.

The truth was that Josiah had not, even for a moment, considered the possibility that one of his own servants might have had anything to do with the incident. He simply could not comprehend the idea that he might not have complete, omniscient control over his own household. The thought stunned him, in a way it ought not to have done in a man so generally sensible.

Josiah had always thought of himself as a man who ran an impossibly tight ship. He prided himself on it, and felt that his servants were a testament to his success in this regard. The reputation for Larkspur Manor staff was unassailable, everyone knew that. Why, every detail of the Presentation tonight—with the exception of its unfortunate and dramatic conclusion—was the perfect example of this fact. And yet here stood this soldier, questioning the integrity of his household.

On any other occasion, Josiah would have had the man thrown out for even suggesting such a thing. Tonight, however...

"Braxton!" Josiah called, and at once, Braxton appeared, materializing from the shadows of the staircase like an apparition.

"Yes, sir?"

"Can you provide Commander Forrester here with a complete roster of the staff, so that he might question them as a part of his investigation?"

Josiah was quite sure that Braxton's face betrayed, for a moment, the same indignation he himself had felt before settling back into its general expression of calm competence.

"Of course, sir. Right away. Would the Commander like to accompany me downstairs while I ready it for him?"

Josiah turned to the Commander and gestured deferentially. The

230

WHAT THE LADY'S MAID KNEW

Commander nodded, slipping his notepad back into his breast pocket. "If that suits you, Elder Hallewell, I believe I will. I don't believe we've had the chance to look around downstairs. Braxton, is it? Lead on, then." The Commander beckoned a second, more junior officer to accompany him, and followed Braxton through a nearby doorway.

"A shame, Josiah. A damn shame," said a voice from behind him. Josiah turned to see Elder Carpenter walking toward him, shaking his head. "On tonight of all nights. What a disappointment for poor Jessamine. I hope she is quite well?"

Josiah mustered up a diplomatic smile. "She is, I thank you, brother. She is strong of spirit, but also of faith."

"Which is all that any man could ask in a daughter... or a wife. Reginald Morgan is a lucky young man." The words were spoken warmly, but there was no warmth to be found in Elder Carpenter's eyes. "And so are you, it would seem. Very lucky indeed."

Josiah felt his smile harden upon his face. "I think we all know that luck has very little to do with it, brother. Opportunity does not fall into one's lap. Blessings are but the tools we have to carve our path."

"And some of us dig a bit deeper than others," Elder Carpenter replied, the warmth evaporating from his voice. "It is clear that a challenging and tumultuous time is upon us, Josiah. It is a time to work together, surely, not a time to alienate one another."

"Alienate? I do not follow, brother," Josiah insisted, opening both of his hands in a gesture of innocence. "I seek only to bring two families together in a blessed union."

"You seek power, and you are exploiting a moment of chaos to snatch it," Elder Carpenter hissed through clenched teeth, so that none of the surrounding guards still milling about would hear him. "I do not know what bargains you have made, what promises have been kept or broken, but I do know this: you have no hope of ascension without the support of the majority of the Council. Mark upon whom you tread, and treat each step with the utmost caution, or you shall find you have neither hand nor foothold to slow your descent."

Josiah took a step forward, tightening the gap between them by half and causing Elder Carpenter to tense like a bowstring being drawn. "You underestimate me to your detriment, brother. I am not a man who miscalculates, and I do not brook threats or even insinuations thereof. And let me assure you, brother: if I make a gambit—and there will be no mistaking it when I do, no closed doors or backroom dealings—there is only one direction I intend to move, and my intention is my word."

Josiah watched with satisfaction as Elder Carpenter turned steadily deeper scarlet as the words he could not muster caught in his throat and choked him. Josiah did not break eye contact, but waited for Elder Carpenter to drop his gaze, which he finally and grudgingly did, turning on his heel and marching right out the front door without a backward glance. The satisfaction was short-lived, however. He had expected trouble from some of the other Elders when news of the match was broken, but he had not expected it to be so direct. It was possible he would have more open hostility to contend with than he had anticipated. The prospect, rather than dampening his determination, lit a fire beneath it.

Fire everywhere he looked, Josiah thought to himself. Now, which flames to quench and which to stoke, that was the question.

§

For the first time in the many years of Larkspur Manor's history, the chaos above stairs stood in stark contrast to the eerie calm and stillness below. Everything had come to a standstill—the trays of food half-filled, the glasses empty, uncorked bottles of wine and champagne standing beside them, unpoured. The clattering bustle of the kitchen was silenced, and no shiny pairs of servers' shoes pounded up and down the staircases. Task upon task lay abandoned upon tabletops and counters. No one dared to speak above a whisper. They stood or sat, huddled together against the horror of the blasphemy still raging in a billowing inferno out on the grounds. They could have watched the fire being put out from the servants' entrances that led out into the very courtyard where the garage was located, but no noses were pressed to the glass in curiosity, no bodies crammed into the open doorways to goggle at the spectacle. The staff was too engulfed in fear and uncertainty to have any desire to act as spectators.

It was upon this unnatural silence and stillness that Eliza descended after Elder Hallewell had dismissed her from his presence in the hall above. She expected the maids to pounce on her at once, demanding to know what was happening, but no one met her upon the stairs or beckoned her into a whispering knot of speculation. Eliza was met instead by tear-stained faces, wide, fearful eyes, and quiet, brooding disappointment. For as much as the night had belonged to Miss Jessamine, the Presentation had been the culmination of months of toil and preparation by the staff, and to watch it fall apart in such a violent and sudden manner was as devastating for them as it had been for their mistress, now lying awake in her bed upstairs. Eliza spotted Bridie in the corner of the kitchen, a cup of tea clutched in her hands. She looked up at Eliza for only a moment before dropping her eyes back to her tea again. Eliza slipped through the kitchen without a single person uttering so much as a word to her, and hurried down the hallway toward the servants' sleeping quarters. She was mere feet away from turning down the corridor that held the peace and quiet of her bedroom when she heard something that stopped her in her tracks—the unmistakable sound of crying.

She crept along to the door at the corner and pressed her ear against the wood. Someone—a man, by the sound of the voice—was sobbing as though his heart would break. Without thinking, without hesitation, Eliza carefully twisted the knob and eased the door inward, peering around the edge into the darkened room beyond.

Peter Bennett sat upon the edge of the bed, his elbows upon his knees, his face in his hands. His entire body was wracked with terrified sobs, his legs and arms trembling violently. Upon the floor at his feet, a can of red paint stood open, the wooden handle of a paintbrush protruding from it. Streaks of red paint were visible on the sleeve of his white shirt and the knee of his right pant leg. He was so wrapped up in the emotions that had overtaken him that he didn't notice Eliza until she had already slipped through the door and closed it behind her.

He leapt up from the bed at the sight of her and stared wildly around like an animal cornered by a hungry predator. Eliza had never seen a person so out of his head with fear.

"Eliza! What... what are you..." He shot a glance down at the bucket of paint and dropped to his knees, shoving it beneath his bed and throwing the bedclothes down over it. "It's... it's not what it looks like. Please, please you have to go..."

"Peter, for Creator's sake, control yourself," she hissed, throwing a nervous glance at the closed door behind her. "The house is still crawling with Praesidio guards, and if anyone sees you behaving like this, you'll be interrogated at once."

Peter blinked at her. "I... but I didn't... I haven't done..." He

233

licked his lips and his eyes darted around the room as though looking for an exit.

"Peter, what kind of fool do you take me for?" Eliza shot back, her voice as sharp as a blade. "I saw the message on the garage wall! And I saw you outside right before it happened. You were a nervous wreck. I should have realized something odd was happening, but I was too distracted, too caught up worrying about Miss Jessamine."

Peter twisted his hands in front of him. "Please, Eliza, I'm begging you. Just give me a head start, all right? Just let me get out of here before you tell your father what I..."

"Peter, calm yourself!" Eliza hissed. For half a second, she considered ripping off her gloves and calming him with her Riftmagic, but she pushed the thought away almost before she'd conceived it; the Creator would probably strike her dead on the spot for using her magic for a purpose like that. Instead, after a moment's pause, she added, "I'm not going to tell my father."

Peter's eyes went as round as coins. "You're... you're not?"

"No," Eliza said, making the decision even as she said the words.

"But why not? I... I thought for sure..."

"Because I like you, Peter, and while I don't agree with what you've done, I don't much fancy watching you swing from the gallows for it, all right?" Eliza replied. She thought of the stolen book, now hiding somewhere in her bedroom, and her own throat felt constricted. "It's not as though you've... you've hurt someone." She looked up at him, suddenly fearful. "You haven't hurt anyone, have you?"

"No!" Peter whispered, putting both hands up as though Eliza were pointing a weapon at him. "Honestly, Eliza, I didn't even set the fire. All I did was paint the words on the wall, I swear it."

Eliza narrowed her eyes at him. "Who set the fire, then?"

Peter hesitated for a moment, but seemed to decide it was best to answer her questions, as he was clearly at her mercy now. "James Whippet, what works in the stables."

"Are any of the other servants involved?" Eliza demanded.

"No," Peter said, shaking his head violently. "It was just the two of us."

"And where is James now?"

"He was hiding out in the stables, making himself scarce, but now

I expect he's been helping the other stable hands get all the guests' horses and carriages sorted and ready to leave."

"And do you suppose he's managed to hold himself together better than you have?" Eliza asked.

Peter sniffed and shrugged, looking sheepish. "I expect so. He's the one who recruited me to help."

"I hope he's had more sense when it comes to the evidence!" Eliza chided, gesturing to the bucket of paint still partly visible under the bed. "What could you have been thinking, bringing the paint inside the house with you! What do you think will happen if someone finds it in here?"

"I... we were told to destroy as much evidence as we could," Peter replied, his voice still shaking. "I didn't want to... I just ran with it, I didn't know what else to do. I thought if I could hide it I could destroy it later when the guards had all left."

"Wait a minute," Eliza said, her eyes narrowing. "You just told me that no other servants were involved. So who told you to destroy the evidence?"

Peter bit his lip. "I... no one. Please, Eliza, don't get involved. It's bad enough that you know what I've done. I can't catch you up in this."

"I'm already caught up in it!" Eliza said. *Perhaps even more than you realize*, she added silently to herself. She hesitated a moment, trying to decide how direct she wanted to be, and then just as she resolved to say nothing at all, the question burst from her lips. "Do you know a man named Eli Turner?"

Peter's wide-eyed expression was all the answer Eliza needed, but she held her breath, waiting for him to respond just the same. "How... how do *you* know Eli Turner?" he asked, confirming her suspicion.

Eliza didn't answer his question. Her heart was racing and she was having trouble keeping her breathing under control. She knew Eli Turner was some kind of... rebel. She thought it was possible he might be involved in a formal organization—a true resistance movement—and here, at last, was the proof. The isolated incidents of defiance against the Illustratum weren't isolated at all—they were coordinated, and Eli Turner was a part of it.

"Eliza?" Peter was still staring at her as though seeing her for the first time, still waiting for an answer she was not going to give him—not yet, anyway.

235

"Change out of that uniform and give it to me. I'll get the paint out of it. Change into a fresh one, splash some water on your face, and pull yourself together. Wrap that can of paint in something—some sacking or something like that, and hide it in the bottom of your closet until it's safe to get rid of it."

Peter nodded, looking relieved that someone had taken charge of the situation.

"What are you going to say to the Praesidio, if they question you about all this?" Eliza asked.

Peter's hands began to shake again. "I... I don't... I hadn't...why would they ask me?"

Eliza suppressed an urge to reach out and shake him by the shoulders. "Because I reckon they'll ask all of us before this is all over! They may not suspect the staff here, but they'll certainly want to know if we've seen anything or anyone suspicious!"

Peter ran a hand through his hair, sending it flopping down over his forehead in disarray. "Right. Okay, yes. I'll... I'll be ready for that."

Eliza had her doubts about that, but now wasn't the time to express them. She waited in the empty hallway while Peter changed into a fresh uniform, and handed her the soiled one in a canvas sack.

"If I wanted to see Eli Turner, could you bring me to him? Could James?" she murmured.

Peter's eyebrows disappeared into his hair. "Yes, but... what on earth would you want to see him for?"

"That's my affair," Eliza replied. "But you're going to owe me a favor after this, and I'll expect you to make good on it, Peter Bennett, do you hear me?"

"Yes," Peter said with a vigorous nod. "Whatever it is, just say the word."

"I shall, I promise you."

"I couldn't have been more wrong about who you are, Eliza Braxton," Peter muttered.

"I'm starting to feel that I couldn't have been more wrong about myself," Eliza said, so quietly that Peter hardly seemed to have caught the words at all. She did not repeat them for his benefit, however. Instead, she reminded him, "Now, fix your hair and compose yourself," and hurried off toward her room.

236

(Excerpt from "An Historical Account of the Downfall of the Lamplighters Confederacy" by Elder Hiram Pratt, published 1875)

"...It became apparent that the aberration did not appear solely in Riftborn families, but that children born to the Dignus could also succumb to the terrible affliction of Riftmagic. How this came to be—and, more importantly, how it can be prevented—is the subject of much study and experimentation to this day among the highest levels of the Illustratum leadership.

The stigma of producing a Riftborn child was a heavy burden to bear, and so it was the regular practice in the lower ranks of the Dignus to abandon the children or otherwise dispose of them. Workhouses and orphanages were the most common places to leave the unwanted offspring, and some were even abandoned on the steps of the Illustratum itself, until restrictions and increased policing of the barriers ended this practice. Families soon learned that children abandoned in this manner could easily be traced back to their parents. The most devout would sometimes resort to killing the children rather than bear the shame of having produced a Riftborn, and though this practice was never condoned by the Illustratum, it was rarely, if ever, punished, and the leadership made it a policy to look firmly in the other direction.

It became a matter of concern among the Riftborn community that Riftborn children born to Dignus families were being left to violent fates, and a resistance movement sprang up with the aim of rescuing these children and either rehoming them with Riftborn families or, in the case of high profile children, smuggling them out of the country to mainland Europe. This operation was formalized by a group of insurgent rebels led by London lamplighter John Davies.

Davies, a Catalyst from the Barrens, gathered a network of Riftborn accomplices who arranged an elaborate scheme of kidnappings, safehouses, and transportation in an effort to identify, abduct, and smuggle Riftborn children from Dignus families. The Illustratum launched a massive investigation to uncover the plot, which operated in secret for years. During that time, it is estimated, by Davies' own admission, that his network abducted hundreds of Riftborn children, using Riftborn in all manner of professions, from teachers to midwives, to nurses and shopkeepers. But the key to the entire scheme lay in the use of lamplighters.

The Riftborn whose job it was to transport the children from safehouse to safehouse needed a way to communicate when it was safe to move and also what routes through the city to take. Davies devised a system of signaling his accomplices using the gas lamps throughout the city, lighting and flashing and extinguishing them in a kind of code that the others were trained to understand. Davies was eventually caught when one of his abductions went awry, and he was sentenced to imprisonment in the Praeteritum for life. Though it was clear that Davies' crimes warranted a swift execution, it was the opinion of the Elder Council that Davies had become too popular, too well-known among the Riftborn population, and his death would surely lead to uprising and insurgency on a massive scale. Many of his co-conspirators were put to death quietly, and their involvement in the elaborate scheme was never made public.

This account will detail the evidence collected that led to the disbanding of the so-named Lamplighters Confederacy, and offer a number of proposals as to how the Illustratum can identify such organized efforts to undermine its authority in the future, while..."

TWENTY

E LIZA SAT UP IN BED, her candle burned down to a flickering
stub, her eyes aching and itching with a tiredness that refused to
penetrate her frantic thoughts. Her brain felt as though it was
racing around and around in circles, traveling miles at a time, but
ending up right back where it started.

In her lap, still open to the very last page, lay the book she
had taken from Elder Hallewell's desk. True to her word, Bridie
had slipped the book beneath the mattress, right under the place
where Eliza would lay her head, but it had been many hours before
anyone in the servants' quarters would retire to bed. Two members
of the Praesidio guard had appeared below stairs with Eliza's father,
and their very presence seemed to cast a frost over the entire staff.
Where before there was sadness and shock, there was now the chill
of anger and resentment: how dare anyone suspect that they had
anything to do with the horrifying events of the night, after all they
had done to ensure that every detail of the Presentation was a paragon
of perfection? Eliza was sure that Mrs. Keats would lash out at the
men as they sat in her kitchen, taking down the names of the additional
staff who had been taken on especially for the Presentation. Indeed,
the woman looked like a kettle that was slowly coming to a boil, and
it was all Penny and the other kitchen maids could do to keep her from
boiling over and landing herself in trouble for insubordination.

Eliza, meanwhile, had been half-mad with fear that Peter would
fall apart at the sight of the guards; but he managed to pull himself
together well enough to blend in with the rest of the staff in their
collective grief. When the guards left at last and the house settled into
empty quietness, Eliza lay in her bed beside Bridie, neither girl daring

to speak of the night's events. Eventually, the tense wordlessness between them was replaced by Bridie's gentle snores, and Eliza felt it safe to creep from her bed, pull Peter's soiled uniform from the wardrobe, and scrub all evidence of his crime from the fibers of the fabric. She used every last trick she knew from her extensive experience of treating Miss Jessamine's many frocks and undergarments, and when she finally hung the suit back in the wardrobe to dry, she was satisfied that it was as clean as ever it had been. Then and only then, her arms and back aching from the labor of cleaning Peter's suit, did she slip the book out from beneath the mattress, light her candle, and start to read.

It had not been her intention to read the night away, but once she began, she could not stop. She flew through the pages, mind reeling, and even after she had finished, sat staring at the final page, trying to absorb what she had just read; but her brain felt full of a blank buzzing horror that rendered her unable to interpret her own thoughts. It was Bridie, rousing to begin her duties of lighting the fires, that shook her from her stupor. Shoving the book beneath her pillow, Eliza blew out her candle and pulled the blanket up to her face just as Bridie sat up, yawning and stretching. She held very still, pretending to be asleep until she heard Bridie pick up her bucket and close the door behind her. Then she rolled onto her back and stared up at the ceiling in the dark.

She had never, in all her life, heard that a Dignus family could produce a Riftborn child. It was not spoken of—the Riftborn and the Dignus were treated as separately and distinctly as if they were two entirely different creatures. And yet, now that she stopped to think about it, she felt like a bloody fool for not realizing that of course, this must be true. The Riftborn had not dropped from the sky. The first of them had to be born to someone—after all, there had been a time before the Awakening. But how could the Illustratum hide such a thing? How could they condone the abandonment and even the killing of such children?

Eliza understood that her Riftmagic was a curse—a sign of her weakness and her sin—but it was a curse that could be tamed and used for good. She had lamented the inherent difficulties and challenges that came with being Riftborn, but never had she considered it a reason she deserved simply not to live. Didn't every human being deserve to live and make the best of the life and lot they'd been given?

240

Didn't they deserve to prove themselves? To stay the Path and earn their place at the Creator's side?

Yes. She knew in her heart that this was so. Every human being, Riftborn or Dignus, deserved that chance.

She cast her eyes to the now empty place in the bed where Bridie had lain. Every night for the last ten years, Eliza had lain beside Bridie Sloane without once wondering how she had come to be in the orphanage from which she had been chosen to enter service. Never once had she contemplated what circumstance in life might have led her friend to such a dreadful place—but then, Bridie didn't know herself, had no memory at all of her life before she had been abandoned upon the steps of the place. Now, Eliza couldn't help but wonder if Bridie herself mightn't have been one of those children, abandoned for the crime of being born with Riftmagic to parents who had none. Eliza supposed she would never find out whether it was true or not, but now she knew it was, at least, possible.

And what of Eli Turner? He had looked Eliza in the face and proclaimed John Davies the hero who had saved his life. Did that mean that Eli himself had been such a child? Had his Dignus family abandoned him to starve or worse, tried to have him killed? Eliza's mind could hardly fathom such cruelty, and yet the Elders had allowed it to continue—it was conceivable that some of them had even participated in the abhorrent practice themselves. How could this be? To question an Elder of the Illustratum was something Eliza could not have imagined doing even in her wildest dreams just a day ago, but a day ago now felt like a lifetime. She felt as though her life had now been divided into two unbridgeable islands—the time before the Presentation and the time after it.

Eliza opened her bedside drawer and pulled out her old copy of the Book of the Rift—it had been her mother's, left behind when she disappeared. Eliza stared at its leather cover, worn to velvety smoothness. She ran her fingertips along the edges of the pages, now curled and tattered from constant thumbing. She had learned to read by studying the words in this book—she had read each verse so many times that she felt she could have recited the entirety of the book by heart, and there was one thing that she knew unequivocally to be true: the Creator would not condone the murder of a child simply because they were Riftborn. And that meant that the Elders—and everyone else who allowed the practice to continue—were in the wrong.

241

She did not understand how this could be—she only knew that it was. And now she had to decide what she would do with this knowledge. But what *could* she do with it? She was one insignificant Riftborn girl in possession of a single book, and a stolen book at that. Who could she tell, and why would they believe her?

And as she lay in her bed, rays of the early morning light creeping in the narrow window near the ceiling, lighting her intentions on fire, she knew who she could tell. She knew who would listen to her, and who would know exactly what to do with the book. She also knew that finding him would be more dangerous than anything she had ventured so far.

§

"Peter."

Peter looked up from a rack of freshly shined shoes, his expression wary. "Eliza? What is it, what's wrong?"

"Nothing's wrong," Eliza replied, keeping her voice low and glancing behind her into the hallway to ensure their solitude. "I just wanted to let you know that I took care of the uniform. It's back in your wardrobe now, and it looks immaculate."

Peter's face crumpled with relief. "Thank you. I owe you one, Eliza, I really do."

"I know you do. And it's on that score that I wanted to talk to you."

"Is that so? Well, as I said, whatever I can do…"

"I need to see Eli Turner. I need you to take me to him."

Peter's face, already pale, turned ghostly white beneath his spattering of freckles. "T-take you to him? But I… I don't know how to find him."

Eliza frowned. "How is that possible? He coordinated your little stunt last night, didn't he?"

"Well, yes, but that doesn't make us chums, Eliza. I don't pop 'round his place for tea."

Eliza refrained from rolling her eyes, but it was a near thing. "But surely you communicated with each other?"

"Yes, but only twice in person, and then it was always in a public place—once in a pub in the Barrens, The Bell and Flagon, and then again in a busy street," Peter explained.

"Well, how did he get in touch with you, to set up the meetings?" Eliza asked.

Peter squirmed. "There's a boy he used to pass written messages along—name's Colin Webb."

Eliza felt a small shoot of hope sprout in her chest. "Well, if this Colin Webb can pass messages from Eli Turner, then he must know where I can find him. Do you know where to find Colin?"

"No, but I reckon James Whippet does," Peter answered reluctantly.

"Excellent," Eliza said briskly. "I'll need you to take me to him tonight."

Peter dropped his shoe brush in his shock. "Tonight? But... I... you can't be serious!"

"On the contrary, Peter, I've rarely been more serious. I have business with Eli Turner that cannot be delayed. It is of vital importance that I see him as soon as possible."

"I don't suppose you're going to tell me what this important business is?"

"You suppose right," Eliza replied. "I expect there are many details you haven't told me about last night, and I haven't pressed you. I'll thank you to do me the same courtesy. I've promised to keep your secret, but I have no intention of divulging my own."

Peter scowled, but nodded just the same. "Very well. I'll head out to the stables to speak to James as soon as I've finished with the shoes. Where shall I find you?"

"Don't you dare go looking for me!" Eliza snapped, more out of fear than temper. "We barely speak two words to each other most days, and I don't want you rousing suspicion among the others by searching me out. I'll be back down after my morning duties with Miss Jessamine around eleven o'clock. Just mind you've spoken to James before then."

"All right, all right!" Peter cried, looking quite alarmed and raising his polish-blackened fingers on either side of him like a criminal in surrender. "I won't go looking for you! I can see I'm going to be the one taking orders around here."

"If you were content to take orders, we wouldn't be in this mess," Eliza retorted, but she couldn't help giving him just a shadow of a smile, and she saw him register it blankly as she turned to leave the room. What had gotten into her?

243

Bridie seemed to be avoiding her, which was all well and good, as far as Eliza was concerned, because she dreaded the prospect of admitting she'd read the book, and even more so the revelation of what she had found within its pages. Because if one thing had become clear to Eliza it was that Bridie had more right than most to know what Elder Pratt had documented for his privileged inner circle of brethren, and that she would not be able to keep the information to herself if Bridie asked her for it in earnest. It was a blessing then that, at that moment anyway, Bridie appeared to want to put as much distance as she could between herself and the book. And so it was without any further discussion of the book that Eliza was able to slip away upstairs to attend to Miss Jessamine.

She was surprised, upon opening the door, to see Jessamine sitting by her window rather than lying in bed. Indeed, upon closer examination, the bed looked hardly to have been slept in. Eliza closed the door behind her and cleared her throat gently to announce her presence, but Jessamine did not acknowledge her, so she cleared it again.

"Miss Jessamine? Good morning," she said, trying to put a smile in her voice.

Jessamine started and twisted around in her chair. Her face was pale and drawn, and there were deep circles under her eyes. "Eliza! You startled me."

"I do apologize, miss. I did try to announce myself."

"No, I'm sorry. It's not your fault. I do believe I'm in another world this morning," Jessamine said with a sigh.

Eliza approached the window, from which Jessamine had already pulled back the drapes, and her stomach dropped. From Jessamine's window was an unimpeded view of the burnt-out shell of the garage, its message still starkly visible even under all the soot. Quickly, she pulled the curtains shut.

"That view isn't likely to brighten your day, miss, if you don't mind me saying," Eliza said, trying to sound robustly cheerful, but ruining the effect slightly with the tremor in her voice.

"No, it certainly isn't. But I don't think I'm in any sort of humor to have my day brightened. Honestly, today I think I'd just rather be blue," Jessamine sighed. "Haven't you ever had a day like that, Eliza? A day where you just couldn't bear to be cheered up? A day when you'd much prefer to wallow?"

244

Eliza looked at her mistress' stricken face, her red-rimmed eyes, and felt a lump rise in her throat. It took her several seconds to swallow it back before she could reply. "I've had days when I needed a good cry, miss, if that's what you're getting at."

"Yes, that's precisely what I'm getting at. I simply can't bear to have anyone tell me that things are sunny or that they'll get better if only I put on a happy face. Is that all right?"

"I reckon it's all right for a day, miss, if that's what you want, but not any longer than that," Eliza said, rather sternly. Then an envelope on the dressing table caught her eye. "Would you like to read your letter?"

Jessamine cast a forlorn look at the envelope, winced, and then looked away again, as though the sight of it caused her physical pain. "No."

"No? But why—"

"It's from Teddy. I can't do it, Eliza. I can't bear to read his excuses. I just can't. Not today."

Eliza bit her lip, then marched forward, opened a silver box on the dressing table and shut the letter inside it with a snap. "There you are, then. If you're not ready to read it, there's no point in letting it stare at you all day. You have no engagements today—no functions to attend. Do you want me to get you dressed?"

Jessamine shook her head, staring blankly at the expanse of closed curtains.

"Would you like me to call for the breakfast tray?"

Another shake of the head.

"How about just a nice hot cup of tea?"

And again.

Eliza had never felt so helpless in her mistress' presence, so at a loss for how to help her. "Isn't... isn't there anything I can do for you, miss? Draw you a bath? Brush your hair, perhaps?" She started forward for the hairbrush, but Jessamine's hand shot forward, snatching up the brush before Eliza could touch it.

"No!" she cried, before composing herself and continuing in a quiet voice. "No thank you, Eliza. I know you are only trying to help, but I need to be sure that my thoughts and feelings are my own today."

Eliza could feel a burning sensation in the corners of her eyes, and she knew she was dangerously close to tears. She struggled to master herself, to smile and nod as she replied. "Of course, miss. I understand. Shall I just come to check on you later?"

"Yes, Eliza, that will do just fine," Jessamine said, and returned to her state of blank preoccupation.

Eliza barely made it out of the room and closed the door behind her when the tears sprang into her eyes. She felt as though the walls were closing in around her. Jessamine didn't want Eliza near her—didn't want Eliza to use her Riftmagic on her anymore. And honestly, thought Eliza ruefully, who could blame her after the previous night's events?

"For all she tried to reassure me last night, she probably never wants to see me again," Eliza whispered to herself, and she felt as though her lungs had collapsed, as though her legs had turned to water. What was she—who was she—if not a lady's maid? What purpose could she have without a mistress to serve after a lifetime of preparing to do so?

A sudden distant sound of wailing startled her out of her miserable musings. The sounds came from upstairs, and there was little doubt as to who had made them. It seemed the pall that had settled over the whole household had affected its most fragile occupant as well. Eliza wiped the tears from her cheeks and started toward the door that led to the upper staircase. If Mrs. Hallewell had been out of sorts for very long, Mrs. Spratt might be grateful for an extra pair of hands, and as her own charge wanted nothing to do with her...

She brushed the thought away, along with a fresh wave of tears, and reached for the doorknob. She had barely turned it when the door burst open, sending her gasping and tumbling to the floor.

"What the devil...?"

Eliza looked up to see Elder Hallewell standing framed in the doorway looking like a man possessed. His hair was disheveled and his eyes were wild with something dark and consuming—grief, perhaps? He was wearing his official Elder garb, but his sash had been torn, and his robe was askew. He stared down at Eliza for several seconds before it seemed that he registered who she was.

"Eliza?"

Eliza scrambled to her feet, frantically straightening her cap and smoothing out her uniform.

"I... h-hello, Elder Hallewell, sir," she stammered, flustered beyond the ability to think. Out of sheer muscle memory, her body contracted itself into a deep curtsy. Once looking at her own feet, Eliza found it almost impossible to raise her eyes again.

"I'm sorry I... are you quite all right?"

"Yes, sir," Eliza breathed. "I'm sorry I startled you, sir."

Elder Hallewell gave a bark of a laugh, running his hands through his already tousled hair. "I think it's safe to say we startled each other. I was visiting with Mrs. Hallewell." His eyes narrowed. "What are you doing here?"

"I was just leaving Miss Jessamine's room when I heard... a disturbance upstairs. I was making my way up to see if Mrs. Spratt needed my assistance," Eliza said. Her heart was hammering so hard that it felt as though it were thudding its way right up into her throat.

"Are you crying?" He asked the question with the air of a man who had never before considered the possibility that a servant could cry. His head was cocked to one side as he observed her.

Eliza very nearly allowed the word "No" to escape her lips, but stifled it. It would be a demonstrable lie to say so, and the last thing she wanted was for the master of the house to think her capable of lying, especially now. She raised her eyes and forced herself to look at him. "Yes, sir."

"Are you hurt?"

"No, sir. I just... I was pulling the blinds in Miss Jessamine's room just now, and saw the state of the garage outside. It's so terrible, what happened last night."

Elder Hallewell's face cleared, and he nodded his head solemnly. "Ah, yes. Yes, naturally it would make you upset to see such a thing, a faithful girl such as yourself. You mustn't worry yourself, though. The culprits will be caught and hanged, I have no doubt. Such a flagrant misdeed against an Elder cannot stand."

"Yes, sir," Eliza replied breathlessly, praying she would be able to hold herself together in his presence. Her mind flew to her room, to the book she had stolen, now hidden once again under her mattress. Had he realized yet it was missing?

"How is my daughter this morning? I had thought about looking in on her..." Elder Hallewell's voice trailed away, and his arm swung awkwardly at his side. It seemed the thought of "looking in" frightened him rather more than it appealed to him.

Eliza made a show of wiping the tears from her face with her apron while she tried desperately to think how to respond—to spare

Jessamine the trauma of seeing the man who had bargained away her future happiness while also ensuring that Elder Hallewell did not feel slighted. "That's a kindly thought, sir, and no doubt Miss Jessamine would be glad to see you, but she's had such an ordeal, sir. She's not yet risen from her bed, nor dressed for the day. The shock of the night's events, you understand. I'm not sure her constitution has quite recovered from it. I don't reckon she'll be up for visitors today, though I'd be happy to announce you just the same, if it's your wish to look in on her."

She gestured for him to follow her back down the hallway toward Jessamine's room, but Elder Hallewell raised his hand to stop her, and it could not have been clearer from the expression on his face that he was nothing short of relieved to have the excuse that Eliza had presented him. "No, please do not disturb her. Of course, I should have realized—a delicate feminine constitution is bound to be much troubled by such things. I trust you'll see to her throughout the day—make sure she has everything she needs?"

"Of course, sir, as always," Eliza replied with another curtsy.

"Very good, very good," Elder Hallewell replied. A strange shadow passed over his face, and when he next spoke, he hardly seemed to remember that Eliza was standing right there in front of him. "Even my wife, in the dream world where she resides, is troubled by the night's events. It should come as no surprise that Jessamine is similarly... well, as I say, feminine constitutions are delicate and easily disturbed."

"Yes sir," Eliza replied, though her mouth was reluctant to wrap itself around the words. A feeling dangerously close to resentment was welling up inside her, threatening to reveal itself in her expression or her tone. To hear Jessamine be called weak, after all that she had endured the previous night... Eliza was quite heady with anger. Thankfully, Elder Hallewell was as oblivious to this as he seemed to be to everything else involving his daughter. He gave an awkward sort of nod to Eliza and strode off down the hallway toward the staircase and out of sight. Eliza watched him go, and realizing that all was now quiet above, made her solitary way back down to the servants' quarters.

§

"I must be out of my bloody mind," James Whippet muttered. He stood shaking his head as he rolled a cigarette for himself.

"I'll admit, I'm having doubts about my own sanity as well," Eliza replied tartly.

It was well after midnight, and the house had settled into silence. With Miss Jessamine shut up in her room, only grudgingly taking some tea and a bit of toast at dinnertime, Eliza had had very little to keep herself occupied throughout the day. And so when she tracked Peter down in the middle of the day, it was with a sense of relief that she learned that he had spoken with James, who had agreed to help. That relief was slipping away now as the deepening darkness swallowed the grounds, and Eliza was left only with a growing fear in the pit of her stomach.

"I don't suppose you're going to tell me why I'm risking my neck to bring you to Turner?" James asked, scratching at a pimple on his chin.

"No, I don't suppose I am," Eliza said stiffly. "My business with him is my affair."

"Seems to me it's my affair now, too, seeing as I've agreed to help you," James countered.

"Your affair is to keep yourself out of the Praeteritum," Eliza snapped. "You mind your affairs, I'll mind mine, and we'll get along just fine."

James appeared to be chewing on his tongue, but he did not reply. He turned to Peter. "You sure about this?" he asked, cocking his head in Eliza's direction.

"No, but what choice do we have?" Peter said. Then, in answer to Eliza's glare, he added, "Look, she's kept her mouth shut so far. It would have been a simple thing just to turn me in."

James took a last drag on his cigarette and flicked it into the nearby water trough, where it extinguished with a sharp hiss. "All right, then. Let's get this over with. He glanced down at the basket Eliza had clutched in the crook of her arm and smirked. "D'you fancy we might stop for a jolly little picnic or something?"

Eliza pulled the basket more tightly to herself and ignored the remark. "When are we leaving?"

"Now, so long as the coast is clear out on the road. You ever ridden a horse before?"

Eliza blanched. She had ridden a horse only a handful of times, and none of them had been pleasant. The creatures seemed to be able to sense her fear and rarely if ever obeyed her feeble attempts at commands. "Is it not possible to take a carriage?" she asked.

"Not unless you want to be caught," James replied with a snort. "The front gates are too conspicuous from the house, and there's no other route we can sneak a carriage out without causing a fearful racket. But a horse can jump the back border hedge quiet as you please."

"Jump?" Eliza asked, her voice weak.

"That's right," James said. The fear in her tone caused his smirk to broaden into a grin. His teeth were stained yellow from tobacco. "You sure you still want to go?"

Eliza took a deep breath and pulled her cloak around her. "Lead the way, Mr. Whippet, before I lose what precious little's left of my nerve."

Peter remained outside the barn as a lookout, ensuring the yard was empty as James saddled one of the quarter horses, a chestnut who kept tossing his head and snorting at the indignity of being woken in the middle of the night. Eliza's fear must have shown on her face because James laughed at her as he fitted the bridle. "No need to look like that. We're going on the same horse. I'll do all the riding, you just hang on, nice and cozy like."

He winked at her and Eliza felt her stomach roll over. She was starting to wonder if she ought to just take her chances with her own horse. She might be thrown to her death, that was true enough, but at least she could avoid James' leers. Before she could question it much further, James had swung himself up into the saddle and reached a hand down to help her clamber up behind him. With no choice but to hang on to him for dear life, she adjusted her basket, wrapped her arms tightly around his waist, and braced herself. James urged the horse to the door of the barn and waited. At the sound of Peter's signal—three loud hooting noises—James dug his heels into the horse's flank and it took off at a speed that sucked the breath from Eliza's lungs and forced her eyes shut. All worries of propriety forgotten, she pressed her face tightly between James' shoulder blades, squeezed her legs against the sides of the horse, and whispered a prayer under her breath.

250

The horse surged through the grounds, James keeping him close to the treeline. The hoofbeats pounded through every muscle of Eliza's body, and she thought surely each one must be as loud as cannon fire, but no lights appeared in the windows, no figures rushed out into the yard to investigate the ruckus. The cool night air stung her skin and threatened to tear the cap from her head—the pins that secured it there felt as though they were being wrenched from her scalp. The shadowy shape of the border hedge loomed ahead of them under an inky, star-strewn sky.

"Here we go! Brace yourself!" James told her, just in time for her to cling desperately to his coat as the horse launched itself upward, soaring over the hedge and landing with a clatter on the other side in an open field. From there, Eliza could see the narrow ribbon of the road with which they would be able to meet up once they were out of sight of Larkspur Manor. She heaved a sigh of relief and pulled herself back from James, determined to put as much space between them as she could without risking slipping off the horse's rump.

"Where are we going now?" Eliza asked him.

"To the Barrens first, for your guide."

"My guide?"

"You'll see."

The ride into the city took much less time than ever it had in the carriage, and much sooner than Eliza expected, the city rose up around them. James slowed the horse to a trot as the cobblestones began to replace the dirt roads, but pulled him to a complete stop when they were at the border of the Barrens.

"We walk from here," James muttered, swinging out of the saddle and lifting Eliza down. "There's no sense in drawing unnecessary attention to ourselves, not with a curfew on."

"Aren't you worried we'll get caught by one of the patrols?" Eliza whispered.

"Not at this end of the city, no," James said, tying up the horse. "The patrols have been concentrated in the areas where the Barrens border the Dignus-inhabited districts of the city—trying to keep all the Riftborn in their place, you understand. They aren't much concerned with the outskirts of the city. But you'll have to tread very carefully indeed once you get closer to the Market District, so that's why you need Colin. He's the best hope you've got. Come on."

James didn't elaborate, and Eliza didn't have the breath for more questions as they rushed from one darkened alleyway to the next, avoiding the vagrants and drunkards for whom curfew was little more than a vague and passing suggestion. Eliza clutched the basket she was carrying so tightly that her fingers had begun to go numb, but she did not loosen her grip; she was terrified that someone would discover what was concealed within it.

Just when she thought she must surely ask James to stop so that she could catch her breath and tend to the searing stitch in her side, he stopped short in front of a grubby row of tenement houses.

"You wait here. Don't talk to anyone," James hissed, then left her, alone and breathless, on the street corner as he approached the third house in the row. Eliza stood shivering on the cobbles, her cloak pulled tightly around her, her eyes darting wildly around at every sound. It was so dark on this road that she could barely make out James' figure on the doorstep. As she squinted, anxious not to lose sight of him, she heard his knock upon the door, the creaking as it was opened, the low murmur of voices in conversation. Then the door closed again, and there was silence, broken only by the howl of someone's dog, and a violent coughing fit from a window overhead.

A few moments later, James' shuffling footsteps began again, and he appeared out of the gloom walking back toward her. He had his hands in his pockets and he was grinning again.

"Well? Did you find Colin? Will he help me?" Eliza asked.

James grinned more broadly. "You can ask him yourself."

Eliza felt her patience waning under the crushing weight of her ever-sharpening anxiety. "What are you talking about? I can't talk to someone who isn't here. And will you wipe that ridiculous grin off your face?! I see nothing here to smile ab—"

The rest of Eliza's lecture was lost to a soft scream which she had to stifle quickly with the hem of her cloak. Even as she watched, the darkness behind James rippled strangely, and a boy emerged as though he had pulled the night right over him like a blanket he was now peeling away.

"I'm Colin Webb, miss, at your service," the boy said, his eyes twinkling at the look of shock on her face. It could not have been clearer he was rather pleased with himself for startling her.

"I... I don't... how did you—" Eliza's voice died away as understanding hit her. "You... you can Manipulate darkness?"

"That's right, miss," Colin said with a little bow.

252

Eliza hardly knew what to say. She'd never before met a Manipulator whose magic worked in such a way—never even knew it was possible. She stared down at the little boy in wonder, even as he fidgeted with his fingers, tugging a shadow closer to him and then casting it away again, the way a normal child might play with a ball or a piece of string.

"That's the first reason you need Colin," James said, reaching down and ruffling the boy's hair. "He's the only one who can get you to Eli undetected with the patrols out."

"What's the other reason?" Eliza asked, still staring, awestruck, as Colin played with the shadows.

"He's one of the only people who knows where Eli lives," James said with a shrug. "Eli doesn't give out his address—he'd be a damn fool if he did. But he's set up a few ways to get in touch with him, and Colin is the most reliable of them all."

Eliza smiled down at Colin. "Sounds like you are quite the important chap, eh?"

Colin threw out his chest. "I'm doin' my bit, miss."

"So you'll need to hang around to collect her when she's finished at Turner's place," James said to Colin. Then he turned to Eliza. "How long do you expect you'll be?"

Eliza blinked. "I... um... I'm not sure. Not... not long." She'd been so intent on setting out to find Eli that she hadn't considered for even a moment what she would say to him when she arrived. She only knew she needed him to see the book, to know that she understood now about Davies. She was full of a thousand questions she was not even sure she dared ask, but she knew he was the one to answer them if she did.

James was chewing his tongue again, clearly aggravated at her for her vagueness. "Right, then. Well, as I said, hang around until she's done, and bring her back here. You got that?"

Colin looked Eliza up and down, as though he were sizing her up. It was an extremely odd expression to see on a child's face, and it made Eliza feel, for a moment, like the child. "How do you know we can trust her?" he asked. "She ain't the usual type we got in the ranks, is she?"

James gave a derisive chuckle that made Eliza blush. "You're right there, lad, she ain't. But she says Eli knows her, and she's kept her mouth shut about the Larkspur Manor job, so I reckon we've got no choice but to trust her."

Colin still looked dubious. Eliza fumbled for a moment for something she might say to reassure him, but before she could seize upon a single word, the boy had shrugged, turned, and doffed his cap to James. "I'll take her, as you say, Mr. Whippet, but I ain't takin' the fall for her, that's sure and certain."

"That's a good lad, and don't worry your head. If anyone's taking the fall for her, it'll be Peter Bennett. He's the one got us into this mess," James replied.

Colin nodded, then cocked his head over his shoulder. "Right then, miss. This way, and keep close to me, or I can't do nothin' to hide you."

"I... thank you, Colin. James, I'll see you back here as quickly as I can manage," Eliza said.

"See that you do," James said. "I can only wait until four. After that, we'll be cutting it too fine to get back to Larkspur Manor before the house wakes up. I promised to bring you here, but I'll not risk getting caught for anything, not with the Praesidio sniffing around questioning folks."

Eliza nodded curtly. "I'll not keep you that long. I assure you, I do not want to be caught either."

James touched his cap and stepped back for Eliza to pass. Colin waited just long enough to be sure she was behind him.

"Grab a hold of my vest, miss, and keep up," he said, and then took off toward the nearest alleyway at a pace that soon left Eliza breathless yet again.

The gas lamps in the Barrens were few and far between, and many of them were smashed or damaged. This suited their purposes just fine, however, as they were keen not to be seen, and the darkness gave Colin all the shadowy material he needed to work. Eliza stumbled along behind him as he slipped from shadowy place to shadowy place, wrapping them in the darkness as he went. Eliza could see almost nothing, even her own hand stretched out in front of her, clutching like mad to Colin so that she would not lose him. She wondered if Colin could see better than she could, or if he was simply so familiar with the narrow passages and darkened corners of the Barrens that he could traverse them blind.

They'd gone perhaps ten blocks when they encountered their first patrol. Colin stopped suddenly, causing Eliza to lose her footing and stumble into his back. He shot out a hand and pushed her backward so that they were both pressed against the wall of a soot-blackened brick building. Then, with a motion like drawing a curtain, he gathered the deepest darkness from the corners and crevices around them and draped it over them. Although it was weightless, Eliza could still feel it, a sort of tingling of energy or buzzing of natural things disturbed. She held her breath. Although she could not see the guards anymore, she could hear them passing mere feet from where they stood. Their boots pounded. One of them spat upon the ground. Another coughed loudly and muttered something about "...filthy vagrants... ought to be allowed to shoot them on sight." It was not until their footsteps had died away completely that Colin released his hold on the shadows and they retreated to the places from which he had gathered them, leaving him and Eliza free to travel once again.

"Your Riftmagic is remarkable, Colin," Eliza whispered as they resumed their traversing of the streets. "I've never seen anything like it."

"Thank you, miss," Colin replied.

"You needn't call me miss," Eliza told him. "My name is Eliza."

"Me mam told me to call anyone as clean as you, 'miss,'" Colin replied promptly.

Eliza smothered a laugh. "Well, I wouldn't want you to disobey your mother."

"Too right you don't," Colin said ruefully. "I couldn't sit me arse down proper for a week if she ever heard me using your given name."

"Do you mind if I ask you another question about your Riftmagic?" Eliza ventured.

"Don't much mind, miss, so long's you keep your voice down," Colin said good-naturedly.

"It's so well developed. I mean to say, you have excellent control over it. And it doesn't seem to tire you at all, using it. How can that be?"

Colin shrugged. "Ever since I stopped drinking the Riftmead, it's been easy as whistling."

Eliza stopped short, tugging Colin back as she did so. "Since you... what?"

"Stopped drinking the Riftmead," Colin repeated. "I reckon Eli's told you all about that, if you're so familiar with him as to visit his house."

"I... I'm afraid not," Eliza replied. "Why would you stop drinking Riftmead?"

Colin looked suddenly wary. "I'd better not say anything else, miss. It's not my place."

"But what do you—" Eliza began, but Colin shushed her at the sound of a second patrol approaching.

There was no more opportunity to talk now that they had reached the border of the Market District. Patrols were plentiful, and it was all they could do to keep moving, even with Colin's prodigious gift for keeping them concealed. It took every ounce of their concentration to slip through undetected, and only when they had emerged into the neat, well-kept streets of the Commons did Colin finally dare to utter another word to her.

"We're nearly there. It's right up here, that one there, with the blue door."

Eliza let her gaze follow his gesture and found herself looking at a perfectly respectable dwelling with neatly trimmed hedges on either side of the stairs and a single light burning in an upstairs window. She wasn't sure what she had expected, descending upon the dwelling of a shadowy resistance leader in the middle of the night, but this tame, respectable-looking domicile certainly wasn't it. Wasn't she supposed to sidle up to a door cleverly concealed behind a fence and whisper a secret code word to a pair of suspiciously narrowed eyes glaring at her through a tiny opening before being whisked into the most seedy and clandestine of hideouts? If she hadn't been so shocked, she might even have been mildly disappointed.

"Go on, then," Colin said, ushering her forward.

"What? Aren't... aren't you coming with me?" Eliza asked.

Colin shook his head. "I don't let meself get spotted here. It would look too suspicious, see, a Barrens urchin like me visiting a house in the Commons."

"But what do I do?" Eliza asked, ashamed to hear the note of panic in her voice.

Colin chuckled. "Just walk up the front steps and knock on the door, miss," he replied, shrugging. "Ain't any more to it than that."

TWENTY-ONE

ELI STARED DOWN at the white-faced figure on his doorstep and his mouth fell open.

"Eliza? How did you... what are you...?" The questions swirled and tossed like stormy waves in his head but wouldn't form on his tongue.

"Please let me in, before someone sees me," Eliza whispered, an edge of terror in her voice. She was wrapped in a long, thick black cloak and carried a small basket over her arm.

Automatically, because he did not dare refuse the request of any person who looked so wholly and desperately frightened, he stepped back into the hallway and ushered her inside. He glanced up and down the street and thought he caught a glimpse of a slight figure melting into the shadows at the end of the block. Colin.

He closed the door swiftly behind them, shutting out the dark of the night and leaving them both huddled together in the half-light of the entrance hallway, lit only by the candle Eli had carried from the drawing room, now clutched in his hand.

"How did you know how to find me?" Eli asked, still staring down at Eliza as though she were an apparition. He had been so sure he would never see her again after he'd rescued her in the Barrens, sure she'd stay far away.

"I didn't know," she admitted, dropping her gaze so that her wide grey eyes were hidden beneath a fringe of thick, black lashes. "I asked Peter Bennett and James Whippet to help me find you, and they led me to Colin, who agreed to bring me here."

Eli's pulse quickened. "Peter and James? But they weren't supposed to—"

"I didn't give them a choice. I discovered what they did—the fire at Larkspur Manor, and I forced them to help me find you," Eliza explained, still not looking at him.

Eli felt panic welling up inside him. "You discovered what they did? But who else—"

Eliza's face shot up and the look she gave him was fiercely resentful. "Nobody else knows! I told no one. And I helped Peter wash the paint out of his uniform, so I guess I'm an accomplice now as well."

Eli's relief was short-lived as he watched her eyes fill with tears. "Thank you for not turning him in. I'm grateful."

"I haven't decided yet whether I regret it," Eliza replied. "But it's done, and I won't betray their trust now, however foolish that decision might be."

"But why did you ask them to find me? Why are you here?" Eli asked.

Eliza bit her lip but did not answer. Her hands were twisting together, gloved fingers wound into tense knots.

"Eliza?"

Rather than offering him a reply, she reached into the basket she carried on her arm and began handing things to him—a jar of jam, half a loaf of bread, a glass jar of milk, an embroidered handkerchief.

"You came all this way in the middle of the night to invite me to a picnic?" Eli asked blankly, staring down at the items now piled in his arms.

Eliza looked sharply at him. "Of course not. But I couldn't risk it being found."

"Couldn't risk *what* being found?"

She ignored him, but dug around in the bottom of the basket and tugged out what appeared to be a piece of the basket itself, shoving it into Eli's already full hands, and he understood: the basket had a false bottom, and she had concealed something beneath it. But before he could ask what it was, she reached into the basket once more and pulled out a book. She stared down at it for a moment, as though steeling herself, and then held it out to him.

Eli looked down at the blank cover and then back up at her. "What is it?"

"It's about the Lamplighters Confederacy."

Eli's eyes went wide, and it was all he could do not to drop everything he was holding. He turned and deposited the entire lot upon a horsehair chair beside the hat stand, wiped his hands on his trousers, and reached out to take the book. It was slender and bound unpretentiously in fabric, not gold-gilded leather. He opened the cover with numb fingers and read the words upon the title page: "An Historical Account of the Downfall of the Lamplighters Confederacy."

He looked back at Eliza whose face was tense with fear, as though she could not believe what she had just done.

"How in the Creator's name did you get your hands on this?" Eli asked weakly.

Eliza hesitated, then said, "I found it in... at Larkspur Manor. You were right. Elder Hallewell was in possession of it."

"And you... you took it," Eli said. He couldn't believe it. He stared down at the pale face, the defiant eyes.

"I borrowed it. I intend to return it. It's more than my life's worth to keep it."

"But why? Why did you take it?"

The doubt in her face was arresting—it stole Eli's breath right out of his lungs.

"I don't know. I... just had to know. I had to understand."

He nodded. "Knowledge is power."

She frowned. "I don't seek power."

"But you do not want to be powerless."

She considered this. "No."

Neither of them spoke. They both stared down at the book in his hands.

"Why have you brought this to me?" Eli asked suddenly.

Eliza gave a helpless bark of a laugh. "I don't know. I honestly don't know."

"You could have put it back," Eli suggested with the faintest trace of a smile.

Eliza's face fell. "No, I couldn't."

"You've read it?"

"Yes. From cover to cover."

"And?"

Eliza paused. "And I know how foolish this is. But I couldn't put it back in that drawer to be buried again. I couldn't bear to leave this in the dark."

Their eyes met, and Eli found something in them—fear? Honesty?—that settled his mind and made a decision for him.

"Come with me."

Eliza hesitated, her feet planted in the entranceway. "Where are we going?"

"To see Sully. She'll know what to do next."

Eli expected her to ask more questions, or perhaps to turn around right then and there and walk back out the door, but she didn't. She took a deep breath, regained what appeared to be a tenuous hold on her composure, and followed him into the house. He took her down the long hallway, and through the drawing room. He heard her gasp quietly and turned to see her gaping around at the walls, which were lined with bookshelves from floor to ceiling. Eli had grown used to being surrounded by books; they were piled on side tables, crammed onto stools, stacked in corners, and spread across surfaces, and so it took a moment for him to register the reason for her shock.

"Yes, we, uh… have a lot of books," Eli said rather lamely.

"But where did you get them all?"

"Sully is a book dealer."

Eliza's eyebrows disappeared under her cap. "A Riftborn book dealer? But that's illegal."

"Everything is legal if you're doing it for the people in charge," Eli replied.

"What do you…?"

"Sully translates and distributes texts for the Illustratum. She's the best there is. That's why she's allowed so many books."

"She… she works for the Elders?"

"Yes."

"But you…" She took a step back, looking suddenly fearful. "I thought you didn't trust the Illustratum."

"Oh, I assure you, I don't."

"Then why—"

"Have you ever heard the saying, 'keep your friends close, but your enemies closer?'"

She looked resentful for a moment, but it passed. "No."

"Well, it's a saying for a reason. By doing this work in plain sight for the Elders, she can conduct other work without attracting attention or suspicion. I assure you, she's very good at what she does," Eli added, for Eliza had that look again, like an animal scenting danger

260

and preparing to flee. "If she weren't, she'd already be swinging from the gallows."

Eliza cringed but seemed to relax slightly. "I suppose there's some little comfort in that."

"We take it where we can find it," Eli said with a sad smile, before turning and continuing through the drawing room and through a second, narrower hall that led to a staircase down to the basement. He could hear Eliza right on his heels, keeping close behind him.

Eli paused in front of a door behind which strange clacking and hissing sounds were issuing. "Now might be a good moment to warn you."

Eliza went pale. "Warn me about what? Surely there can't be anything more dangerous waiting for me on the other side of that door than what I've already undertaken tonight?"

Eli smiled grimly. "Not more dangerous for *you*, no. My own safety is another matter."

"You're scaring me now."

Eli allowed his smile to broaden. "I'm sorry. What I mean to say is that Sully may seem a bit hostile that I've brought you to see her, but you must understand that it has nothing to do with you. It's me—I told her I wouldn't speak with you again, and I've broken that promise."

Whatever Eliza had expected him to say, it clearly wasn't that.

"Not speak to me again? Why ever not?"

"Because she wasn't sure if you could be trusted."

Eliza snorted incredulously. "*Me*, the one who can't be trusted? You were running from the Praesidio when we first met, and I'm fairly confident you had something to do with blowing up a building at Larkspur Manor two nights ago. How am *I* the untrustworthy one in this scenario?"

Eli laughed gently. "I think I'll let her explain." And with a deep breath, he knocked upon the door. The sounds within the room ceased and a sharp voice snapped. "What the devil is it at this hour?"

Eli took this as an invitation to enter and pushed the door open. Sully stood next to a work table scattered with bookbinding materials, her leather apron covered in inky streaks and blotches. She removed a glove and brushed several tendrils of hair out of her face before pushing her glasses up her nose and squinting at Eli.

"Eli, what are you—" she stopped speaking at once as her eyes focused on Eliza standing nervously in the doorway behind him.

Her face, momentarily slack with surprise, hardened into a mask of wariness.

"That better not be who I think it is," she said without preamble.

"Miss Lila Sullivan, I would like you to meet Miss Eliza Braxton," Eli said slowly, gesturing between the two women. Eliza dipped quickly into a polite curtsy, but Sully, her face flushing with anger, removed her other glove and threw them both onto the wooden tabletop behind her.

"Eli, you bloody fool, what have you done?" she hissed.

Eli took another step into the room. "Sully, it's not what you think. I didn't bring her here. She just showed up. I was as surprised as you are to see her here."

"Somehow I very much doubt that," Sully exclaimed. "You can't possibly expect me to believe that you kept your word to me after you met the girl, when you swore you'd forget about her entirely."

"Not... not exactly, no," Eli said. "But it's not as bad as you think..."

"It's exactly as bad as I think!" Sully began to shout. "She's standing in my house, Eli! What the devil is she doing in my house? How did she find it? How did she find *you?*"

Eli glanced over at Eliza, who was frozen upon the threshold, watching the argument escalate with mounting horror upon her countenance.

"I've just told you, I didn't invite her here!" Eli repeated, endeavoring to keep his voice as calm as possible even as Sully's anger expanded until it seemed to suck all the air from the room.

"Well, then someone had better explain to me how—"

"It was my idea." Eliza's cracked squeak of a voice rang out shrilly, causing both Eli and Sully to turn to her in surprise. "I... I forced Peter Bennett to help me find you."

Sully narrowed her eyes. "Peter Bennett doesn't have this address."

"No, but he and James Whippet knew how to find Colin Webb, and Colin knew where to find you," Eliza explained.

"Well, I'll be sure to give that boy a whipping when I see him next," Sully cried, throwing her hands up in exasperation. "Is there no one I can trust?"

"Please, you mustn't blame Colin either," Eliza burst out, stepping forward and then hastily back again, not daring to enter the room

262

without invitation. "I left him no choice. I had to find Eli. It was a matter of utmost importance."

"I see," Sully said, skepticism dripping from her voice like honey from the comb. "And what was so important that you felt obligated to risk all of our lives?"

Eliza threw a pointed look over at Eli, who started and remembered that he was the one holding the book. Swiftly, he held it out to Sully, who glared at it for a moment before wiping her sweaty palm on her sleeve and snatching it from his hand.

Eli watched her expression transform as she examined it, anger and contempt melted away by dawning comprehension at exactly what it was she held in her hands.

"Saints alive," she whispered, thumbing through the pages. She looked up at Eliza, every trace of fury gone. "Where did you find this?"

Eliza cast another anxious glance at Eli, who nodded encouragingly for her to continue. "In Elder Hallewell's study at Larkspur Manor."

"You stole it?"

"I... I borrowed it." She drew herself up defensively. "And I mean to return it. I am not a thief."

Sully turned the book over, examining the spine, the fabric covers, the pages within. "I don't think anyone will care what your intention was. This is official Illustratum property, printed and bound for their personal library. It's likely the only copy that exists. You see, it's got the Council seal on the inside back cover."

Her eyes were aglow at this realization, but Eliza looked quite ill. She swayed on the spot and clutched at the doorway to steady herself. "I... I think I might need to... could I please sit down?"

Sully was still absorbed in the book, but Eli rushed forward and offered her an arm, which she clutched tightly as he guided her through the door and onto a straight-backed wooden chair in the corner.

"Thank you," Eliza whispered.

"Are you all right?" he asked her. "You're looking peaky."

"I've just discovered that I absconded with a rather priceless artifact from my master's study. I will admit that I've been better."

The corner of her mouth managed a tiny twitch of humor. Eli laughed aloud.

The sound snapped Sully out of her reverie. She looked at Eliza and held the book up. "And why have you brought this here?"

Eliza shrugged. "I... I don't know. I guess I wanted to show Mr. Turner here that he was correct when he told me the answers to my questions were right under the same roof."

Sully looked sharply at Eli, who sobered up at once. "You disobeyed me?" she asked.

Eli stiffened at the word—he was not a child, after all, though Sully would argue he had behaved like one. "I did," he admitted, raising his chin. "I do not regret it. I took a chance, I warrant you, but here she is."

"Here she is, indeed, and who's to say she wasn't followed?"

Eli scoffed. "Colin brought her here. You know damn well she wasn't followed."

"All right then, who's to say she won't turn us in at the first opportunity?" Sully pressed, undeterred.

Eli opened his mouth, but it was Eliza who spoke up in her own defense.

"I'm not turning anyone in," she insisted, and though her voice was still weak from her moment of dizziness, there was an edge of defiance to it. "If I'd wanted to turn Mr. Turner in, I'd have been quite capable of it in the very first moments I met him. I could have turned Peter Bennett in as well. I'm the one who's taken the book. I'm the one to blame, if blame is to be cast. I certainly didn't come here to bring trouble to anyone else."

Sully eyed her anew. "You've really got no idea what you've stumbled your way into, Miss Braxton, have you?"

Eliza looked as though she would have liked nothing better than to supply a different answer. "No. I'm afraid I don't."

"Then why are you here, Miss Braxton? What is it you want?"

Eli was sure for a moment that the girl was fighting back tears, but when she answered, there was no trace of tears in her voice. "The truth. I want the truth."

For the first time since she'd set eyes on Eliza, the open hostility faded from Sully's expression. "Well, you'll find a damn sight more of that here than you will at Larkspur Manor, so I reckon you've come to the right place after all."

Eli released a breath he didn't realize he was holding as Sully heaved a sigh, tossed her glasses onto the tabletop beside her, and sank down onto a rickety stool.

"All right, Miss Braxton. You're here, and there's sod all I can do about it. You want the truth? Go on, then. I imagine you have questions."

Eliza's eyes widened. "You... you mean I can ask you whatever I'd like?"

Sully laughed, a sharp, dry bark of a laugh that was nevertheless amused. "Oh, you can ask what you'd like. And I'll answer what I'd like."

Eliza licked her lips, and it was clear from her expression that she was casting around in her head for her first question. It burst from her before she had quite decided how to express it.

"Is it true?"

Sully narrowed her eyes. "Is what true?"

"What it says in the book... about the Riftborn children."

Sully cast an exasperated look at Eli, who smiled gently. "I'm afraid you'll have to be more specific. We haven't yet had the privilege of reading it."

"It says that Riftborn children are sometimes born to Dignus families."

"Yes, that is true," Eli confirmed.

"Why have I never known that could happen?"

"Because they do not want us to know it," Sully said. "To admit that they can produce a Riftborn child is like admitting some kind of weakness within themselves. They will never acknowledge it publicly, you can be sure of that."

"How do I know you're telling the truth?" Eliza asked.

"You don't," Sully admitted freely. "But you certainly don't need to take my word for it. An Illustratum Elder wrote the book, Miss Braxton. If you don't want to place your faith in me, place your faith in him."

"Faith is a subject I'd prefer not to discuss at present," Eliza replied, her cheeks flushing.

"What else do you want to know?" Sully asked.

Eliza squirmed a little in her seat, her blush deepening. "It's a question for Mr. Turner, really."

"I've told you, I'd prefer Eli to Mr. Turner," Eli replied.

If Eliza heard his request, she ignored it. She met Eli's eyes and said, "Mr. Turner, you told me, when last we met in the Barrens, that John Davies saved your life."

Eli threw a quick glance at Sully before answering. After all, it wasn't only his story to tell. "I did."

"Well, I just wondered... if you meant that... that is to say... are you one of the Riftborn children born to a Dignus family that he helped to rescue?"

She asked the question with a quiet breathlessness, and it was clear she had been wanting to ask it from the moment she'd seen him standing in the doorway.

"Yes. I was," Eli said quietly. "If John Davies hadn't organized the Lamplighters Confederacy, I would likely have been abandoned in an orphanage to be worked to death in a workhouse, or else killed before I could tie my own shoes."

Eliza shook her head in wordless horror. Eli found himself wondering what it must be like for her, watching her perception of the world crumble to dust. He had never harbored the illusions she had carried all her life, that the Illustratum was unassailable, a force for good in the world. He could actually see the wheels turning behind her eyes, see the desperate struggle to reconcile the world she knew with the world she was discovering. What a blow it would be, when she finally realized they could never coexist—that they were, in fact, illusion and reality.

"Their own children. I don't understand," Eliza whispered.

"They fear us. They fear our magic, and what we might be capable of," said another voice from the doorway. Eliza jumped right out of her chair and spun around. None of them had realized Jasper was standing in the doorway. But he wasn't even looking at her anymore. He was staring at Eli, his expression a mixture of pity and exasperation.

"A manor girl, Eli? Really?" he said with a snort. "And here I was, wondering if my taste in company at Madam Lavender's was foolish."

Eli felt the color rise in his face, but did his best to match Jasper's playful tone. "Far be it from me to do anything that might call your foolishness into question. Jasper Quinn, meet Eliza Braxton of Larkspur Manor."

Jasper spoke not a word of greeting, but merely raised an eyebrow in Eliza's direction before turning to Sully. "I can't imagine you authorized this."

266

Sully pursed her lips. "I did not," she replied.

"Well, shall I pull up a chair for the lecture, or am I the only one whose poor decisions meet with shouts and cursing around here?" Jasper asked, crossing his arms over his chest.

"Oh, there was shouting and cursing in abundance, I promise you. Before you call for another round, however amusing you might find it, you might like to have a look at this," Eli shot back, picking up the book from the table and tossing it to Jasper, who caught it instinctively.

"Go on," Eli encouraged him. "Have a proper look."

Jasper dropped his eyes to the book, turning it over in his hands before sighing and opening the cover. Eli watched his eyes grow wide and his mouth fall open despite his best efforts to remain unimpressed. When he looked back at Eliza again, it was with a renewed interest.

"You don't mean to tell me a manor girl—a *Hallewell* manor girl, of all people—actually stole this?"

"I didn't—" Eliza began hotly, but Eli cut her off.

"Took it from the master's study. Brought it here herself."

Jasper let out a low whistle, then turned to Sully. "So, what are we doing with it? We can't just sit on it."

"No," Sully agreed. "No, we certainly cannot. This is dangerous, but it's an opportunity that will not fall into our laps again. We have to think this through carefully."

It was only through a monumental effort that Jasper refrained from rolling his eyes. "Of course we do."

Sully ignored him and looked at Eliza now, with a gaze that Eli knew very well—a gaze that seemed capable of excavating from inside you the very deepest of your thoughts and feelings. Eliza squirmed under it now, and Eli did not envy her the experience.

"Eliza, this is your decision," Sully said, ignoring Jasper's groan of frustration from the doorway. "You are the one who brought this book to us. You must have had a purpose in doing so. What is it you want us to do with it?"

Eliza appeared, for a moment, paralyzed with horror at being asked to make a decision. It was as though she thought that, in putting the book into someone else's hands, she was absolved of further responsibility. Her eyes drifted from Sully's face to the book, however, and a shadow fell across her features. "I don't want this to be buried again. This proves that the Illustratum lied about the nature of

John Davies' crimes. It's not right, that he is known only as a criminal, when all he tried to do was save children's lives. It's not fair that his death has been buried."

Sully nodded encouragingly. "I agree."

"Can you… is there any way to… to tell people? Like you did with the notices? I know it's just one book, but…" Eliza's voice grew small and trailed off, as though she was embarrassed she'd even considered it.

Sully looked down at the book, her brow wrinkled in concentration. Then she looked up at Eliza and pointed behind her. "Jasper, pull that sheet up, will you?"

Jasper, his expression still dark, ambled out of the doorway and approached a great bulky shape in the corner, which was covered in a length of white fabric. With a flourish, he pulled the fabric off, revealing a large machine.

"Have you ever seen one of these before?" Sully asked, crossing the room to rest her hand upon it.

Eliza shook her head. "I'm afraid not."

"It's a printing press. Not a very fancy one, of course, nothing like the one the Illustratum's got to put out their notices and primers and whitewashed history books. But it's serviceable. If I get her moving, with all hands on deck, she could knock out two hundred copies of this book in a matter of days."

Eliza's eyes widened, and she looked at Eli, who nodded in confirmation.

"Does the Illustratum know you have it?" Eliza asked.

"No, indeed, they do not," Sully replied, "or I'd be a resident of the Praeteritum right now. I rebuilt it from scraps and smuggled parts. Took me the better part of five years to manage it."

"What… what do you intend to do with it?" Eliza asked.

"How much reading do you do, Eliza?" Sully asked, scratching her chin and leaving a streak of ink there.

Eliza fidgeted. "Not… not much at all. There's not a lot of time for reading, what with all my duties at the manor."

Sully nodded, as though this were the answer she expected. "And when you do read, what do you read?"

Eliza blinked, as though the question were a strange one. "Why, I read what anyone reads, I suppose. The Book of the Rift. My religious primers. My handbooks and devotionals. The poetry of the prophets. The occasional penny dreadful cautionary tale."

"And have you ever wondered why those are the only books available to you? Why you have never read a single text that has not been produced by and distributed by the Illustratum itself?"

Eliza did not answer. She was looking from Eli to Jasper to Sully, as though expecting one of them to answer it for her.

"Come with me. There's something I want you to see," Sully said, and she turned and walked abruptly out of the room.

Eliza threw a startled glance at Eli, who nodded and gestured for her to get up and follow. He allowed her to pass him, and then followed behind her, down the narrow hallway that led to Sully's sanctum sanctorum.

Sully stopped sharply just before the door and turned back to Eliza, who also halted at once, looking wary. Sully held up the book that Eliza had given her. "I'm accepting this as proof that you'll keep quiet about what's on the other side of this door. I'm trusting you, which is not a thing I have much practice with anymore. I am taking a chance on you, and that chance is our lives, do you understand me?"

Eliza was trembling from head to foot, but she nodded solemnly. "You have my word, Sull—um, Miss Sullivan."

One corner of Sully's mouth crooked into a smile. "A Braxton's word. Never thought I'd be taking that again."

"What do you—" Eliza began, but Sully had already turned and pushed the door open, and the sight on the other side of it dissolved the rest of Eliza's question into a gasp of wonder.

The room beyond was massive, covered floor to ceiling in bookshelves set into the walls and set up in rows, so that the only places to walk were down long, narrow alleys between shelves, each and every inch of which were crammed with books of every size, material, and description. Even Eli, who had first stumbled upon the room when he was six years old, could barely repress a shiver of awe every time he entered it. The very air seemed to tingle with the temptation of forbidden secrets.

"This is my great rebellion," Sully said, turning to look at Eliza, whose mouth was still hanging open. "Every book in this room is a crime."

"A crime?" Eliza repeated.

"Every one has been banned. Copies of them removed from libraries, routed out, and burned during the Awakening."

"Why?"

"Some of them depict a time before Riftmagic came to be—before the Illustratum came to power. Others come from other countries, where the Illustratum holds no sway at all, where life for the Riftborn is very different than it is here."

Eliza walked forward, as though an irresistible, invisible finger were beckoning her. She stopped before the first of the shelves, gazing at spine after spine, some labeled in English, others in languages she could not comprehend.

"The world before Riftmagic?" Eliza whispered. "But how can that be?"

"You know that the world far predates' the appearance of Riftmagic," Sully said. "You know this from your primers, and from the Book of the Rift itself. But do you know how long ago it was, that Riftmagic came to be?"

"You mean the Awakening. I... no, not exactly," Eliza said, surprising herself even as she said it. She cast her mind around, sifting mentally through all the religious texts she had read, all the lessons that had been ingrained in her. "I don't know exactly how long—I don't think the texts ever say. But it's been ages and ages."

"It has been eighty-seven years."

The girl tore her eyes from the books. "Only eighty-seven years? That... that can't be right."

"Eighty-seven years," Sully confirmed. "There are people alive today, in this very country, who can remember a time when there was no Riftmagic at all—when the Illustratum was merely a fringe religious sect on the outskirts of society, trying to gain a foothold in our culture and our politics." She turned to the shelves, walked along the far right wall, plucked a book from among its fellows, and held it out to Eliza.

"Here is a collection of correspondence from a member of our Parliament—that was what we called our government at the time. In it, he discusses the rise of the Illustratum, as they gained both prominence and power."

Eliza hesitated, then took the book, handling it as though it were made of glass.

"When Riftmagic first appeared in children, everyone was

terrified. They did not understand what was happening. Many thought it might be an illness, or have some sort of medical explanation. The greatest medical minds of the day were baffled. This book," and Sully lifted another down from the shelf, "documents their theories."

Eliza looked over at Eli, who nodded at her in silent encouragement to keep listening, though she looked pale and frightened.

"When science and logic and history could offer no explanations, the Illustratum swooped in and said they had the answer. They claimed a prophet—a prophet who had the ear of the Creator, and knew the truth."

"Yes. The Great Elder, Prophet of the Rift," Eliza said, with an air of great relief that she could seize upon this single scrap of familiar information.

"That's right," Sully said. "But what else do you know about him? What do you know of him before he told the world the Creator spoke to him?"

Eliza bit her lip. "Nothing." She knew nothing of him before his ascent to Prophet. "The Book of the Rift began with his words, as though there were nothing that had come before."

Again, Sully nodded, as though she had expected nothing less. "His name was William Tibbet. He was a powerful man. He had already used his pulpit in the growing Church of the Rift to win himself a seat in Parliament and was gaining followers everywhere. Citizens flocked to his speeches in droves to hear him preach about the dangers and sin of Riftmagic. He whipped their fear into terror, and then into rabid anger. This book recounts some of his early sermons, transcribed from his notes by one of his secretaries who later fled the church."

A third book was piled into Eliza's shaking hands.

"The people began to riot in the streets, demanding the Riftborn be rounded up and contained before they could infect any more of the population. This was how the city began to be divided up, first with the Praeteritum and then the sectioning off of the city's districts. The majority party in Parliament tried to quell the uprisings, but was met with resistance on all sides. The monarchy could not command the confidence of the people. There was a great upheaval, and coup, if you will, and Tibbet and his supporters wrested control of the government. The royal family fled to Scotland, and the Illustratum was formed as both the governmental and religious seat of power in the country. The royal family had it all documented for posterity. It took me nearly a decade to acquire a copy of it."

Another book upon the pile. Another blow to the girl's understanding of the world.

Sully gestured to the farthest wall. "A collection of books from all over the world—books conceived of and produced outside of the Illustratum's influence. Writers of great stories, philosophers, historians, poets. People who wrote what they knew of the world and of humanity, not what the Illustratum told them to be true."

Eli watched as Eliza wandered over to them, shifting the books to one arm so that she could reach out a tentative finger to run along their spines. "So many of them."

He followed in her wake as she walked along, taking in all the familiar names, names he had grown to know almost as friends during his many hours of wandering these shelves—devouring the words between the covers, losing himself in their magic: Byron, Keats, Shelley, Austen, Paine, Goldsmith, Moore, Wheatley, Rousseau, Voltaire, Goethe, Shakespeare, Wordsworth, Cervantes. He sometimes forgot how fortunate he was, that these names were not just a meaningless collection of letters to him, but keys that unlocked doors within himself that opened onto the wider world.

Sully remained quiet, allowing Eliza to wander the aisles. When she emerged at last, looking dazed, Sully cleared her throat. "These books are more than words. There is truth here, and humanity, and history. I have made it my life's work to ensure it has not been lost, that they survived the purging that came with the Awakening—as ironic a term as ever was wielded."

"What will you do with them?" Eliza breathed.

"Someday, I will find the means to scatter them like seeds to the wind. Until then, I will protect them. But I wanted you to see them—to understand the scope and purpose of what it is I do. And now, I make a proposition to you."

Eliza looked at Sully, all trace of awe dissolved in the sudden return of tension. "What proposition?"

"You don't want this information buried again," Sully said, holding up the book Eliza had brought. "Nor do I. In fact, I think we have an opportunity to distribute it, to spread the truth to as many people as possible. What do you think about that?"

272

Eliza bit her lip. "But don't... don't the people in the Barrens already know about Davies. I mean, they are in an uproar about his death, aren't they?"

"Oh, they know the name, sure enough. They know he was a Resistance leader. But you'd be amazed what fifteen years and a relentless campaign of propaganda and lies can do to the truth about a man. And you've got to remember, of all the things Davies did, the rescuing of Riftborn children was the most secret– it had to be, for everyone's safety. When Davies was arrested, the Illustratum charged him with murdering Dignus children. He was forced to publicly confess to it. And while some of us know the truth, the distribution of this book could change everything. It proves his greatest crime was naught but a fabrication, and it also proves that the Illustratum lied to the public about all of it. This book could turn the rumblings of discontent into a full-scale rebellion, and that's what we need. So, what say you?"

Eli was sure the girl was going to balk, to turn tail right then and there and flee the place. But to his relief, her face hardened and instead she replied, "How would we do it?"

"With my printing press, which you've already seen. If you would be willing to leave this book with me for, say, three days, I could have it reproduced in its entirety and ready to distribute among the Riftborn," Sully said.

"A few days? But what if Elder Hallewell finds out it's missing?" Eliza asked, a hysterical edge to her voice.

"What if he's already discovered it?" Jasper suggested. Eli turned to him, throwing him a disgusted look. Jasper raised his eyebrows innocently. "What? She risked taking it in the first place. She smuggled it out of the house. She brought it here. She's already accepted the possibility of being caught."

"Yes, but do you have to be a complete tosser about it?" Eli snapped at him.

"Two days," Sully countered. "I'll get it done in two days."

Eli grimaced. He knew that meant none of them would sleep for forty-eight hours.

"Two days? You're sure you could get it done?" Eliza asked, her hands twisting around the books in her arms.

"Yes," Sully replied. "I'm sure of it."

Eliza looked at the book again, then back at Sully's determined

273

face. "How do I know you'll return it to me? How do I know I can trust you?"

"We're the ones who ought to be asking you that question," Jasper said pointedly.

"She's got as much to lose as we have, Jasper," Eli said, rounding on him. "And maybe even more. Why don't you do us all a favor and shut your bloody trap."

But Eliza was ignoring Jasper. She had eyes only for Sully, and she was awaiting her reply.

"I'm giving those books to you," Sully said, pointing to the stack in Eliza's arms. "Read them or don't, it makes no difference to me. But as long as you have them, you've got leverage over me. The discovery of any one of those books will mean a noose around my neck."

Jasper swore under his breath. "And you lecture me about taking unnecessary risks!"

Sully ignored him. "When I've finished with the book, I'll arrange to have it sent back to you. Slip it right back into your master's study where you found it, and we'll all be in the clear."

"What do we do with the copies?" Jasper asked. "How are we going to get them out among the Riftborn in the Barrens?"

Sully frowned, looking bad-tempered. "I hadn't gotten as far as that, yet. I can assure you, though, we won't be affixing them to lampposts while running from the Praesidio guard. Anyway, that's our watch, not Miss Braxton's. As long as she agrees to my terms, she's free to go tonight."

Eli turned to Eliza, who was clutching Sully's books in her gloved hands and looking down at them as though they might explode. "What do you say, Eliza?" Eli asked.

Eliza met his gaze, and though her pupils were dilated with fear, her mouth was set in a grim, determined line. "Once I have the book back, and I return these to you, am I finished?"

Eli shrugged. "If you wish to be."

"I don't have to... to take any further part in your... your *activities?*" She spoke the word with such fear that Jasper snorted again. Eli ignored him.

"Of course not. You keep our secret, and we'll keep yours."

Eliza nodded slowly. "Very well."

"Eli, why don't you show our guest out," Sully said briskly.

"We've got quite a lot of work to do, all of a sudden. And Miss Braxton?"

"Yes?" Eliza replied, eyes snapping over to Sully.

"I thank you for the risk you took tonight. I know it must have been difficult for you. But you have done a great service to the Riftborn of this city, by uncovering this truth. I hope you will remember that."

"I... I will."

Sully pointed to the stack of books in her hand. "I hope you'll consider not just hiding those away while they're in your possession. If it's truth you're interested in, you'll find quite a bit more of it within those pages."

"Yes, I... that is, I'll consider it," Eliza said breathlessly, tucking the books into her basket.

"Come along," Eli told her. "I'll walk you out."

They spoke not a word all the way back to the front door. Once there, Eli handed Eliza back the food and other items from her basket, so that she could better hide the new and illegal contents she now carried.

Eliza settled the basket against her hip and inclined her head. "Well. Goodbye, then."

"Can... can I ask you something?" Eli asked tentatively.

Eliza looked wary, but nodded. "You can, although I do not promise I can answer it."

"Something's changed," Eli said. "Since that morning in the Barrens, something's changed in you, and I think it's down to more than what you read in a book. What is it?"

Eliza was silent, and Eli cursed himself for asking so personal a question. He watched her carefully; he could see her flexing her fingers beneath her white cotton gloves and remembered how, all those weeks ago, a single touch from her bare skin had left him unable to resist her command.

Her voice was barely more than a whisper when she answered at last. "The night of the attack at Larkspur Manor, I was asked to use my Riftmagic in a way I have never been asked to use it before—in a way that made me question everything I've devoted my life to."

"What did—" Eli began, but Eliza shook her head.

"Please don't ask me. I can't bear to... I don't care to discuss it. But Mr. Turner... Eli... the very first time we met, you said to me,

275

'Creator help you to see whom it is you serve.' I am determined now to understand. From now on, I will seek the truth, and I will not let anyone else judge for me what that is. And if I can help others to find that truth as well—so much the better."

Eli looked into the girl's eyes. They were bright and dilated with fear, but her gaze and her voice were quite steady.

"Will I see you again?" The question was out of Eli's mouth before he could stifle it, before he even knew why he was asking it.

"I don't know," she said. "But whatever happens, I do not regret my coming here tonight."

(From the collected sermons of William Tibbet, founder of the Illustratum, formerly the Church of the Rift)

"I come to you today a man blessed—blessed in ways I still cannot comprehend. These ears are those of a humble man—a man who has only ever looked to the Creator for guidance and tried his utmost to do His will. Like the rest of you, I have sometimes struggled to understand what He wished of me. I have had to dig deep, deep into my soul to divine His meaning, and I have not always been successful, for who among us can truly know Him? I would never presume I could.

Until today, my children. Until today.

Last night I woke with the Creator's voice in my ear, speaking to me as clearly as I am speaking to you now. At first, I was sorely afraid. Could it truly be Him, or was it a devil, determined to hoodwink me? And then, within my mind, He opened a door onto vistas I could only dream of. He showed me truths that only He could know. And when He spoke, His voice was within me and without me, and it planted His will directly into my heart.

"Take these truths!" He told me. "Shout them from the mountaintops! Let all My children hear them, for with them they shall build My new kingdom and find their way into My arms!"

And I began to write, not my own words, but His. I wrote all night, unceasingly, for there could be no rest until He had been heard. I lost all sense of time, all sense of who or where I was. There were only His words, His truths, His will flooding through me. And when I had finished, when at last He released His hold on me and the pen dropped from my hand, I had written the Book—His Book—the Book which I share with you now, the Book which shall, at last, make sense of the madness that has befallen the world, and bring comfort and answers to us all.

I give you—nay, He, in His infinite wisdom and mercy, gives you—The Book of the Rift."

TWENTY-TWO

S ULLY WAS AS GOOD AS HER WORD. Two days later, Peter Bennett found Eliza doing the ironing and slipped a brown-paper wrapped package back into her hands.

"Colin Webb just brought this for you," he murmured. "Don't suppose you'd like to tell me what it is?"

"Don't suppose I would," Eliza replied, but she smiled for the first time in two days, so profound was her relief at having the book back in her hands. She slipped it into her pocket where it felt like a hot coal burning a hole through her apron until she could at last sneak back to her bedroom and open it. There was a note tied to the top of the book.

Copies made. Thank you for the risk you took in getting this to me. We are grateful. -E

And just like that, anxiety extinguished the feeble spark of relief in her chest. Eliza wondered if she would ever feel properly calm again, but there was no time to dwell on it. A choice lay before her. On the one hand, she could return the book to its proper place and never take such a risk again—simply do her best to return to her life as she had known it, to go through the motions of her duties and try to be the obedient and faithful servant she had always striven to be. On the other hand, she could push wide the door she had opened by going to Sully's and continue to unravel, layer by layer, the world she thought she knew, until she arrived at whatever truth lay at the heart of it all. There was, after all, a stack of Sully's illicit books still hidden behind her dresser that would throw that door wide open, though she had not yet dared read even a single page of them.

She was much more tempted by the former path—and yet she could not resolve herself to walk it. She could not shake the feeling

279

that she had done something irreparable—that even if she returned the book and never saw or spoke to Eli Turner again, she would always be looking over her shoulder, always wondering what might have been if she'd made a different choice. A determined life of obedience had not left much room for experiencing regret, but Eliza could already feel the tendrils of it twisting themselves insidiously around her heart at the very suggestion of returning to such a life. However, she was not ready to turn and walk down the second path, the darker and more uncertain of the two. She looked down at the book, indecision roiling in her belly, and could resolve herself of only one thing: regardless of which path she chose in the future, her next step was clear: the book had to be returned to Elder Hallewell's study as soon as possible.

The Praesidio guard had already come and gone that day, still interviewing the servants about the events of the night. She still had not been called in to meet with them, and she was beginning to wonder if she had already been eliminated as a suspect—after all, she had been with Miss Jessamine and then with Elder Hallewell himself most of the evening, and she was accounted for at the time the crime had taken place. The constant topic of conversation among the staff was the ongoing investigation, and so Eliza was able to glean from their huddled whisperings that not a single one of them had been asked about a missing book. She was hopeful, then, that the book's absence had not been discovered yet.

Trying to replace the book during the daytime was entirely too risky. It would be simple enough to ensure Elder Hallewell was out of the house, but there were too many other people bustling through the hallways and rooms, cleaning and polishing and dusting and the like, to ensure she would not be spotted coming in or out. She decided, therefore, to return the book at night, when the rest of the house was asleep. The wait was agonizing—surely the clocks had never ticked so slowly before—and Miss Jessamine was little help in keeping Eliza busy to pass the time. She was still keeping to her room, pacing about the chamber in her nightgown like a sleepwalker, refusing meals and carrying around Teddy Potter's letter which she still had not found the courage to open. Eliza exhausted every resource she had to cheer her mistress up, but Jessamine still seemed to be avoiding contact with her, and without the usual calming influence of her Riftmagic, Eliza felt nearly helpless to do her job. It was practically a relief when darkness and silence had settled over the manor like a blanket, and

Eliza, clad in her nightgown, her feet bare, slipped from her room and up the stairs to cast away, at last, this most damning piece of evidence.

The study was still, the last glowing embers of the fire long since gone cold. The desk stood as though Elder Hallewell had just stepped away from it—a letter, half-finished, with the fountain pen resting atop it. The smell of brandy lingered around a not-quite empty glass abandoned beside the inkwell. Wasting no time, Eliza tiptoed across the room, opened the drawer, and slid the book beneath the others piled inside. A cursory glance at the drawer's contents further reassured her that the book's absence had not been discovered; the contents appeared untouched from the last time she had opened it. She slid it shut carefully and straightened up, her eyes falling upon the letter. A phrase caught her eye.

"*... more regular dosing of the general population with Riftmead...*"

Eliza froze. Before she could stop herself, before she could remind herself that she needed to get out of that office as quickly as possible, she was bent over the desk, reading every word on the page.

Francis,

In light of the seriousness of the injuries inflicted by Davies during his attempted escape, and the recent uptick in discontent in the Barrens, it is incumbent upon us to consider more stringent methods of suppression. I know many of our brothers favor increasing patrols and prolonging the curfews, but surely you can see how this has only made the situation more tense. The harder we push, the harder they will inevitably push back, which will lead to further violence in the streets, an outcome that will have negated all our prodigious efforts to contain the news of Davies' death. I feel we should strongly recommend to the rest of the Council that alternative methods of Riftborn suppression be considered, methods that will not be detected for what they are by the Riftborn themselves, but will be nonetheless effective in dulling the will to resist.

The very first method we ought to recommend is more regular dosing of the general population with Riftmead. I realize our studies suggest higher doses could have adverse health effects in a small number of subjects, but this would be an acceptable price to pay for restoring the general peace and ensuring the continued authority of the Illustratum. If we recommend this measure—and I strongly believe we should—we must have access to the Riftmead research out of the workhouses, orphanages, and asylums. Can you send word to your brother and ask him to compile the relevant details for us? You know Carpenter will demand the hard numbers, and we must have them ready to present. If we can ensure the outcomes—that is, if we can provide enough reassurance that Riftmagic will be rendered less effective and therefore less of a threat—then we can move on to recommending methods of ensuring all Riftborn are dosed. Here I will need your help, for I have yet to conceive of another avenue apart from the weekly services...

The letter ended there. Eliza read it through three times before her overwrought brain would accept the meaning of the words.

"*...dosing...*"

"*...adverse health effects...*"

"*...Riftmagic will be less effective and therefore less of a threat...*"

Poisoned. They were being poisoned. Every week she was kneeling and praying to the Creator to help her tame her Riftmagic, and every week the Elders were handing her a chalice to drink from, a symbolic promise to cleanse herself, to fill herself with the Creator's blessing and strength. And what was it she was really filling herself with? What was really in that cup? Whatever it was, it was intentionally dulling her magic and perhaps even making her sick.

And what was this about the orphanages and workhouses—it sounded as though the occupants were being experimented upon. But that couldn't be true. It just couldn't be. It was too much, too terrible... and yet...

There was a sudden murmur of voices in the hallway outside the room, and the echoing of footsteps. Eliza listened, frozen in horror, as the footsteps approached the door to the study and the knob began to turn.

She looked frantically around for an escape and her eyes fell upon the plum velvet drapes drawn over the nearby window. She dashed over to them and hid behind the folds, making sure her feet were obscured just as the door to the study opened.

"I do apologize for the late hour, but this message cannot be delayed." It was Elder Hallewell's voice. Eliza's fear expanded inside her, crushing her lungs and fogging her brain.

"I understand, sir. It shall be delivered at once. Do you anticipate an immediate reply?" Eliza did not recognize the second voice, but

282

she knew that Elder Hallewell used a private messenger service to communicate with the other Elders. This must be one of the couriers.

"I do. I would appreciate it if you would wait for it, and return it immediately to me," Elder Hallewell said, and she heard his footsteps approach the desk. She heard a scribbling sound—the addition of his signature, perhaps—and then the crisp sound of paper being folded. A moment later she smelled the scent of something burning, and knew the official wax seal of the Illustratum must have been applied to the missive.

"There you are. With all haste, man," Elder Hallewell said, and the courier's footsteps could be heard echoing across the room, followed by the shutting of the door. Trapped alone in the room with Elder Hallewell, Eliza fought a mad desire to simply run. What would happen if he decided to draw the curtain to watch his message be carried away? What would she say if she were discovered?

Elder Hallewell sighed, a deep and tired sound. There were more footsteps and a clinking of glass upon glass—he must have been pouring himself another brandy from the decanter beside the desk. Silence while he drank—and then the clink of the glass being set down again before the silence returned.

Eliza held her breath and prayed. *Please. Please let him leave. Please let him go to bed.*

A soft knocking sound startled them both. Eliza managed not to cry out, but Elder Hallewell cursed under his breath.

"Yes?"

The sound of the door creaking. "Forgive me, sir, but I heard a disturbance. Is all quite well?"

Eliza felt tears welling up into her eyes. It was her father—the only person who could possibly have made her situation worse.

"Braxton. Thank you, yes. I needed to send an urgent message, and called for a courier. He has just left."

"Is there anything I can do to help, sir? Do you require anything now that you are up?" Braxton's voice was so mellow and accomodating. Elder Hallewell might have asked for the moon, and Eliza doubted her father would have admitted it was out of reach.

"How would you characterize the morale below stairs, since the Presentation?" Elder Hallewell asked.

Eliza heard the slight hesitation in her father's voice. "The staff is as dedicated as ever, sir, but much disturbed by what occurred.

They all understand that the continued questioning by the Praesidio is necessary, but I will not deny that it is disheartening."

"I completely understand," Elder Hallewell replied, sounding sympathetic. "I want to raise their spirits and thank them for all their patience and persistence in spite of everything that's gone on. I'm going to send down a cask of Riftmead from my private stores. See that it is served at dinner this week, for all the staff, with my compliments."

"Thank you, sir!" Eliza could envision her father prostrating himself in a deep bow. "I shall see to it personally. They will all be very grateful."

"It's nothing at all," Elder Hallewell said magnanimously, and Eliza felt such a surge of anger that it frightened her. "Well, good night then. Could you make sure my valet is waiting? I expect I may be up for some time, and I wish to get properly dressed in case I have to leave for the Illustratum in a hurry."

"Of course, sir. Right away." Eliza heard her father back out of the room, heard the door close behind him. A few moments later, she heard the clink of the glass, the shuffling of feet and, at long last, the final opening and closing of the door. She allowed the silence in the room to linger as she counted to ten, and then sank, with an exhalation that was half-sigh and half-sob, to the floor behind the curtains.

When the shock of nearly being caught had passed, and her heartbeat had steadied from its galloping crescendo to a steady thrum, Eliza rose carefully to her feet and crept, shivering, back down the stairs and to the safety of her own room. A narrow strip of light bled out from beneath the door to her father's office, but she did not check on him. Instead, she went straight to the tiny writing desk in the corner of her room, lit her candle, and began to write down the letter that had composed itself inside her head on her walk back downstairs. A sensible girl would have been scared out of her wits at nearly being caught in her master's study, and would have resolved never to do such a foolish thing again.

But, Eliza observed ruefully as she climbed into bed and opened the first of Sully's books, the sensible girl she once had been was gone.

(Eliza's Letter to Eli)

Eli—

The book has been returned to its proper place without incident, and I am fairly confident that its absence has gone unnoticed. I do not believe we need to worry about anyone discovering it has been tampered with until you decide what next to do with the copies you've made. And on that score, I have a suggestion. It might be completely mad, but then, from the little I know of you, you seem quite at home with madness.

The second time we met, you chanced upon me while delivering charity baskets in the Barrens. The other lady's maids and I embark upon this duty every Tuesday morning. Each week, the daughters of the Elders take it in turns to host a charity circle, where all the daughters assemble the baskets. This coming Sunday night, after several weeks hiatus due to the unrest in the Barrens, it will be Larkspur Manor's turn to host the circle. If you can find a way to get copies of the books to me, I can conceal them inside the baskets before they are distributed on Tuesday morning. In this way, we can disseminate the books widely among the people who most need to read them, and the maids who are delivering them will not even be aware that they are doing so.

By making this suggestion, I realize I am getting involved in ways I promised myself I would never allow. All I can say is that my eyes have been opened, and it has proven impossible to close them again. I want to be perfectly clear that I am taking full responsibility should the use of the baskets be discovered. I will not allow any of the other girls to face consequences for what I alone have chosen to do, nor will I betray anyone else's role in the scheme. I anxiously await your reply, and stand ready to do what I must.

—Eliza

TWENTY-THREE

T HE BACK ROOM OF THE BELL AND FLAGON, brimming
with loud and raucous argument just minutes before, had gone
completely silent. All eyes were on Sully as she read the letter
Eli had just handed to her. Her eyes flew back and forth across the
page, her expression utterly indecipherable. Finally, she looked up at
Eli, her eyes burning into him above the rims of her glasses.

"When did this arrive?"

"Less than an hour ago. Colin wouldn't have caught me at all if
I hadn't been waiting on the crates of paper to be delivered. And she
sent these back with it."

Eli reached out and set a stack of books on the table in front of
Sully. They were her own books—the ones she had loaned to Eliza as
collateral in their bargain to protect each other.

Eli couldn't be sure, but he thought the corner of Sully's mouth
might just have betrayed a hint of a smile, however it was gone the
moment he saw it.

"What's going on, then?" Zeke asked, looking from Eli to Sully.

"I think you're all familiar with the charity baskets that get
delivered around the Barrens every week—some of you may even
have been on the receiving end.

"Aye, my family gets one regularly," Fergus replied.

"As does mine," added Michael Webb, Colin's father.

"The lady's maid I was just telling you about, Eliza Braxton, has
come up with a plan to distribute the books secretly in the charity
baskets. She's volunteering herself for the job."

A stunned silence met these words. Jasper was the first to break it.

"Let's just put aside for a moment the fact that trusting a manor girl with anything is borderline suicidal," he said, rubbing his hand over his eyes. "Certainly she doesn't suppose that she can deliver hundreds of books on her own. Unless she is suggesting getting the other maids involved, in which case, she's as mad as a hatter."

A rumble of agreement went around the circle.

"Them girls is sanctimonious as they come," Fergus wheezed. "Can't imagine a single one of them agreeing to it."

Eli held up a hand. "No, no, she doesn't want to involve the other maids—not knowingly, at least. She's proposing to hide the books in the charity baskets—conceal them, so that the other maids don't know they're inside."

"But how would she conceal them?" Zeke asked. "We couldn't risk one of the other maids discovering the books before the baskets were delivered and sounding the alarm." He was trying his best to sound skeptical, but Eli could tell he was intrigued.

"When she arrived at Sully's place the other night to deliver the book, she had created a false bottom for the basket she was carrying and concealed the book beneath it. Perhaps she could do the same for the charity baskets?"

"That's a big undertaking," Michael said, scratching at his chin. "I've seen those girls gathered in the High Street before they start their rounds. There's got to be a hundred of those baskets if there's one. Maybe even more."

"She sounds confident she can manage it," Eli said.

Sully let out a short, incredulous blast of laughter. "My God. Manor servants in Illustratum liveries delivering Resistance literature into the hands of the masses. Is it really possible?"

Eli shrugged. "I think it may be."

Jasper leaned back in his chair, his expression shrewd. "It's inevitable that the Illustratum will find out about the books, and maybe even how they were distributed. Once they're out there, there will be no turning back—that bell can't be unrung. She puts the other maids at risk of being thought accomplices. Is she going to let her friends take the fall?"

Eli opened his mouth, but it was Sully who answered, holding up the letter. "She professes here she's prepared to take the blame, should the baskets be discovered as the method of distribution."

"I don't like it," Jasper said dismissively.

288

"You don't like it because it wasn't your idea," Eli shot at him. "And also because it doesn't put you in the center of the action."

The legs of Jasper's chair clattered to the floor as he sat up. "I don't like it because it involves so many manor servants. We can't trust them, Eli. They're all indoctrinated. Flocks of mindless sheep, the lot of them."

"One of those mindless sheep put that book in our hands, lest you forget," Eli snapped.

"Yeah, and then she couldn't get out of there fast enough," Jasper said dismissively. "She's not cut out for this, Eli, none of them are. They're too cozied up to the enemy."

"We've used manor servants in the Resistance before," Zeke said slowly, sucking on his pipe.

"Yeah, but usually we've put them there," Fergus pointed out. "But a born and bred manor servant?" He shook his head ruefully.

"Exactly," Jasper said.

"She wouldn't be the first," Sully said quietly. "There were a few, in the days of the Lamplighters Confederacy. Not many, but a few. And they fought like hell, just like the rest of us. Some people in this room likely wouldn't be here without their efforts, and I'll thank all of you not to forget it."

There was something in Sully's face, a fierce and defiant something that kept Jasper's tongue still in his head for once. None of the dozen people gathered dared to step on the silence that followed her words, but waited instead for Sully to continue.

"I see an opportunity here," she said, pulling her glasses off and rubbing at her eyes, which were ringed with dark circles from several sleepless nights. "Unless of course, one of you has a brilliant plan up his sleeve as to how to distribute the books without being caught. If you have, now would be the moment to reveal it."

Aside from some uncomfortable squirming and a few smoke rings, there was no reply.

"I see. So this manor girl remains, at present, the only person to offer up a solution to our problem. Let's discuss it on the merits, setting aside for the moment from whom it comes."

She looked around expectantly, and the rest of the group hastened to meet that expectation.

Cora Jackson, the local herbalist, cleared her throat. "It's efficient," she said. "It gets every book into the hands of the people in a matter of an hour or two."

"It avoids the issue of patrols," Zeke added. "No guard is going to stop a girl in manor liveries and bother her for papers or question what she's doing there. They'll be able to move about freely."

"It keeps us out of suspicion," Michael Webb said, gesturing for the whiskey bottle and pouring himself a dram. "Say what you will of the girl, but she's taking this on herself, which leaves us all free and clear of blame."

"That's something, isn't it?" Fergus agreed. "I'm glad to let someone else risk their neck on this one."

"You're always glad to let someone else risk their neck," Liam Mills, a sign maker, teased, roaring with laughter and slapping Fergus on the back, causing him to hunch over in a fit of coughing.

"I still don't trust her," Jasper said, sounding petulant now.

"I do," Eli replied.

"And why's that, I wonder?" Jasper sneered. "Can't trust 'em just because they bat their lashes at you, brother."

"Best reason not to trust 'em," Zeke muttered darkly, more to himself than to anyone else.

"Let's have a little less romance advice from the man who lost his shirt to a whore in a game of whist," Sully suggested with a smirk.

"Lost his trousers too, I heard," Cora sniggered. Jasper glared at her, but she merely winked back.

"Look, I'm not in love with the girl, for Creator's sake!" Eli cried. "I barely know her. But I think we've got an opportunity here, and I thought so from the first time I met her. She's not just some scullery drudge who's never seen the upstairs. She's a lady's maid! She was able to get into an Elder's private study! When have we ever had that kind of access before?"

No one spoke, because they all knew the answer was never.

"She came to us, first with the book and now with the plan to distribute the copies. We didn't have to convince her to our side, she came of her own accord! She's also an Influencer, and a damn powerful one at that. Imagine the possibilities, if we could turn that magic to our advantage in Larkspur Manor, of all places? She's a gift to this movement the likes of which we haven't seen before, and we'd be a pack of bloody fools to waste this chance!"

Heads were nodding in agreement through the low-hanging fog of pipe smoke, but Eli had eyes only for Sully. He had made this appeal to her once before, but the circumstances had changed dramatically since then. He knew her approval would be the only one that mattered in the end, and he knew he would not get another chance to secure it.

"We will need to ensure some details," Sully said at last, all business. "First, the books cannot be discovered before the baskets are delivered. Secondly, we have to ensure the Riftborn families will find the books– perhaps the false bottoms are a step too far in concealment– perhaps wrapping them will be sufficient? Let's discuss it. And thirdly, the books must come with clear instructions for the families who receive them: read this book and then burn it. Tell no one how it came into your possession."

"We can't guarantee everyone who gets a book will follow those instructions," Zeke said.

"We can't guarantee anything, Zeke," Sully agreed. "But most will follow the instructions once they see what's in the book. Even if a copy or two escapes the purge, the scale of the thing will be concealed from discovery."

There were a few murmurs of discussion, as the wording of the instructions was debated. Only Jasper remained stonily silent. Finally, Sully called everyone to attention with a sharp rapping on the tabletop.

"Let's put it to a vote, then. Who's for letting the lady's maid do the dirty work?"

All hands rose into the air except for Jasper's. He looked around the room as though every one of them had betrayed him, then heaved an aggrieved sigh, and grudgingly thrust his hand in the air as well. "I'm only agreeing to this because I know if I don't, those books will sit in our basement for a year catching dust while we bicker over what to do with them. But don't say I didn't warn you."

"Thank you, Jasper. Let it be noted that Jasper's warning has been acknowledged, with only a passing reference on my part to the distinct irony of Jasper having the unmitigated gall to hand out warnings while patently ignoring them himself," Sully remarked. "Very well then, if no one else has any comments, let us draft a letter back to Miss Braxton accepting her proposal. If all goes well, we may have set into motion the first mass distribution of unfiltered Illustratum material in more than fifty years."

"And if it doesn't go well?" Jasper asked, eyes on Eli.

"We'll cross that bridge if we get to it," Zeke replied, a warning in his tone as he looked between the two. "Remember, I won't hesitate to throw your arses out of my pub if it comes to blows, back room or no back room."

"Well," Sully said, slapping her hand on the table and raising her glass. "It begins, then. To Davies. May his legacy be known again."

Twelve glasses rose into the air. Twelve voices echoed the sentiment. "To Davies."

Eli threw back his whiskey. It burned all the way down, fueling the fire of excitement and fear already roiling in his belly. He poured a second, and whispered the toast.

"To Eliza. May the Creator be with you."

(Correspondence from the personal records of Thomas Platt, member of the House of Commons, dated 11 October, 1800)

Dearest Alice,

I hardly know what to write, such is my shock at the violence with which common sense and order have been overturned. Parliament is descended into chaos, and I fear the worst. Tibbet and his band of extremists have whipped the people of this country into a frenzy. Their wild and frankly unfounded claims about the origins of this so-called "Riftmagic"—I hesitate even to use the term, as he has coined it—have no basis in verifiable fact. Who is this man to claim God speaks directly to him? And why are we to believe such claims?

Tibbet takes the floor tomorrow with a speech, and I worry the effect it may have upon the populace. They are already rioting in the streets, their terror fed by Tibbet's minions preaching his words on street corners and in pubs. Families are being attacked and affected members being locked away, as though their abilities might spread like a disease. I beg you to take the children and get out of the city. Go north, to my sister, and wait for me there. Take what you can and abandon the rest. If all goes as I suspect it might tomorrow, those of us who are speaking out against Tibbet will be at great personal risk. I will not abandon my duty to the people who elected me to represent them, but I do not want my family to suffer as a result of that duty. Already, more prominent members of Parliament are being harassed in the streets. Lord Pruitt was assaulted and taken to hospital after he denounced Tibbet on the floor. I cannot ensure your safety, my darling, if you remain.

If a vote of no confidence is forced and allows these lunatics to

293

take over, I shall have no choice but to flee, but I shall face my duty with a stouter heart and a peace in my soul if I know that you and the children have already found a safe haven in which to wait out this storm.

Yours,
Tom

TWENTY-FOUR

"**S**IR, THE CARRIAGE HAS BEEN BROUGHT 'round for you. And you asked me to alert you when Miss Jessamine would be coming down to receive her guests."

Josiah looked up into Braxton's perpetually calm face and wished for a moment that he could trade places with the man, that he could have the same unflappable demeanor; it would make what he was about to do much easier, that was certain.

"Thank you, Braxton. Has she come down yet?"

"No, sir, but Eliza has already begun arranging the supplies for the baskets in the sitting room, so it cannot be but a moment before she makes her way down."

Josiah dismissed Braxton with a wave of his hand and rose from his seat at the desk, where he had been reading Francis' most recent correspondence. Tonight they would be offering up the legislation they had co-written, as well as presenting the research they had been able to acquire regarding the use of Riftmead in various strengths. It would no doubt mean many days of debates and amendments and counter-proposals, which meant that if he didn't take the opportunity to talk to Jessamine now, he might not get another chance for weeks, and he had let the silence between them go on for much too long as it was.

He stepped out into the entrance hall just as Jessamine turned the landing and began to descend the last set of stairs. She was dressed in an emerald green satin day dress with a matching jacket that made her eyes glow like jewels. She paused on the steps at the sight of him, then seemed to gather herself with a breath and continued to descend the remainder of the stairs, her face composed.

Blast it all, why did the girl have to look so much like her mother? It made the whole thing damn near impossible.

"Jessamine," he said, and she gave a small curtsy of acknowledgment at the greeting. "I fear I have been neglecting you since your Presentation."

"Not at all, Father," she replied, keeping her eyes carefully on her own hands, which were clasped tightly in front of her.

"It grieves me that we have not had the chance to speak since that night," Josiah began, struggling for the words he needed—and realizing that, for all he knew he ought to tell to her, he hadn't the faintest idea what it was he ought to say. "I feel it has been an oversight on my part, not to ensure that you are properly recovered."

Jessamine raised her head and looked Josiah quite steadily in the eye. He took an involuntary step back from her. "Recovered from what, Father?"

"The... the shock of the night. The explosion must have been quite terrifying. And of course, there were... other things that may have caused you distress."

He was floundering and he knew it. Surely he had been planning to be more direct? Surely he had a litany of explanations and excuses he could use to justify his actions in promising her to Reginald Morgan without so much as a warning? Every one of them shriveled to dust on his tongue as he looked into those startlingly green eyes.

"What is it you fear has distressed me?" Jessamine asked. She was regarding him with the strangest expression on her face—Josiah could not decipher it at all. His confusion angered him, and he felt a defensiveness rise in him unbidden, like a tidal wave. He would not be questioned. He would not be doubted. Any notion of guilt or apology vanished beneath the rising water, and when he replied it was louder and harsher than he had intended.

"After your outburst, I was afraid you had perhaps lost sight of your obligation and duty. We are all of us making difficult decisions for the good of the Illustratum and in service of our greatest obligation of all: to serve our Creator and preserve His peace."

Jessamine dropped her eyes, but not before Josiah saw the glimmer of moisture that had appeared in them as he spoke. "I thought perhaps you were going to apologize to me," Jessamine whispered.

Josiah bristled. "Apologize to you? For ensuring your future prosperity? For seeing the High Elder's will done? For securing the

296

prominence and power of your future children? Am I meant to be sorry for these things?"

A strange sound escaped her—something between a laugh and a sob. "No, sir. I suppose not."

"Miss Jessamine, what's keeping you, miss? Your guests will be arriving at any—oh, I do beg your pardon, sir."

The lady's maid had bustled around the corner and stopped in her tracks at the sight of Josiah standing there. Her face turned instantly crimson and she dropped her gaze quickly to the floor, sinking into a curtsy.

"Nothing's keeping me, Eliza," Jessamine replied. She looked up at her father, a remarkable coolness in her expression. "Nothing at all. If you'll please excuse me, Father. I have guests to attend to, and my charitable obligations to fulfill. I bid you good night."

She curtsied and, without waiting for her father to respond, she turned and walked away from him and into the adjoining sitting room. The lady's maid threw an anxious glance at him and then scurried along in Jessamine's wake.

§

Jessamine made her rounds of the room that had been prepared for their activities. Eliza was hovering near the last of the baskets, fussing with the tops and spacing them along the tables.

"Are there more of them than usual?" Jessamine asked, frowning.

"I think there are a few more this week, yes, miss," Eliza replied. She smoothed out the corner of a napkin. "But I'm sure we'll manage."

"After what we saw a few weeks ago, I would have thought you'd want your trip into the Barrens to be shorter, not longer," Jessamine said. "Are they quite sure it's safe now?"

"It seems so, miss. We were told that the deliveries would resume this week. I expect the increased patrols have quieted things down some."

"I had wondered... after what happened at my Presentation, if... if things hadn't gotten worse. Father is never home anymore. I'm afraid that's... that's the first I've seen of him, just now in the entrance hall." Jessamine felt a lump rising in her throat and struggled to force it down.

"Miss Jessamine? Are you all right, miss? You're looking awfully pale all of a sudden. Would you like me to fetch you a cup of tea?"

Jessamine looked up to see Eliza gazing at her with an anxious expression and gave a helpless laugh. "My goodness. Apparently, I'm not doing as admirable a job of keeping a stiff upper lip as I imagined I was."

"Is there anything I can do, miss?"

"Can you cure me of being a silly, sentimental school girl?" Jessamine asked, fingering the rolls of ribbons that had been laid out for the charity circle.

"I'm sorry?" Eliza asked in evident confusion.

"Never mind," Jessamine said. "It was just that conversation you walked in on just now—the one with my father. I had been hoping—foolishly, it seems—that he might have felt badly for what happened at my Presentation—that he might even offer me an explanation or an apology. Instead, I received a lecture on the importance of my duty."

"Oh, I'm... I'm terribly sorry, miss," Eliza replied in barely more than a whisper.

"You see?" Jessamine laughed bitterly. "It was very simple for you to say, and you didn't bargain me away to Reginald Morgan, did you?"

"I don't think apologies come very easily from fathers generally, miss," Eliza said. "They certainly don't from mine."

"Hmmm. We have that in common, it seems," Jessamine said. "Now, about that tea..."

"Yes, miss."

"Have you got anything stronger?"

Eliza's smile faltered, and Jessamine knew the girl was trying to work out whether or not she was quite serious. "S-stronger, miss?"

"Oh, never mind. I suppose I'll have to face Sadie Carpenter fortified with nothing but my own determination, then. Would you please ensure all is prepared to meet them in the entryway?"

"Yes, miss. Of course."

Jessamine watched Eliza go, then turned and stared into the fire. She wasn't sure what would be the worst to bear—Kitty's wide-eyed looks of pity, Sadie's snide commentary, Rebecca's red-faced stammerings, or the rest of the girls, falling all over themselves and each other to interject just the right rehearsed expression of sympathy or shock or whatever other manufactured imitation of emotion the moment called for. She felt as though she could play out the entire evening in her head without even having experienced a moment of it.

She still hadn't read Teddy's letter. She simply couldn't bring herself to open it, mostly because she knew what it would say, and she wanted to hold on to the illusion that Teddy could not write such things. If she kept the letter sealed, she could imagine that there was still a chance it was filled with passionate declarations of undying devotion and elaborate plans to run away together, perhaps even to Europe, where the politics of the Illustratum could hold no possible sway over their future together. She did not really think she could ever do such a thing—leave her home and her father and the only life she'd ever known—she was not sure she had that kind of courage. But she clung to the idea that Teddy would wish it—that he would even risk it—just to be with her. It was easier to cling to this dream than it was to unseal the envelope and see the empty apologies, the excuses, the long-winded treatises on duty and responsibility and the sacrifices one must make to stay the Path. She longed for an apology from her father, but from Teddy, she did not think she could bear it.

Part of her longed to fly up the stairs to the furthest reaches of the house and fling herself into her mother's lap. She longed to cry bitterly into the soft folds of her mother's nightdress, and feel her mother's fingers stroke her hair as she poured every ache of her heart out in salty torrents of tears. She felt her mother could have helped her to bear it, could have explained things in a way that allowed little glimpses of sunlight to penetrate the bleak darkness of her outlook. But of course, her mother wasn't upstairs anymore, was she? No, wherever she was, she was far away, sailed off out of reach, borne adrift on the tide of her own unrelenting sorrow.

She had nowhere to empty her tears, no one to whom she could unburden herself. Eliza was sweet and attentive, but she could never provide the kind of comfort Jessamine needed, not when she was so full of sensible, obedient advice. If she spoke to Eliza about how she really felt, she'd soon find herself nodding along to the dawning realization that yes, she did owe it to her father to marry Reginald Morgan, and she did not think she could bear betraying her own heart in this way. And so the sorrow continued to eat away at her insides, hollowing her out, until she wondered if there would be anything left of her at all upon which to hang the smile she presented to the girls now walking through the door.

It was every bit as bad as she had anticipated.

"Jessamine, darling, how *are* you?"

"You poor thing, I can't imagine how you're coping."

"...said to my mother just the other day, how does one even recover from such a shock?"

"It was *simply* terrifying..."

"My father says they've still no idea who was behind it..."

Jessamine had barely to utter a word. The flurry of conversation spun around her like a dervish and she stood at its center. She felt something thrust into her hand and looked down, dazed. It was a cup of tea. Eliza stood beside her. Before she could thank her, Eliza leaned forward and murmured, so quietly that the other girls couldn't hear, "Whatever you do, sip it slowly, miss."

Curiously, Jessamine bent forward and sampled the tea. It was all she could do to stop from coughing and spluttering. The heady aroma of whiskey filled her nostrils. She looked up at Eliza again, amazed. Eliza simply winked at her, and pressed a peppermint into her hand.

"Courage, miss," Eliza whispered and hurried away.

Jessamine grinned to herself and, ignoring Eliza's advice, knocked back the tea in a single go, then popped the peppermint into her mouth.

"Jessamine, did you hear what I said?"

"Hmmm?" Jessamine looked up from her empty cup, insides still burning, to find Kitty giving her a curious look.

"No, I'm so sorry. What was that, Kitty?" she gasped.

"I said, what's become of Sadie? Why hasn't she arrived yet?"

Jessamine looked around properly for the first time as the girls settled themselves at their assigned places and noted Sadie's absence. "I've no idea. She hasn't sent word that she would be missing."

"I should think not!" Kitty hissed. "Sadie Carpenter, miss a chance like this to gloat over the disruption of your Presentation? I imagine she'd sooner part with a limb."

Jessamine shrugged. "Well, I'm certainly not going to complain. Perhaps she's having trouble deciding which gown goes best with an expression of smug superiority."

Kitty snorted. "You'd think that would be a specialty of hers by now. But how *are* you?" she added in a whisper. "Forget about the fire for a moment, I'm talking about Teddy. I've been just sick with worry about you."

Jessamine kept her face as smooth and impassive as she could. "You needn't worry about me, Kitty."

"Not worry! But I don't understand! Are you saying you *knew*?"

Jessamine did not reply. It was more than she could bear to have others pity the fact that she was nothing more than a pawn in her own life.

"Well, Teddy looked ready to murder someone. His face when you and Reginald took the dance floor! Why, it took my breath away! I've never seen Teddy Potter look anything but good-natured in all my life."

Whatever composure Jessamine had left was slipping from her face. Kitty must have noticed, for she put a hand over her mouth and shook her head apologetically. "I'm terribly sorry, Jessamine. What can I be thinking of, prattling on about it like this? Come sit, and we'll talk about something else entirely. You won't hear the name Teddy Potter cross my lips again tonight."

The charity circle was quieter than usual without Sadie to spur the conversation along with well-timed barbs. It seemed no one had the nerve to bring up Reginald Morgan to Jessamine, which suited her perfectly, as she had no desire to speak of him. Every girl in the circle knew about Reginald, about his well-publicized dalliances and roguish behavior. When they were younger, it had been a source of much giggling and speculation, but now that they were all having to think seriously about the realities of matrimony, none of them found much to laugh about anymore. In fact, Jessamine suspected that she was silently being pitied, which she could hardly bear. For once in her life, Jessamine was grateful for Bette and her running commentary of dark predictions about the fickle nature of Riftborn morality. It gave Jessamine something to focus on while she tried to ignore the sidelong glances and whispered asides. Indeed, she was putting so much energy into feigning interest in Bette's sermonizing that it was rather a while before Jessamine noticed that Rebecca Potter had barely spoken a word since she'd arrived. She sat demurely before her assigned task—wrapping muffins in cheesecloth—and kept her eyes down. It was not until Kitty remarked on Sadie's extended absence that Jessamine noticed that Rebecca was sniffing and rubbing at her downcast eyes rather more often than was normal.

"Rebecca? Are you quite well?" Jessamine asked. The question caused Rebecca to start violently, sending a muffin tumbling, forgotten, across the carpet.

"What? Me? Oh. Oh, y-yes, I'm quite well, thank you," she stammered, but Jessamine caught sight of her face and saw that she had almost certainly been crying.

"What's upset you? Kitty, lend her your handkerchief," Jessamine prompted. Kitty looked startled, but produced a lacy scrap of fabric at once and handed it to Rebecca, who wasted no time in blowing her nose loudly into it.

"Come on, now, what's troubling you?" Jessamine prompted again.

But Rebecca looked around at the circle of girls, half of them practically salivating at whatever she was about to say, and shook her head.

"Here, let's go along to the washroom," Jessamine said briskly, standing up and holding out a hand to Rebecca. "We'll get your face washed and I'll find Eliza to get you a nice cup of tea."

It felt good to be tending to someone else's delicate feelings rather than her own, and Jessamine put her arm around Rebecca and guided her out of the room and down the hallway to a little powder room that was rarely used, except when there were guests. She wetted a soft cotton cloth and handed it to Rebecca, who sighed and dabbed at her eyes as she sank onto the chaise lounge in the corner.

"Oh, I... I just... I know it's not my place to question how these things are done... it's not any girl's place, but... oh, I just can't bear it!" And Rebecca burst into a storm of crying.

"What can't you bear, dear?" Jessamine asked, patting the poor girl on the shoulder.

"I was... was so looking forward to being able to call you my sister," Rebecca sobbed. "You're one of the only girls who's ever been nice to me. I'm such a dunce at social gatherings. I never know what to say, and the other girls know it, and I always feel like I'm making a frightful mess of everything."

"Nonsense, you're a lovely hostess," Jessamine said, more out of kindness than honesty. "You mustn't let them get to you so."

"Oh, but... but Sadie is the worst of them all, and now I... I'm afraid..."

"Afraid of what?" Jessamine pressed. "Go on. You can tell me."

302

Rebecca looked up at her, the handkerchief pressed to her mouth so that her next words were muffled. "Elder Carpenter was at my house this afternoon and I... I think he might be trying to negotiate a... a union. Between Teddy and Sadie."

Jessamine felt as though the floor had vanished beneath her feet. There was nothing to stop her from falling and falling down into nothingness.

"Are you sure?" she managed to whisper.

"No, I'm not sure," Rebecca whimpered, still dabbing at her eyes. "But I definitely heard them mention her name, and Father's been pacing in his study ever since. He always paces when he has a big decision to make."

"Does Teddy know?"

"I don't know."

Jessamine felt a wild something trying to escape her—whether it was a sob or a scream or something altogether different, she had no idea, but she fought it down with every ounce of her resolve. She would not give in to it, whatever it was, not in front of Rebecca, and not with a dozen other girls sitting two rooms away.

"Well, put it out of your head, Rebecca, for it is useless to worry over anything until you are sure. And if you must worry about it, in the meantime, remember this: Sadie Carpenter has had no more say in this than I have. Creator knows I would relish the chance to blame her for it, but I cannot. Whether she will gloat over her good fortune at being matched with Teddy or whether she will cry into her pillow at her misfortune has mattered not at all to the men making the decision. Do you understand me?"

Rebecca stared, wide-eyed, up into Jessamine's face. Perhaps she had never heard anyone speak so openly of the power that fathers held over their daughters—or perhaps she had simply never felt the weight of it before.

"And so, if the day comes when she waves that ring in my face as she will undoubtedly do, because when has Sadie Carpenter ever shown herself capable of passing up such an opportunity, I will not hate, but pity her. And you must do the same, Rebecca. For all her life she will know the truth behind that ring, and she will have to live with it just I will have to do, and there is no happiness to be found in that."

Rebecca dropped the handkerchief and nodded once, slowly.

"I don't know why this has happened," Jessamine continued. "I don't know why we have been denied the opportunity to become the sisters we had imagined we would be, but I do intend to find out. I may not be included in the decisions that chart the course of my life, but I will not be ignorant of them, I promise you that."

And though Jessamine continued to address Rebecca Potter, the promise she made at that moment was to herself. If her father wouldn't explain to her why she had been bargained away to a man she detested, then she would find out all on her own. If she was to come to terms with her role in the world that the Illustratum had built, she had to know the reality of it.

She stood Rebecca up and helped her to compose herself. Then she marched her back into the charity circle, noting the sudden silence that descended upon her reappearance, which was no more than she expected; certainly, the girls would take the opportunity of her absence to gossip and speculate freely on the subjects of her Presentation and impending engagement—she would have done the same herself, had the roles been reversed, so she could hardly fault them. A few of them made the obligatory remarks—asking after Rebecca's health, hoping she was *quite* all right—but otherwise allowed her trip to the powder room to pass without further investigation.

They worked quickly. Eliza spent the entire evening whisking back and forth along the table, taking the piles of completed items almost as quickly as the girls could put them down and arranging them in the baskets. Usually, she did this at the end of the evening, when all the work had been completed, but Jessamine suspected she was hovering out of a motherly instinct to ensure that her mistress was faring well, and she was grateful to be able to catch her eye and see a sympathetic smile once in a while. As a result, the baskets were closed, tied, and on their way out to the carriages before the charity circle had even risen from their seats, and as Jessamine was so subdued, no one seemed eager to prolong the evening beyond the traditional small talk and bidding of good night. And so, it was barely nine o'clock when Jessamine flopped down onto the sofa near the fire. Eliza closed the door behind the last of the girls, looking every bit as relieved as Jessamine felt.

"You're in luck, Eliza. We've worked quite quickly this evening. I hope that means that you can have an early night of it as well," she said.

304

"Very good, miss. And how did you fare?" she spoke the question mildly, and Jessamine knew Eliza was leaving it up to her, which version of the question she wanted to answer. She decided she did not have the fortitude to address the more personal of the two, at least until the morning.

"Well enough, Eliza," she said, and tried to smile. "But I think I've had enough for one night."

"Up we go then, miss. Let's get you settled into bed."

"More welcome words were never spoken," Jessamine replied gratefully.

TWENTY-FIVE

WHEN ELIZA ARRIVED IN HER BEDROOM an hour later, Bridie was sitting on the edge of the bed. Her arms were crossed over her chest and her freckled face was creased into as serious an expression as ever Eliza had seen upon it.

"Bridie? What's wrong?" Eliza asked at once.

"I had to lie to a Praesidio guard today. I looked him in the face and lied to him."

Eliza sank onto the edge of the bed. "A Praesidio guard? But why?"

Bridie looked at Eliza as though she were mad. "What do you mean, why? The Presentation! The guards are still questioning people about it. Surely you've been questioned?"

"Oh," Eliza sighed, trying to hide her relief. "No, not yet. But what would you need to lie about, Bridie? You've done nothing wrong."

"Oh, haven't I?" Bridie asked, with a toss of her tawny head.

"Of course you haven't," Eliza said soothingly. "You had nothing to do with that explosion. You have nothing to worry about."

"But I lied, Eliza!" Bridie cried out before dropping her voice to a whisper. "He asked me if I'd seen any servant do or say anything they ought not to, and I lied to him!"

"But what do you—"

"That book!" Bridie hissed. "The one you made me smuggle down here for you, the one that belongs to Elder Hallewell! I suppose it's still here, isn't it, and I'm still an accomplice to—"

"Calm down, Bridie!" Eliza interjected. "I've already returned the book. It was never missed, and no one need ever know it was gone. I'm so sorry, I should have told you right away."

Bridie's shoulders which had been huddled up around her ears, now settled back where shoulders ought to be. "You promise?"

"Cross my heart, Bridie."

Bridie sighed and dropped her arms to her sides. "I still had to lie to that guard. For you."

Eliza placed a hand on Bridie's arm, and though Bridie frowned, she did not shrug it off. "I know, and I'm so sorry to have put you in that position, Bridie. But thank you for not saying anything."

Bridie looked affronted. "Of course, I didn't say anything! I'm your friend."

"I'm glad to hear that," Eliza said with a smile. "I was afraid you mightn't ever talk to me again."

"I was angry! And confused and... well, yes, and scared, too. You scared me. I couldn't understand what had come over you! For Creator's sake, Eliza, you're the one who's always reminding me to hold my tongue, to stay the Path, to mind my actions, and then all of a sudden, it was as if I didn't know you at all! And then you dragged me right into your madness! Truly, what was I to think?"

"I... I lost my head, Bridie. I'm not sure what else I can say."

"Well, have you found it again?" Bridie cried, throwing her hands up in exasperation.

"I... well, I certainly hope so," Eliza replied evasively. And then, before she could help herself, she blurted out "Bridie, did you... um... look at the book at all?"

Bridie folded her arms again. "I most certainly did not. Gracious, Eliza, I was in enough trouble as it was, simply carrying it in my pocket. I never want to see that book again!"

For one mad moment, Eliza was overcome with a desire to confess—what the book had revealed, what she knew—or suspected she knew—about Riftmead, about the baskets upstairs and what they contained, and that Bridie herself would be an unwitting conspirator in distributing them. But as quickly as the impulse seized her, it passed. The whole of Riftborn London would know the truth inside that book soon enough, and if Bridie could stay ignorant of her role in spreading that truth, Eliza would spare her from it for as long as she could.

"I'm sorry, Bridie," Eliza repeated. "And I won't ask you to do anything like that again."

"I should think not," Bridie said, but she seemed pacified, and when she spoke again, it was with a softened expression and tone.

"That night was hard on all of us, Eliza. I know how devoted you are to Miss Jessamine, and I'm sure it must have been difficult, being asked to use your magic like that. But after all, a girl's got her duty to do, and an Elder's command is as good as the law. Miss Jessamine wouldn't want you to break the law. I'm sure she forgives you."

"Yes, I'm sure she does," Eliza said, and dropped her gaze before Bridie could try to scrutinize her expression. "It's forgiving myself that's less certain."

Bridie reached across the bed and squeezed Eliza's hand. "Enough of that foolishness. You did your duty, and that's an end to it. We've all got a responsibility to do what we know is right, even if it's hard to do it."

Eliza placed her other hand on top of Bridie's. "You never spoke truer, Bridie Sloane."

§

Eliza would gladly have slept the next two days in full just to escape the constant gnawing fear in her belly, but sleep was as elusive as peace. When she finally climbed out of bed on Tuesday morning and dressed to head into the Barrens, it was with an overwhelming sense of relief. It was somehow comforting to know that she would prefer actually committing the crime rather than sitting around planning for it—the anticipation of the act was far more nerve-wracking than the act itself. She pinned on her cap, slipped down the stairs, and entered the bustling kitchen to retrieve the baskets.

Kitchen maids milled around carrying baking pans of fresh bread and platters of eggs. Steam rose from the pots bubbling on the stove, but the baskets were nowhere to be seen. Eliza's heart began to beat faster, but she told herself not to panic. It had been several weeks since they'd been allowed to make the deliveries into the Barrens. Mrs. Keats had probably just forgotten to put them out for her. Eliza maneuvered her way through the early morning kitchen choreography, murmuring a few "good mornings" and "pardon mes" until she reached the dry goods pantry door. She pushed it open and froze in her tracks.

Mrs. Keats sat upon a bench by herself, a basket open at her feet. In her hands, unwrapped and open, was one of the books.

The world spun. Eliza gripped the doorframe, sure she would

lose all ability to remain upright. Mrs. Keats looked up at her, her expression an enigma.

"Close the door behind you, Eliza. Be quick about it," she muttered.

Eliza did as she was bid, and turned back to Mrs. Keats, who patted the bench beside her, indicating that Eliza should sit down. Her mind a swirling fog of panic, Eliza did so.

"One of the baskets was leaking. A badly sealed jar of jam. That's what you get for letting Madge MacCoul handle the preserves instead of me." She smiled gently.

Eliza could not return the smile. Her face, like every other part of her, was numb with terror.

"I suppose you have something to do with this?" Mrs. Keats asked, holding up the book.

What was the point in denying it? The confession burst out like water breaching a dam. "Yes. Every basket has a copy. They'll soon be all over the Barrens."

Mrs. Keats looked down at the book, and Eliza braced herself for the explosion, for the falling apart of everything she had worked so hard to organize.

"I was always afraid John would be forgotten by everyone but me," Mrs. Keats whispered.

Eliza's mouth fell open. "John? Are you... did you know John Davies?"

Mrs. Keats nodded, and her voice when next she spoke had become muffled with tears. "He was reckless and passionate and brave and a bloody fool, and I loved him for all of it."

"You... *loved* him?"

Mrs. Keats gave her a severe look. "You needn't look so surprised. I know I'm an old goose now, but I was young once."

"No, it's not that, it's just... I didn't realize you *knew* him."

"Not many people did. Good little manor girls and upstart boys from the Barrens weren't meant to mix, were they?" she said ruefully. "But I was taken with him from the first time he smiled at me, and it was no good telling myself otherwise. The heart wants what the heart wants." She sighed. "But he lived in a world I couldn't understand—or rather, I suppose I didn't want to understand it. Even back then, he spoke of changing the world we lived in, of fighting back. It all sounded very glamorous, to hear him talk of it, but the reality isn't glamorous at all, is it? I felt none of the restlessness he felt, none of the discontent, I suppose, because my lot in life was so much more comfortable than his. I didn't want to give it up. I wasn't brave enough to choose uncertainty and insecurity, even if it meant love. I was a coward. And so when he asked me to marry him and join him in the Barrens, I refused. I stopped answering his letters and eventually, he stopped writing them. It was years later I read he was arrested and sentenced to life within the walls of the Praeteritum."

"That's why you were so upset that day in the Barrens, when you saw his name on the notice. I thought it was because you knew he was a criminal."

"Oh, how they vilified him," Mrs. Keats whispered. "A murderer, they called him, a kidnapper and a vicious murderer. They waved around signed confessions and paraded him through the streets like an animal before they locked him away. I knew better, of course. Many of us did, but there was nothing we could do. We dared not speak out. It was terrible, watching them bury him in lies. And now they're trying to do it again."

"I'm trying to make sure they *don't* do it again," Eliza whispered. "We want the truth out there, in their own words, so they can't deny it."

"And they'll certainly try to deny it," Mrs. Keats said, wiping her eyes. "You can be sure of that, if nothing else." She looked frankly at Eliza. "Who is 'we?'"

"What?"

"You just said, 'we' want the truth out there. Who have you got yourself mixed up with, Eliza?"

Eliza dropped her gaze to her hands. "I can't tell you that, Mrs. Keats. I'm sorry. But there's no point in telling me to back out now. The wheels are already turning. I have to see it through."

Mrs. Keats narrowed her eyes. "Yes," she sighed after a moment's hard consideration, "I suppose you must. You were never one to give up on something once you set your mind to it, were you?"

"I suppose you think me a fool," Eliza said.

But Mrs. Keats shook her head, running her fingers over the book one last time before wrapping it back in the brown paper and tying the ribbon around it. Then she tucked it carefully back in the basket. "No, I don't think you a fool. I was a fool once, for not following my heart. I can't very well call you a fool for following yours, now can I?"

Eliza looked skeptical. "What my heart is leading me into is a lot more dangerous than falling in love."

Mrs. Keats threw her head back and laughed. "Spoken like a girl who's never been in love."

Eliza ignored the remark. "Does that mean you... you aren't going to say anything?"

"Not a word, love. Not a blessed word."

Eliza leaned forward and threw her arms around Mrs. Keats, who gasped at the force of the embrace before wrapping her own arms around Eliza in return. "I should have known. I should have known this day would come. You are your mother's daughter, Eliza."

Eliza felt the shame creep through her veins. She lay her head on Mrs. Keats' shoulder and gave a humorless laugh. "And why's that? Because I'm destined to stray from the Path and right into trouble?"

Mrs. Keats took her face in her hands and looked Eliza right in the eyes. "No. Because you are too bright for a world that will never let you shine as you were meant to, and so was your mother."

Eliza blinked. "I... I've never heard you talk about her like that before."

"Not many of us dare speak about her at all, with your father running things down here."

"*He* certainly never speaks of her, if he can help it. It's like she was never real, just a lesson to be heeded, like one of the morality tales in our primers," Eliza said.

"Ah, well, that's because he loved her, not because he hates her. You see, my love, when women are broken, they are expected to mend themselves and soldier on. But when men are broken, they are expected to lock those broken pieces away and pretend they never existed at all; and it broke your father, when your mother left. I don't know why she did it, and neither does anyone else, but I know she was a good woman at heart just as you are. You must have faith that it will all make sense, in the end.

"I'm not sure how much faith I've got left, Mrs. Keats."

"Well, you'd better find it, my girl, along with every bit of luck and grit you can muster," Mrs. Keats said, picking up the basket and handing it to Eliza. "You're going to need it."

(From the morality tale "Mary Far Astray" from the Riftborn Children's Primer, 2nd ed. published 1811)

"...It is my magic! I shall do what I please with it!" said Mary, and she let the cursed magic rise into her fingertips. The sweets she so desired flew into her hands, and she laughed with glee.

"How easy! How fun! I shall have whate'er I please!" she declared.

But as she bit into the first of the sweets, it turned to ash in her mouth, and she coughed and sputtered at the bitterness. She looked down at the sweets in her hands and saw they were no longer brightly colored, but black and grey and rotting. She cried out and dropped them to the ground, where they turned to snakes and beetles and all manner of creeping vile things that scuttled over her shoes and up her skirts.

"No! No! Get them away! Get them off!" she cried, trying to brush away the crawling beasts, but they multiplied and swarmed about her, and their buzzings and hissings became as one voice, whispering in her ear.

"Your Riftmagic belongs to your Creator. You have stolen it from His service. Never again shall you taste of sweetness or joy, for you are a selfish and wicked girl."

And Mary could not even protest, but kept her lips pressed tight, for fear that all the creeping things would crawl into her open mouth..."

EPILOGUE

T HE SHADOW BOY SLIPPED UNNOTICED through the streets of the Barrens, but it was not his magic that protected him from discovery now. It was nothing more or less than the fact that he belonged here, slinking through the gutters of the soot-blackened streets; and so he was as much a part of them as the shadows themselves. No one took the slightest notice of him, which was how he liked it best.

He was late and he knew it. He ought to have been in position a quarter of an hour ago at least. It was unreasonable to expect a bloke to be up before the sun, he told himself. If it was too early for the Creator Himself to shed light on things, it was too early for him. No one would accept this excuse, but he clung to it anyway in an act of private defiance.

By the time he dashed around the corner into the High Street, the group of manor maids were already gone, dispersed through the side streets and alleys like a flock of crows to deliver their bundles of chaos wrapped in conformity. He swore under his breath and turned on his heel, taking back off in the direction he'd come, hightailing it toward Wentworth Street. Almost right away, he spotted a basket on a front stoop, a woman bending down to examine it. As he watched, she picked it up and brought it into the house, two small children already tugging at her skirts for the contents. He smiled and kept jogging.

Further along Wentworth Street, he caught up with a pair of maids, whom he watched carefully from a distance. Neither was the maid he was looking for—they were both too dark of hair and sturdy of build. He watched as they knocked on several doors, placing baskets into the hands of residents. He noted that no one refused the basket when it was handed to them — it seemed the crackdowns were working. A few weeks ago, the resentment in the Barrens had been high, but brutally strict curfews and near-constant patrolling had beaten the population down into a rancorous but subdued quiet. His own elder brother had earned himself a dreadful beating and three nights in the Praesidio pens for coming home a few minutes late from his shift at the docks. Even as the boy watched, kicking a rock casually along Wentworth Street, three pairs of guards strolled through, and every Riftborn eye dropped to the ground at the sight of them.

He wound his way through narrow rutted lanes and muddy roads, and everywhere he looked, black-cloaked maids dropped sedition upon doorsteps. At last, as he rounded the corner into Dorset Street, he spotted her — the lady's maid with the grey eyes and the fair hair. Her eyes widened when she spotted him, but she made no sign that she recognized him. He tipped his cap and meandered toward her. As he did so, she pulled away from the other maid who accompanied her, who was still standing in a doorway, talking earnestly to a woman who was bouncing a baby on her hip. She kept her eyes down, pretending to be adjusting the remaining baskets upon her arm.

The boy approached and held out a grubby handful of twisted paper flowers. "Spare a venia for a lad to get a blessing, miss?" he asked.

"Yes, of course," Eliza replied, and she dug into her pocket, adding in an undertone, "Hello, Colin. I suppose you're here to keep an eye on things?"

"You suppose right, miss," Colin said with a grin. "All shipshape, then?"

Eliza nodded. "So far. None of the other girls seem to suspect a thing." She placed a venia in his hand and pretended to be deliberating over which of the flowers she wanted to choose. "Have you got any further instruction for me?"

"No, miss," Colin said. "I'm just meant to look out for trouble."

Eliza nodded and selected a red flower, which she tucked into the buttonhole of her cloak. "Oh, I think there will be plenty of that, after today."

"I'd have a flutter on that, for sure, miss," Colin replied. "I must say, I owe you a 'pology, miss."

"An apology? To me? Whatever for?" Eliza asked, looking startled.

"I told me dad I didn't think you was up to it, this plan you came up with. Told him you looked too scared when I met you."

Eliza gave him a small smile. "You needn't apologize for that. I *was* scared. I don't think I would have been up to it, that day."

"Still. Apologies all the same, miss. You got more backbone than I reckoned you did. When I'm wrong, I like to own up to it, proper-like." He spit into his palm and held it out to Eliza. She stared at it for a moment, then, with a surreptitious glance around the road to ensure no one was watching, she took his hand and shook it quickly.

"Good luck, miss," he whispered.

"And you, Colin."

"Eliza! Don't let that urchin swindle you out of all your money, now! Come along!" Bridie was calling to her from down the road, looking disapproving.

Eliza turned to go but halted as a patrol rounded the corner into the road, pulling a large wooden cart behind them. As she and Colin stood and watched, the guards stopped in front of a door, pulled a bottle from the clinking contents of the cart, and handed it to the woman standing in the doorway, the woman to whom Bridie had just finished speaking.

"For your family to celebrate the Feast of the Awakening, with the blessings of the Illustratum," the guard grumbled.

The woman stared wide-eyed at the bottle, as though she couldn't believe her luck, and then dipped into an awkward curtsy with the baby still balanced on her hip. "Thank you, sir. And our thanks to the Elders as well!"

The guard nodded gruffly and he and his companion continued down the road, stopping at every door, handing out bottle after bottle.

Colin shook his head. Something about this wasn't right. He would have to take to his heels and let the Resistance know. He turned to tell Eliza as much, but she was still staring after the guards, her face stony.

"Miss? Miss, I should be heading on my way, and so should you. It ain't smart to linger in..."

But Eliza did not let him finish. She fingered the little paper flower in her buttonhole and then looked down at Colin, her expression set in grim lines of determination. She no longer looked like a proper lady, Colin thought. She looked quite fierce, in fact, like a true Barrens lass. "Tell Eli, I'm in," she hissed in Colin's ear. "Whatever they need.

Whatever's next. I want to be a part of it." And before he could reply, she was gone, hurrying off after the other maid.

And so the shadow boy slunk away down the alley, and the lady's maid disappeared from his view. There was not much he could count on in the hardscrabble streets of the Barrens, but as he pocketed the coin she had given him, he was confident in one thing: he had not seen the last of Eliza Braxton.

Then he laughed, beckoned to the edge of a nearby shadow, and vanished.

Also by E.E. Holmes

THE WORLD OF THE GATEWAY

The Gateway Trilogy (Series 1)
Spirit Legacy
Spirit Prophecy
Spirit Ascendancy
The Gateway Trackers (Series 2)
Whispers of the Walker
Plague of the Shattered
Awakening of the Seer
Portraits of the Forsaken
Heart of the Rebellion
Soul of the Sentinel
Gift of the Darkness
Tales from the Gateway

THE RIFTMAGIC SAGA
What the Lady's Maid Knew
The Rebel Beneath the Stairs

E.E. Holmes is a writer, teacher, and actor living in central Massachusetts with her husband, two children, and a small, but surprisingly loud dog. When not writing, she enjoys performing, watching unhealthy amounts of British television, and reading with her children. Please visit www.eeholmes.com to learn more about E.E. Holmes, *The World of the Gateway*, and *The Riftmagic Saga*.

Made in the USA
Monee, IL
18 February 2023

28177364R00194